SNOW ANGELS

Jenny Loudon

ooo WHITE MOTH PUBLISHING ooo

Snow Angels

Copyright © 2020 Jennifer Loudon

The right of Jennifer Loudon to be identified as the Author of the Work has been asserted by her in accordance with the Copyright, Designs and Patents Act 1988.

All the characters in this book are fictitious and any resemblance to actual persons, living or dead, is purely coincidental.

All rights reserved. Any unauthorised broadcasting, public performance, copying or recording will constitute an infringement of copyright. No part of this book may be reproduced or transmitted in any form or by any means, electronically or mechanical, including photocopying, fax, data transmittal, internet site, recording or any information storage or retrieval system without the express permission of the author.

Published in 2020 by White Moth Publishing, United Kingdom.

ISBN: 978-1-9998630-2-9 (paperback)

ISBN: 978-1-9998630-3-6 (e-book)

For every single one of us who has loved and lost.

And for our own angel, Connor.

'As freezing persons, recollect the snow—
First—Chill—then Stupor—then the letting go—'

Emily Dickinson

1

Saturday, 28th October

When the worst thing happens, how do you survive it?
It was not a question that had yet crossed Amelie's mind. She lay on her back, relishing warmth beneath the duvet as Nick slept beside her. Daylight glowed around the edges of the curtains and a car door slammed in the street below. She pushed a strand of hair from her face and moistened her lips. Her child's cry intruded on the quietness. She nudged Nick who murmured but did not stir.

Amelie rose and opened the curtains, appreciated the morning light falling on her husband's thick auburn hair and the curve of his freckled shoulder. As Bertie's cries grew more insistent, she moved swiftly across wooden floorboards to his bedroom.

He sat rubbing his eyes in a nest of duvet in his cot, surrounded by a collection of soft toy animals. He had been playing for a while—many were upside down and a few had been thrown out onto the rug. His hair was matted against one side of his precious head, his cheeks were pink, and his flawless blue eyes were rimmed with teardrops.

'Mama,' he mumbled, stretching out chubby hands.

A nameless place deep inside Amelie's being lit up as she gathered her warm bundle of a child into her arms, and hugged him. He pressed his wet mouth against her neck in a loud kiss and nuzzled his head under her chin.

Downstairs, she moved with the infant on her hip, noting cobalt sky through the window as she entered the bathroom and changed his sodden nappy for a dry one. Bertie clutched his soft toy rabbit, and blinked at the ceiling, still too sleepy to wrestle with her. Astride her hip again, he watched silently, thumb in mouth, as she heated his milk.

Amelie carried her son back upstairs, past the photographs on the stairwell wall—several of her, Nick and Bertie, the black-and-white portrait of her mother that had been commissioned from a professional, and the snapshot of her grandmother Cleome, at home in Sweden with her dog.

In her bedroom, she re-arranged pillows and settled Bertie up against them with his bottle.

Nick woke and muttered, 'What time is it?'

'It's quite late. Bertie decided to give us a lie-in,' she whispered, leaning over her child to kiss her husband on the lips. 'And it's time for my run.'

She changed quickly into leggings and a long-sleeved top while Bertie watched her silently, sucking his bottle, and Nick, yawning, watched her too, idly stroking his son's hair.

'I wish you could come back to bed.'

Amelie smiled and raised her eyebrows in Bertie's direction. 'Fat chance.'

Stepping out of the front gate and turning right toward Iffley Road, Amelie took her first deep breath of fresh air. She experienced a rush of gratitude for this life she had always wanted—for her husband, her child, the good nursing job in her beloved Oxford—all her dreams come true. She walked briskly at first to warm her muscles as the air was cool and autumnal, and then broke into a gentle jog. After crossing the main road, she ran down a wide, tree-lined footpath towards the heart of the city. At the roundabout, she veered left, well into her stride as she ran over Magdalen Bridge. At her side, the River Cherwell sparkled and trees in the Botanic Gardens clung to gowns of copper and yellow. Sunlight brightened the cream stone of Magdalen Tower as it rose triumphantly into the cerulean sky. As Amelie passed by, the weathervanes atop four of its crocketed pinnacles spun in a sudden easterly breeze.

At this time of day, there were few vehicles on the road; the occasional bus rumbled past, a handful of cyclists hissed quietly over the asphalt, and a few Lycra-clad runners like herself padded between the maze of stone buildings that formed the heart of Oxford. Amelie revered her city, especially in the early mornings when the streets were devoid of students and tourists, and there was a sense of space and peace about the place. As she ran up the High Street, the earthy aroma of fresh coffee wafted from a café, lacing the air. She crossed the almost-deserted road to Queens Lane and raced past abandoned bicycles propped haphazardly against limestone walls, and the bricked-in doorway of a deconsecrated church. The spires of Hertford College came into view. A rough sleeper slumbered on the ancient stone, covered with a clean donated duvet, his huddled body a stark contrast to the wealthy institutions that towered around him. This was her Oxford, a place of extremes. She had been born in this city whose streets she flew through, as had her son. It was the place where she had friends whom she had known all her life, the place where she belonged. It was home.

Back at the house, Bertie had reached the limit of time he was prepared to spend lounging in bed, and so Nick pulled on his jeans, t-shirt, and glasses, dressed his son in warm clothes, and then holding his hand, carefully descended the stairs with him.

'Let's get you some breakfast, chap,' he suggested fondly, closing the stairgate behind him.

While Bertie watched cartoons and played with his toys, Nick turned on the radio, and set about making a stack of pancakes. He whistled as he cooked, piling them onto a plate to keep warm in a low oven, so that his family could eat together when Amelie returned.

Amelie dashed on past Wadham College where Nick had studied for his DPhil. The trees bordering the footpath were hung with tawny leaves. She passed the Natural History Museum and reached University Park where she saw other joggers, children on scooters, and a dog carrying a large stick in its mouth. She admired the might of the Wellingtonia sequoias as she always did, and sped on towards the riverbank, circling the pond where a heron stood poised in the reeds. The Cherwell flowed sleepily, its dazzling surface reflecting sparkles of sunlight. Amelie noted the man standing at the entrance to the footbridge. She often saw him, and always recoiled from the darkness cast over his closed face and hunched shoulders. She avoided his gaze, and sprinted on, thankful for other people in the vicinity. Looping around the circumference of the park, she was now halfway through her run, and heading in the direction of home.

Earlier that morning, while it was still dark and before Amelie had awoken, Darren Ackerman stood in a timber yard in Witney, rubbing his palms together in a nervous gesture, a roll-up hanging from the corner of his mouth. He grinned lopsidedly at Billy the groundsman's weary expression as they waited, as usual, for their chaotic boss to find the paperwork for the morning's tree surgery job. The Unimog lorry was loaded with chainsaws, ropes, cans of fuel, and rakes, and the chipper was already hooked up; they had been ready to leave for ten minutes or so. Darren took his roll-up between thumb and fore-finger, sucked it fiercely one last time, and threw it down onto the scalpings. He scratched his head, flattening a patch of sparse hair.

Overtime was good, he told himself; he needed the cash. He shivered. Breakfast had been a Kit Kat found in his kitchen drawer and washed down with scalding black coffee. Last night's beer made his stomach growl. Stamping his feet and plunging his hands into the pockets of his Kevlar trousers, he looked about and noticed that yellow stripes had appeared in the sky while they had been waiting. It looked like it might be a clear day. Of course, the ground would be sodden from the recent rain, the felled beech would make the usual mess in the garden, and the customer would moan. People expected tree work to be carried out nicely and tidily—like trees were not full of dust, dead leaves and insects, like severing a limb never created any sawdust. You did not fell a tree without consequences, Darren knew that. The beech would make a fuss when she came down; she would groan and splinter, and say her piece. It would be all right though, he reassured himself; he was a dab hand at dealing with clients these days, and it was amazing what Billy could do with a chipper and a rake. With any luck this customer would want to keep the logs, and Darren would be in the pub by lunchtime.

Paperwork finally in hand, the two men climbed into the cab of the Unimog, and Darren started the engine. He pulled his pouch of tobacco from his pocket and chucked it onto the dashboard before he forgot. He did not want to lose it, halfway up the tree. The Unimog was a proud beast of a vehicle, and Darren enjoyed the way people turned to look as he drove by. Other road users tended to be respectful too. You could say that for the boss; he had some good kit.

Amelie's ponytail swished from side to side as she jogged, and a few loose wisps of hair framed her freckled face. Her limbs were long and slender; she was a natural runner. Working as a children's nurse for the past six years, from time to time she mouthed silent prayers of gratitude for her own wellbeing and that of her family, knowing only too well that good health was a precarious state of being, not to be taken for granted, and often beyond anyone's control. She squinted in the sunlight; a passing car honked its horn in warning, and she hastily stepped back from a kerb.

Kerstin Lindberg was having palpitations again. She lay alone in her modern, four-bedroomed townhouse, wearing satin pyjamas and with a manicured hand splayed across her chest. She took deep breaths and willed the tremors to stop. Within seconds of her heartbeat steadying, she leapt out of bed, not wanting to waste any more precious time. In the bathroom, she discarded her pyjamas, dropping them into a well-placed laundry basket before stepping into the power shower, and turning it on full force. She massaged her head with shampoo, flannelled her armpits and between her legs, and allowed a hot stream of water to wash over her for a moment before turning the tap firmly off. She wrapped her head and body in tight plump towels and paused beside her bedroom window to watch the small children next door playing on their huge plastic climbing frame. The sight of the little ones inspired her; she would call in to see her daughter Amelie, Nick, and little Bertie, to kill some time before she headed off to Bicester Village. That would take care of the day, she decided, satisfied with her plan.

She raked mousse through her short blonde hair with her fingers, massaged expensive cream over her long arms and legs, lavished balm from another gleaming pot onto her face, and applied concealer to cover the dark rings beneath her china-blue eyes. After that she dabbed her face with foundation, brushed on blusher, eye liner and shadow, mascara and lipstick, carefully co-ordinating the colours to give her appearance a peachy glow. She threaded gold hoops through her ear lobes, found a red cashmere cardigan, black trousers, flat ballet pumps, and a colourful scarf. Running a hand over her neck, Kerstin mused that while she did not believe in plastic surgery, the idea was increasingly tempting.

On Amelie's return, Nick opened the door and caught her in a warm embrace. They shared a lingering kiss. Amelie smiled broadly. 'I'm very sweaty.'

'I love you when you're sweaty,' Nick murmured. His accent had a faint hint of Irish brogue, inherited from his father. 'I've made us a stack of pancakes.'

'Let me take a quick shower?'

He nodded. 'Sure.'

She gestured to a photograph of the two of them, hanging on the wall nearby. It was her favourite, from the time when they had met, seven years earlier, while she was a student nurse at Oxford Brookes and he was a postgraduate at Wadham. Nick was living on a houseboat on the Oxford Canal not far from where Amelie, ever the home-bird, still lived with her mother. In the photograph, he wore a chunky chestnut-coloured jumper and jeans, brown-rimmed glasses, and a wide and sexy smile. In those days, he still wore a silver band around his left forefinger and kept his auburn hair tied back in a ponytail. His arm was around her shoulder and she nestled beside him, her hand spread over his belly. Her hair was longer then too, its pale waves almost reaching her waist.

'I love that picture of us. I want us to always feel that way about each other.'

'I want you,' he teased.

She grinned and stroked his hair with her fingertips. 'I want you too, but we'll have to wait until later. I love you, you know.' She kissed her husband, leant into him again, and stroked his back.

Thank goodness she had said that, done that.

By the time Kerstin had dashed out to the local bakery in Walton Street, returned home and climbed into her shiny white Audi, the city had woken up and the streets were crowded with a mix of locals, students and the hundreds of visitors who came to shop ahead of Christmas or to see the sights or to eat in one of the many restaurants. An irritating breeze had whipped around her ankles as she had darted out to the shop, and Kerstin now shivered and turned the car heater up high. Traffic clogged her route, and she made tediously slow progress across the city centre. Once over Magdalen Bridge, however, she sped up Iffley Road, swung into Percy Street, and snatched a parking space close to Amelie and Nick's terraced house.

Should I have called? she wondered. Well, I'm here now, she shrugged, and having looped her tote bag over her arm and grabbed the bag of patisserie from the passenger seat, she stretched one elegantly-clad leg from her vehicle.

'Mum!'

'Darling. I thought I'd bring you some fresh croissants for breakfast.'

'We've already eaten a stack of pancakes. But come in! This is a surprise.' Amelie relieved her mother of the bulging paper bag.

'You know me. Full of them. Hi, Nick'

'Hello, Kerstin.'

'Who's my favourite grandson?' Kerstin crooned.

'Nick's just getting him ready to take him out.'

'Oh?' Kerstin's pencilled eyebrows shot up.

'I've got to work on my dissertation,' Amelie explained.

'Oh, so I'm interrupting?'

'Come in and have a coffee, Kerstin, while I load up the car and get Bertie's things organised. Here, you can keep him from running outside while I have the door open.' Nick handed the infant to his grandmother.

'I don't want to get in the way if you're busy.' Kerstin dropped her tote bag, and took Bertie, who wriggled in her arms and grabbed at her earring.

'I am never too busy for a coffee,' Amelie stated firmly.

Thank goodness, she had said that too. Had offered. Had been kind to her lonely parent.

'Let me take Bertie off you, Mum. He's dribbling all the time. Teething.'

'I don't need a coffee. I can see you're busy. I'm on my way to Bicester.'

'Shopping?'

'Yes. Do you need anything for Bertie?'

'Not that I can think of.'

Nick gathered a rucksack, changing bag, and pushchair, and loaded them into the boot. When he returned, Bertie squirmed impatiently, and so Nick wrestled him into his little duffle coat, said a rushed goodbye to Amelie and Kerstin, and carried the child out to the car where he strapped him into his seat before turning to wave.

Amelie and Kerstin stood outside the front door with their arms folded against the chilly breeze, and waved back, and then watched as Nick turned the key in the ignition. Nothing happened. He tried again, several times. Nothing.

He got out of the car and cursed. He raised the bonnet and poked about in the engine, and tried several more times to start the car while Amelie and Kerstin clustered around it. 'No good,' he declared.

Bertie kicked his legs playfully in his car seat.

'Do you have any jump leads?' Kerstin asked.

'No.'

'Me neither. Where are you two going? I can give you a lift.'

'They were off to the Cotswold Wildlife Park for the day,' Amelie said.

'I'll take them!'

'You can't do that, Mum. They're going for the whole day. And you hate animals.'

'No, I don't. Well, not animals in cages. I don't mind animals in cages. And that place is more like a garden.'

'I'll think of something else to do.' Nick scratched his head.

'I promised Bertie you were going to the zoo,' Amelie pointed out.

'Zoo! Zoo!' shouted Bertie from inside the car, kicking his legs furiously now. Amelie lifted him out of his seat.

Kerstin spoke up. 'I'll take you; that's decided. We'll just have to call in to my place on the way, Nick. I can't visit a zoo dressed like this. And I need a different handbag if I'm going to be able to help with Bertie.'

Once the new idea was agreed upon, Nick transferred Bertie's gear to Kerstin's car, strapped him into his car seat yet again, pecked Amelie on the cheek, and murmured, 'Wish me luck,' before lowering himself into the front passenger seat of the Audi.

Kerstin fluttered her fingers at Amelie, and blew her a kiss. 'I hope the dissertation goes well, darling.'

'With any luck I'll never have to look at it again after today!' She waved and blew kisses as they disappeared up the street.

Kerstin drove them back to her house in Merrivale Square, and Nick took Bertie to run around on the rectangle of clipped grass in her back garden while she changed into warmer trousers and designer walking boots, and swapped her tote for a crossover body bag. When she was finally ready, she suggested to Nick that they might wish to stroll, with Bertie in his pushchair, up to Walton Street for a coffee before they took off for the zoo. Nick agreed all too willingly, envisaging a tall mug of steaming latte, and twenty minutes of peace with a copy of The Guardian while Kerstin entertained his son.

By the time they returned to Merrivale Square after coffee, changed Bertie's nappy, got everyone loaded back into the car, and eventually left the city, it was just gone a quarter to twelve.

The tree had fallen like a beauty. Fat rings of her trunk lay sectioned across the customer's lawn, which was mercifully dry and had not got too churned up. While Billy laboured, feeding the tree's limbs into the chipper, Darren clutched a mug of milky coffee and smoked a roll-up, his tree climber's harness hanging limply around his backside. He reflected on the job. When he had climbed the tree's slender branches, a profound sense of sadness had circled them both. He had grasped her limbs, trusting her to hold him despite his impending treachery, and levered himself into a safe position. Pausing for a moment with his weight cradled in a fork of her living wood and his chainsaw idling, high above the patchwork of suburban gardens, he had felt the beech flex, and had closed his pale eyes and lifted his stubbled chin to the east wind. Sunlight was filtered by foxy-coloured leaves which rustled prettily, and there was a moment when he considered not making the first incision or starting the murderous process of dismembering her; but then he remembered the money, and knew that if he did not bring her down, some other tree surgeon would. The so-called "owner" of the beech was scared by evidence of squirrel damage and terrified of her financial liability, should a limb fall on something or someone: understandable really, in these days of litigation. He had revved the engine of his saw.

Now, with the job done, he was awash with regret as he sucked on his cigarette and surveyed her graceful limbs, lying chopped and dead on the grass. There was no going back, no saying he was sorry, and it meaning anything. His deed struck him as profoundly wrong, and not fair on the voiceless woody life-force. In another time or another place, she would have lived to old age, shedding an occasional limb as the years passed, slowly decaying but playing hostess to a million other living creatures as she did so, all the time with her arms stretched out for the sky. Darren believed in karma, and was not convinced that a career in tree-felling boded well for him. He stubbed out his roll-up on the top of a low brick wall before chucking it behind a garage. He swore that the trees cursed him as they fell, full of reproach and fury. This one had groaned. He scratched his chin with sap-stained fingers, and grimaced.

Still, at least they would get out of there early; the customer wanted to keep the logs and the wood chips. They would be back in the yard by one, and he could get straight to the pub. Happy days.

The A40 from Oxford to Burford was busy with weekend traffic. Perhaps Saturdays were not such a bad thing after all, Kerstin reflected as she joined the flow of vehicles out of the city. Here she was, with her handsome son-in-law and cute grandson, enjoying some quality family time. One did need a day off occasionally, even if so many unstructured hours were a challenge. She glanced in her rear-view mirror. Bertie had fallen asleep clutching his soft toy rabbit in his chubby grip, and Nick, who was a man of few words at the best of times, sat gazing at the scenery as it flashed by. Kerstin was not sure how she would keep the conversation flowing all day without Amelie there.

'How's work?' she asked.

'Oh, it's grand, thanks.' Nick ran his fingers through his thick auburn hair. 'Do you always drive this quickly?'

'I'll slow down if it makes you feel better,' she replied, crisply.

As they approached the Eynsham roundabout, the traffic decelerated to a crawl. Kerstin turned on the car radio and drummed her fingers on the steering wheel. There was a stream of coaches and cars in front of her, creeping along like a lumpy caterpillar. When they finally reached the dual carriageway, she pressed the accelerator down, and then was forced to slow again by road works at Curbridge. As she drove, she mentally mapped the rest of the day. She would take them all for lunch on arrival, and then allow Bertie to see the zoo animals. There would no doubt be another trip to the café for tea, and the shop after that, and then they would be able to head for home. She drew a blank at what to do with the empty evening that lay ahead. She glanced at her scarlet fingernails as the traffic grew sluggish again before the Minster Lovell roundabout. After it, she flew past ranks of trees in full autumnal splendour and onwards to a landscape of sudden wide-open sky, broad grassy verges and dry-stone walls lining open fields.

'I should get out of town more often!' she exclaimed to Nick who gazed to his left, at the magnificent scale of field and sky.

Darren drove the Unimog out of Burford, glad to be out of the tangle of traffic, finally. The sun blinded him. His stomach grumbled from lack of food and his scalp itched. Through the windscreen, he witnessed the terrain open up dramatically; undulating hills, for as far as the eye could see. He reached onto the dashboard for his tobacco pouch, and glanced at a lone, scrappy, verge-side tree, which had somehow been spared by the farmer. He wondered why that tree got to survive—what made it so special?

'Here, fix us both a roll up,' he said to Billy, handing him the tobacco pouch. As he spoke, the packet slipped between his fingers and fell into the footwell. Instinctively, and without a moment's thought, he released his seatbelt and stooped to pick it up. As he did so, his right hand still gripped the lorry's steering wheel, and drew it fractionally round. The Unimog swung violently across the central line of the road.

'Watch out!' Billy cried, and Darren reared back. Suddenly, all he knew were crashing sounds like nothing he had ever heard before in his life—a splintering, groaning, confusing tangle of noise and pain, and then... seeping darkness.

It happened out of nowhere. There was no warning. A white lorry with a flat silver grill beneath a high cab veered into her lane and came straight at her. Kerstin's first reaction was disbelief. A split-second later, she rammed her foot against the brake pedal and swung her Audi towards the grass verge, desperate to avoid the looming giant monstrosity. The screeching clamour of clashing metal pained her ears, and as her airbag inflated, and the car collapsed, she knew that something about her body was terribly, terribly wrong.

Nick, who was looking away from the Unimog at the benign view of brown rolling hills, did not see the lorry, did not anticipate what was coming at all, and as he gazed at the landscape, his body was propelled forcefully sideways and the world that he knew simply slipped away.

Bertie, still clutching his rabbit and dreaming, saw a thousand stars.

Billy the ground worker glimpsed the startled expression of a blonde woman behind the steering wheel of a white car, and then heard the appalling shattering crunch of crumpling metal as her vehicle disappeared beneath them. The Unimog windscreen fractured into a million mosaic pieces, obscuring his vision, as he was flung painfully against the full restraining force of his seat belt. He watched Darren's head, propelled by the same force, smash against the dashboard. His body buckled, slithered downwards and wedged itself in the gap between the steering wheel and the seat.

A Volvo travelling behind Kerstin swerved and bounced over the grass verge and collided with a dry-stone wall. The car behind that attempted to screech to a halt, leaving strips of rubber on the road's surface, but was unable to stop smashing into the back of the Audi. Another car piled in behind it. A van travelling behind the Unimog steered to the left, hurtled over the grass verge and, with its tyres losing purchase, rolled onto its roof and skidded down the incline where the bank fell away from the road. Two further vehicles skidded; one smashed into the brushwood chipper. For a brief moment, all was still.

Amelie ran her fingers back through her hair and took a deep breath, as she heard her phone ringing. The dissertation that would complete her master's degree was almost finished. As she had worked on the final draft that morning, she had grown excited by the prospect of no more studying—for a while, at least. There would be more time for Nick and Bertie. She answered her mobile phone. It was her reclusive grandmother Cleome, calling from Sweden.

Cleome, who was English but had lived in Sweden for most of her adult life, had been named after her mother's favourite garden annual, the colourful and sumptuous cleome hassleriana; her mother not realising (or perhaps not caring) that Cleome would spend her life spelling out the name or explaining how it was pronounced (Klee-*oh*-mee) to almost everyone she met.

'Have I caught you at a good time?' Cleome asked brightly.

'Yes, perfect. I'm about to take a break from studying and get something to eat.'

'Ah good, good. Where are Bertie and Nick?'

'They've gone to the wildlife park for the day.'

'Bertie will love to see the animals.'

'He was excited; he kept shouting, "Zoo! Zoo!"'

'I can't wait to see him again. He is a true joy.'

'They have gone in Mum's car, actually. Ours wouldn't start, and she happened to be here.'

'My Kerstin—in a zoo?'

Amelie chuckled. 'Exactly. She had to go home and change her shoes and find the right handbag before she could go.'

'Ha, ha, ha! We are wicked to laugh. But she hates animals.'

'She said she didn't mind them in cages.'

'Ho, ho, ho! You are making me hurt with laughter. Now Trassel is barking. You know I love my daughter—but she baffles and amuses me too.'

'I know you love her; don't worry. How is my favourite dog?'

'Like her owner, her whiskers are turning grey, and she is getting fat. Helen keeps scolding us both about our weight; you know how bossy she can get.'

'How *is* Helen?'

'Oh, you know, still working all hours, as doctors do. Very busy with her refugees and looking after us waifs and strays. She's in love with Daniel but she denies it, and gets cross with me if I make hints. But enough of me; tell me about you.'

'I'll be glad to finish my master's, and then hopefully I can apply for a promotion.'

'You're a good, hardworking woman, Am. You make me very proud, you know.'

'Oh, I don't know about that.'

'And Bertie had a good week at nursery?'

'He did but he's grouchy from teething. Nick's great with him when I'm on nights.'

'His work at the university goes well?'

'He grumbles about his students but he loves his research work, and yes, it goes well. But I want to hear all about your week in beautiful Sweden. I miss you, and I miss *Det Lilla Huset*.'

'I'm an old lady, haunted by her memories and her aching joints. Not much to tell. And I'm facing another Swedish winter. It's enforced hibernation some years. *Det Lilla Huset,* for all its charm, is a draughty wooden house in the middle of nowhere.'

'But you still love it there?'

'I would not be anywhere else. Ignore me: I'm grumbling.'

'Just think of all that beautiful white snow in the forest!'

'Pah, you romanticise it!'

Billy struggled to pull Darren upright. The weight of him was unnatural and leaden; his eyes were open and blank like there was no-one at home, and his arms flopped like a rag doll's. Billy did not know much but he suspected that Darren was dead. He sat him upright, clambered out of the cab, staggered to the verge, and threw up. Looking about, he realised that there were cars stopped at odd angles, all over the place, and a strange quiet had descended on the scene. One van was on its roof. A fat man ran up to him, yelling into his mobile phone, and asking if he was all right. Billy could not speak. His legs gave way, and he collapsed into a praying position, his gaze fixed on a patch of dandelions.

Along the road from Burford, vehicles slowed to a halt with their engines running. Drivers wondered what the delay was about. From the Oxford direction, there was already a queue back beyond the Minster Lovell roundabout. The chilling easterly breeze swooped between the tangled vehicles and over the debris that was strewn across both carriageways and the verges on either side of the road. Motorists who could see what had happened and had escaped the carnage made fevered calls to the emergency services, and rushed to the assistance of others who were less fortunate. Only one man was brave enough to approach the mangled wreckage of Kerstin's Audi before turning away with his arms wide open to keep others from the sight.

A family, having abandoned their car, stood huddled and pale-faced at the edge of a field. A woman who said she was a nurse attended to Billy, throwing a shawl around his thin shoulders. At Billy's gesture, she ran to the cab of the Unimog.

One man shouted that he had to get by, and would people get out of the way and let him pass.

When they came, the sirens and flashing blue lights were a relief. In urgent convoy, two police cars, an ambulance, a rapid response vehicle, and a fire engine wove their way past the stopped traffic to the mutilated heart of the accident. Officers and ambulance staff swarmed around the tangled mass of Kerstin's car and the Unimog, like flies.

Darren Ackerman's body was extracted carefully from the cab. It looked unscathed apart from the area just above his left temple which had swollen like a purple fruit.

'Oh, mate!' Billy cried.

Paramedics worked to stabilise the head injury and resuscitate Darren, and Billy turned away. Firemen with cutting equipment set about Kerstin's Audi.

'There's a child in here!' a fireman shouted.

Billy thought his heart might stop.

The scene of the accident was cordoned off and bystanders were led from the immediate area. An air ambulance appeared and hovered above the scene. One car which had collided with the brushwood chipper had occupants still trapped inside while another, which had been travelling in front of the Audi and had miraculously avoided collision by spinning out of the way, had come to a halt facing the carnage, its driver distraught from shock. The passengers of two further cars which had ploughed into the melee—one into the back of the Audi and the other into the back of the first—were being carefully extracted from the wreckage. One man emerged and was able to stand up, albeit gingerly.

Billy watched confounded, as another man wriggled out of the window of the upside-down van further down the bank, merely nursing one hurt arm.

When he had been checked by ambulance personnel, Billy was taken to one side by a police officer and asked to sit in a panda car. He heard the officer request that forensics be contacted. The sun had gone behind a cloud and Billy could not stop shivering.

Out of sight of Billy, the fight for Darren Ackerman's life was soberly abandoned, and his body was covered. A paramedic filled in a form.

Amelie ended the call to Cleome. She made herself a quick sandwich, slicing one of the fresh croissants that her mother had bought, and stuffing it with cheese and tomato. As she ate, she worked out that all she needed to do was check her footnotes and bibliography, do a final read-through, and then she would be finished. She read a message from her closest friend Esme, who was also a nurse at The Children's Hospital. They had known each other since childhood, attending the same schools, and eventually choosing the same profession. Esme invited Amelie, Nick and Bertie to supper that evening. Amelie replied that they would love to come. While she chewed her last mouthful, she transferred a load of Bertie's clothes from the washing machine to the tumble dryer, set the machine going, and then leant against the worktop. She gazed up at the patch of blue sky visible through the window, and tried to call Nick but he did not answer his phone.

He would be busy with Bertie, who would be a handful, toddling around in such a wide-open space. Amelie smiled to herself as she imagined her son's face, and his innocent delight at seeing so many animals.

She made herself a mug of coffee, and had just sat back down in front of her laptop when the doorbell rang.

2

It was a warm March morning, a few days after her nineteenth birthday, when Amelie first met Nick Tierney. At the time she was a student nurse, and most mornings before taking the bus across the city to Oxford Brookes, she would go running. Her usual practice was to leave the home she shared with Kerstin on the northern tip of Jericho, and head down Rutherway. Always drawn by the water, she crossed to the towpath beside the Oxford Canal, and ran past houseboats that in those days were permanently moored there. During these runs, she met early morning dog walkers and other pedestrians on the narrow spit of land between the canal and Castle Mill Stream, a parallel waterway. She relished the damp green scent in the air, and always jogged in the direction of the city, and then, depending on her mood, either wound her way home through the narrow, homely streets of Jericho or took a longer route past the ancient colleges and museums.

Nick's narrowboat always caught her eye because of its neatness and fresh coat of racing green and cherry red paintwork. Some boats in the small community were neglected, with furniture or other items stored against dirty windows or piled in cockpits, but Nick's shone. Living on the water in such a beautiful vessel struck the teenage Amelie as pioneering and romantic.

On that particular March morning, bags of charcoal briquettes were stacked neatly on the cabin roof of Nick's boat, replacing the potted herbs and geraniums of the previous summer. Smoke rose from a short chimney. Nick was outside, kneeling on a small patch of grass at the water's edge, attempt to fix a tyre on his bicycle. She had never seen him before; she would have remembered if she had. His auburn curls were tied loosely back, and his broad shoulders were clad in a woolly jumper. He bent over his machine. As she approached, he looked up and smiled. 'Nice day for it,' he said, the hint of Irish brogue clearly discernible.

'Yes, isn't it? What happened?'

'Some bastard took the wheel. Teach me to leave it out here. I'm fixing in a new one. Could I ask you to help me, and hold the bike upright while I tighten this nut? It won't take a second.'

'Sure.'

As she held the bike, they chatted. When he asked, Amelie told him that she was studying paediatric nursing. Nick told her that he was working towards a DPhil in Earth Sciences.

Amelie had defied convention; when most of her friends from The Cherwell School had left Oxford to study at universities around the country, she had chosen to stay in the city that she knew and loved. As the lone child of a single parent, she was close to her mother. Kerstin had been born in Sweden, and the two of them always spoke Swedish at home—a private language which made their domestic world a little bit different and special. Her father had flown many years before, on the Christmas Eve before she had turned three. They had not heard from him since. Amelie occasionally felt his absence like a small hole somewhere in her being, but she had never sought him out. The type of person who walked out on a young daughter at Christmas was not someone she wanted to know. Kerstin earned a good salary at a management consultancy, and they often took exotic holidays together, but all the travelling had a curious effect on Amelie; far from wanting to see more of the world, she had decided that new places were over-rated. Everything she needed was available in her beloved Oxford—her mother, her friends, the parties, the culture, the shops, the history, the modernity; and, given her ambition to be a nurse, some of the best teaching hospitals in the world.

After that first day when she helped him with his bicycle, Amelie often saw Nick—or if he was not actually visible, she might catch the aroma of fresh coffee or fried bacon as she ran past his narrowboat. Occasionally, as the weather warmed up, books lay strewn across the cockpit, and she became curious about his subject. Earth Sciences had an enchanting ring about it.

One evening, after a placement of night shifts when she had not run for about ten days, she bumped into him in a bar in Walton Street. A live band played loud indie rock music, and Nick tapped her on the shoulder and mouthed hello. He gestured with his thumb toward a quieter corner of the pub. The two sat and talked until the place closed, walked back to his narrowboat, and continued talking until dawn when they both fell asleep. For Amelie, it was as if her heart had known Nick for millennia, and on that first night a voice had whispered that he was 'the one' despite her young age.

Nick's parents lived a few miles away in a hamlet called Toot Baldon. Nick was an only child too, born late in his parent's marriage, when his mother Hilary was almost forty and his father fifty-two. Patrick was Irish, and Nick had spent a lot of time as a child visiting grandparents, aunts, uncles and cousins in County Sligo. Like his father, he loved a good pint of Guinness, and a great *craic*. Unusually for an academic, laughter danced in his chestnut-coloured eyes and joy played around the corners of his mouth, lacing his life blood, lightening his intense study and later, enhancing his outstanding research work.

On the evening when he met Amelie in the pub, he had recently ended a long relationship with an undergraduate called Jessica. His mother Hilary still held Jessica in high esteem and mourned her departure. Hilary was a somewhat sour Englishwoman who clung to her only child. When Nick had taken his place at Oxford, she had moved house to stay close to him.

The hours that Amelie passed with Nick were a complete contrast to the ordered way of life she had always known at her mother's Merrivale Square townhouse, a stone's throw away. Where Kerstin was neat, practical and driven, Nick was spontaneous and affectionate, and his flourishing work ethic involved chaotic piles of books, discarded coffee mugs and irregular hours, although he always took fastidious care of his boat and his bicycle. His effortless genius dazzled Amelie who grafted to gain her degree. She saw straight to the heart of him though, to the goodness that was the fuel of his fire, and he saw the same qualities in her.

'D'you know what I love about your face?' he asked her one evening in those early days, 'apart from these fine Nordic cheekbones, eyes that are the colour of the Baltic on a winter's day, and the cute way your two front teeth cross slightly?'

'No, tell me, what?' Humour flickered about her lips.

'It's the way your beautiful soul shines through everything you do.' He pulled off his glasses and studied her for a moment before wrapping his arms around her. It was the first time he told her he loved her.

Nick was seven years older than Amelie, and although she was only nineteen, she began to spend her nights and days on the houseboat.

Kerstin was philosophical and buried herself in work. Amelie continued to meet a small group of friends, especially Esme and Marsha who had stayed in the city too. Kerstin travelled abroad on business after gaining a promotion. Nick was awarded his DPhil a year later, and gained a position as a postdoctoral researcher at the university. As life got busier and they sought a more convenient lifestyle, they left behind the narrowboat and moved in together permanently, to a one-bedroomed flat in Princes Street. Amelie graduated in 2011 and started work as a paediatric nurse at The Children's Hospital.

In the scorching summer of 2013, Amelie and Nick married in a simple ceremony at the Oxford Register Office, to the disapproval of Hilary who had always dreamed of a church wedding for her son. Nick was thirty and Amelie was twenty-three. The honeymoon took place in Ireland, beginning in a smart hotel in Dublin and continuing at Patrick's cottage in the beautiful countryside beside Lough Gill. Yeats' famous poem The Lake Isle of Innisfree was written there—it was the only poem that Nick knew, and he could recite it from heart. The sun had shone for their entire honeymoon, lighting up the emerald landscape like a blessing.

Two years later, after Amelie had begun the master's degree and while she still worked full-time, she became pregnant unexpectedly—news which Nick greeted with whoops of delight. Amelie was uncertain about how she would cope, but as her grandmother Cleome said, women did not always get to choose such things; sometimes a greater force was at work, and it was best for Amelie to focus her energy on acceptance. Everyone would support and help her.

Bertie, named after Albert Einstein (whom Nick greatly admired), was born on the twenty-third of May, 2016. Shortly afterwards, despairing of the couple ever being able to afford a home of their own, Hilary and Patrick gifted them a deposit for the terraced house in Percy Street. Bertie joined Oxford Brookes' nursery and Amelie returned to her studies and her job at The Children's Hospital.

And throughout all the hard work, the exhaustion and the small tests they faced every day, Amelie and Nick remained kindred souls. Sometimes they had furious arguments, and there were days when Nick drove Amelie to distraction; but their bond was strong, and their joy mutual.

The doorbell rang again, and Amelie moved swiftly to answer it. She was surprised to find two policewomen standing on the path outside her door. Her first reaction was fear that she had done something wrong, but she could not think what.

Frowning, she asked, 'Yes?'

One of the policewomen asked if they could come in, and Amelie panicked, unsure about her rights, and still convinced that she must have done something awful.

'Tell me what I have done first,' she demanded.

The overweight policewoman with scraped-back blonde hair and shiny pink skin reassured Amelie that she had done nothing wrong, and quietly insisted that they come into the house. Something about her tone made Amelie step back from the door. She led them to the sitting area beside the fireplace, and the other police officer who was small and dark-skinned suggested that Amelie take a seat on the sofa. The concern in her brown eyes was startling, and Amelie quickly complied, her heart thudding. The officer sat in Nick's armchair.

'Can you confirm your name for me, please?' she asked, and after Amelie had given it, she added, 'And can you confirm that you are the mother of Albert Patrick Tierney?'

Oh no, Amelie thought. Oh, no.

There were a couple more questions about her mother and Nick which she answered, her mind a blur. The overweight policewoman, who perched at the opposite end of the sofa, cleared her throat, and with unwavering kindness, began to speak slowly and clearly, explaining that she was here to tell Amelie that, very sadly, her husband and mother had been killed in a road accident, and that her son had been taken to hospital by air ambulance, unconscious and not breathing.

Amelie was so shocked that she could not take in what the policewoman said. She asked where her family were, and the officer replied that she did not know, explaining in a voice musically softened with sympathy, that she had not been briefed properly yet, and did not know exactly what had happened.

'But they're at the wildlife park—they left hours ago,' Amelie asserted. 'There must be some mistake. They called at my mother's place first. Nick messaged me from there. My mother was changing her clothes.' The policewomen listened. 'They went for a drink and a snack in Walton Street before they set off. He told me that too. Bertie was grizzly. He's teething. They are at the wildlife park. The Cotswold Wildlife Park.'

'We have identified your family from information in your mother's and your husband's possessions. Your son has been taken by Air Ambulance to the John Radcliffe Hospital,' the dark-skinned officer stated, her brown eyes watering.

'But I don't understand. There must be some mistake.'

'There is no mistake. We're here to take you to see your son. We need to leave now.'

'I am a nurse. I work at The Children's Hospital. Is that where he is? I want to see him. Now.' Amelie stood up and stumbled on the rug.

'He is at Accident and Emergency at the John Radcliffe. If you would like to gather your things, we'll drive you to the hospital.'

'It's okay. I can drive. Wait, no, I can't. The car won't start. They didn't go in our car because it wouldn't start. My mother drove. Are you sure you have this right? They were not in our car.'

'I believe the car in the accident was an Audi.'

'My mother has an Audi.' Amelie frowned, unable to register the implication of her own remark. It was as if her brain had frozen, and life played out in slow motion. 'Mum just left here this morning. And Nick… Nick must be all right. He is always all right, he's so strong. But I need to see Bertie!' she exclaimed suddenly, and grabbed her handbag and slung it across her body. She picked up her phone.

'See, Nick messaged me this morning. And I rang him back at lunchtime. Here, see. He didn't answer because he was busy with Bertie at the zoo. Where is Nick now? He will explain to you.'

'We don't know where your husband is now but we can make enquiries and find out for you. Have you got your house keys with you? Maybe you need a coat.'

'My coat. What about Bertie, what does he need?'

'I'm sure the hospital will take care of that.'

'You can just drop me off there; it will be fine.'

'We'll stay with you—all day, if necessary. Come with us now. Is everything turned off, nothing on the cooker? Your computer?'

Amelie closed the lid of her laptop. 'I could take the bus.'

'We'll be going in the police car, with the blue light on.'

'He'll be all right? Bertie will be all right?'

'He was unconscious when the paramedics reached him. The last report was, he wasn't breathing but they were trying to resuscitate him.'

Amelie let out a little cry. She folded her arms and began to pace. 'It will be all right, you know. My mother is a good driver. Nick is resourceful and clever. And Bertie is a strong kid.'

'Let's go, get you into the car now, and you can see your son.'

'I hope he's not frightened or scared. He's quite a plucky kid when it comes to being with strangers so he should be okay.'

The two policewomen glanced at each other.

'Bertie is unconscious,' the blonde one repeated quietly, putting a hand on Amelie's shoulder. 'Your mother and your husband have passed.'

At the scene of the accident, all the casualties had been transported to hospital but the A40 remained closed. The sun shone from a bleached blue sky. A flock of migrating birds flew overhead. A bee landed on a lone field poppy at the side of the road. The autumn breeze had changed direction, and a gentle south-westerly caressed the mangled wreckage. Recovery vehicles and a specialist road cleaning service vehicle waited a short distance away, ready to move in once the police had finished gathering and recording evidence. Appointed officers dealt with curious onlookers in both directions. Billy had been asked to give a witness statement, and the tree surgery company had been contacted. There would be a full investigation into the safety of the Unimog. Darren's family in the Midlands were being informed of their loss.

The policewomen led Amelie through alien hospital corridors. She could not speak, and walked between them, docile as a lamb. They entered a small, windowless room where there were four chairs and an empty table. A doctor came in straight afterwards, and closed the door behind him. He was an older medic, an Indian with combed-back grey hair and a kindly expression. Amelie recognised him. He sat beside her and told her in quiet, respectful tones that he was very sorry but that she was too late.

Bertie was dead on arrival at the hospital.

'He would not have known anything,' the man reassured. 'His passing would have been very peaceful.'

Amelie glanced up at the doctor, and knew instinctively that what he told her was true. Being a nurse, she was used to death. She knew the procedures, recognised the doctor's quiet voice, the awkward sadness in his eyes, his concern for her, his awareness that she might become his next patient, his professional readiness.

She took a deep breath, and nodded at the doctor. 'Where is he?' she whispered. 'I want to see him.'

She was led to another room, and registered the presence of a nurse. 'What is this cut, here on his head?' she asked.

A small neat crescent, like a new moon, not awful at all but somehow miraculous, scarred Bertie's smooth forehead, just above his eyebrow. His face was serene and still. His long eyelashes rested on his perfect cheeks. His clothes were neat, as if someone had taken care, and tidied him up.

Her question remained unanswered.

'This is him. Yes, this is Bertie,' Amelie confirmed in a whisper, confused.

She had seen death before, but not like this. Oh, never like this.

Ever so gently, she scooped her child's limp body into her arms, perched on a nearby chair, and cradled him, stroking his hair. He still smelled of the shampoo they had at home; the fragrance of his skin was still unique to him. His hands were still chubby and small, each little fingernail perfect.

'It cannot be,' she whispered.

When she looked back on it, she could not remember all that happened next, only snatches. She had to give all sorts of details about Bertie, clinging to the small hope that by giving the information, there might be a tiny chance that someone would realise they had made a mistake.

At one point she begged a doctor to try again to resuscitate Bertie, and bring him back.

The nurse gave her Bertie's soft toy rabbit, and she clutched it.

'I don't understand,' she repeated, over and over.

She stood in a corridor with the policewomen, waiting for something, and a hospital porter came up to her, a kind Brazilian man called Luiz, whom she knew.

'I got him up this morning. I gave him his milk in the usual way. He was really looking forward to the zoo. I don't know how this can happen. I don't understand,' she told Luiz.

'Your boy is an angel now,' Luiz murmured, and took one of her cold hands in his warm one and held it for a long time while she stood, waiting.

'He has gone to join the angels,' Luiz whispered again.

She was not allowed to see Nick. Or her mother. Their bodies had been taken to the mortuary at the coroner's office. She was furious. Surely, that was not right? She shouted at the blonde policewoman. Nick was her husband. Kerstin was her mother. Why were total strangers interfering, and telling her what she could and could not do with the people she loved? The policewoman was very understanding, and gently let her know, repeatedly let her know, that this decision was for her own sake.

From another small room with no windows, Amelie telephoned Nick's parents. Someone put a coffee on the table in front of her but she did not touch it. Hilary answered the house phone, and Amelie asked to speak to Patrick.

'There's been an accident, Patrick,' she managed, her voice hoarse. 'It's Nick.'

I am telling a man he has lost his son, she thought bleakly. How do I do this in the very best way? Tears streamed down her cheeks and her shoulders shook.

'And Bertie.' She whispered his name and stalled. Blood pounded in her ears, and she heard a sound like rushing wind tearing through her body. She could not grasp what to say to Nick's dad. She no longer knew what was right and wrong. 'Patrick,' she repeated blindly. 'Oh, Patrick.'

One of the policewomen gently took the telephone, identified herself, and spoke in hushed tones with Nick's father, answering his questions quietly and professionally. The road number was mentioned. The time: twelve thirty-eight. The vehicles involved. Where the body was.

Patrick said he would speak to his wife, and he would call them back.

Kerstin's Audi and the Unimog were winched onto separate recovery vehicles and removed from the accident scene. The Volvo which had hit the dry-stone wall, the van which had overturned, and the other vehicle that had crashed into the back of the brushwood chipper were also towed away. The road cleaner set to work. At four twelve in the afternoon, the A40 was re-opened to traffic.

Amelie did not know where to go next. Like a wild animal, she sensed that it was not safe to return to her ravaged home. The policewomen drove her to Esme's house, a little way up the street. Amelie rang Esme's doorbell. Esme flung open her door. In the room behind her, her son Joel toddled around, pushing a baby walker full of wooden bricks.

Joel looked over at Amelie and said, 'Bertie!'

Esme's face broke into a smile until she registered the state of her friend, and noticed the policewomen, who lingered beside the gate. She frowned, and spread her hand over her chest.

At the sight of Joel, which was something she had not anticipated, Amelie swivelled to leave but Esme, knowing that something was terribly wrong, caught her friend's arm and barked at her husband to take Joel into the back garden. She led Amelie to a sofa, and guided her to sit down.

The dark-skinned policewoman explained what had happened, and Esme, her face streaming with tears, took her silent friend into her arms. At some point, Paul and the blonde policewoman made mugs of tea, and Paul left the house to take Joel to his parents. The policewomen left, and together Amelie and Esme telephoned Cleome. Amelie's voice was weak; she could not think clearly or explain, and Esme prompted and then eventually took over the phone.

Amelie spent that night curled up between Esme and Paul in their bed. She insisted that they both stay with her. Esme cradled her, while Paul, not knowing what was appropriate, lay flat on his back, unable to touch the distraught woman sandwiched in his bed. When he thought that Amelie might have finally fallen asleep, he crept away into the spare room.

Amelie feared that she might forget to breathe if she were left alone for a moment. Or else freeze to death without the warmth of Esme's body.

❄

In a red-painted wooden cottage known as *Det Lilla Huset*, deep in a forest clearing beside Lake Båven in Sörmland, Sweden, Cleome Sjögren lurched about her bedroom. Her blotched face was riven by grief and she clutched a crumpled handkerchief in her arthritic hand. Ancient silver bangles jingled as she dabbed her tears. Trassel, a black and white border collie, tiptoed beside her as she selected items for a suitcase—underwear, nightwear, and a clean skirt that concealed a full bottle of bootleg Russian vodka.

Really, all she wanted to do was to *go*.

'Have you got your pills?' Helen checked, coming into the bedroom. Helen was tall, and some thirty years younger than Cleome. Tousled dark hair framed her coffee-coloured eyes and long, elegant nose.

Cleome retrieved a packet of tablets from a bedside drawer and flung it into the case. Her grey hair, escaping from its bun, hung in wisps about her pink face.

'I have made a soup for us to eat before I take you to the airport,' Helen said.

'I cannot think of eating.'

'You must. Just a spoonful.' Helen put a hand on her friend's shoulder, and then sensing the need, drew Cleome into an embrace. 'I can come with you, you know.'

Cleome pulled away and squeezed her friend's forearm. 'You must stay and look after Trassel, make sure Josef comes to feed the hens every day. He can sleep here when he doesn't have school, if he wants.'

'He will enjoy that, and Trassel will be fine with us at *Båvenshult*.'

'She will. I know she will… *Oh, how could this happen, Helen?*' Cleome cried, suddenly overcome.

Tears welled in Helen's eyes and the tip of her nose turned pink. She shook her head and struggled to regain her composure. 'I really don't know,' she replied.

The day after the accident, the clocks went back, as they always did at that time of year. Paul and Esme walked up Percy Street on either side of Amelie while it was still early, and before most of the neighbours had stirred. Amelie wore clothes from the day before and her hair was scraped back off her face in a rough ponytail. She trembled constantly. She did not want to return to the house but knew she must.

Paul led the way into the tiny patch of front garden, carrying Amelie's house key. Bunches of flowers were propped against the front door and reached partway down the garden path. Someone had left a dish of food wrapped in layers of clingfilm. Paul picked it up. Esme reached forward and stooped to collect the bouquets. Behind them, Amelie stood and sobbed.

Inside, it looked the same. It smelled the same. Everything of theirs was there, and yet *they* were not. Amelie slid straight to the kettle, and filled it from the tap. Esme searched cupboards for vases and Paul put the dish of food in the fridge.

No-one spoke until Paul said, 'I'll leave you two to it, then. I'll be back later.' He was going to collect Joel, of course, but nobody acknowledged that.

Amelie and Esme sat at the table, and drank scalding sweet tea. 'Maybe you should have a shower, get changed,' Esme suggested gently. 'I'll be right here if you need anything.'

Amelie drifted past the family portraits on the stairwell wall, and oh God, quickly past Bertie's open bedroom door and into her own room where she faced Nick's discarded clothes, lying on a chair.

She cried out—the strangest sound, part scream, part howl—and Esme was there, hugging her, holding her, and saying, 'You can do this. Come on. You can do this. Let's find you some clothes. Start with a shower and then we'll decide what to do next. One step at a time.'

Downstairs in the bathroom, Amelie stood in the shower and sobbed; she did not use shampoo or soap. The towel she grabbed off the radiator smelled of Nick, and she held it to her face, inhaling deeply, as water dripped onto the floor. Esme appeared, rubbed her dry, and handed her clean clothes.

Amelie sat on the sofa. A bite of toast and jam stuck in her throat. Toys were strewn around, abandoned after the departure for the zoo.

'Shall I tidy?' Esme appealed. 'Maybe I should clean.'

'Do what you want, Ez.'

'I want to help but I don't want to do anything that will upset you and I don't know what…'

'Whatever you think. Just do whatever you think.'

❄

Cleome sat in the back seat of a taxi, occasionally fingering the chunk of turquoise on her vintage silver necklace. She pulled a cherry-red pashmina tighter around her shoulders, and stared blindly at the English countryside, unable to register the freshly-ploughed fields. The bald driver listened to the car radio. Out of the blue, her heart cramped. She inhaled and exhaled deeply, her lips forming a crinkled 'O', her knobbly hand spread over her chest. Fumbling in her bag, she sought her hip flask, and told herself to keep calm. The car slowed as they entered the city suburbs. After a time, she leant forward to indicate Amelie's house. The driver set her wheeled suitcase on the pavement and handed over her folded coat. She paid him in cash, adding a decent tip.

Esme opened the front door, and helped Cleome into the narrow hallway. In the sitting room, Cleome engulfed her granddaughter in her arms. 'We will get through this somehow. I promise we will,' she whispered into her hair.

Esme made tea. The three women sat around the dining table that was pushed against one wall, and analysed each detail of the accident. There was a witness now, apparently; the passenger in the lorry. The police were interviewing him.

'I want to see my daughter's body, to say goodbye to her,' Cleome declared, straightening her back.

'They won't let us, *Mormor*. Not Mum or Nick.'

'Oh God.' Cleome's green cat-like eyes shrank to slits. 'It was that bad.'

'Don't say that, please. I can't…'

'I'm sorry… Oh, I'm sorry. Come here, darling, come here.' Cleome leant over, cradled Amelie's head, and stroked her hair. 'We'll not mention it again, I promise.'

The doorbell rang.

Marsha, Amelie's dear childhood friend and colleague at The Children's Hospital, stood a little back from the doorway clutching a plate that bore a lemon drizzle cake. Tall and dark, with eyes like melted chocolate, she dissolved into tears and whispered, 'Sorry, sorry.'

Amelie took hold of the plate as the cake threatened to slide.

'It's your favourite. I couldn't think of what else to do so I baked.' Marsha fingered the gold crucifix which shone against her ebony skin.

Inside, Esme said, 'Hi Marsha,' sadly, before moving to put the kettle on again.

'The accident happened at twelve thirty-eight on the A40 near the Minster Lovell roundabout,' Amelie told Marsha. She put the cake down on the table, overwhelmed with an urge to repeat the facts—in the same way that they did on the ward to check that a patient's care was in place. Details tumbled from her lips. 'A lorry… A lorry swerved into their lane. It was a head-on collision. Mum and Nick died straight away. Bertie was taken in the air ambulance but was…*gone*…by the time they reached the JR. He would not have known anything. The consultant was clear on that. Bertie would have known *nothing*.'

Marsha held Amelie's pale hands in her strong dark ones. Cautiously, she informed Amelie that news of the accident was everywhere on social media. The pileup had featured on the television news with filmed footage of the accident scene. It would no doubt be reported in the Oxford Mail. She might want to consider protecting herself.

"Protect yourself" was what Kerstin had always taught her. *Protect yourself.* When you love, there is no protection, Amelie realised. She was exposed, raw and vulnerable. Completely unprotected.

Esme made more tea the way each person liked it: black, no sugar for Amelie, one sugar for Marsha, white for Esme, and mint for Cleome. She sliced up the cake. She continued to tidy—toys to the toybox and coats to the hooks in the cupboard under the stairs. Amelie, Marsha and Esme were used to each other's company and worked together for long hours, at all times of the day and night. She removed the booster seat from the fourth chair at the dining table, and stashed it away. She disappeared into the kitchen, and allowed tears to spill down her olive-skinned cheeks as silently as she could, before blotting her eyes dry on kitchen towel. She emptied the dishwasher, storing Bertie's bottles, bowls, and special little spoons reverently at the back of a cupboard.

Was it helpful? She had no idea. She had lost her compass, could never have prepared for this. Was tragedy contagious? She told herself sternly that it was not, but it took all her courage to stay with Amelie. She wanted to flee from her friend's appalling situation, find her own family, hug them tight, and never let them go.

More flowers were delivered to the door. Marsha left for a shift at the hospital. Another pair of Amelie's nursing colleagues visited with food and red eyes. The Family Liaison Officer arrived to discuss unbelievable practicalities—the coroner would register the deaths of Kerstin, Nick and Bertie. Amelie needed to collect their death certificates from the registrar. She must contact Kerstin's motor insurer; the police would provide the accident details. She was advised to employ a solicitor and appoint a funeral director. Would she like Kerstin's and Nick's property returned? She would need to inform certain institutions about what had happened—employers, the nursery school, tax people, mortgage company, bank, pension providers.

Pension providers? Amelie let out a crooked laugh.

Cleome listened with her head in hands. Eventually, she looked up.

'We need a list we can work from and tick off,' she demanded. 'We will never manage otherwise. You are very kind but we are not fit enough to remember these details.'

Patrick entered the house stiffly, with Hilary following behind. Amelie hugged them, although they were not the hugging kind. She offered them seats beside the littered dining table. Esme made more tea, and offered slices of the lemon drizzle cake.

Hilary perched on a dining chair, eyeing the room while Amelie replied to Patrick's gently probing questions. Her face, unusually devoid of make-up, appeared waxen. Patrick reassured Amelie that they knew a good solicitor, and offered to help with the practicalities. 'It would help me, if you would allow me. It will be better if I have something to do.'

'A good idea to keep busy,' Cleome approved.

'Exactly, if I can keep busy… Do something useful.'

'And Nick went to the zoo because you were studying?' Hilary spoke suddenly, her wandering gaze fixing on Amelie. 'Nick went because you were too busy to go?' The unspoken implication soiled the air.

'Yes,' Amelie whispered.

'We will have none of that!' Cleome thumped the table and glared ferociously at Nick's mother.

Hilary hunched her shoulders. She stood and made for the door, leaving her tea and cake untouched. Patrick followed her, promising to return soon.

That evening after Esme had left, Cleome extracted a pouch of herbs from her suitcase, all grown and dried at *Det Lilla Huset*. She made *tisanes* from camomile and lavender flowers mixed with valerian root and sweetened with honey. As she prepared for bed, she sent silent prayers into the Oxford night sky for strength and healing.

Amelie lay beside her grandmother under a clean duvet on the large bed in the attic room. She kept still until she heard her relative's gentle snores and then rolled away and sobbed, as quietly as she could. Her own death strutted about the quiet bedroom, never far away—she sensed the shadow of it, stalking her.

3

Monday 30 October

Cleome was clad in a blue corduroy skirt and chunky turquoise cardigan. Wisps of her hair escaped from a bun, framing green eyes that turned up at the corners and a wrinkled heart-shaped face. Amelie sat at the dining table and stared at the wall, her pale hair hanging down her back in a tangle.

There was a knock on the door, and Cleome answered it without thinking. A journalist clasping a notepad stood uncomfortably close to the threshold. Cleome stepped towards the woman in an attempt to establish a clear boundary. The journalist did not budge although her chin drew back a fraction. 'My condolences to your family. I'd like to speak to Amelie Tierney to record her thoughts on the terrible tragedy.'

Cleome peered at her dyed black hair and beak-like nose, the ring through one nostril. Something about the reporter shimmered; a subtle mirage that most people would not discern. Cleome grasped a fleeting impression of dark feathers and a beady eye. A raven? It could be so hard to tell with city folks.

'Is Mrs Tierney at home?' the journalist persisted. A knobbly black-clad knee raised as she set a narrow foot on the doorstep.

'Go away!' Cleome shooed her as she would a bird, before pushing the door shut.

It was not the first visit from the media. They pecked at the meat of misfortune like carrion-feeders in the forest back in Sweden, and infuriated her with their lack of dignity or compassion. As she lingered in the hallway for a moment beside the closed door, she realised that she must take charge and protect her granddaughter, even if it meant blocking out her own grief for the time being. When the doorbell rang again moments later, her shoulders dropped with relief as she peered through the peephole, and saw it was Patrick.

'Hilary is not well. A headache. I have left her at home with our cleaner who's fussing but will look after her well enough,' Patrick explained, as he stepped inside. His tweed jacket, corduroy trousers, polished brogues, and checked shirt, open at the collar, gave the impression of order and common sense. His grey hair too was neatly combed but his cinnamon eyes betrayed his real state, and were liquid with sadness.

'Come in, come in,' Cleome encouraged. 'Would you like a coffee or tea, and a slice of cake? We have so many cakes now—people keep bringing them,' she said as they walked through to the main room.

'Thank you. Coffee would be grand, but no cake, thanks. I've quite lost my appetite. I have come because I would like to be useful. Hello, dear,' he said to Amelie, and placed his hand on her shoulder.

Amelie gave her father-in-law a watery smile.

'Patrick, can you help me with something?' Cleome signalled from the kitchen. 'Her work. Nick's work. They need telling,' she whispered. 'Bertie's nursery too. I mean, I'm sure they've all heard by now but it is only right that we speak to them. Would you do that? She cannot possibly do it; she can barely speak. I have her phone here, and the code for it. You will find the numbers you need on it. Do you know how these things work?'

Patrick took the phone, and the scrap of paper with the code scrawled in Cleome's hand. 'I do, and I can certainly make some calls,' he said.

'Maybe sit upstairs at the desk in the attic room?' she suggested. 'You can compose yourself there, and have a bit of privacy. Amelie?' she called, poking her head around the kitchen door. 'Should Patrick call your work and Nick's work, the nursery—explain?'

'Oh… please.'

While Patrick dealt with the phone calls upstairs and out of earshot, Amelie took a shower and washed her hair properly, and then dozed on the sofa. Cleome sat at the wooden dining table with her head in her hands and despite her resolution to stay strong, wept silently.

At around midday, Patrick reappeared and offered to drive them to Kerstin's house.

'I don't think my daughter had many friends. She was a loner, you know—a bit like me that way,' Cleome confided as they arrived at Merrivale Square.

Amelie gazed out of the car window, mute at the sight of her empty childhood home.

'Oh, what's that?' Cleome pointed at Kerstin's front door.

'Flowers!' exclaimed Amelie. She slipped out of the car as soon as it stopped, leaving the door ajar, and moving swiftly toward the building. A dozen colourful bouquets were sympathetically arranged beside the front door. A candle in a jar had burned out.

'Oh!' Cleome cried, covering her mouth with her hand.

Amelie tucked her hair behind her ears and crouched down to pluck several small hand-written cards from the bouquets. She handed them to Patrick who read aloud messages of condolence.

'She *did* have friends,' Cleome whispered, swiping at her eyes.

A neighbour appeared; her face crumpled with concern. Patrick intercepted, led her away from Cleome and Amelie, and spoke with her in hushed tones.

Amelie used her key, and together they stepped into the silent house with its peculiar layout, first entering the kitchen which was on the ground floor, behind the garage. Nobody knew what to do with the flowers and so Cleome filled the sink with water, and they stood the wrapped bouquets there.

On the first floor was the living room and Kerstin's suite of bedroom, dressing room and bathroom, and on the top floor—once Amelie's domain—was Kerstin's office, a couple of spare rooms and another bathroom.

'Please search her desk. She is—*was* very organised, you will find everything no doubt,' Cleome said to Patrick who had sat down, somewhat awkwardly, in Kerstin's office chair. He opened a drawer cautiously, and with reverence. 'My Kerstin was a management consultant, and never left a stone unturned,' Cleome added proudly.

'He knows, *Mormor*,' Amelie murmured to her grandmother, placing a gentle hand on her arm.

'Of course he does. Silly me.' Cleome shook her head. She wandered back down a flight of stairs clutching the handrail, and entered her daughter's bedroom, pausing on the spotless cream carpet. The bed was neatly made with an orderly row of five purple scatter cushions that matched the lampshades and bed runner.

Cleome pressed her hands together, as if in prayer.

She recalled her stubborn, fiercely ambitious daughter. Kerstin's tough energy was vanished, never to be seen in this world again. *How could it be? Where was she now?* She spread a hand across her bosom, and fumbled with her necklace. She poked her head into the dressing room. It was pristine; the furniture new, the hanging clothes neat above rows of matching shoes, the colours—creams and purples in the rooms, reds, blacks and whites in the wardrobe, all co-ordinated. The sight of her daughter's possessions evoked a swell of savage emotion. Cleome stumbled into the adjacent living area and sank onto a cream sofa. For a moment, she feared that she might make a mess, and then realised that it did not matter. Nothing really mattered any more.

Leaving Patrick to search the study, Amelie explored the bedrooms and bathroom on the top floor. Each space was immaculate and sumptuously furnished. Bedcovers complemented clean painted walls. There was no clutter or dust. In the bathroom, unused towels were folded neatly over a shining rail such as you might find in a hotel. It was sterile. Amelie shivered, folded her arms, and squinted down at the rear garden. It consisted of grass, with not a flower in sight, and a patio where new garden furniture sat, protected by expensive covers.

What had life been like for her lone parent since she had left home?

Turning her back on the empty rooms and Patrick, who now studied a pile of documents, she descended the thickly-carpeted stairs, and joined her grandmother who sat silently in the living room gazing out of the window.

Amelie picked up a silver-framed photograph of herself and Kerstin, taken by a professional when Amelie was fourteen, at the time when black-and-white portraits of people wearing white shirts were all the rage. Amelie recalled the new t-shirt, and her mother's expensive silk blouse. Her mother had been excited that day. They had gone to a salon, sat in adjacent chairs while their hair had been blow-dried, and then had waited in the photographer's studio, both smelling of hairspray and looking not quite themselves, for the portrait to be taken. Amelie would keep the photograph. She tucked it under her arm.

'I had better clear out her fridge, put the bin out,' Cleome fretted, levering herself off the sofa.

'She has a cleaner for all that. Oh God, we need to tell her.'

'Everything is here. Her will, her insurance documents, her pension and so on.' Patrick placed a pile of pristine folders on a low coffee table, ran his fingers back through his wiry grey hair, and looked suddenly weary.

'You've done enough here for now. Let's take these things and go. The Family Liaison Officer is returning at four. We will need all our strength for that,' Cleome said.

'Did Nick... Had he made a will?' Patrick asked.

'Yes, we both did, when Bertie was born.'

'Would it help if I approached your solicitor?'

'Oh...Oh... I can't believe we're having this conversation!' Amelie cried.

The police officer gathered a little more information from the group before setting a box of tissues on the table. She had brought the personal belongings of Kerstin, Nick and Bertie that were not needed for the police investigation, and bent to pick up a large bag.

Amelie pressed Bertie's soft toy rabbit to her blotched face and sobbed. Patrick stood up and swayed as Nick's wristwatch was laid out on the table; his attention remained fixed on it, as if it might bite him. Cleome reached for Kerstin's newly-cleaned handbag. She pulled open the zip with her arthritic fingers and extracted the contents, lining them up in a row. When the bag was empty, and Kerstin's wallet and lipstick, packet of Nurofen, miniature bottle of perfume, spare gold earrings, and sundry items, were all on show, she staggered to the kitchen, poured a large vodka and tonic, and downed it in one.

On Hallowe'en evening, Amelie and Cleome sat in the living room with the lights off and the curtains drawn. They were silent with exhaustion and could hear the chatter and laughter of trick-or-treaters—excited, still-living children—in the street outside. They need not have feared disturbance; nobody knocked on their door. The children were guided to happier homes.

Cleome paced and brooded, overrun by concern for the lost souls who roamed the earth that night, both living and dead. After the road had emptied of children, she peering between the curtains and observed a fine white mist lit by pools of streetlight. She glanced up at the night sky for signs of the thinning veil between the living and the dead on the auspicious night. She looked for a message from Kerstin, if she was honest. Did not see one.

The tributes were many, and cards littered every shelf. Friends, neighbours and colleagues brought dishes of curry, macaroni cheese, and fish pie, along with bottles of wine, to Amelie's door.

Overwhelmed, Amelie gave away the food to Patrick, Esme and Marsha. In a cruel twist of fate, she and her grandmother were unable to enjoy any of it. They nibbled, dutifully and silently, on tiny portions that clogged their throats.

Esme appeared between nursing shifts, using her own key. She tidied and cleaned, and folded away clothes discreetly without consulting Amelie, driven by the need to support her friend. Nick had so little, it seemed, apart from a few clothes and mountains of books which she straightened on shelves in the living room, bedroom and landing.

Other visitors had a common look about them of stunned disbelief, restless fingers, and pink, watery eyes. Several could not speak and simply wept. Others offered wild advice. 'Learn to knit like that woman who lost her daughter,' one schoolfriend of Amelie's suggested, three days after the accident. 'Book yourself in for a marathon,' a nursing colleague whom she barely knew, advised. And the worst one, coming from another mother at Bertie's playgroup: 'It will be all right, you'll see. You'll get over it eventually.'

'What an idiot!' Cleome fumed after she had shooed the white-toothed woman from the door.

'She was doing her best. Nobody knows what to do in these situations.' Amelie was calm.

'It's true, I suppose I should be more patient. We are their worst nightmare.' Cleome shook her head. 'We are taboo now, you know. That one won't come around again.'

There would be an inquest into the deaths. They had to inform GPs, and communicate with the coroner's office, contact executors, apply for probate, sort out bank accounts and household bills, contact funeral directors, begin funeral arrangements.

'We must stick together throughout this chaos, us three,' Cleome insisted, wagging her finger at Patrick and Amelie. 'It is how we will survive.' Her cat-like eyes glinted as she spoke. She took a swig from the hip flask that she now kept in a colourful woven pouch suspended from a belt about her waist. She offered the flask to Patrick who took a slug, and to Amelie, who shook her head.

The three of them trudged about the city, visiting the solicitor, the coroner, the funeral parlour, Kerstin's house again, and various banks. They preferred being out of the house and walking, and frequently stopped to drink coffee or something stronger in one of the many pubs in the city.

The life of Oxford continued to unfold around them with its own ceaseless momentum. Pedestrians, cyclists, cars, buses, shoppers, students, tourists—the combined energy of humanity—flowed through the ancient city streets like a river, as it had done for centuries. Nothing halted it, not even this latest horrific tragedy which was merely one of thousands that the city had absorbed over time.

Leaves fell from the trees, swirling through the air, and tumbling over pavements and lawns. The Cherwell was swollen after rain. A funeral date was fixed. Hilary insisted that Nick's funeral must take place at their village church. She would not hear of cremation; he must be buried. Cleome and Amelie were emphatic that Kerstin and Bertie must be cremated, and wanted a humanist service. In the end, one momentous day was planned with a joint service for Kerstin and Bertie at the crematorium in the morning, and a church funeral and burial for Nick in the afternoon.

Was that the proper way? Was there a better plan? Nobody knew.

'We will be noble in the face of this,' Cleome raged.

Patrick took a deep breath and murmured, 'Amen.'

Amelie pressed the palms of her hands together as in prayer, held them up to her face, and squeezed her eyes shut.

4

Wednesday, 15th November

Amelie and Cleome clasped hands in the back seat of the funeral directors' pristine black Mercedes. The vehicle was the first of a convoy that followed a hearse bearing Kerstin's coffin, resplendent with red flowers, out in front, and another transporting Bertie's small white casket, that sat atop cascades of hand-picked dahlias, foliage and ivy, cut from friends' gardens and hedgerows.

After careful thought both women had bought new dresses and colourful pashminas to keep them warm on the pale November day. Amelie wore cornflower blue. Her long wavy hair was parted in the centre, and tied back with a scrap of lace. She wore Nick's wedding band on a gold chain around her neck. Cleome was clothed in burgundy with a fuchsia shawl, and had piled her hair up in her trademark bun. Her many vintage silver bangles gleamed and her flat red-laced boots had been polished until they shone. On the seat beside her was her green leather handbag with the trusty hip flask tucked inside. They had agreed that the funeral dress code be bright colours to denote gratitude and celebration for the lives of those lost. Hilary was the lone dissenter, determined to wear black.

Amelie chewed her lip as the funeral cortege crawled out of the city and up Headington Hill, past the park, college, houses, shops and pedestrians who hurried to appointments or walked dogs or pushed small children in buggies. For most of the local population, it was an unremarkable Wednesday when life continued as it always had, and even the weather appeared undistinguished; simply cool and grey.

The celebrant had come to Percy Street the week before. Kindness had emanated from her—in the gentle way she spoke, in her unwavering focus on Amelie and Cleome's needs, and her helpful suggestions. She was perhaps forty, with blonde shoulder-length hair, and over her black polo neck and trousers she had worn a turquoise shawl. She had been quietly efficient, establishing whether they had any particular readings in mind for the service, and going through in careful detail things they would like her to mention about the lives of Kerstin and Bertie.

A man called Chris, whom neither Cleome nor Amelie knew, but who claimed to be a good friend of Kerstin, had contacted Amelie and offered to read the eulogy. Anthony, who was Bertie's godfather and Nick's oldest friend from school, would do the same for both Bertie and Nick. Amelie and Cleome had accepted all such offers with humility. Neither could truly grasp what was happening.

As they approached the chapel with their arms linked, Cleome leaned in slightly toward her granddaughter while Amelie walked tall, determined to be strong. Debussy's Clair de Lune played over the crematorium sound system. The chapel was already filled to overflowing, and many of those who had gathered would have to remain outside and listen to the service on speakers. When Amelie took a programme and saw photographs of her mother and Bertie on the cover, she bit back her tears. Cleome squeezed her hand. They took their place in the front pew, beside Cleome's younger sister Antonia, Helen and Daniel her neighbours from Sweden, Marsha, Esme and Paul, and Nick's parents.

That there were so many mourners for Kerstin astonished Cleome. It was clear who had come to pay their respects to her—the smartly-dressed cohort of men and women in their fifties, who filled several pews. One woman in particular stood out as somehow familiar. She was tall with dark hair streaked exotically with grey that curled over stiffly-held shoulders. She wore an expensive-looking black coat. Cleome could not see her face, and was so grief-stricken that she soon forgot her. Kerstin, it seemed, had a whole life that she had never appreciated.

Bertie's little friends stayed away of course, but many of their parents attended, as did several of Amelie's old schoolfriends, alongside her nursing colleagues, staff from Bertie's nursery, and even the Asian couple from the local newsagents. Nick's friends, colleagues and students packed the aisles, smartly dressed and in sombre mood.

So many stricken faces, so much grief.

The celebrant, who today wore a bright pink shawl and matching reading glasses, began the ceremony by talking about the lives of Kerstin and Bertie.

When it was his turn, Kerstin's friend Chris spoke clearly and confidently, of a strong woman who was fair, intelligent, hard-working—and fun. He told anecdotes which made a section of the congregation laugh out loud in recognition. Cleome sobbed noiselessly, her shoulders bent and shaking. Amelie sat with her arm about her grandmother, and her gaze fixed on Chris, remembering her parent. One of her mother's friends stood up and read the poem, Death Is Nothing At All. Everyone sang Morning Has Broken.

The manager of Bertie's nursery spoke of the cheerful little boy who was always smiling and keen to learn, the way he liked to sing and clap and dance and play outdoors. How the sandpit and painting were his favourite activities. She said he was popular with the other children, and much missed by all his little friends and the nursery staff.

When it came to her turn, Amelie walked determinedly to the lectern, a piece of paper clutched in her hand. She cleared her throat. 'Our grief is one way of expressing our thanks for those we have lost,' she stated, her chin held high, her gaze alighting on close friends and family in the pew over to her left. 'We loved deeply and now we are heartbroken. It is the way of the world. It is our time now, to gather here like we are, to let our tears flow and our hearts break open with the pain of our loss. Our disturbed sleep, the way we shiver in the sunshine and have no appetite, our loneliness—all of these things are natural. They honour the souls we have lost and show that we truly loved them. Only people who felt nothing for my mother and my little boy… can let this moment pass unnoticed. For those of us who *did* love Kerstin and Bertie, who continue to love them, and will always love them, this moment will never be forgotten. We will mourn, and at the same time give thanks for the lives they were given, the moments, hours and years we spent with them, and for the lives we all still have. Would we choose to live without such love in order to avoid this despair? I don't think so. I certainly would not. I give thanks for the precious lives of my mother Kerstin and my son Bertie, and I am honoured that I was able to love them, and that they loved me in return.' She pressed her mouth closed and returned swiftly to her seat where Cleome took her hand, and Esme put an arm around her.

One of the women who had looked after Bertie at nursery sang Amazing Grace with such force and beauty that Amelie's skin broke out in goose bumps, and her tears which had been tightly contained, spilled down her cheeks.

At the close of the service, everybody sang Somewhere Over the Rainbow. The words caught in Cleome's throat, and she could not join in, but raised her chin and closed her eyes.

The large crowd lingered outside the chapel after the service had finished. Several of Kerstin's colleagues and a few of the nursery staff who had worked with Bertie expressed their condolences and said their farewells.

Esme stepped aside to return a call to her mother who was looking after Joel. After she had finished, she slipped her phone into her bag and smiled at the woman with the dark and silver curls who stood separately from everyone else. The stranger clasped her jewelled hands together and peered through the crowd as if straining for a glimpse of someone. She pushed a strand of hair behind one ear. Tears dampened her handsome sallow face. Esme smiled, and asked if she was alright.

'Oh yes, just sad. Of course.' The woman recovered, revealing white polished teeth in a fleeting smile that looked somehow familiar to Esme.

'Are you a friend of the family?' she asked politely.

'A distant relative.'

'Days like this make you think, don't they?' Esme said, the weightiness of the occasion making her more conversant than she would normally be.

'We have to make the most of our loved ones while they're here,' the stranger agreed.

'Shall we go over and re-join the group?'

'Oh no. I will stay here, thanks.'

'Of course.' Esme nodded her farewell, and wound her way back to Paul.

The remainder of the congregation returned to their vehicles to prepare for the twenty-minute drive to St Lawrence Church in Toot Baldon where they would be joined by more of Nick's co-workers, and distant friends and cousins who had not been able to make it to the morning service.

'You are kind,' Patrick had told Amelie the week before. 'So very kind, to allow this. I know what Nick meant to you, and you to him, but organising Nick's funeral according to her own wishes has kept Hilary going.'

As planned, the hearse containing Nick's coffin was waiting for them, adorned with lilies ordered by Hilary and hand-picked bouquets of dahlias and berries from Amelie and Cleome. Amelie sat beside her grandmother again in the funeral director's car, and chewed her fingernail as they made the slow journey to the church which once upon a time, Hilary had advocated as the venue for their wedding. Nick had objected to that just as strongly as he would have fought against a Christian funeral today. He was a man of science who, while he did not discount the existence of God, certainly did not approve of any religion. On the journey, Amelie brooded, fearing that she had let him down. Did he—would he have—understood how it was beyond her to fight his mother, to resist, to put forward an alternative? Would he see how her strength was depleted since the accident, her willpower drained away?

She stepped out of the Mercedes, smoothed her dress, and looked about her at the lychgate with its crooked gate wedged open, and the lichen-spattered tombstones which, worn and greying, studded the grass. Would Nick have reassured her and insisted she was doing the best she could? He was a kind and unselfish man but suddenly she was overcome with guilt that she had not organised his funeral herself, had so easily stepped down. He was the love of her life; how could she have left this day to his mother? She swiped a tear from her cheek. Cleome looked at her questioningly.

'Nick was not religious! I don't know whether he even wanted to be buried,' she blurted. 'We have never discussed it.'

'And why would you?' Cleome reasoned. 'You cannot blame yourself for not knowing. If Nick is looking down, he will see that you are being kind to his mother. It is all as it should be. Don't worry.'

Amelie blinked back her tears. She sent a silent prayer to Nick, asking him to forgive her. With her shawl pulled tightly around her shoulders, she entered the church porch, where Patrick and Hilary stood waiting to greet everyone. She inclined her head to Hilary and mustered a warm smile for Patrick.

The white-painted space had a dark-beamed ceiling and stone arches that ran the length of the church. There were scented white lilies and abundant green foliage for decoration, and an organist played Bach. In the sea of faces, she spotted a glamorous woman who looked familiar but she could not place her. She registered the presence of Nick's colleagues, his old college friends, several of his cousins from Ireland, and the ex-girlfriend Jessica. She saw Antonia, Marsha, Esme and Paul,

Helen and Daniel, people from work, the couple from the newsagents, and many of the new friends they had made since having Bertie. Ahead of her, Cleome sneezed loudly, before they took their seats in the pew, and riffled in her large leather bag. With a subtle gesture, she took a slug from her hip flask and gestured to Amelie, who shook her head.

The music changed, and they all stood. The bearers carried in Nick's coffin and placed it carefully on a stand, a couple of feet away from Amelie. The sight of it made her heart thud, and she took a deep breath to compose herself. That Nick's beautiful body lay dead in the oak casket was impossible to comprehend. She longed to touch him again, to kiss his skin one more time; despaired that they had not been given a chance to say goodbye. Even the authorities had deprived her of a private moment with him after his death. She could not take her eyes off the polished wooden box where her beloved soulmate now lay. The wild thought occurred to her that at any moment someone might confess, and say there had been a mistake. She shook her head, bit her lip.

After the vicar had made his introduction and offered a prayer, the congregation sang Dear Lord and Father of Mankind, and then Anthony stood at the lectern and gave the eulogy. He spoke fiercely, of a man who was brave and honest, who had a brilliant mind and a madcap sense of humour, who had loved Amelie and Bertie with a passion rarely seen, and whose future had been cruelly snatched away. Anthony read defiantly from Albert Einstein, stating that he was one of Nick's heroes.

For the first time since the accident, a smile reached the corners of Amelie's mouth. In Einstein's statement on the mystery of eternal life, was her Nick. He would have loved it. When it came to her turn to speak, her fingers sought Cleome's before she stood, and Cleome squeezed them reassuringly. She avoided the lectern, instead taking her place beside Nick's coffin. For a moment, she stalled, transfixed by the wooden box with its mass of lilies, dahlias, and green foliage. Slowly, she placed her hand on the corner of it, and then looked up, to focus on the light that flooded through an arched window at the far end of the church. She would recite the one poem that Nick knew; the one they had learned together on their honeymoon, laughed at, made jokes about—shared. "Their" poem. She knew it by memory.

'*I will arise and go now, and go to Innisfree,*
And a small cabin build there, of clay and wattles made;
Nine bean-rows will I have there, a hive for the honey-bee,

And live alone in the bee-loud glade.
And I shall have some peace there, for peace comes dropping slow,
Dropping from the veils of the morning to where the cricket sings;
There midnight's all a glimmer, and noon a purple glow,
And evening full of the linnet's wings.
I will arise and go now, for always night and day
I hear lake water lapping with low sounds by the shore;
While I stand on the roadway, or on the pavements grey,
I hear it in the deep heart's core.'

She kissed her fingertips and pressed them against the wooden casket before returning to her seat.

The congregation sang Make Me A Channel of Your Peace, and moved outside for the committal and burial. As she watched Nick's coffin being lowered into the earth, Amelie trembled. She questioned her decision to deny Bertie a place in the graveyard beside his father, but when it was all done and they eventually turned away from the graveside, her resolve rekindled, and she knew that she could not have left her son here, in this churchyard that meant nothing to her. She would make it all right for Nick, she would make it "his" place—but she would not do that for Bertie too.

When she looked back on it, she could barely remember the wake at Patrick and Hilary's house in the village, or the people she spoke with or what was said. All she recalled was Nick's Irish grandmother Sinéad, telling her in a warm Dublin accent, 'You made him very happy, I'm in no doubt about that. I am praying for you.'

One bright cold afternoon not long after the funerals, Cleome and Amelie scattered Kerstin's ashes in the River Thames above Oxford. They floated lilies and sprinkled rose petals on the water's surface too.

'She would never forgive me if I took her ashes back to Sweden, the place of her birth; in fact, I think she would haunt me,' Cleome said, her arm linked through Amelie's as they stood on the riverbank.

'You must take her jewellery home though, look after it, keep it safe,' Amelie said.

'I will do that for you, if that's what you'd like. What will you do now, Am?' she asked.

'Carry on, I suppose. I have no idea.'

'Don't rush back to work.'

'I have to—they don't give you much time off. Besides, it will keep me busy..'

'Why don't you come back with me for a while?'

'Thanks, but I don't know—'

'You always have a home with me.'

'I know. And thank you. You have a home with me too, any time, for as long as you need... Oh, how will we survive, *Mormor*?'

'I don't know—but somehow we will.' Cleome eyes glittered in her wrinkled-peach face, and she raised her chin to the river breeze.

Amelie had Bertie's ashes placed in a cherrywood box. She printed photographs of Nick and Bertie, and the few she could find of Kerstin, and blu-tacked them to the walls and doors downstairs at Percy Street.

She arrived fifteen minutes early for her first shift back at work. It was still dark outside, and the night staff looked weary. A senior nurse reported on how each patient had been, which treatments had been given, and what specimens collected and sent to the laboratory. She related each patient's baseline observations for temperature, pulse and blood pressure. Amelie's head spun at the volume of information. A consent form needed signing for a boy who was having an early procedure. A teenage girl's parent needed updating on her test results. Before the accident, she had no problem retaining the details of her patient's care, but now she struggled to remember what had just been said.

As her shift got underway, her hand trembled when she took a young girl's temperature. She forgot to get the consent form signed; a near-disaster that was remedied by her colleague. She could not concentrate on what a patient's distraught mother was telling her. At mid-morning, she sat down at the nurse's station and rested her throbbing head in her hands. Her chest was tight, and she felt nauseous and breathless; she was terrified, she realised, of being in the hospital building again. She had a flashback to the day of the accident when she had arrived at the site in a panda car with blue lights spinning and the siren wailing. She suspected she was experiencing post-traumatic stress symptoms. She wanted to pick up her life again and care for her patients but did not trust herself to make the right decisions. She was also ravenous as she had not eaten breakfast. As she sat on the chair, she shivered. The ward manager approached her, and took her into a side room. After interviewing her at length, she sent her home.

Back in Percy Street, Amelie paced up and down her living room, deeply troubled by her experience on the ward. She sat down on the sofa, rested her head back, and promptly fell fast asleep. When she awoke, she was disorientated. She checked the clock above the dining table and realised that she had slept for most of the day. She made herself a strong coffee and feverishly typed out her resignation notice to the hospital, convinced that she would never be able to face the hospital building again. With the holidays she was owed and compassionate leave due, she would not need to return there. After sending the email, she tore a chunk from a white loaf, dunked it into an open tin of tomato soup and crammed it into her mouth. She wiped her fingers on a cloth, and emailed her dissertation to Brookes, not caring that the footnotes and bibliography had never been checked.

Outside, the street fell quiet as the neighbours closed their doors at the end of another day. Amelie sat on the sofa, staring out of the front window. Clouds gathered in the sky above the roof tops while below the east wind played idly with litter and city dust. She drew the curtain against the night, and made a mug of coffee and swallowed some paracetamol to soothe her throbbing head. She approached each of the photographs that she had stuck on the walls and doors, and gently peeled them off, picking off the blu-tack, before placing them in the pocket of an open suitcase.

'Amelie, I know you're in there, please let me in,' Esme shouted through the letterbox, early the following morning. 'Take the door off the latch, so I can use my key. I'm worried about you.'

'Go away, I'm fine.'

'Am, please, you can't go on like this!'

'Just go away!'

'Right, I'm going away but I'm coming back in an hour and I want you to let me in or I swear I'll break a window.'

Amelie peeped through the gap at the edge of the curtain and saw Esme strut down the street, with her arms folded. The sight left her strangely unmoved. She looked around the downstairs room one last time while fingering Nick's wedding ring where it hung on the chain around her neck. The large suitcase where she had stashed Bertie's best little clothes and treasured toys including his rabbit, Nick's watch and jumper, the silver-framed photograph from Kerstin's house, the cherrywood box containing Bertie's ashes and more besides, was zipped shut. Her rucksack was crammed with essentials. She blew her nose, swallowed another paracetamol while standing at the kitchen sink, and left the upturned glass on the draining board. She called a taxi, and wrote a note for Esme, telling her not to worry. Outside, as she waited by the kerb, the sun broke through the cloud and shone in her face, making her squint. She held her face up to it for a moment, for surely it was a signal of hope.

5

Lake Båven, Sweden

Waning Cold Moon

Cleome stood in the low-ceilinged kitchen of the eighteenth-century wooden cottage where she had lived for many years, yawning. She warmed her arthritic hands by the Aga. She had done it again—nodded off in her chair, and now it was dark outside, and her border collie Trassel was whining. Exhaustion dragged at her bones. She pulled hand-knitted socks off the Aga rail and, plonking herself on a kitchen chair, struggled to fit them over her feet. She wound a colourful scarf around her neck, fetched her hat, coat and a pair of fingerless gloves, laced up her walking boots, and took a swig of vodka and tonic from a tumbler. Trassel's tail thumped against her calves.

'What a palaver, and all for you,' she muttered, fixing a coat in place over the dog's quivering body. She grabbed a torch and her walking pole, and headed out of the door.

Det Lilla Huset (The Small House) stood on a finger of land that protruded into Lake Båven with forest on either edge of the promontory, and facing the door, a wide glade that led down to the water. The lake herself was shaped like an octopus with many coves and islands, and was renowned for her natural beauty, abundant fish and crystalline water.

'How do I keep going, Trassel? Can you tell me that? How do I go on, with my Kerstin gone before me?'

A chill wind blew from the east across the partially frozen lake. Cleome shivered, and took the track round the side of the cottage and into the forest, out of the bitter breeze. Her path was lit by a waning gibbous moon, aptly known as the December Cold Moon. At this time of year in Sörmland, darkness fell at around three in the afternoon and lasted until past eight in the morning, and even when it did make an appearance, the sun stuck stubbornly low in the sky, causing the temperatures to plummet.

In the forest, Cleome turned on the torch, wary of stumbling in a patch of shade. Black boughs were lined with the first snowfall of the year, and naked birch trunks shone like skinny ghosts in the beam of light. Only her muffled footfall, the occasional crunch of a breaking twig hidden beneath snow, or the dog's excited scarper over hummocks of dead grass that poked up through the whiteness, broke the silence. As she plodded on, Cleome was overcome with a wave of sorrow. Something about being outdoors illuminated the truth of her situation. She stood, lifted her chin and roared at the forest.

'How could you?' she screamed. The "you" echoed. She plucked a stick from the snow and hurled it at a tree trunk. She kicked the white stuff violently, making an arc of fresh flakes. Trassel barked.

Cleome had telephoned Amelie repeatedly over the past two days, and had not been able to reach her. 'God, you'd better keep her safe!' she threatened, shaking a fist at the treetops. Her only grandchild, although English and bound up in Kerstin's world of city living, had always been special to her. She had spent many summers at *Det Lilla Huset* when she was young, while her mother had worked back in Oxford. She was a strong character—conscientious, but not always predictable.

Cleome kicked the snow again and shook her head as if to free herself from worry about why Amelie did not answer the telephone. As the elder matriarch, she knew she must keep going for Amelie's sake, and be of some use to her, yet she did not know the best way to do this. She stared up at a swathe of inky sky, visible through a gap in the canopy. Despite the huge moon, she could still discern the splendour of Orion and trace the distinctive line of stars that formed his "belt". The stars were named Mintaka, Alnilam and Alnitak—Arabic words that alluded to a belt of pearls. She savoured the exotic names, and spoke them aloud in the forest to soothe herself, relishing the way the stars connected her to an ancient world, long gone. Squinting up at the sky again, she sought the orange glow of Betelgeuse, for reassurance. Stars were a constant in a topsy-turvy human life; you could rely on them to turn up with pinpoint consistency, to carry on, regardless of any human plight.

After all these years, she knew every tree on her route. She was more at ease in the forest than she had ever been in any city; she recognised every scent, noted every shift of a season, where a new seedling grew or a rotten tree fell. Tonight, the air smelt clean and watery after the fresh snowfall, the amber browns of autumn replaced by the blanket of bleached white. A tawny owl hooted. Winter was getting into her stride now; there was no avoiding it.

She plodded on, taking her familiar circuit through the wild woodland, crossing back over the track halfway through the walk. She noted that the Bengtsson's place, down by the forest road, sat in darkness. *Det Mörka Huset* (The Dark House) as she called it, privately. Lotta Bengtsson had hung curtains a few years back, and had closed them after nightfall ever since, an unusual thing in Sweden. Lotta was convinced that she was being watched—though by whom or why, she could not say. It struck Cleome as a very tall tale, for who would drive out here to the forest to watch Lotta Bengtsson? And what could she possibly be doing that was of any interest? The woman spent most of her time watching soap operas and cleaning up after her sloppy menfolk. Lotta suffered from nerves, was the truth of it—and after her long marriage to Magnus with his dirty fingernails and purple cheeks, and with having to care for Robban, her full-grown son who had Asperger's, it was hardly surprising.

Trassel returned from bolting through the snow, and trotted with her head and tail up, glued to Cleome's ankles.

'What is it?' Cleome tutted. Trassel let out a low growl, and Cleome looked about. She had turned off her torch. Moonlight shone over the clearing, casting shadows from her and the dog on the blue whiteness. She heard a buzzing noise, like a swarm of bees and looked upward but could see nothing. 'If that is you, Robban Bengtsson, don't you dare film me with your drone!' she cried out, before prodding her pole into the virgin snow. In this area, thinly-iced puddles lay beneath the surface, waiting to soak her boots.

The humming noise faded and ceased, and she heard the crackle of wood caused by footfall. Trassel heard it too, and flew into the trees barking. Robban Bengtsson had recently bought a drone camera, and she often came across it hovering over the forest like a giant spider. It was his latest obsession. He did not answer her, which was not unusual, and while he was a harmless man, she felt suddenly vulnerable.

'*Kom hit*, Trassel!' She pursed her lips and whistled. 'Let us head for home.'

Pausing at the top of the gentle incline, Cleome glimpsed the twinkling lights of her friend Helen's farmhouse, beyond a moonlit, undulating field. She would not visit Helen this evening to exchange the day's news; the wind was perishing and she was far too weary for Helen's bossy insistence that she eat with them. Helen scrutinised every decoy that Cleome threw in her path—particularly when it came to the matter of the bootleg Russian vodka that she bought secretly from Helen's lover Daniel, for cash. Cleome did not want Daniel's soulful Muscovite sympathy tonight either. Nor could she face the young Syrian refugee who lived with them; compared to him, what right did she have to grieve? No, she wanted to be alone.

As she turned toward home, she caught sight of a possible Geminid meteor shower; it was hard to be sure with the moon so bright, and her eyesight not what it was. She followed the hunter's trail down the wooded hillside, past a scattering of natural boulders, and on through a coniferous part of the forest to the rutted, icy track which led back to her cottage. It was with some relief that she caught sight of her little wooden house, nestled at the top of the glade. As she drew closer to it, she paused at the sight of the moon's reflection, glittering on the lake's half-frozen surface. How *could* it carry on shining on the lake so beautifully when her own life was filled with dark horror? She pressed her lips together in fury. Why did the moon not falter? Why did the lake not shrivel and go dry with misery? She studied the little homestead bathed in silver light—the cottage, barn and orchard—and recalled Kerstin playing outside in the garden in summers past, riding out on the pony she kept in the barn, and learning to drive a car along the track. She recollected Kerstin's father, her first husband, Per Lindberg. Per knew how to light a fire without using matches, and which trees to cut for the warmest fuel. His hair had been long, tangled and blond and he had grown a wild ginger beard. He caught fish in the lake using an old net, and gutted them with a sharp blade kept in a little hut beside the jetty at the lake's edge. He had made the pudgy English boys of her youth, with their urban affectations and stupid ideas about life, pale into nothingness. At twenty-two, she had married Per Lindberg, and the two of them had set up home here, in this very place. After Kerstin was born, the gloss of Per's fishing and campfire-building skills had soon worn off though, as the realities of heating a small wooden house and earning a living to pay the bills had struck home. Any further talent in Per had proved to be somewhat lacking. He had been showing off, she had soon realised. He would rather drink and philosophise than put bread on the table. Swedish childcare was abundant, and she had found herself working full-time while Per whittled strange sculptures out of wood and blew all her salary on hashish. Love had blinded her, though whether it was actual love of Per or love for the lake and the forest, she remained unsure. During the divorce, and with some help from the bank, she had bought Per out of his share of *Det Lilla Huset,* and toiled to care for young Kerstin.

She had tried to trace Per to tell him what had happened and to send him the funeral details but she had failed. The last anyone had heard of him, he was living in Indonesia, and nobody seemed to know where.

Kerstin had not kept in touch with her birth father, either. When she was ten, Cleome had married Wilhelm, who had turned out to be a good husband and stepfather. Wilhelm was a businessman, committed to making a proper, warm dwelling out of the dilapidated summerhouse. He had helped her to renovate the cottage, installed an Aga on her insistence, and heaters and insulation, so they no longer froze in the Swedish winters. He would have preferred that they lived in his apartment in Stockholm and only visit the cottage in summer, but Cleome could never agree to that. Her heart was in this wild place.

Kerstin had liked Wilhelm. They used to go riding together, and she had worshipped his skilled approach to money and business. In a similar manner to the way that Cleome had fled from England, Kerstin returned there as a young adult, in part influenced by Wilhelm who had once worked in London, and in part swayed by childhood memories of her English grandparents' thatched cottage in the Home Counties, a place where rolling gardens were home to beds of delphiniums, roses and lupins in summertime and the lawn was mown in neat stripes. Cleome had sent Kerstin there for a fortnight's holiday each year while she was growing up, sensing that it was the right thing to do, and yet unable to bear being there herself.

After she had left Sweden to live in England permanently, Kerstin had thrived in what was then "Thatcher's Britain". Wilhelm had died, quickly, from pancreatic cancer in 1987. Kerstin had not taken it well, had built her shell a little tougher.

A child had never been a part of Kerstin's life plan, and it had come as a shock to find herself pregnant, and then hastily married. Motherhood had not come naturally to her but Cleome had helped as much as she could, and she had to hand it to her daughter; despite being abandoned by Amelie's father Julian, she had worked hard and done a good job of raising her child.

Cleome stood with her gloved hands on her broad hips, and sighed.

'It is all my fault,' she mumbled to the inky sky, and swiped a tear from her cheek as she turned towards the cottage. The accident was the type of punishment her mother had warned her would always come, all those years ago.

Back inside the wood-panelled hallway, she threw down her gloves onto a wooden chest and peeled off her layers, hanging her hat, scarf and coat on pegs beside the door, and abandoning her boots on the mat. She winced at the pain in her red fingers as she removed the dog's coat.

'Thank God that is done,' she announced to the dog, in an attempt to rally herself. 'Now let us feed you. Oh God, no dog biscuits. I will fetch some lake fish from the freezer, boil you some rice.'

In the kitchen, reeling with tiredness, she grabbed the tumbler of vodka and tonic, and drank deeply before setting about the cooking.

6

Sunday, 10th December

'On the radio, they are talking about heavy snow, you know,' warned the Asian taxi driver. 'I hope you're not inconvenienced on your journey.'

'I don't care what it says on the radio.'

'Sorry, Ma'am, just being cautionary. Probably all bollocks anyway.'

Amelie did not want to make conversation. Her head throbbed and her nostrils stung. She stared out of the window as the taxi idled on Magdalen Bridge. The last time she had run over this bridge was on that fatal morning when she had been so blissfully ignorant of what was about to happen. The sun had shone and the water had sparkled; there had been no inkling of the darkness that was coming.

Or had she missed some little omen? Tears rolled down her cheek.

'You are upset, Ma'am!'

'Just drive. Please.'

Amelie's thoughts returned to the man who had knocked on her door the day before. She could not get him out of her mind. He was tall and scrawny, with a heavy fringe that flopped over one eye. At first, she had wondered if he was an addict come to beg, but then he had thrust a bunch of cellophane-wrapped freesias at her, clasping them so tightly that she feared the stems might break. There had been a desperate look in his eyes. He had tried to apologise for the accident, had even suggested that the lorry driver was a good person. She had baulked at that, screamed at him and thrust his paltry bunch of flowers at his chest. She had threatened him with the police and been unable to stop crying after he had left. Her nose had run, her head had throbbed and her body had not stopped shaking. And then, after she had recovered, she had felt wretched, and riddled with guilt. The man had meant well; she had seen it in his eyes but ignored it. Now she fretted that by turning him away, she had missed an opportunity; she did not know what.

She paid the taxi, somehow managed to find the right coach, and stowed her suitcase in the hold. She boarded, and found a seat near the back. Waiting for the coach to depart, she wept again, turned her face to the window, and wiped her tears on her sleeve.

As predicted by the taxi driver, fat snowflakes began to fall from a huge white sky shortly after the coach left Oxford. A swirling shroud surrounded the largely empty vehicle, slowing progress along the M25 and M11 to a crawl. They reached Stansted Airport one hour and fifty minutes late. Snow carpeted the approach road, creating havoc. Abandoned vehicles littered the airport entrance. The coach wheels spun in slippery, freezing slush. The driver advised passengers to disembark, collect their luggage from the hold, and walk the remaining distance to the terminal building. Amelie zipped up her coat, hoiked her rucksack onto her back, and trudged over rutted, brown-stained mulch, with her suitcase bumping behind her on its little wheels. The bedlam continued inside the overcrowded airport as hundreds of people whose flights had been cancelled waited to see what would happen next.

Outside, it was going dark. Amelie's nose ran and a high temperature made her sweaty and weak. For a while, she simply sat on her suitcase in a small space beside a wall, with her head in her hands. Eventually she roused herself, and found a departures board which confirmed that her missed flight had anyway been cancelled. She joined a long queue to re-book it. She sneezed repeatedly, and dabbed at her sore nose with tissues. Eventually she managed to secure a flight for the following day, and found a patch of floor to bed down on for the night. She took two paracetamol and lay shivering beneath a blanket, donated by airport staff. Throughout the night she woke continually, dazzled by bright lights or disturbed by other passengers.

When she stepped off the aeroplane, she could barely speak, her throat was so sore. After making it through the airport security and baggage collection, she told a taxi driver where to take her, and dozed.

As the vehicle drew to a halt, it woke her up. Her heart lifted a little. Snow fell all around, more beautifully than it ever did in England, the flakes appearing like fairies in the forest. She paid the taxi driver, and he trundled off, back up the track.

She tried the door handle and then knocked, concerned that no dog barked, and that the door—normally always open—was locked. She shivered, unaccustomed to the freezing temperature. Abandoning her rucksack and suitcase beside the porch, she strode out towards the lake, her feet sinking into soft, deep banks of drifting white. Cold penetrated her trainers and snow melted on her jeans, chilling her to the bone.

All around her, the lake and forest were eerily silent. It was as if she had landed on another planet, so deep and penetrating was the quiet. There was wonder in the air; magic, she thought.

Sensing peace for the first time in forty-four long days, Amelie allowed herself to sink back into a snow pile, trusting it to catch her. While flat on her back and with her arms splayed, flakes of snow kissed her face as cold cooled the back of her hot head and neck. She moved her arms up and down, up and down, and spread her legs and brought them together, apart, together…

A snow angel—she would make a snow angel.

7

Winter Solstice

'I gave Magnus Bengtsson some cash to run the snow plough up the lane earlier,' Cleome remarked to Helen as she steered her Volvo cautiously up the long, rutted track that led to *Det Lilla Huset*.

'You'd think he'd do it out of kindness!' Helen frowned.

'He doesn't know the meaning of the word. Do you know, he did not even mention Kerstin's passing?'

'Oh, he does annoy me! It's just as well you had the foresight to ask him to clear the snow or you'd be stranded now. He knows full well how snowfall affects you, and has nothing better to do since he retired.'

'I should do it myself, I suppose.'

'At your age?'

'Never mind, the job is done. Lotta compensates for him; she chatters on nervously and makes exaggerated sad faces at me. At the last knitting group she sobbed on my shoulder and I ended up comforting her. She and the others don't really know how to be with me now. I am even more of an outsider. First, I was English, then divorced, now this. They all watch me, as if they are waiting for the next thing to happen.' She slowed the car. 'Will you come in for coffee?'

'Sure, just a quick one. Look, there are footprints to the house. Somebody has paid you a visit.'

'I don't know who that can be. I locked the door. I don't entirely trust Robban Bengtsson with his blessed drone these days. He is so enthusiastic that he forgets about a person's privacy.'

'Oh, he is harmless and he does know right from wrong. Perhaps he called by to show you his latest aerial photographs, or maybe one of your friends came.'

Cleome parked her Volvo next to Helen's in a wide car port at one end of a long, red-painted barn. Trassel bounded out of the car and tore off towards the cottage, barking.

'Let me transfer my shopping into my car, and then I'll be in for that coffee and to warm up a bit,' Helen said.

Cleome collected two hessian bags from the boot and trudged across the snow-laden grass towards the main door of her house, following footprints softened by further snowfall. She hesitated when she saw a suitcase and rucksack dusted with a fine covering of snow crystals, abandoned beside the porch. Further down the glade, Trassel danced in excited circles and yapped.

'What on earth?' Cleome set down her bags, and squinted as she traced a further trail of footprints down the glade. Her gaze fell on someone lying in a snowdrift in front of the scattering of boulders, on the left-hand side of the open space. Trassel still barked feverishly. 'Helen, I think you'd better come here!' she shouted, hurrying as fast as she could, her feet swinging in wide semi-circles over the deep snow, as she ran towards the pile of colour. 'Oh, my God! Oh my God!' she cried.

'What is it?' Helen followed, taking big bounds through the heaped drifts.

'It's Amelie!' Cleome screamed.

Helen fell to her knees beside Amelie, pressed her neck with her fingertips, and put her ear close to Amelie's mouth. 'She's still breathing. We need to get her inside, now! Can you lift her feet? We need to carry her gently, keep her horizontal, no sudden jolts.'

Before they attempted to move Amelie's unconscious body, Helen took off her padded coat, and placed it over her patient. She then lifted Amelie under the armpits while Cleome took her feet, and they struggled to the porch with Amelie slung between them. Cleome set down Amelie's feet, while Helen knelt and cradled her head and Cleome fumbled to open the door. They carried her in, to a sheepskin rug in front of the warm *kakelugn*—the tall blue-and-white tiled stove—which stood in the corner of the living room.

'Gently and slowly, let's lay her down here. It's better if she can remain flat. Let me get these damp clothes off her. I need blankets, anything warm that you have. Put the kettle on too.' Helen worked fast, peeling sodden garments from Amelie's frozen body. Amelie groaned; her eyes flickered open and then closed again while Helen worked on.

Cleome dashed about. She shut the door, set the kettle on the Aga, and handed over woollen shawls, blankets, socks, and towels.

'Amelie, can you hear me?' Helen asked. 'Do you have a hot water bottle or two?' she requested of Cleome as she placed blankets over Amelie's trunk.

Cleome riffled through a cupboard, grabbed a hot water bottle, and as she filled it from the kettle, her hand trembled.

'Do you have a thermometer?' Helen called from the living room.

'No.'

Amelie murmured. Cleome handed over the hot water bottle. Helen wrapped it in another towel and placed it over Amelie's groin.

'Here are my keys. Get my medical bag from the boot of my car, as quick as you can. I need to take her temperature and listen to her heart. We might need an ambulance.'

Cleome fled to Helen's car, leaping through the snow with an energy she did not know she possessed. She found the medical bag and rushed back to the house with it.

'She's pale,' Helen muttered. 'Amelie, can you hear me? I'm going to take your temperature now.'

'She's always pale.' Cleome knelt over her granddaughter and took her hand.

'Let's see, thirty-one degrees. Hypothermic, but not as bad as I'd feared. I still think it would be safer to call an ambulance.'

'No ambulance!' Amelie croaked.

'Amelie? Amelie, can you hear me, darling? It's *Mormor*.' Cleome bent closer. Amelie's eyelids fluttered.

'Make her a warm, sweet drink, please. Amelie, I want you to lie flat for now. I'm going to cover you some more.' Helen felt Amelie's feet and hands, and then wrapped her legs in another blanket, placed a towel around her long damp hair, and covered her arms. Amelie's teeth chattered.

'I've warmed these bags of wheat,' Cleome offered.

'Brilliant. Amelie, I'm going to put these warm bags in your arm pits to help you heat up a bit.' Helen stood up, and addressed Cleome, 'I'd be much happier if we called the ambulance.'

'No ambulance!' Amelie wheezed.

Cleome knelt down again beside her granddaughter, and stroked a long damp tendril of hair from her face. 'Helen knows what she is talking about, Am.'

'I will refuse to go. I will refuse to let them near me.'

'But, darling…'

'It's okay,' Helen soothed. 'I want to listen to your heart please, Amelie.' Disturbing the blankets as little as possible, Helen placed a stethoscope on Amelie's chest. 'It's regular; that's good—but it's a little rapid. Do you know how long you were out there in the snow?'

'No, I must have passed out.'

'You have mild to moderate hypothermia, and it is advisable to get checked at the hospital. I will outline the possible complications…' Helen ran quietly through a list of symptoms.

'I don't care. I'm not going anywhere.'

'It's your decision,' she nodded reassuringly, her concerned gaze fixed on Amelie's pinched face, so like her grandmother's with its high cheekbones and eyes that turned up at the corners. 'But if you deteriorate, I will have no choice,' she said, firmly.

Helen opened the stove doors and added more logs so that the fire crackled. Cleome helped Amelie to sip warm ginger tea and honey through a straw.

'I will stay here tonight,' Helen told Cleome. 'This is too much for you to cope with alone. I'll just call home to let them know where I am.'

The cream Mora clock which stood in the downstairs hallway marked the minutes with its steady 'tick, tock' and the hours with its mellow chime, and was noticeable only because of the silence that prevailed in the little wooden house, after Helen returned home.

Slowly, Amelie recovered from the hypothermia. She sat in a daze on Cleome's colourful sofa beside the *kakelugn*, coughing, sneezing, blowing her nose, and staring out of the window at pirouetting snowflakes. She rarely spoke, nor did she explain her sudden appearance at *Det Lilla Huset*. She frequently burst into tears, distressing Cleome (who cried quietly and privately, upstairs in her room) and prompting Trassel to nuzzle her thigh.

Grief circulated like a dark mist, swirling around each woman, and encasing them in shadow. After ten days, the ancient homestead grew dusty and neglected, and every piece of furniture, artwork, houseplant and colourful rug, took on a jaded appearance as Cleome's strength faded in the face of Amelie's sorrow.

Each day, Helen bustled in through the front door bringing a blast of fresh air in her wake. Her sharp intelligence missed nothing, and she monitored her friends' physical health whilst also delivering homemade broth, fresh bread, and news of the outside world. She attempted to keep the kitchen hygienic without being intrusive. Privately, she fretted that it would take more than a bowl of warm soup and a snippet of local gossip for Amelie and Cleome to heal. Some force had been unleashed, and they grieved at a depth she sometimes saw among the refugee community in Sörmland—where the entire physical body was affected. Helen thought that Amelie might be anaemic, but Amelie refused a blood test. An outbreak of psoriasis on her scalp made her scratch distractedly and the skin around her hairline grew red raw. Helen prescribed medicated shampoo but it was not helping. Cleome frequently placed a hand across her heart as if her angina was playing up, but refused to admit that it was. While she had coped alone, the extra burden of Amelie was casting her down, and all Helen could do was trust her instincts, be a good neighbour, and hope that they improved soon. Lying awake in her bed, she gazed out at the waning crescent moon hanging regally in the sky, with worries racing through her mind. The night was clear and star-studded. The temperature was plummeting. The snow would freeze. Bones would be broken. She fretted over Amelie, seeing how she hovered half-alive, but could not work out how to help her.

The snow melted and the cottage was engulfed in dense, freezing mist. Pearly air clouded the glade, hiding the lake from view, and in the hours when the mist suddenly lifted, splotches of snow could be seen, splattered over the swathe of sodden green. The days rolled, one into the other, and Cleome lost track of time. She and Amelie dozed on sofas, taking it in turns to rouse themselves and put another log in the *kakelugn*.

'Mum and I always spoke Swedish, unlike *Mormor* and I, who talk in English,' Amelie told Helen during one of her visits. 'I like to hear Swedish being spoken; it is a comfort.'

'Well, I will speak Swedish with you any time,' Helen offered.

'Did I tell you that I begged the consultant to try again?' Amelie confided. Her conversation frequently hopped from one subject to another. 'I begged her to save Bertie... but deep down I knew it was too late. You know how it is with a patient? That moment when you know they have passed? Before she had even answered me, I gathered his small body in my arms.' Her voice cracked. 'Why did I study that day and not take the day off, like a good mother? If I had done that, none of this would have happened.'

Helen placed a hand on Amelie's shoulder. 'It was not your fault. None of this was your fault, I promise you that much.'

'I left Esme a note,' Amelie continued, not listening. 'The truth is that I cannot stand to be with her. When I see her happy with Paul and Joel, it makes me want to scream. It's horrid of me, and I'm a coward, I know, for running off without speaking to her—but I was frightened of my own terrible thoughts.'

'You did well to come here. Esme will understand, and when you are ready, you must call her. In the meantime, you can rest here, regain your strength,' Helen consoled. 'I must dash now. Eat the fish and potatoes before they go cold. I'll see you tomorrow.' She hurried from the kitchen, waving as she did so.

'I keep wondering what I was doing at the precise moment. Was I at the table studying, or was I eating the croissant? Was there a clue that I missed, that something awful was happening? I cannot believe the way it slipped past me unnoticed, while I carried on doing whatever I was doing. And then I wish… Oh, I wish that I could turn back time, and relive that morning all over again—do it differently.'

Cleome wrapped her arms around her granddaughter. She did not attempt to speak or reassure. Sometimes, there were no words. She replayed the morning of the accident over in her mind too, in an attempt to make sense of it. She wished that she had picked up the phone that day and exchanged some kind words with Kerstin. She had rung Amelie, but not Kerstin. To be truthful, she had not had the energy for Kerstin, and it haunted her now. If she had made the call, might her daughter have been delayed, her journey time different, the accident avoided? And the thing that really bothered Cleome—that she would never admit to Amelie—was her hunch that Kerstin had known she was dying at the accident scene, had been afraid, had suffered. The medics in England had reassured her that she would not have known a thing—but how did they know? Was it something they said to everybody? Cleome suspected that Kerstin had died agonisingly, and could not quell her unease.

'We will plod on, you and I,' she told Amelie. 'We will keep on, getting through each hour, until this horror abates.'

'Our lives have changed forever.'

'It's true, they have. Nor should we ever try to pretend otherwise.' Cleome sighed and gazed out of the window. 'You know, the lake here is sacred. She will take our tears and help us heal.'

Amelie frowned. 'Did I tell you? They offered to take me to visit the crash site, but I couldn't do it. Should I have found the courage? Paid my respects?'

'Not if you weren't ready. You can go anytime. It will still be there.'

'Nick had an organ donor's card; they donated his beautiful eyes. And Bertie... I said yes to organ donation, to help another child. I know how valuable that will be for someone—but I wonder if I did the right thing?'

'It was a compassionate gesture, very brave.'

'I'm sorry I am rabbiting on, dumping all my emotions on you. Let's try to eat. Afterwards, I will borrow a warm coat and take Trassel through the forest. It will do me good to get some air. Will you come with me?'

'No, no, dear. I'll have a little nap while you are gone.'

Trassel ran off through the undergrowth while Amelie picked her way beneath a canopy of dripping branches at the side of the cottage. Her breath formed clouds of vapour. The patter of melting snow, felted crunch of her own footsteps, and the dog's excited rush were the only sounds to break the deep silence surrounding the small cottage. A milky mist lingered over the lake.

In the forest, there was space to be as emotional as she liked, and no-one to witness it but the trees, birds and wild animals. As she walked, the name Darren Ackerman conjured in her mind, persistently. She had never laid eyes on the man, had purposely avoided photographs of him in the media, and yet now she imagined a dark-haired person with a cold and careless stare. Overcome with rage, she snatched a dead branch off the forest floor and smashed it repeatedly against a burnished pine trunk. The branch splintered into jagged pieces and fell to the forest floor. She roared like a lioness, filling the air with her fury. Trassel barked. She flung down the branch stub and strode between the trees, diverting from the track, and stumbling down a shallow dip. She puffed up a small hill, consumed with dark thoughts of what she would do to Darren Ackerman if he was still alive, and all the ways in which she would make him suffer. She realised fleetingly that she had lost sight of the lake but her attention soon turned back to plotting her revenge. How did you punish a dead man? There must surely be a way.

Up ahead, the woodland changed character. She faced a dense area of spruce trees that at first appeared impenetrable. She decided to turn around and make her way back but Trassel growled and her tail rose rigidly as her attention was caught by something hidden in the thick stand of conifers. The dog tore into the undergrowth, barking noisily. Amelie called her back but she did not return, and so she had no choice but to push the dripping branches aside, and follow the dog.

'Trassel, *kom hit*!' she called. 'Come here!' She whistled. She paused and listened but could not hear any sound of the dog. 'Blast,' she muttered, picking her way carefully through the copse, climbing over fallen wood and soaking Cleome's coat as she brushed past low wet branches. 'Trassel!' she bellowed again. 'Trassel!'

Eventually she caught sight of the dog, sniffing around a tree stump. 'Come here!' she repeated. Her fingers stung, pink with the cold. She blew on them to warm them up. The dog came, and it was only then that she realised she was lost. She had been so absorbed in her own thoughts that she had rampaged through the forest blindly, not taking note of where she was going. She had long since lost sight of the lake which would have enabled her to find a quick way back to *Det Lilla Huset*.

The daylight was fading and the temperature was dropping fast. How foolish she had been. Rather than attempt to retrace her steps which would take a long time, she decided to follow a faint animal track, in the hope that it would lead her to the forest road. All around her, the woodland was silent apart from a faint humming noise in the distance, like some kind of gardening machine. She reached the deserted road at a point where it carved through an area of pine trees and huge rocks. It was unfamiliar but she had a good sense of direction, and figured that if she set off in what she thought was an easterly direction, she would soon recognise where she was. She put Trassel on her lead. Most of the snow had now melted; it would be an easy walk.

After a short distance, the road turned a sharp corner and she came across a man, standing at the verge. He clutched a drone in his hands and wore a canvas bag across his body. He gazed skywards. Trassel froze, before letting her tail wag slowly.

'It's Robban, isn't it?' Amelie approached the man. His skin looked dry and flaky, and was blotched pink from the cold. 'What are you doing, out here?' she asked

'I was taking photographs with my drone. But I think it's getting too dark now.' His attention flickered to the inky sky.

'I got lost, walking the dog. Can you direct me back to my grandmother's please?'

'You must be careful getting lost in the forest, my mother says. The cold can kill you. I'm going to walk home now too.' Robban was suddenly enthusiastic, and took off at fast pace along the road without her. Amelie hastily followed.

'I'm sorry your baby died,' he said, tonelessly, not turning to look back at her. 'And your husband.'

Amelie nodded. 'Thank you,' she whispered.

'Your mother was very beautiful. You are very beautiful too,' he went on, as he loped along, his body leaning at a slight slant. After a short silence, he added, 'I would like to get a job but nobody wants me to work for them. Mother and Father say it's because the immigrants took all the vacancies.'

'You used to work with your father at the vehicle maintenance plant in Flen, did you not? I remember you helping to fix *Mormor's* Volvo one summer, many years ago.'

'Oh yes, I was there for one summer, and then they didn't want me anymore. Father was made redundant. He says Sweden is not the place it used to be. It's full of foreigners, let into our country by numbskulls in Stockholm.'

Amelie felt uncomfortable. 'What are you carrying?' She changed the subject.

'My drone camera. I like making films and taking photographs.'

They continued to stride out in silence. Robban led them off one road, and turned right at a T-junction onto another. Amelie recognised where she was then. After a time, he strode onto a narrow track through the trees, telling her that it was a short cut.

'You must have this small tree, at least.' Helen came through the kitchen door, bearing a tiny fir in a pot, and a cotton shopping bag, full of goodies. She had already hung a wreath on the front door, and set a gingerbread house on the kitchen table. 'Josef iced that house for you,' she said.

'I bet that made him happy.' Cleome raised an eyebrow doubtfully.

'He wasn't terribly thrilled but he had a girl round and was trying to impress her. She was very keen on making it pretty—you can thank her for most of the decoration.'

'It's very colourful, definitely got the feminine touch.'

'Look,' Helen continued, extracting items from the bag which she had set down on the kitchen table. 'I bought a small packet of decorations for the tree. I know you won't want to make the place beautiful like you normally do but this will be something, at least. Oh, and here, this candle is scented with orange—I know you love orange.' Helen pushed her shiny dark hair from her face, and grinned. Her cheeks were rosy from the cold. 'What are you doing here?' she asked, noticing several stems of mistletoe and a collection of candles laid out on the worktop.

'It's the solstice, and I'm preparing to welcome the return of the light. It is one of my favourite moments of the year. Have I never told you about it before?'

'Maybe. I forget these wild things you do.'

'The mistletoe will be hung in a doorway for good luck and peace in the house. Let's face it, we need some of that around here…'

'And all the candles?'

'I will turn off the lights tonight and we will spend the evening quietly, in candlelight.'

'Sounds romantic,' Helen teased.

'It is for me and Amelie—to honour a tradition that is as old as time! Get away with your "romantic" remarks!' Cleome chuckled. 'But here, perhaps you'd better take a few bits for you and Daniel, if you're in the mood?' she teased.

Helen burst out laughing. 'I don't think so!'

The front door was pushed open, and Amelie and Trassel walked into the hallway.

Cleome poked her head around the kitchen door. 'I was getting worried about you!'

Trassel, set free from her lead, trotted across the kitchen floor and lapped noisily at the water in her bowl.

'I got lost in the forest, but luckily I found the road, and then I came across Robban Bengtsson. He knew the way back.'

'Was he out with his drone?' Cleome asked.

'Yes, taking shots of the forest, he said. He also shared some horribly racist views with me, obviously put into his head by his parents.'

'Nothing new there then—they are peculiar people,' Cleome shrugged. 'Amelie, changing the subject: tonight is the solstice, the darkest day of the year, when we give thanks for this beautiful planet of ours, and welcome the return of the light. Will you join me, sitting in candlelight and listening to some music?'

Amelie and Helen exchanged knowing glances, and Amelie hugged her grandmother from behind. 'You are so cute sometimes,' she said.

Cleome stood, weighing the letter in her hand, uncertain what to do about it. She was alone beside the mailbox on the forest road. By the handwriting on the envelope and the postmark, she knew immediately who had sent it. A warning pain spread across her chest. She took a deep breath and looked at the missive again. Her name and address were written with a fountain pen using navy ink. The handwriting was a flourishing Italic. She tucked the envelope into her coat pocket, and hardly noticed the walk home. Back in the safety of her kitchen, she eased it open with shaking hands. A Botticelli angel adorned the card. She opened it.

'Thinking of you at this sad time. With my love, Catherine,' she read out loud. She clutched the card to her chest and shook her head. 'Why now?' she whispered. '*Oh God, why now?*'

In the supermarket, gaudy displays of *Julskum* reminded Amelie of childhood Christmases in Sweden. The sweets in their red and green shiny packets had always been her favourite. Other shoppers stared at her and her grandmother. Her grandmother wore a long purple coat and laced blue leather boots. She had pulled off her woolly hat and revealed her matted hair. Amelie was aware that she too must appear eccentric as she clumped along the aisle in wellingtons that flopped about her leggings, her hair pulled back in a messy ponytail, and her psoriasis no doubt showing at the edges of her face. It had been a bad couple of days.

'Let's make this quick,' she murmured, and Cleome nodded.

'For all the fuss about Christmas, the Swedish have no idea about Christmas food,' Cleome complained. 'I will roast us a chicken, here put this in the basket. And I can make us a *julskinka* too—a Christmas ham?'

'That looks nice. And I really don't mind what I eat—we can have whatever you want.'

'Do you remember the tradition of leaving out a bowl of buttered *julgrot*—like a Swedish rice pudding—for the spirits who live in the forest? We always did it when you were little, and I still carry on the tradition. I must get some rice now. It's there, up that aisle. That is one thing we do not need right now—the mischievous ones of the forest upset with us.'

'Surely they would not kick us while we are down?' Amelie jested.

'Oh, you can never be sure. I think one needs to respect such things. All the ancient traditions came about for a reason. Our ancestors were not as dim as we like to think.'

They turned into the aisle, just as a woman further up it started to shriek at her two young sons. One boy froze at the sound of his mother's voice and twisted his small hands together; the other who was perhaps only three, burst into tears. The mother's hair hung about her face, dark and bleached white at the tips, as she continued to rant at her children.

'Don't shout at them!' Amelie cried out, unable to bear what she saw.

Cleome stepped close to her side, instinctively supportive. The two boys and their mother turned and gawped.

'Whatever your sons have done, I'm sure it's not too bad,' Cleome suggested diplomatically, speaking in Swedish.

'Oh, and what right do you have to tell me how to treat my kids? Keep your nose out of my business, you hippy,' the woman snapped, and turned away with her arms protectively around her sons' small shoulders.

'I think we have spent enough time in here,' Cleome observed and led them towards the till.

'I am losing it,' Amelie reflected. 'I could have hit that woman.'

'We are all out of sorts, Am. It's the grief; it has taken us to a different place. We live in the same world but we don't see things the way we did before. I'm not sure we'll ever see things the same way again, in fact. I am not defending that woman but we both know how small children infuriate, and she wasn't that bad, really.'

'I am so emotional. I really could have hit her…'

'I yelled at Kerstin when she was younger, believe me. We had the most blazing rows. I am ashamed when I think of my behaviour now.'

'Not when she was little, surely?' Amelie frowned.

'Oh, I don't know. I was not the best parent.'

Amelie loaded the shopping into their wicker basket. 'It is such a cruel, horrible world we live in,' she fumed. 'I don't know how I'm going to cope.'

'It certainly has its imbecilic moments,' Cleome agreed.

On Christmas Eve, Cleome and Amelie rose, both groggy from lack of sleep and rigid with dread at the prospect of the day ahead. They each had a shower, and sat and drank coffee at the kitchen table while their hair dried.

'I forgot to get you a present,' Amelie said quietly.

'Me too. "No presents" is okay though. We don't need them. It wouldn't feel right.'

'True.'

Cleome placed three tall beeswax candles on the table and lit them in memory of their lost ones. They began to prepare the meal of roasted chicken, potatoes, and vegetables, to the background of some Bach organ music. The simple actions of peeling and chopping helped to keep some of their emotion at bay. While they worked side by side in the kitchen, there was a stream of interruptions. Helen rang, a little tipsy, her voice full of fun, and Cleome told her to stay at home and celebrate; they were fine. Cleome's sister Antonia rang too. The Christmas call with her sister was always brief and formal, and this year was no different. Esme messaged, as did Marsha. Amelie replied to them. Patrick made a brief call to wish them both well.

While the dinner roasted in the Aga, they walked with Trassel to the edge of the frozen lake and back. A bitter wind circled the old homestead. The low winter sun occasionally pierced the cloud, and flashed between black silhouetted trees. One sunburst caused a moment of dazzling brilliance as glittering light bounced off the lake's glassy surface.

'Tomorrow will be Christmas in England,' Amelie said. 'And then three days after that, it will have been two months.'

'Yes. And then, after that, we will both begin a new year,' Cleome added, defiantly, linking her arm through her granddaughter's.

8

Sunday, 31ˢᵗ December

Sunshine bounced off the blanket of snow that lay outside the cottage. It glowed through the low windows casting white light and soft shadows into the rooms. By lunch time, the sun had disappeared behind a fat bank of cloud and thousands more milky flecks drifted from the sky. They gathered in the corners of the windowpanes as all afternoon, the snow continued to fall.

Around dusk, Amelie took her grandmother's car and drove along the deserted road through the bleached forest. Few would venture out in such weather, if they had a choice, she reflected. She wondered how many would attend the party later. The car headlights lit a tunnel through the white-flecked darkness, and the effect of the falling specks was hypnotic. She had been tasked with dropping off spare glasses, plates and cutlery from *Det Lilla Huset* to help with the catering, before the snow became too deep. She was not in the mood for festivities, if she was honest. To go to a party felt disloyal to her mother, Nick and Bertie—and besides, she was tired. She yawned expansively.

When she turned onto the track to Helen's farmhouse, she noted that the entire winding driveway through the trees had been snow-ploughed to allow access. She parked the car as close to the house as she could, beside ranks of neatly-stacked logs in an open section of the barn. As she stepped out of the vehicle, a feral cat watched her with its bright eyes, and she heard the muffled bark of Kaia the Dobermann, coming from the main house. The footpath to the front door had been shovelled clear with a spade, and snow lay in jagged piles beside it. Outdoor lights lit her route but she still trod cautiously.

When Helen's husband Victor had left her, fourteen years previously, Helen had been determined to get out of the city and find a place in the country where she could raise her young son Josef—a place where he would learn the values of Swedish outdoor life and benefit from all that the forest and lake had to offer. *Båvenshult* was the first property she viewed, and she had immediately fallen in love with the farmhouse and its assorted collection of outbuildings. These days, Josef was a strapping teenager who would no doubt fly the nest in a year or two, but Helen's love for her smallholding had grown year on year, and Amelie could see why. She paused, and looked up at the cloud-laden night sky. She watched the snow swirl down to the peaceful, undulating field at the side of the house—it was like a scene from a painting. She closed her eyes and allowed tiny flakes, like cold kisses, to fall on her face. She listened to the sounds of the landscape—so quiet tonight, blanketed in white.

Somebody let Kaia out of the house and the dog came bounding towards her. At the door she was met by Tarek, the Syrian refugee whom Helen had given a home a couple of years previously, in the one-bedroomed cottage adjacent to the barn. He was a tall man, slender but with broad shoulders. He wore a woollen jumper which matched his dark curly hair and the short stubble of his beard. His brown eyes shone brightly, as if he was waiting for her to say something. They were not autumn-brown like Nicks but dark like coffee, and radiated concern.

'Hi,' she said.

'Hi,' he replied.

She smiled and he smiled back, and there was warmth in his eyes then, along with the hint of sorrow. She had met him before, briefly, the previous summer. There had been a gathering down beside the lake one afternoon with beers and a picnic. They had all sat on the small beach that was a part of *Båvenshult* land. Tarek had played with Bertie for a while, she recalled. He had been a natural when it came to entertaining a toddler. Bertie had trusted him, had gripped his hand while they had paddled in the lake. Amelie drew in her breath.

Helen's generosity to this young immigrant had caused much gossip and speculation in the neighbourhood, and had ruffled the feathers of several local inhabitants who feared for both her safety and her sanity, and predicted that no good would come of her naïve hospitality. But Helen's instinct about Tarek had been proved right, time and time again. For the past two years, he had worked hard and watched over

Josef like an older brother. He had cooked for him, and driven him to sports practice, music lessons and meet-ups with friends while she was at work. These days, Tarek also had a part-time job teaching at the local sports centre. He had been a newly-qualified teacher when he had fled from war-torn Raqqa, and was taking steps to build a good new life in his adopted country. He had proven himself to be kind and conscientious, and was an increasingly popular character in Flen, both in the immigrant community and amongst some of the more open-minded natives.

He offered to help her carry in the boxes of crockery and glassware, and when he spoke, his accent was soothing, like velvet, if there could be such a thing. She had forgotten it was that way, and was now reminded of his enduringly warm and reassuring manner, the previous summer. He pulled on some boots and they went out to the car to fetch the cardboard boxes. As she placed one on the table, she inhaled the fragrance of cooking spices scenting the warm kitchen air, and was struck by the cosiness of the scene around her.

Daniel, Helen's Russian boyfriend, stood at one end of the large central table, chopping pickles for a salad. A navy apron was tied around his firm midriff, and his thick white hair stood in tufts from the exertion of preparing the various Russian dishes that he insisted on eating at this time of year. He broke off from what he was doing to engulf her in a bear-like hug. She had met Daniel many times over the years, and was fond of him.

'Is Helen not back yet?' she asked.

'She is held up at the *vårdcentral*. There's been an outbreak of flu. She won't be long now. Thank you for bringing these things over; she will really appreciate it.'

'Something smells delicious.'

'I'm making *kibbeh*, a special dish from his home for our young Syrian friend. Middle Eastern meatballs, to you and me.'

'He is very kind!' Tarek grinned.

'We émigrés need reminders of home from time to time. We are all looking forward to seeing you and your grandmother later,' Daniel added.

'Are you staying with your grandmother over the holidays?' Tarek asked.

'I'm staying with her for the time being, yes.' She caught sight of a vase of yellow freesias on the kitchen table, and experienced a vivid flashback to the incident when the tall, skinny man had come to her door in Percy Street, offering the same type of flower to her, wrapped in cellophane. She recalled his pleading expression, and her subsequent explosion of rudeness and anger. She shook her head. She kept having these moments when snapshots of the past came at her out of nowhere. She realised that she was gripping the table edge.

'Are you okay?' Tarek asked.

'Oh yes, I'm fine. Thank you.' She looked up to find him watching her. He moved as if to say something but then stopped himself, and continued to watch her, empathy written in the softness of his expression.

He knows what it's like, she thought. *He understands.*

After she had collected her thoughts and said her farewells, and as she drove back through the snowy forest, Amelie considered Helen's unconventional household. She imagined what it must have been like for Tarek, making his way from Syria alone. The sea crossing would have been dangerous and he must have known that he was taking his life into his hands. The reception on landing, or even where he might land, would have been unknown. He had literally thrown himself into the hands of fate. She seemed to recall that he had spent over a year in a Greek refugee camp, and remembered news footage of bitter winter weather and harsh living conditions at the camps, seen on the television at Percy Street. It was extraordinary to think he had been one of those people, and had battled on, and somehow made it to Sweden. She considered his courage, and the determination it would have taken to strike out across strange lands in such a way, when he did not even speak the languages, and all in order to seek a better life. He was similar in age to Nick, who had had such a privileged life by comparison.

Snow spiralled outside the car windows. A thousand white flecks drifted past brown tree trunks.

She turned her thoughts to Daniel and recalled that he had rented Helen's *lillstuga* in the grounds of the farm, for many years. He was a lecturer in poetry at the university in Stockholm, and regularly escaped his city apartment to spend hours fishing out on the lake in the summer. Many years ago, he had had a wife, a tall, sad-looking redhead who hated the mosquitoes that were an inevitable part of Swedish summers. She had left him for another man, a city dweller but Daniel had continued to rent the *lillstuga*, and when his love affair with Helen had begun, he had invested in proper heating and insulation for the little cottage, and spent more and more of his time there. For some reason, Helen had never invited him to live in the main house.

Back at *Det Lilla Huset*, all was peaceful. Cleome had lit candles that flickered in the dark rooms. She played soothing classical music and appeared to be lost in her own thoughts. Sensitive to her grandmother's mood, Amelie moved like a phantom through the cottage, quietly tidying. She left Cleome sitting beside the *kakelugn*, and took Trassel for a walk to the frozen lake's edge and along the icy shore, using a torch with a strong beam to light her way. Snowflakes melted in her open mouth when she stopped and lifted her face to the sky. Fat marshmallows sat on the fence posts around the orchard, and snakes of white lay in perilous ridges along the wires. Icicles fringed the cottage fascia board and the roof was padded with a plump duvet, making *Det Lilla Huset* look like something out of a fairy tale. The advent candlesticks lit in the window made a mirage of good cheer.

Despite all the tricks that Cleome had learned from living in this Scandinavian country, she could not get warm. On the final day of an abysmal year, it felt like the end of the world was coming, and as she loaded the stove with more wood, there was a lump in her throat. She had taken a bath in a bid to get some heat into her bones and bring some solace. It had not worked—although she did feel fresher for having had a wash, and realised to her shame that a good scrub had been long overdue. She did not want to go out to a party later. She could not muster one ounce of goodwill and fretted that she would burden the other revellers with her misery and inhibit people on a night they should all enjoy. She simply wanted to sleep while one year slipped silently into another, and wake up when the transition was over. She took down the card depicting Botticelli's angel from the mantlepiece and re-read it, tracing her finger over the inked words. Why had Amelie not noticed it or asked who Catherine was? If she ever did, what would she say? Would she lie?

As she heard Amelie return from her walk, she replaced the card and composed her thoughts. She needed to decide what to wear, to find her sparkling moon brooch perhaps. It always raised her spirits.

'Why did you not drive?' Helen exclaimed. 'I saw your torches flashing around the sheltered edges of the field but never dreamt that it was you two! And you are so late; it must have taken you ages! You must be frozen. Come in, come in!'

'Not at all! We left late, couldn't get ourselves going. The track was impassable. Old man Bengtsson did not clear it as he said he would, and as the snow kept coming, I could not face it myself. We had to leave Trassel at home; she would have got frozen cold.' Cleome took Helen's hand, climbed the house steps and hobbled over the threshold. Kaia approached Amelie, and nuzzled her hand.

'Come in, let's take off your coats and warm you up with a drink and some food before we all troop outside for the fireworks. I still can't believe you walked in this weather!' They slipped off their boots, and Helen took their coats.

'Oh, it wasn't too bad. There's no wind, the snow has stopped now, and everything looks so pretty.'

'Rather you than me! Here—have a glass of *glögg*. There's still plenty left.'

'Where is everybody? It's not a very big party.'

'The weather stopped several people coming and others were nervous about it, and only stayed a little while. My colleague and her husband left an hour ago, and so did the Ahlbergs. Tarek's football buddies went on to another party in town. He is the team's captain this year and they gave him a hard time for not joining them but he said he wasn't interested, and he can be very determined when he wants to be. He is charming with it too, of course, and so they departed on good terms. Three of his Syrian friends from home are still here, along with Josef and his school chums, my colleague Sven, and Daniel.'

'Where *is* your handsome poet?' Cleome squinted.

'Ha! He would be flattered to hear you call him that. They are all in the sitting room where there's a warm fire.'

'But he *is* so handsome, that man of yours!'

'And you possess such rare beauty too,' Daniel regaled Cleome as he appeared in the kitchen doorway. 'You have the eyes of a wild cat and the spirit of a tiger.'

'Oh goodness, and how much have you drunk, Daniel?' Cleome chuckled, offering her wrinkled cheek for him to kiss.

'And the beautiful Amelie has returned. You have your grandmother's eyes, although yours are paler in colour, like the lake in summer.'

Amelie felt the heat rise in her cheeks. 'Good to see you again,' she said.

'Let's get you a drink and some food, and you can take a seat by the fire. You can eat there where it's warmer,' Helen suggested.

'Here, have some of the dish I was making for our Syrian friend earlier.' Daniel fetched two plates, and served three *kibbeh*, a large dollop of tahini sauce and some salad on to each, and handed it to his guests, along with a knife and fork wrapped in a napkin. 'Come through,' he gestured. 'Tarek fantasises about this dish but we don't ever have the right flavour of lamb for him. Swedish lamb is not a patch on Syrian lamb, so I am told,' he joked, as they walked through to the sitting room and took their places on a sofa beside the fire. They sat and balanced the plates on their knees. Helen brought through a tray with glasses of *glögg* and set it on a low table in front of them.

'Oh, but these are delicious.' Amelie nodded, pointing her fork at the *kibbeh*. Kaia sat beside her, and leant against her knee.

'And I am so grateful to you for making them.' Tarek strolled over. In the tactile way of all Syrians, he put an arm around Daniel's shoulder, and nodded hello to Cleome and Amelie with one hand over his heart.

The log fire crackled, and flames danced in the wide fireplace. Daniel presided over the party like a host, his rolling laughter billowing through the spacious room. Josef and his friends clattered around upstairs. When they had finished eating they stood up, and Helen introduced Cleome to her colleague Sven, a tall pale man with a serious disposition who struck up a polite conversation. Tarek introduced Amelie to his friends—three fellow Syrians who now lived in Flen.

'This is Ayah,' he said, and a woman in a blue hijab nodded her head demurely. 'Her brother Zain, and our friend Kafi. All friends from home.'

Amelie said hello, and then Helen appeared at her side and updated her with some local gossip. Zain and Kafi drank beer and joked with Tarek while Ayah sipped lemonade from a tall glass. Her watchful eyes studied Amelie, and sensing her gaze, Amelie glanced up and smiled at her. Ayah looked away, her mouth twisted in private amusement.

Beside her, Tarek clutched a glass of coke and chatted in Arabic to his friends. His animated voice and warm character captured their attention, and the men listened to him, and laughed. Ayah did not join in with the humour. Amelie wondered what he was saying. She had a sense that he knew what mattered in life—and what did not.

Outside, the sky had cleared and was inky and starlit. Everyone waved goodbye to the Syrian guests who had decided not to stay on for the fireworks but to drive back to Flen while the snow had stopped. A gibbous moon bathed the wintry garden in light and cast shadows from the buildings and forest edges. Daniel and Sven prepared the firework display. Josef locked Kaia in a room on the far side of the house, even though the fireworks had been chosen especially for their prettiness and there would be no explosive bangs. Daniel returned to the main group who stood wrapped in coats and hats, stamping their feet on the snowy ground, while in the distance, Sven lit the fuses and stepped away from them.

Josef and his friends stood over to one side of the lawn, drinking beer from cans and laughing raucously. Tarek disappeared inside. Daniel, who wore a Cossack hat and a long, fur-lined coat, stood beside Cleome as the first firework streamed into the sky.

'I used to tell Kerstin that a star had danced and she was born,' she mused.

Amelie linked her arm through her grandmother's, and stood at her side with her chin buried in a warm scarf and a bobble hat on her head.

'You know your Shakespeare,' Daniel nodded.

'And truth. I know the truth.' Cleome sighed. She placed her hand over Amelie's and squeezed gently.

Josef and his group began a rowdy countdown to the new year, and then their cries of '*Gott nytt år!*' rang out into the night air. More fireworks ignited.

Tarek reappeared and stood at the edge of the party, a few steps from Amelie, lowering his gaze from the display in the sky. He wore a short wool coat over his brown checked shirt and black jeans, and a scarf wrapped snugly around his neck. He glanced over at her and smiled, his dark eyes shining. She wondered whether he was ever sad. He seemed to conjure his own happiness from an endless supply, somewhere deep inside him. She tilted her head to one side as she noticed him avoiding the colourful display.

'You don't like fireworks?'

'It looks like war—how do you say in English—it's a fine line,' he shrugged, and ran his hand through his dark curls so that one or two stood up from his head. 'Sometimes, all I see is missiles. It is better for my heart to focus on the beautiful white snow.' He smiled again, as if it was not a problem that he saw war where others saw beauty.

'I'm sorry, that must be hard for you.' She smiled back at him. His unwavering cheerfulness was infectious and her spirits lifted.

'Sometimes it is impossible, sometimes it is okay. You are lucky, to simply enjoy the pretty spectacle.'

'I suppose I am.' It had been a while since anyone had called her lucky, but she could see his point. She wagered that Tarek did not dwell on the loss and heartbreak in his life, the way that she still did.

'I am so sorry for your loss, by the way. I have wanted to say something to you. I remember briefly meeting your husband and son last summer, by the lake.'

'Yes, I remember that day too. It seems like another life now.'

'I am sure it must feel like a different world for you. He was a nice man, your husband—full of laughter and kindness, and your little boy was very cute. Your mother was helpful too, as I recall, correcting my Swedish to help me improve.'

'Thank you.' She was pleasantly surprised to hear her family spoken of with such lightness and compassion. There was something very appealing about Tarek's gentle manner—a great strength in his quiet certainty.

The fireworks finished. She looked up at the sky again, at the sweep of stars that punctuated the blackness. There really was no need for fireworks when the night sky looked so glorious, she thought. She stood, watching the stars with Tarek, and feeling quietly surprised by the sense of ease which had crept over her. He was the first person to speak so naturally, and to mention her mother, Nick and Bertie freely and without any awkwardness. She glanced over at him and smiled again, appreciatively. 'Thank you for what you said about my family. Helen has told me that you lost your girlfriend and many members of your family as well, in the war. You have my condolences too.'

'Yes, thank you, I did. And now I am very lucky to live here where it is safe and I have many friends.'

'Do you miss home?' she asked hesitantly, curious about how he coped but not wishing to be tactless.

'Oh, of course—but I cannot return to Syria while there is war, and with my family gone, and many relatives fled to Europe, what would be the point anyway? I left because I did not want to kill or to be killed—and I stand by my decision. I am a peaceful man and I do not want to fight anybody or hurt anybody, so I have to keep away from my country. One day, if there is peace again, I will go home, of course I will. I miss my homeland every single day, even if the time when my family were alive and we all lived together is now gone forever.'

Cleome had moved off, and Amelie folded her arms, and swallowed hard.

'But please, don't feel sorry for me,' he went on. 'I am okay. Tomorrow I see my Syrian friends and we celebrate the new year our way. We are survivors, and we are very grateful to be here in Sweden.' She saw determination glitter in his dark eyes then, and the stubborn set of his bearded jawline.

There was a sudden commotion behind them as one of Josef's friends was sick in the snow to accompanying cries of disgust. Sven, who like Helen was a doctor, rolled his eyes and strolled over to see whether help was needed.

Amelie turned away; she was in no mood to assist a drunken teenager. 'I need to find a way to survive and live a good life too, somehow... God only knows how,' she confessed. It was easy to speak, outside in the crisp night air, to someone who, like her, had lost so much.

'God *does* know how, if you listen to Him,' Tarek offered. 'People like you and me, we have to dig a little deeper than most. But you will do it. You will survive. Life will not be the same, but people like us, we are sent these great challenges because we are capable of overcoming them. We are strong enough to live on and to learn why we are really here.'

'I don't believe in God. I'm sorry, it was just a turn of phrase.'

'I don't mean your old man who sits on a cloud, you know, not that God.'

'Who then, Allah?'

'You can say Allah. Or for me, more like, it is the divine energy that exists in all things, the universal, the source—in every plant and creature in this garden, and the forest over there, in the snow and the wind, and in all the life on this earth.'

'...and family and friends...'

'Oh sure, yes—the divine energy in all of us. We are being asked to "look inside", to do some work on ourselves—on our own hearts and minds—as we face up to the new truth of our lives. That is all.'

'I'm not sure I want to face up to anything, right now,' Amelie said.

'You know, you look how I sometimes feel. I see it in your face.'

'Oh?'

'We are people who have lost a lot, and I was just like you, hurting so much.'

'But you are so strong, are you not?'

'I don't know about that. I hope this is the year the war ends, and I can go home.'

'Well, I hope that for you, too.'

He nodded, tucked his fists into his armpits, and looked down at the scuffed snow around his feet. 'We don't get to choose these things that happen, you know. We are not in charge, that's for sure.'

The rest of the party returned indoors to the warmth. Someone let Kaia out and she bounded through the snowy garden towards Tarek.

'Would you like to take a walk down to the lakeside? I'd like to show you something.' He was suddenly enthusiastic. She hesitated for a moment, but did not want to disappoint him.

'Sure,' she agreed.

He whistled to the dog, who scarpered ahead of them along the path out of the garden, as if she knew where they were going. 'I hope the snow is not too deep. It's usually not too bad where the forest overhangs the path.'

'I love the snow,' she reassured him.

'I know that.'

'How do you know that?' she teased.

'I just do,' he replied, smiling.

They fell into silence as they walked, and Amelie felt a little awkward, as if she should be trying to make conversation. Around them, the landscape was silent, apart from the distant crackle of flower-like fireworks in green, pink and white that rose above the forest on the opposite shore of the lake. The lake herself was dark with occasional glimmers of silver where the moonlight caught her icy surface. Amelie wondered where Tarek was taking her.

He turned to her with the playful grin of someone who is about to reveal an exciting secret. Kaia ran ahead, rushing through the snow, as if she knew the secret too, and was also excited to share it.

'Not long now,' he said.

When they arrived at the small beach belonging to *Båvenshult*, Tarek pointed to a headland over to their left. She focussed on the bay shore as it curved around the water's edge. Beginning beside the small beach where they stood, a vast swathe of forest festooned the land, coming right down to the water. The wooden jetty where Helen launched her boat in summer glistened with crystals of ice. Amelie squinted, attempting to follow the line of Tarek's arm and pointed finger, to see what the mystery was.

'There,' he said, satisfied, and nodding his head.

She caught her breath as she noticed a tiny cottage, all lit up at the end of the woody peninsular. The small homestead glittered like a shimmering beacon in the night, surrounded on three sides by water, and guarded by the wild forest.

'I've never noticed it before,' she gasped.

'It's new. Some people from Stockholm came and saved it from ruin. Most of the time, it is empty. They only come for a couple of weeks in the summer, and it seems that this year they are here for the new year too.' He turned to her, his eyes gleaming. 'It is my dream place,' he told her. 'It's what I think of, when I am sad. I promise myself that one day, I will live in a place like this, surrounded by the beauty of nature and with peace all around me. I wanted to share this with you. It is a magical place, is it not?'

'Oh yes,' she enthused, a smile spread wide over her face. She gazed at the cottage, perched on top of the rocks, white light pouring from its windows, reflecting off the lake ice, and dispelling the darkness. 'It looks like you could make a real home there.' She felt her shoulders drop as she spoke.

'That's it, exactly. A real home!' Kaia sat beside Tarek, and his fingers reached down to stroke her ears. They turned and made their way back to the party. Amelie's spirits were the highest they had been since before the accident. She was surprised at how quickly and easily her depression had vanished. She felt carefree for the first time in a very long time.

Back at the house, they learnt that Sven had left and Josef's poorly friend had been taken upstairs to bed. The remainder of the young group were in the sitting room, listening to music while the adults were gathered in the kitchen, sitting around the big table, chatting and drinking. Amelie felt exhaustion overtake her like a drug. Cleome sidled over to her and announced that they must leave; the tired lines on her beautiful old face were a sure sign that she too, needed to sleep.

'Let somebody give you a lift,' Helen urged.

'No, no. I want to walk,' Cleome insisted. 'It's not far. I must use these old legs of mine or they will seize up. Amelie, are you ready to go home?'

'I will accompany you both,' Tarek offered.

'You really don't need to,' Cleome assured him.

'I want to. There is lots of ice out there.'

They trailed slowly in single file along a ridge at the edge of the field where the snow lay thinnest. Once they had crossed the open space, Cleome led the way through the trees along the track she knew so well, shining her torch on the forest floor when the canopy was so dense that it obliterated the moonlight. They reached the edge of her property where snow had drifted in the open glade and were able to follow the track they had made earlier. When they were almost at the cottage door, and could hear Trassel's excited bark, Tarek bade them a happy new year, and lit a cigarette before wading back up the slope, a lone silhouette against the whiteness.

'Isn't smoking *haram*?' Amelie mused.

'I think Tarek is past caring,' Cleome replied.

9

New Quiet Moon

'It is a New Moon. We must set our intentions for the coming lunar phase,' Cleome announced.

The women sat on opposite sides of the yellow-painted kitchen table, shoving fish pie around their plates with forks, and eating very little. Amelie looked up with a blank expression on her face, and Cleome could tell that it was not a good day for her granddaughter. She had been fretting about her future ever since the new year, not sure where to go or what to do next. She was obviously not interested in the new moon.

'I keep thinking of snow angels,' she murmured. 'Of the fun and joy in making one, and the pleasing shape… And then, of how they never last, and melt away—and in no time at all, there is no sign that they were ever there.'

Cleome's eyes sharpened in her wrinkled-fruit face. 'You have something there—about the meaning of life, who we are, and what we are doing here.'

'I do?'

'Yes, you just keep thinking about your snow angels.'

'Do you mind if I stay on here for a while?'

Cleome dropped her fork with a clatter. 'Of course, I don't mind! This is your home now! And I would… I would be *lost* without you here. It is often very lonely out here in winter and now, with everything, it would be utterly unbearable, and…' The old woman shook her head. Finishing the sentence was too hard. She reached for her glass of vodka and tonic with a knobbly hand, and took a swig.

'When I came here, I didn't have a plan,' Amelie explained. 'I simply ran away. I will need to return to Oxford at some point, but not yet. I can always rent a little place somewhere near here if it's too much for you having me stay, and we can see each other every day. I have savings, now that…since…' She held up her hands and shook her head.

'I will not hear of such nonsense!' Cleome's eyes blazed, pinpricks of light. 'This is your home. It is *our* home now, and you can be here whenever you want. We have to stick together, you and me.'

Amelie's eyes brimmed with tears. 'I honestly don't know what I'd do without you.'

'You would survive. Things would be different, sure. But you would get through it. You are a warrior.'

'I don't know about that. I feel like an utter failure. Marsha and Esme have both emailed. Esme is still angry with me, though she's trying not to be, of course—but I can tell she is. Marsha is very sweet but constantly worried. They both say they miss me and keep asking when I'll go back to Oxford. I disappoint them by not being stronger, not carrying on…'

'They are no doubt concerned.'

'Mm… I haven't been a very good friend to them—Esme especially. I can't… I can't… It's Joel, and the fact that she still has Paul, like I said. I know it sounds awful…'

'Of course, you see her happy—and you wonder why it is not you. It's natural.' Cleome watched as Amelie stood abruptly, and began to clear their plates and scrape their uneaten food into the bin. Her granddaughter moved like a different person these days—where once she was swift and confident, now her movements were stilted and jerky. Before the accident, she was graceful, and always running, dashing about, smiling and chatting. How quickly things changed. Looking at her now, it was as if grief had formed a separate rigid carcass that she was compelled to carry at all times.

Amelie paused to look out of the window, with a dirty plate suspended in one hand. 'Esme doesn't understand why my phone is turned off. But how can I turn it on when there's a hundred photos of Bertie on there? When my home page is a picture of the three of us?' The plate clattered onto the draining board. 'My arms always feel empty. There's no little hand to hold, no little-boy body napping against mine or asking for a cuddle. The emptiness, *Mormor*! It is shocking!'

Cleome pushed herself to her feet and put her hands carefully and gently around Amelie's bent shoulders. 'There, there,' she whispered. 'Let us sit and change that photograph on your phone. I am not good technically but I will give your moral support.'

'Would you mind?'

'Of course I don't mind, silly.'

'Let's make a cup of tea and do it, then.' Amelie nodded decisively. '…And in reply to what you said earlier, my new moon intention is to stay here with you and try to sort myself out. What is yours?'

'Oh, to muster courage, as always,' Cleome chuckled, a savage smile lighting her face.

The days were short and sparsely lit by the unnaturally low sun. It was like living on a darkened, alien planet. The lake had frozen solid, and while it was apparently safe to walk on or even to drive a car across in places, the notion terrified Amelie, and she stuck to the shore and observed the great plate of ice from a distance. Some days the surface was flecked with snow, like desiccated coconut on a grey sorbet. Occasionally, it shifted and cracked like thunder, making her jump out of her skin. At other times, the dazzling expanse whistled and sang—an eerie, unearthly sound that echoed through the deserted landscape. On rare occasions when the sun appeared, the surface melted and the lake was transformed into a giant mirror, reflecting the forested shoreline and passing clouds with pristine accuracy. One such day, a trail of affluently dressed skaters with poles and sunglasses, beanie hats and neat little back packs progressed towards her, gliding in a human chain across the ice. They sped straight past while she watched from behind a tree, their blades scratching the surface, the sound of their voices boomeranging around the vastness.

Amelie squinted across the frozen expanse to the next headland where Tarek's dream house was barely discernible now that its inhabitants had returned to the city, and lights no longer shone from its windows. From this distance, it looked like another rock on the outcrop, its architecture was so blended with the landscape. It felt like a secret, hidden there, across the bay. A shared secret. If Tarek could survive here with his dreams, she mused, she could too. She turned back towards home with a slight spring in her step.

Life in the Swedish forest was a million miles away from the civilised existence she had known in Oxford. Oxford was a place of ancient stone colleges and brightly-lit shops, bicycles, buses and cars, clutter everywhere, and everyone in a rush to get where they were going. In winter time, everywhere glistened with artificial light and there were distractions galore to help the time pass. The brightly-lit children's ward was a part of that world too, with its constant stream of young bodies to be fixed, disease to be cured or patched up in whatever way possible. When she had worked, she had rarely had a moment to herself, whereas now she spent hours and hours alone, or just with her grandmother, every single day. Would she ever be able to face that bright and busy life in Oxford again? Right now, just the thought of it exhausted her.

That evening, back at *Det Lilla Huset*, the Mora clock ticked in the otherwise silent hallway, Trassel whimpered in her sleep, and her *mormor*'s knitting needles clacked as she concentrated on her knitting pattern. Before long, both women grew tired, and they set about their bedtime routines, and headed upstairs with the clock showing that it was not yet ten.

In this way, the days tumbled past, and Amelie often had no idea whether it was a Saturday or a Monday.

She had a new wallpaper on her phone now—a photograph of *Det Lilla Huset* sitting prettily in the snow, smoke curling from her chimney. She spoke with Esme one day as the sun was setting behind the woodlands in the middle of the afternoon. She was nervous, and thanked her friend for her latest email, and apologised again for bolting from Percy Street in the way she had. It was hard to explain why she had abandoned her promising career so impulsively, what she was doing in Sörmland when she did so little, or to help Esme understand that "doing nothing" and "having no plans" was what she needed right now; it was not that she was "giving up", more that resting and being with her grandmother might just save her sanity. The conversation petered out as Esme was obviously still confused and a little hurt, but Amelie took some comfort that the thread of friendship was still there between them, like a spider's web—delicate but deceptively strong.

At night, her body ached for Nick, and she longed for another chance to hold him, one more time. She felt hollowed out, as if she had a wound that refused to heal and was packed with ice. She pined for the small things—bleary-eyed coffee drinking, watching television slumped together on the sofa after Bertie had gone to bed, taking Bertie to the park and holding hands and admiring him together, as he learned to run and climb and swing. She longed to press her lips against his firm freckled skin once more. She mourned his body heat, his urgency, him wanting her.

Tears came upon her like storms without warning. She could be out at the shops with her grandmother or washing her hair, or worse—wake alone, suddenly in the middle of the night, ripped open by a bad dream, her heart racing and her terror so absolute that she wondered if this was it—if she was not dying too. And on those nights, she wrapped her arms around her body, cupped her sides with her own hands, settled her breathing to a regular rhythm, and tried to figure out a new way to survive.

As January progressed, Amelie felt as if she and Cleome spiralled like the snowflakes outside the window—aimless and destined to melt—but on the rare days when the sun shone, the forest could be a real tonic. Snow glittered prettily beneath her boots, and pure crystalline air cleansed her mind and lungs. On those days, she left Cleome dozing beside the *kakelugn*, and set out with the dog, knowing that she could walk safely for a couple of hours before the sun set again, at around three.

One day, she returned to *Det Lilla Huset* after such an outing, just as dusk was falling.

'Here, I pulled this letter from your mailbox to save you the walk. There's no stamp on it; it must have been hand-delivered. Beautiful handwriting,' she said.

Cleome took the letter, gawped at it behind Amelie's back, and swiftly stashed it in a nearby drawer. Amelie went into the kitchen to make them each a milky drink. She was standing beside the Aga watching the pan so that it didn't boil over when the cottage was suddenly plunged into darkness.

'Oh, bugger it!' Cleome cried from the sitting room.

Amelie felt around and found a torch in a kitchen drawer, and went into the hall where she checked the ceramic plugs on the power board for signs of a broken fuse. All of them were intact. 'It must be a power cut,' she concluded. The house telephone did not work and both mobile phones needed charging so there was no-one whom they could call to check. They lit candles and opened the doors of the *kakelugn* to bring more cheer into the low-ceilinged sitting room, and drank their warm drinks. As time went by and the power did not return, they decided that they had no choice but to wait until morning before investigating any further.

Cleome retired early to bed with a book and a candle; she was more used to unexplained losses of power—but Amelie sensed that something was not quite right, and brought her duvet down to the sofa so that she could doze beside the *kakelugn*. Trassel stayed with her. Even though it was not late, she must have nodded off because she was woken some time later by Trassel barking furiously at the window. She got up and peered outside, but it was a cloudy, moonless night, snow was falling, and she could see nothing. She settled the dog and huddled under the duvet again, her ears pricked for every noise.

In the morning, the power was back on. Amelie walked in the garden with Trassel, the sharp east wind stinging her cheeks. It swirled around the house, lifting the fresh snow and making eddies that danced like ghosts around the property. Frowning, she noticed fresh footprints in the snow—sunken marks, only faintly disguised by the further snowfall. She saw that a car had driven part-way down the track and stopped some distance from the cottage. The trail of footprints came to the back of the house, stopped a few yards from the sitting room window, and then looped back to the tyre tracks. She wondered if that's what had disturbed Trassel, the night before.

She shivered. When she returned indoors, she did not tell Cleome what she had seen.

'Am, do you realise the date?' Her grandmother gripped the back of a chair with her bony fingers, a fierce expression on her face. Amelie frowned; she had no idea, she had lost all track of time. 'It's the twenty-seventh.'

'Nick's birthday,' Amelie whispered.

He would have been thirty-five.

10

Imbolc

Cleome revived a little. She showered, put on new clothes, and tied her hair up neatly. After a warm drink and a simple breakfast, she laid out the table beneath the window in her sitting room with seven candles and added a vase of bare branches from the woodland.

'What are you doing?' Amelie quizzed.

'Imbolc,' she whispered, a twinkle in her eye.

'And what is that?'

'It's the day when I celebrate rebirth, and healing… and purification.' She paused to adjust a branch before stepping back to admire her arrangement. 'All throughout history, our ancestors needed natural light and warmth to grow the food they needed, and Imbolc is the cross-quarter date—the midpoint between the darkest day or the Winter Solstice, and the Spring Equinox—where day and night are of equal length. So at Imbolc, we say farewell to winter, finally, and to darkness, and we welcome spring—in all aspects of our lives not just in the weather. It is a symbolic time. I will light the candles one at a time and contemplate all the light we have in our lives.'

'I cannot see much light!' Amelie observed wryly before taking herself upstairs to clean the bathroom.

'Ah, well, then you are looking in the wrong place,' Cleome called after her, beaming. Ignoring Amelie's scepticism, she went ahead and lit some frankincense resin, her favourite incense with its rich cleansing scent, and stood and murmured several prayers of gratitude with her eyes lowered; and when she had finished, she wrapped up warm and went out of the cottage alone, walking purposefully through the frozen, rain-sodden forest with her intelligent eyes brightly observant of every small change in the landscape.

Neither woman slept well during the remaining long nights of February. Often, during the interminable stretch of pitch-black, one would come across the other sitting in the kitchen with a candle burning or in a pool of light beneath the reading lamp next to Cleome's favourite armchair. Amelie drank mugs of camomile tea during these dark, quiet hours. She wore thick knitted bed socks and an antique robe that Cleome had dug out of a trunk. Cleome's midnight drink of preference was hot chocolate laced with vodka, and she shuffled in her slippers around the kitchen preparing it, a long cashmere dressing gown tied at the waist over the top of her ample flowing nightdress.

Any sense of routine was abandoned, and sometimes one woman slumbered until midday while another paced from dawn. Daylight was precious and sometimes they found it hard to manage to walk the dog, feed the hens in the barn, and to shop, cook and do simple things like laundry at appropriate times. Often, they missed shop opening hours or meals, and left damp clothes in the machine until they smelt and had to be washed again. Amelie's psoriasis raged—nothing would soothe it—and she scratched distractedly, causing the skin at the sides of her face to bleed. Cleome's gut cramped, resulting in rushed trips to the toilet. Her heart pain still flared and she secretly sipped a tincture made from hawthorn berries, not wishing to alarm Amelie.

'Why did this happen to us?' Amelie demanded, one dull morning as they struggled to tidy the kitchen and make a shopping list of much-needed provisions, while both in a state of stupor. Freezing mist lingered outside the cottage windows, an opaque veil that clouded the property with eerie whiteness. She wore the leggings she had slept in, a pair of fuchsia socks recently knitted by Cleome, and a crumpled sweatshirt. Her hair was tied up in a ponytail but loose loops stood out from her scalp where she had been scratching. 'What did we do wrong to deserve such a fate, can you tell me that?' she asked, of no-one in particular.

Cleome clattered an iron frying pan onto the Aga hotplate. 'I am going to make us an omelette before we go out,' she declared, ignoring the unanswerable question. Her hand wobbled as she cut butter from a packet to melt in the pan.

Amelie turned away and caught sight of the suffocating mist that blockaded the view across the garden. Being unable to see the trees or sky bothered her. She felt a desperate urge to sweep the fog away, and be reassured that the grass, trees and clouds were all in their right places. A wave of nervousness caught her off guard, and her vision swam a little. She remembered to breathe.

'I get so scared,' she whispered.

Cleome half-heartedly whisked eggs and poured them into the heavy pan. She lifted it to tip the beaten eggs so that they covered the hot surface. With the omelette safely frying, she turned and made a stop sign at her granddaughter.

'Amelie! You have to stop it. All this analysing—it will get you nowhere.'

'I cannot!' Amelie burst out. 'I'm livid that Bertie had his little life snatched away! It's not fair! He did nothing wrong! He was an innocent toddler! And Nick was a good man, a decent man, intelligent... He had his whole life before him—he was healthy and strong, and it was all stolen away by some stupid tree surgeon!' She clicked her fingers in Cleome's face. 'And Mum, for all her issues, she never hurt a fly. You saw how her friends at work respected her. Why her? Why them? They were only going for a day trip to the bloody wildlife park!' she yelled.

'It was an accident.'

'I am sick of hearing that it was an accident! It wasn't! Some *nobody* drove a massive lorry into them. If he wasn't already dead, I would kill him right now!'

'Amelie, I cannot bear your shouting. You make me feel ill. I cannot...' Cleome spread a hand over her chest.

'I'm not shouting!'

'You are! My nerves... Oh, I am too old to be dealing with all this.' She hobbled to the table, unscrewed the lid of the vodka bottle and took a gulp of the liquid, neat.

'I don't know how you can always be so calm!'

'You think I am calm? You think I can accept all this? You think I don't feel a well of fury inside me that rocks me to my very bones? You think I don't wake in the night with my head full of the blackest thoughts? I, too, could murder someone, Amelie! I, too, could punch a total stranger in the street just because she's wearing the same perfume as my Kerstin, and is still alive! I don't want to see my friends and have to listen to them telling me the latest news about their kids and grandchildren and great-grandchildren, and then watch as they suddenly fall quiet, realising who they are talking to. Like I am some bloody leper! It makes me sick inside and furious, utterly furious!'

'But you never show it.'

'It doesn't mean I don't feel it! We are a different generation. Not everything is put up on computers for everybody to read, not everything is spoken about and analysed all the time! My generation—we do not wear our emotions on our sleeves like badges. Now please, stop your shouting while I try to make this omelette. And grate the cheese, please.'

'I'm not hungry.'

'It doesn't matter. We have to pretend. We have to eat a little and pretend. That way we will get through another day.'

During the warmer months, Cleome's chickens roamed in a large pen in the orchard, managing for the most part to dodge the goshawks and keep safe from other predators, but over winter they lived in an insulated section of the barn where natural light shone through a row of barred windowpanes. Ancient wooden walls safeguarded the flock from icy blasts of wind which would freeze them to death. Abundant sawdust was scattered over the barn floor and straw filled their nesting boxes. Some years, Cleome was able to let them out to forage for a few hours if the sun shone and the wind dropped, but that had not happened at all this winter, and so she regularly fed them treats of leftover raw cabbage, fruit skins and occasionally, crusts of fresh bread. She talked to her birds as she went about the routine of scooping up fouled sawdust with a shovel, and laying down some clean, taking out the previous week's straw from the coop and putting in fresh. She had named all her hens after the poets she loved, and so she had an Emily and a Mary, a Maya and an Alice, a Christina, a Carol and an Edna, plus numerous others. She would no more dream of eating one of her "girls" than she would of eating a friend. She kept them purely for eggs and for company, and when their laying days were over, they lived out their old age strutting free around the pen, or occasionally if they flew over the fence, in the fringes of the forest where they scratched for insects and made dust baths in the earth until their lives were over.

As she worked, the hens helped Cleome with their new bed-making, sticking their tiny heads into piles of fresh straw, and scratching and trampling it down with knotty feet. At the thought of the impending spring, the cockerel she would borrow off Helen, the broody hens and hatching fluffy chicks, she recalled her own pregnancy with Kerstin and brushed a tear away with the back of her fingerless glove. She tried to fight back more welling tears but suddenly, in the middle of the barn, with all her chickens at her feet, she was overcome, and howled, impulsively and unexpectedly. The chickens pecked at the new cabbage leaves, drank fresh water from their shallow trough, and ignored her. After a few moments, Cleome's emotion was spent, and she stopped and sniffed noisily. She felt for the crumpled letter in her pocket and pulled it out once again, feeling safe to re-examine it in the privacy of the barn. She did not have her reading glasses, and squinted and held the paper at a slant so that it caught the feeble light coming through the barn window.

The handwriting was distinctive and easy to decipher. As she re-read the message, she shook her head and sighed. How could this appeal come now, of all times? At first, she had wondered if it was a ploy of some sort, a bad joke by an interloper, given the appalling timing—but she would know the handwriting anywhere. There was only one person who wrote so extravagantly, with such well-formed italic letters and such regular spacing; her writing was like an art form, all of its own. She re-read the message, and considered it again. Intuitively, she sensed genuine remorse and concern. It had been hand-delivered though—there was no evidence of a stamp having fallen off or a postmark only just skimming the edge of the envelope—which was shocking and confusing. It suggested that she had been here, at the end of the lane, and yet had not visited. She had written out a telephone number which Cleome had not found the courage to call yet. She pursed her lips at the sheet of expensive writing paper that trembled in her grip. Life was shuffling the cards again, changing the game. She would not tell Amelie or Helen about it—but perhaps she would contact her sister when she felt brave enough. For all their differences, she could trust Antonia with something like this.

Back in the house, she slid the letter back into the depths of her handbag.

'Hello! Anybody here?' Helen called out as she let herself into the cottage. 'Right you two, get dressed! You are coming to my house for supper. You need air—and to get out of this stuffy house for an hour.'

'I really don't...' Amelie began timidly, the lump in her throat swelling. 'I am in too much pain. I think I might be going down with something.'

Helen put a hand on Amelie's forehead, and asked where she hurt.

'Everywhere,' Amelie mumbled. 'All the time.'

Helen looked deeply into Amelie's eyes. The pain of heartbreak glimmered in them, like a subtle trick of the light. 'It will help,' Helen encouraged. 'I promise.'

'I am not in the mood to be sociable!' Cleome asserted. 'You can go away with all your bossiness. I am not a child!'

'Both of you, just pull on some clothes, please. It is only the family and it won't be late; we're all tired. Daniel has made a huge pot of his Russian *solyanka*—far too much for all of us—and from the looks of things when I left just now, he was also baking a cake. It was he who asked that you come.'

'Oh, very well then,' Cleome relented at the mention of Daniel. 'I will try to find a decent cardigan. That man is too good, always cooking for you.'

Helen shrugged. 'He is driving me mad. He never leaves me alone.'.

'Some women would like that,' Cleome shouted back down the stairs. 'They would be grateful.'

Amelie stood, rigid. 'I really don't think I can,' she said.

'Do you take anything to help with the grieving?'

'What, you mean medication?'

'Yes. Something to take the edge off it for you, to help you get through it all, just for a while.'

'No, I don't want drugs.'

'I can arrange for someone you can talk to, then.'

'Thank you, but I'm fine. Honestly, I think I have a virus.'

'Grief can feel that way. Listen, Tarek will be there. You will enjoy talking to him, surely? You two have a lot in common.'

Amelie's interest was piqued despite her reservations. She tipped her head to one side as she considered whether she might be able to face going out, after all.

'Amelie, come on!' Cleome returned and fussed about, looking for something for her to wear from clothes strewn over the furniture. 'If I can do this, you can too. Here, pull on this skirt over your leggings. Wear this jumper to keep warm. It's clean.'

The light was dazzling in Helen's kitchen, and the cooking smells and rousing classical music threatened to overwhelm Amelie. She sat at the table with Kaia's muzzle resting on her knee and Tarek beside her. Politely, she sampled a mouthful of the sweet and sour beef stew. It stuck in her throat. There was nothing wrong with the food—a part of her, the old her, knew that it was delicious—but her appetite was missing.

Cleome and Helen sat at either end of the table, and Josef and Daniel sat opposite her. Josef was a tall, dark-haired boy, bright-eyed like his mother. The men laughed and joked frequently, keeping up a constant banter about sport, most of which went over Amelie's head. Tarek and Josef exchanged heated opinions on a football match. Nobody asked anything of her, which was a relief.

'All this snow; it is quite a year for it,' Daniel remarked.

'The wonder of snowfall is that it shows us that there are different ways of seeing the same thing,' Cleome opined. 'It changes the look of everything, and makes us pay attention. I believe that when it falls like this, it is a sign for us to take a fresh look at our lives, to examine all our rigid beliefs and our foolish blind habits.'

'Oh, snow is just snow, for heaven's sake! There are no signs in it.' Helen rolled her eyes.

'I am with you, Helen,' Amelie said. 'It's a weather pattern, plain and simple. Geography and climate.'

'You two must feel very cold in this weather, if you don't see the magic of the bigger picture,' Cleome said, a mischievous smile playing around her lips.

'Facts are facts,' Helen stated. 'It is a proven fact that snow falls, given certain conditions—temperature, precipitation, all that stuff. There's nothing mystical about it. Snow just *is*.'

'Ah, but I have to agree with Cleome. There is great mystery in the snow, as there is also in the sun,' Daniel disagreed. 'Poets have known this through time. We are all linked by the mysterious forces of the universe. We are all one. If it snows, there is a reason.'

'I agree with him,' Tarek said. 'The geography is part of it but not all.'

'Well, I wish I could see signals in the bloody snow,' Amelie grumbled. 'But I can't because that is just sugar-coated fantasy, designed to make people feel better when they are really just inconvenienced, cold and fed up.'

'Oh dear,' Cleome shook her head.

'And if anybody tells me I'm not right, I say prove it!' She scratched her scalp.

'Well, you have known moments when the snow has dazzled you with its beauty, surely?' Tarek prompted gently. Amelie fixed her gaze on him, and her bad mood stalled. 'You cannot measure that in a laboratory. Yet you know it happens. Those days when the sight of all the whiteness inspires you to all sorts of thoughts and emotions you didn't have before.'

'That's different!' she objected, feebly.

He shrugged. He was wearing a dusky blue flannelled shirt with the sleeves rolled up, and his forearms were muscled, with a fine covering of dark hair. Amelie suddenly wished that she had changed into some proper clothes before she had come out. She smoothed her hand over her hair, self-consciously. Tarek smiled at her and she felt herself blush. She felt awkward that the others would notice her red cheeks but they were too busy chatting on about the snow and what it did or did not mean.

'So, Josef and I have learnt a new tune on our guitars,' Tarek announced. 'Now that we have finished eating, we will play it for you. Fetch the guitars, Josef!'

'Do I have to?' Josef mumbled but he was already scraping his chair back to fetch the instruments, and looking secretly pleased.

Helen beamed at Tarek. 'You are so good with him,' she whispered while Josef was out of the room.

Tarek and Josef carried their chairs to the space under the kitchen window, and the others turned their seats to face them. It took a moment for them to tune their guitars, and during the process, Tarek's attention was focused solely on Josef, helping him to get each string to sound right. Josef grinned nervously at his mother before they began.

'We are going to play the Beatles song, Blackbird,' he said.

Tarek's attention remained with Josef as he counted them in, and they started to sing the sweet song. Tarek's voice was tuneful and confident, and led Josef's less self-assured singing. The sound of it thrilled Amelie in a way that she had not anticipated, and she felt goose bumps break out all over her body. 'Take these broken wings and learn to fly,' Tarek sang, and as he did so, he looked directly at her. She gazed around at the others, who were also enthralled by the beauty of the tiny performance. While she was delighted, at the same time, as the song went on, she found she had to fight back her tears. Tarek's voice was so beautiful, it moved something deep inside her that she had forgotten existed. He turned his attention back to Josef and nodded the timing of the piece to him, to guide him. As they finished, everyone burst into applause, and Daniel whistled. Josef blushed and looked very pleased with himself. Tarek leant forward and patted his shoulder.

'You did brilliantly,' he said.

Amelie was disappointed when the evening was over. Josef tidied the plates into the dishwasher. Tarek gathered his things and prepared to return to his bungalow. She wondered when she would get the chance to talk to him again. Something about him always made her feel better, and young again, like she had *before*. She did not know if it was the second glass of wine at work but as she looked across the farmhouse kitchen at Tarek, something stirred inside her that she had not felt since she first met Nick. She wished that Tarek would sing again and the song would never end. She watched him move about, putting the chairs back, and pulling on his jacket. Helen, Daniel and Josef were obviously so fond of him. He had made a good place for himself in his adopted family. He smiled at them all as he said his goodnights, his brown eyes warm and lit up with his own special inner fire. He glanced over at her and raised a hand. Their gaze lingered for a moment before he turned and left.

Helen said, 'I'm going to drive these ladies home now, Daniel. Thanks for a lovely dinner. I've got things to do this evening so maybe I'll see you tomorrow.'

Daniel nodded, and went to the cloakroom beside the door in search of his coat. He kissed each woman goodnight, and gave Helen a hug.

'You were harsh to Daniel, after he had cooked such a splendid meal,' Cleome commented in the car as they made their way back along the forest road.

'He never leaves me alone. It's too much sometimes. I need a bit of space.'

'He loves you.'

'You don't know that.'

'Oh, I do. I see it quite clearly.'

'Ugh! I don't have time for silly love stories at my age!'

'I don't know why you are like this!' Cleome grumbled. 'If I was twenty years younger, I would snap him up!'

Helen and Amelie exchanged glances and burst out laughing.

11

First Quarter, Moon of Ice

Amelie and Cleome sat in Cleome's old Volvo at the far end of the car park in Flen town centre, with the car engine running. The parking spaces close to the supermarket entrance were all taken due to the horrendous weather but supplies of food had dwindled at *Det Lilla Huset* and Cleome had run out of painkillers, so they had no alternative but to shop. They had left the house in a rush, and by the time they reached Flen, the rain was tipping down and they were faced with sprinting through the downpour that hammered on the car roof, or waiting. Of course, neither woman had brought an umbrella. Neither even wore a proper coat. Cleome kept the engine running to keep the heater pumping out some warmth.

'I wish I had not dashed out in my slippers.' She compressed her lips in annoyance and pushed a loose strand of hair back from her face. She glanced at Amelie who wore layers of mismatched clothes. 'I also can't think what we need from ICA. I wish we had made a list,' she went on. Her knobbly fingers clasped the steering wheel as they both sat waiting, mustering energy.

Amelie turned to her grandmother. 'Did I ever tell you that Nick and I wanted to have three children? I wanted Bertie to go to The Cherwell, where I went; I wanted us to move to one of those nice houses in Jericho when we had made some more money, and oh, oh, I've just remembered: we have a holiday booked for a campsite in France this summer!'

'Can you remember what we need? Bread, perhaps?' Cleome persisted.

'I'm still so angry all the time.' Amelie shook her head.

Cleome, finally humbled into silence, gave up trying to think about the shopping and stared straight ahead through the rain-streaked windscreen, and sighed loudly. What could she say? What comfort could she give when there was so little to be had?

'I would do anything to get them back, anything!' Amelie whispered.

'I know you would, dear. I know... I cannot register it, myself,' Cleome tutted.

'What do you miss most?'

'I don't know. There is this numbness in me, like I am dead inside or finally fossilised. It is all so bloody unnatural. My family was growing, the generations unfolding as they should, and now our lineage is broken irretrievably.'

'What did we do wrong?'

'I don't know, I simply don't know.'

'We are being punished for something!'

Cleome laid her hand on Amelie's thigh. 'I do wish it had been me who had gone instead of them. That would have made more sense.' She stuck her pointed chin in the air. A hair had started to sprout from it, unnoticed.

'You can't say that. That's awful!'

'Well, one should always be grateful for life, and never wish it away—but I am only being honest. If I had gone, it would have been better. But come now, come now. Let's stop this. It's not helping. We need to get on and sort ourselves out somehow. I will get the food. You go to the pharmacy just across from ICA. I will leave the car open and meet you back here.'

Amelie exited the Volvo and folded her arms, clamping a long purple cardigan to her body, and hunching her head against the freezing rain as she ran awkwardly in loose-laced trainers, past the supermarket and towards the brightly-lit pharmacy. Inside, there was such a long queue that she stalled, and decided that rather than wait, she would dash to the hair salon. On returning, she queued impatiently, clutching a package from the salon. The lighting in the pharmacy was so harsh and unnatural that she was unused to it, and squinted. The shop assistant's gaze flickered disapprovingly over her, as she handed over the pain relief. Amelie felt suddenly self-conscious about how she must look, and her anger rose like a red flag.

'My child died, okay? And my husband, and my mother! In a car accident!' she shouted at the woman, who recoiled, and looked down at her polished fingernails. 'How would you look if that happened to you?'

'*Jag beklagar sorgen*—I am sorry for your loss,' the woman muttered. Amelie paid and snatched the painkillers. As she strode out of the building, she noticed a trio of women, all wearing hijabs, watching her. Their faces were lit with a mixture of amusement and scorn, and they stared at her openly, having obviously overheard her tirade. Amelie realised that one of them was Ayah, Tarek's friend, and so she paused and said *hej* to her. Ayah looked Amelie up and down, her lips pressed together, and her gaze stony. She nodded imperceptibly at Amelie before turning her back on her and examining something on a nearby shelf. Amelie felt a mix of shame and embarrassment that one of Tarek's friends had witnessed her outburst, and fled out of the shop. She was filled with a fury so intense that she did not see where she was going. A car skidded to a halt as she ran over the pedestrian crossing to the alley that led to the car park. She jogged blindly past rows of parked cars, not knowing where she was heading, and it took a few moments for Cleome's shrill voice to pierce her consciousness. 'Amelie, Amelie, where are you going?'

Amelie stopped and turned and looked at the old woman, clothed in turquoise and standing in her slippers with her hands raised, as if to heaven. She ran over to her, fell into her arms, and was immediately comforted by the endearing and familiar scent of lavender.

'There was a hideous woman in the pharmacy with stupid make-up and sprayed hair. How come she gets to live?'

'We cannot think like that, we cannot.'

'I wanted to hit her! I think I raised my fist! I don't know what I did! And then Tarek's friend was watching me. I feel so humiliated.'

'Let's get you home. This was too much for both of us. I could only remember the dog food and just got us some chicken, carrots and bread,' Cleome went on, linking her arm through Amelie's as they made their way back towards the Volvo. 'It all gave me a panic attack too. I paid and got out of there quick. I have been waiting for you. You took a while. I was worried.'

A furious, icy wind blasted from the north east, and temperatures regularly plummeted to minus fourteen or fifteen each night. Chill draughts found every tiny gap in the framework of the old wooden cottage, and it was all the women could do to keep warm. The routine of bringing in logs and keeping the *kakelugn* lit, of walking Trassel every day, and cleaning out and feeding the hens took up their time and energy.

Late one morning, on a rare day when watery sunlight filtered through the windowpanes, Amelie took out the package from the hair salon. She shampooed Cleome's fine silver hair while she bent over the kitchen sink with her bony fingers gripping the ceramic edge.

'You are getting water in my eyes,' Cleome complained.

'I'm sorry, here, take this towel. You did insist on not washing your own hair in the shower.'

'It's too cold and anyway, I wasn't thinking clearly.'

'It will soon be done. I'm putting the conditioner on it now.'

'I never use conditioner!'

'It will make it shine.'

'At my age, what do I want with shining hair?'

Amelie smiled, a rare fleeting reflex. 'There's a lot of grumbling going on today,' she teased, as she tipped another glass of warm water over her grandmother's bent head.

'You are giving me a crick in my neck.'

'Nearly done, nearly done. You will thank me for this.'

'I will, if I can ever stand up straight again.'

Amelie gently wrapped a towel around her grandmother's head and took her hand as the elderly woman stood up straight. 'Come and sit on the chair, over here in the light.'

Cleome hobbled across the kitchen and sat obediently on a chair placed beside the window. 'What are you going to do with it?'

'A bob, we agreed? These scissors are great—they are proper haircutting ones. I talked that hairdresser in Flen into selling me an old pair, and I bought this shampoo and conditioner off him to butter him up a bit. It smells of melons.'

'Don't make me look embarrassing. I don't want to look like one of those old crones who tries too hard—you know the type—desperate to be sexy.'

Amelie giggled, the unfamiliar sound pirouetting through the still air. 'Trust me. Now, relax and look straight ahead out of the window.'

Peace descended in the room as she combed through long lengths of her grandmother's damp hair, carefully taking each section and gently teasing out each tangle. As she began to snip, grey tendrils drifted silently to the wooden floor. She combed, pinned, trapped sections of hair between her fingers, and cut, ensuring that each action was precise and the newly-trimmed ends rested, straight and soft, on Cleome's shoulders. She found the natural parting, and moved in front of her grandmother, combing her hair forwards and making a couple more cuts to ensure that it hung evenly. For a moment, Cleome dozed, her head nodding until she sat up abruptly again, correcting herself. Over on the rug beside the Aga, Trassel stretched out and sighed, and in the hallway, the Mora clock ticked.

When she was happy with the style, Amelie took a hair dryer, switched it onto a low setting, and dried Cleome's hair, curling it under slightly at the ends. When that was done, she checked it and made one small snip at a bit she had missed.

'There,' she declared, her head on one side. 'Beautiful. Here, look.' She passed a hand mirror to her grandmother.

'Well, my, my...' Cleome turned her head and admired her reflection. 'I think I like it. It's very different. Sort of modern.'

'It suits you!'

'I look like a different personality.'

'You look younger.'

'Where did you learn to do such a thing?'

'I watched the hairdressers in the place where Mum used to go to while I was growing up, and they gave me some tips, and then I taught myself over the years. I used to cut my friends' hair after school. I've always loved doing it.'

'I never knew.'

'Well, I'm glad you are pleased.'

Cleome's cheeks flushed and her jade-green eyes sparkled for the first time in many weeks. 'Maybe I do look younger,' she admitted.

Amelie swept the floor and brushed the fallen locks into a dustpan.

'So, will you cut your own hair now?' Cleome asked. 'I don't see how you can do that.'

'Easily, because it's long. I wash it, comb it through and part it, and then I stand in front of a mirror and chop. I cut Bertie's and Nick's too... I mean, I used to...' Amelie shook her head.

'There, there now, let's not think about that. You go ahead and wash yours now, and you can cut it by the mirror in the sitting room, where it's warm. I'll make us tea, and you can take little sips, in between snipping away with your scissors. D'you know, I'm very pleased with this, Amelie dear, thank you. I feel lighter.'

'I'm going to give mine a good prune too,' Amelie recovered. 'I might need you to check the back for me. Sometimes I miss a bit in the middle.'

Amelie went to the kitchen sink, turned on the mixer tap and put her hand under it to adjust the water temperature before she stuck her head into the warm flow. She had forgotten, while she had been cutting her grandmother's hair. Not for long—maybe only for a moment or two—but she had forgotten. And there had been a miniscule hiatus—a precious, tiny interval—of peace.

Cleome watched, nursing a mug of tea in her armchair, as Amelie stood in front of the mirror, and lopped around six inches from her long fair hair. It fell in separate curls onto the wooden floor.

'Tarek sang so beautifully the other night,' Amelie said, as she cut. 'I was completely lost for a moment there. His voice... was enthralling, I could have listened to him all night.' She blushed, and then laughed at herself. 'Listen to me,' she joked. 'I sound like a teenager.'

Cleome raised an eyebrow and the women exchanged knowing glances through the mirror. 'It was hard not to be seduced by that song,' she agreed. 'You know, it's okay, Am—to feel like that, I mean. You mustn't admonish yourself. You must listen to your own natural recovery with all its curious signals and signs. Honour it. Trust it. Pay no attention to what others might think.'

'I'm scared about enjoying anything, if I'm honest. It's confusing.'

'I know, I know. But don't be.'

Later, as she lay awake in her bed with sleep eluding her, it occurred to Amelie that perhaps she had feelings for another man, a man who was not Nick, for the first time in her entire life. They were not the same kind of feelings, nowhere near, but there was a glimmer of similarity. Tarek made her smile, he made her interested in life again. No sooner did she have the realisation than she felt guilt stir inside her, like black sticky tar. She tried to remember what her grandmother had told her, and to trust herself to do the right thing. As she drifted off to sleep, she could think only of Tarek. Of his dark eyes, wild hair and wide smile. Of his kindness. She tried to resist but the thoughts kept coming, and she eventually drifted off to sleep with a head full of memories of him and his dream house on the rocks.

'We must take small steps, be very careful,' Cleome instructed, as the pair stepped out into the snow-covered garden. 'Don't be fooled by this soft, pretty stuff on the surface. After the recent weather patterns, there will be ridges of perilous ice beneath it. It's ankle-breaking weather.'

The wind had dropped and they had wrapped up in thick coats, hats, gloves and scarves, in order to take Trassel for a walk. They trudged through the forest at the side of the cottage, where the snow was not so deep, and as they walked Cleome pointed out tiny icicles that hung like rows of gleaming daggers from blackened branches, and the minute and tender fronds of grey-green lichen decorated with sparkling droplets of frozen water.

'This,' she whispered, 'is treasure. This is the divine at work, right before our eyes.'

Amelie stared at the lichen, and tried to see more than green fur growing on a twig. Further into their walk, they came across animal tracks in the snow, and Cleome identified the imprints from a moose's cloven hoof, and the wide marks with two dew claws to the rear which indicated wild boar. A muddied area showed where the boar had been foraging in the hard earth. They reached the edge of the lake where not a house or a person was in sight. The frozen surface appeared steely and was splodged with patches of startling white. The air smelled clean and fresh.

'Nature is such a great healer. She teaches us, if we listen,' Cleome murmured. 'The lake is frozen as we are frozen. She mirrors our plight. If we allow her, she will help us. We must always treat her with respect though, and acknowledge her power. We must always be mindful to give thanks to her; we cannot just take her for granted.' Cleome gazed out over the frozen mass with her elfin chin raised, and one of her hand-knitted hats pulled down over her ears. Amelie stared blankly at the sheet of ice. Cleome murmured a prayer to the lake and opened both her gloved hands, as if bestowing an invisible gift.

When they were home again, Cleome sat and knitted, with a pair of cobalt blue reading glasses perched on the end of her nose. 'Ach, look at that! I keep making mistakes and not even noticing. My technique is shot to smithereens,' she grumbled, unravelling several rows, pulling the wool out in a long length and re-wrapping it around the ball. She tutted and caught up the loops on her fat wooden needle. Amelie sat on the sofa with a book. As she read, her eyelids grew heavy, and she rested her head against the back of the sofa and pulled a blanket up over herself. Trassel leapt up beside her and pressed her furry body warmly against her thigh. She drifted off into sleep. As she dozed, a lurid nightmare took shape in her mind. Bertie was lost and crying out for her. She searched the streets around Percy Street, and met familiar faces—the neighbour who lived a few doors away was up a ladder painting a window frame, the Asian couple from the newsagent strolled arm-in-arm, and one of the older girls from Bertie's nursery school was out skipping by herself with a rope on the pavement, even though she was far too young to have the skill. She approached each one and begged them to tell her where Bertie was—and none of them had ever heard of him; nobody knew what she was talking about, they could not hear his cries. Yet she could hear him wailing and calling out her name 'Muma, Muma'. And then somehow, he was in her arms but it was too late, *she* was too late, and Bertie had the magic mark on his forehead, and she woke up with a sickening lurch, and the book fell from the sofa arm to the floor, and tears were running down her cheeks.

'Am, you were dreaming,' Cleome whispered, holding her. Amelie smudged her tears with the back of her hand. Sometimes, she felt so afraid, and so utterly, deeply exhausted. She rested against her grandmother, once again comforted by her lavender scent. Cleome stroked her head and held her close. 'It will get better. I promise you it will get easier.'

It was the first of March, Amelie's birthday. A full moon had glowed the night before, occasionally piercing the duvet of dense cloud that was laid over Sörmland, but by morning, snow and a heavy mist met each other outside the cottage door, so that it was not obvious where one stopped and the other began. An arctic chill seeped into every nook and cranny of the forest, and Amelie and Cleome wore layers of Cleome's old clothes to keep warm while they took the dog for her morning walk.

At lunch time, Helen burst through the door, and stamped her feet on the large mat before sitting on the bench in the hallway, and pulling off her boots. 'This weather! We have not had a winter like this for a long time!' she exclaimed. 'Here, happy birthday. I have brought this for a special celebratory *fika*.' She handed over a chocolate Bundt cake and gave Amelie a small present. Amelie sat and slowly unwrapped the gift, peeling away the tissue paper to discover a turquoise journal and matching pen. She was surprised by how much she instantly liked the size and feel of the notebook in her hand, and on opening, how the plain cream pages appealed to her.

'Write everything down. It helps.' Helen smiled, her eyes shining with kindness.

'Thank you,' Amelie mumbled.

'It's my pleasure. I have tens of journals at home, full of my thoughts and fury. I hope it works for you.'

'I would not have thought you needed that sort of thing,' Amelie ventured.

Helen raised an eyebrow. 'Oh, you'd be surprised!'

'Maybe I should get one of these things too?' Cleome said.

'But you meditate, don't you?' Helen said.

'Yes, yes.'

'Well, then—same kind of thing.'

At Helen's comment, Cleome realised that she had abandoned her meditation practice since the day of the accident. She also realised that she missed its calming results. Without her 'quiet time' each day, it was like walking through life naked and unprepared. She privately vowed to take it up again.

The women chatted as they sipped tea and ate the moist cake, sitting around the kitchen table.

'You are both looking a little better,' Helen observed.

'I have been making us a strong herbal infusion in the evenings—with chamomile flowers, oat flowering tops, some cardamom pods and ginger root for flavour, and a little marshmallow root to help my guts. We both sleep better after drinking it.'

'The aloe gel is helping my skin too,' Amelie chipped in.

'And what is your news?' Cleome asked.

'Daniel has gone back to his apartment in Vasastan. The university have a lot of students studying Russian at the moment, and he's been invited to lecture in London—a one-off on Pushkin.' Helen's gaze drifted to the window.

'You miss him?'

'He has his career; I have mine.' She took a deep breath, and fixed a smile on her lips. Helen's eyes were like a deer's—dark and watchful, and her long nose lent elegance to her face. She kept her feelings buried deep but Cleome knew her well, and did not question her friend further.

After Helen had left and while Cleome dozed in her armchair, Amelie opened the journal. She tried to do as Helen had said, and not to think but to tune in to some deeper part of herself, and let her pen be guided by whatever random thoughts came up.

Bertie, she scrawled. She dropped the pen and notebook, and raced swiftly and silently upstairs where she cried, taking big gulps of air as quietly as she could, in the hope that she would not wake her grandmother. Writing his name, seeing his name… the stab of pain was so savage, it terrified her.

12

Full Moon of Ice

The days grew longer but winter lingered. When Amelie expected daffodils and the first flush of green on bare branches, the forest around *Det Lilla Huset* remained stubbornly brown and naked. Snowdrops flowered in drifts in her grandmother's garden, uncannily late. Everything seemed out of step and not quite right.

The rooms in *Det Lilla Huset* were stale from lack of ventilation, and cluttered with detritus after the long winter. There were discarded coffee mugs and plates, dead geraniums in pots on window sills, and cardigans and socks abandoned in unlikely places. Spiders' webs were strung across corners and balls of dog hair lurked in hidden spaces. Even though outside the spring still refused to appear, Amelie was filled with an urge to clean. She extracted her grandmother's vacuum cleaner from beneath a pile of empty cardboard boxes in the utility room, and plugged it in.

She ran the brush over the low ceiling of the sitting room, methodically sucking up cobwebs. She took down each painting, dusted frames, and polished glass. She peeled off her sweatshirt before hoovering the walls and rehanging the pictures. She found white vinegar and an old newspaper, and polished the windows. It was astonishing how quickly they sparkled. Enthused, she cleared away the discarded crockery and clothes, the old copies of *Dagens Nyheter*, junk mail, and burned-down candle stubs. Cleome's knitting basket was surprisingly well-organised so she left that alone. She tugged cushions off sofas, and collected lost hair grips and coins before hoovering the upholstery, and plumping and replacing pads. She shifted furniture and rugs, and hoovered every inch of the wooden floor, discovering pens and paperbacks, dog toys and magazines, all long since abandoned and lurking unseen beneath heavy sofas. She beat the rug outdoors. Finally, she applied her energy to the low table in the centre of the room, and the messy area around the *kakelugn* which was littered with broken shards of bark and sawdust, and yet more tangled cobwebs.

When she had finished, she felt light-headed, and made herself a coffee and some buttered rye toast which she ate enthusiastically. Cleome and Trassel returned from outdoors, and Cleome took in the pile of dirty crockery in the sink, and the dead plants and collection of assorted garments on the kitchen table.

'What have you been doing?' she asked, her old-apple cheeks rosy from the cold, and her chest heaving.

'Go and see,' Amelie gestured towards the living room.

Cleome hobbled to the doorway and poked her head into the sitting room. 'Oh,' she cried, and put a bony hand to her chest. 'Oh!'

'What is it?' Amelie frowned.

Cleome turned to Amelie with tears rolling down her cheeks and Amelie, concerned, placed a gentle hand on her grandmother's shoulder.

'You have no idea how happy this makes me,' Cleome sobbed.

'Then why are you crying?'

'I have no idea.' She reached out her hand and softly cupped Amelie's cheek. 'You are an angel,' she said.

'Let me make you a coffee.' Amelie gestured to a chair at the table. 'I will sort out all this stuff in here next.'

When, sometime later, the women took Trassel for her afternoon walk, an invisible bird sang in the mist like a symbol of hope. The lake was thawing and had grown watery around the edges. Blocks of ice floated in it like discarded white islands. A young moose careened past in the distance. Cleome froze but it was gone so quickly that Amelie wondered if she had imagined the cartoon-like creature, with its oblong head and extraordinarily long legs. She called the dog back from chasing it, and they continued on their way. An icy wind blew up and numbed their faces. Gusts whipped through the trees, lashing the softer branches so that they danced helplessly in a howling, unsettling din. Trassel trotted with her nose up, sensitive to the weather change. On the way home, they checked the mailbox beside the main road, opposite the Bengtsson's place. It was empty, and they turned for home, hunching their shoulders against the aggressive weather.

As they passed, Lotta Bengtsson scurried around the corner of her house, wearing only an apron over a cotton top, and carrying a dustpan and brush. She looked frozen and harried.

Amelie called '*Hej*!' to her in greeting. '*Fy, vad det blåser!*' (Gosh, it's really windy!)

Lotta muttered '*Jo,*' in a non-committal tone. Her gaze flickered from them back to the house, her irises black with nerves, her pink and white fingers clutching the plastic. From inside the open doorway of the dark house, they heard Magnus Bengtsson shout at his son, calling him an imbecile. There was a crashing sound, as if something had been thrown. Lotta flashed a rictus smile, turned and scuttled back towards her husband, gabbling something that they could not catch.

'Is everything alright, Lotta?' Amelie called.

Lotta's shoulders hunched a little higher, rising from her plump body in defence, and she did not answer.

13

Vernal Equinox

As March unfolded, the snow melted and so did the silence around *Det Lilla Huset*. Birds sang and running water trickled in the stream that ran down to the lake. The earth offered tentative fronds of green that rose up to meet the brighter daylight. On some days, there was a canopy of pure blue above the little wooden cottage, and weak sunshine cast long hesitant shadows.

Cleome clutched the bannister as she descended the stairs. In the kitchen, she fetched the vodka bottle from the cupboard and tipped its contents into the sink; it was a shocking waste but a magnificent gesture, and that was what mattered. After a night of little sleep and some serious soul searching, she had decided that it was time to accept the new shape of things, and stop railing against the universe. She made a pot of strong nettle tea for courage, using leaves she had dried the previous year when life had looked very different. As she waited for the tea to infuse, the deep knowledge welled in her, as it had so often before, reminding her that all things change, all things pass; life was one big energetic shifting entity that was never still, never fixed. She was a tiny part of the ever-changing story, one diminutive pinprick of light in a vast universe. No point in trying to fight it. More important to accept, step into the flow of life, and do her best.

During the drive to the airport, Cleome stopped the car at a red traffic light. Amelie observed a trio of little girls dressed in colourful skirts, shawls, headscarves and wellingtons, standing at the side of the road with a young woman acting as chaperone. The girls' cheeks were painted with disks of rouge and their small noses spattered with kohl freckles. Their skirts blew sideways in a playful breeze. Each girl clutched a small coffee pot full of sweets. When it was safe, the girls skipped across the road. 'They dress as Easter witches—*påskkärringar*—and give out hand-made cards in exchange for sweets,' Cleome explained. 'A bit like your trick or treat, except that they don't threaten you with a trick. That wouldn't be very Swedish.'

'They look so sweet!'

'Look, they have stopped to wave at us,' Cleome said, and raised a hand. Her bangles jingled as she waved back enthusiastically. 'It is a sign…'

Amelie waved and smiled too. 'Yes, their joy is a sign of better things to come,' she agreed—and then wondered if she was becoming as batty as her elderly relative.

Cleome had invited her younger sister Antonia, who lived in England, to spend Easter with them. Skavsta airport was smaller than Amelie remembered. She linked arms companionably with her grandmother as they strolled towards the modest arrivals area. Antonia emerged from Customs, a head taller than the surrounding crowd. She had neatly-waved grey hair and wore peach lipstick. A single string of pearls lay over her beige polo-neck sweater, beneath a long, belted camel coat. When they embraced, Amelie inhaled her familiar expensive perfume and the scent of wool wash. As they all walked back towards the car, the sisters exchanged a glance, and for one moment Amelie had the impression that they exchanged a private message, a secret that she was not party to. The moment passed when Antonia briskly turned the conversation to the weather and their plans for the weekend ahead.

After they had returned to *Det Lilla* Huset and had tea and cake, Amelie declared that she would take Trassel for her walk so that the sisters could talk in peace.

As soon as she had gone out of the door, Antonia fixed her searchlight stare on Cleome.

'Well?' she hissed. 'What does she want? I don't know why you couldn't just tell me over the phone. I've been itching to know.'

'To meet up,' Cleome replied meekly.

'After what happened last time?'

'I know. That's why I wanted to discuss it with you. I need your advice.'

'She's changed her tune.' Antonia's eyes narrowed.

'But surely that's allowed?' Cleome said.

'After the way she treated you?'

'There is such a thing as forgiveness, as we all know. I wonder if this isn't the time for it.'

Amelie paced her bedroom, trying to decide what to wear. She had very few clothes of her own at the house, and none that made her feel attractive. She wondered whether Tarek would join them for the lunch at Helen's on the eve of Easter. Did Muslims even celebrate Easter? Ashamed by her own ignorance, she vowed to learn more about Islamic culture, but in the meantime, decided that he would probably be there, as he was a part of Helen's family these days. As she pulled on a checked skirt, she wondered if he would talk to her at the party, and what excuse she might make to speak to him. What could she ask him about? She stood before the long mirror, smoothed the skirt which fell below her knees, and corrected the sleeves of a short mohair jumper that her grandmother had knitted for her. Easter: it was all about rebirth, she thought. *What did that even mean?*

Downstairs, Cleome and Antonia sat waiting for her in the kitchen.

'I'll drive so you can have a drink,' she offered.

'That's quite all right. I have resolved to give up drinking,' Cleome declared stiffly.

Antonia raised her eyebrows. Amelie squeezed Cleome's shoulder and nodded; both women sensed that it might be a difficult day as it was the first Easter without their loved ones, and they did not question each other's actions.

At *Båvenshult*, the usual chaos reigned. Trassel greeted Kaia and they barked at each other and chased around the kitchen wagging their tails. Daniel took his visitors' coats and ushered them through the kitchen, and across the hallway into the spacious white sitting room where one wall was lined with shelves of books, and bright Kilim rugs were scattered over the wooden floor. A fire was lit in the hearth, and the three large cream sofas were adorned with cheerful throws. A *påskris*— an Easter tree made from birch branches and hung with painted eggs and brightly-coloured feathers—adorned a low table. A generous vase of scarlet tulips was placed on another.

'Let me get you all a drink.' Helen approached them, looking flushed and bright-eyed. Her skin was glowing, and Amelie noticed how well she looked, and admired her friend afresh. It seemed they were the last to arrive, as usual. Tarek was there, with his back to them, talking quietly to Ayah and her brother Zain. Ayah glanced at Amelie, and immediately looked away. Josef and his friend chatted, over by tall windows which led to the garden. Helen's colleague Sven, whom Amelie recognised from New Year's Eve, greeted them and introduced his friend Anna, another doctor from Katrineholm. They all shook hands.

After the drinks, during which Tarek had remained deep in Arabic conversation and had not come over to speak to her, they moved through to the dining room where a long table was laid with a white cloth and a huge array of dishes. Helen shepherded everyone to their places, telling each guest where to sit. She directed Tarek to take a seat beside Amelie, and it was as they sat down that his eyes met hers, at last. He smiled.

'Hello,' he said, and she replied 'Hello' back. His eyes were like Turkish coffee and shone with their usual warmth. Her stomach somersaulted as they exchanged glances. Daniel and Helen took their seats at opposite ends of the table and the remainder of the guests found their places on either side. Spread before everyone was a whole salmon decorated prettily with dill, a platter of pickled herrings, a lamb dish, bowls of potatoes, and numerous salads and baskets of bread. Daniel raised a toast to springtime and to good health before they passed dishes and plates to each other, chatting merrily as they spooned out the food.

Cleome, who sat at the centre of the table opposite Amelie, began a conversation with Ayah, who sat beside her. Ayah wore the same dusky blue hijab that she had worn on New Year's Eve, and made frequent furtive glances across the table at Tarek. Amelie was discomforted, and wondered what the situation was between Tarek and the young woman. She had smooth brown skin, and cheeks that dimpled as she smiled. While she checked Tarek frequently, he did not seem to notice. Whenever she made eye contact with Amelie, her mood changed and her dislike was barely concealed by her small pout.

Antonia, who was a retired publisher, fell into deep conversation with Daniel. The two doctors talked among themselves, and Josef, who sat on Amelie's right, chatted happily with his school friend. At the far end of the table, Helen talked animatedly to Zain about her charity work with refugees. Zain shovelled food into his mouth and frowned, as he listened. He barely spoke, and Amelie wondered if he struggled with the language.

Tarek passed Amelie a plate of boiled eggs. The eggs had been cut in half and were decorated with shrimps and dill.

'You didn't get any,' he said to her.

'Thanks,' she said, helping herself to one.

'In Sweden, we don't need churches. Nature is our church—all the God we could ever need is in the forests and lakes,' Cleome asserted loudly.

Amelie rolled her eyes affectionately, and exchanged a secret smile with Tarek.

'We Muslims revere Jesus but we don't agree that he died on the cross,' Tarek said to Cleome. 'Then again, what does it matter who believes what? The food is good, there is much to celebrate and I'm sure most of us are not here because of what happened to Jesus.'

'I'll drink to that,' Amelie agreed, raising her glass of lime soda. Her thoughts were not on the sacrifice that Jesus had made or the celebration that He had risen again; they were rooted in the here and now. The nearness of Tarek's body, sitting next to hers, was making her feel like a teenager again. She caught the faint scent of him—a fragrance of cedar. She was distracted by his hands resting either side of his plate. I have a crush on him, she realised bleakly, shocked to find herself in such a predicament. Embarrassment took hold of her and her armpits grew sticky. She tucked her hair behind her ear, and swallowed hard.

'Your hair looks pretty like that,' he said.

'Thanks.' She smiled, feeling the blood pound at her temples. She gripped her cutlery and resumed eating.

'How do you celebrate Easter in England?' he asked.

'Last year, I painted hard-boiled eggs with my little boy. My husband and I ate rather a lot of chocolate. But I was shattered. I'd been on nights. All I wanted to do was sleep.'

'Nights?'

'I'm a children's nurse. I used to work in a hospital. I'd been working the night shift.' She put her cutlery down.

'Ah.' Tarek put his knife and fork down too. 'Are you okay or shall we just ignore the tears?' He moved his head closer to hers and the cedar fragrance filled her senses

'Just ignore them, thanks,' she managed, and looked up to see Ayah watching her, her small mouth twisted.

'Bet you are glad you shared that chocolate together, and I bet it tasted good,' Tarek encouraged, in an obvious effort to make her feel better.

She tore her gaze from Ayah, glanced at him, and smiled gratefully.

'Be glad you did that.' Tarek nodded. 'You know, changing the subject completely, and since we were discussing the meaning of Easter, Daniel has told me that a man cannot live for sport alone, and that I need to get some culture in my life. What do you think of that?'

'Education doesn't stop, just because you left school,' Daniel interrupted, winking at Amelie.

'He keeps giving me poetry books to read but I find football is much easier to understand!'

'There are some who would say that football is but another form of poetry!' Daniel laughed.

'Now you're talking!' Tarek raised his glass of coke.

Amelie recovered, glad that the conversation had moved on and her own emotions were settling again. She avoided looking across the table at Ayah, but sensed that she was still being watched as she finished her plate of food.

When the long lunch was over, Amelie, her grandmother and great aunt prepared to leave. Daniel helped to find their coats, holding each garment for them to slip their arms in. The dogs ran out through the open door and dashed about the garden excitedly. Tarek stepped outside beside Amelie.

'Your grandmother tells me you are going back to England,' he said.

'Yes, we have the inquest.'

'I am going to look after your grandmother's dog and chickens while you are away, and I will think of you, and pray that it goes as well as these things can.'

'Thank you, you're very kind.'

He touched her forearm and their eyes met briefly. He then hastily withdrew his fingers, nodded, and turned back towards the house where Ayah lingered in the doorway.

On Easter Sunday, the three English women donned thick coats and boots to go for a walk.

'Your skin is looking much improved,' Cleome remarked to Amelie, as they tramped through the forest.

'Yes, that salve you made seems to be making a difference.'

'I hate to say I told you so.' Her emerald eyes twinkled.

'And of course, I'm less stressed. Stress is a big factor.'

'Of course,' Cleome nodded, a quiet smile playing around her lips.

Antonia dawdled, peering through the trees as if she expected danger, and testing each step as if she did not trust the earth beneath her smart walking boots. While Amelie and Cleome waited for her to catch up, Trassel sniffed about in the undergrowth, and Cleome's attention was caught by the miniscule changes taking place in the forest.

'You see, look at this,' she remarked, touching a tightly-furled bud on a tree branch. 'Isn't it a miracle? You can read me all the science you want about how plants grow and when they grow, but there is such magic about it. *Why* do they grow? That is what I'd like to know. I ask myself this question, over and over again. *Why? What for?* And the only answer I come up with is that there is no reason, no answer. Trees and plants are simply a manifestation of a wider, beautiful universal energy.'

Amelie looked around. Tiny, fairy-like, nameless insects danced in a pale sunbeam that pierced the tree canopy. The air was full of music—cheerful tunes from a multitude of hidden birds. The sounds were beautiful and heartfelt, and her grandmother was right to question it: why did they sing like this? Why bother?

'Of course, many would say that the birds only sing to defend their territory or attract a mate, to reproduce and ensure the continuation of their own species,' Cleome said, as if reading her granddaughter's mind, her face tilted up toward the maze of branches above them. 'But sex would go on, whether they sang or not, let's face it.' The skin around her bright eyes crinkled with mischief. 'Birds sing to celebrate, to express joy, in all this...' she swept a hand through the air. 'And who can blame them? This...' she paused, '...this is paradise. This is the heaven everyone talks about.'

'What are you two discussing?' Antonia asked, as she caught up. Her breath came noisily, and her creamy cheeks were flushed pink. She stopped and dabbed the corner of her eye with a clean cotton handkerchief.

'Cleome says this is the real heaven,' Amelie replied, and looked about her, as if considering the notion.

'I very much doubt that,' Antonia huffed.

Cleome rolled her eyes behind her sister's back, before leading the way along the uneven track through the woodlands. Their chosen path was strewn with roots and rocks, and they had to tread carefully. Patches of blue anemones, known locally as *blåsippa*, decorated the forest floor on either side of their route, a sure sign that winter was finally over. At one point, their way forward was blocked by a fallen tree. A pointed stump and large teeth marks in newly-exposed heart wood indicated that a beaver had been at work.

'Good grief,' Antonia muttered. 'Do they bite?'

Nobody answered. The older women wended their way through the scrub around the fallen trunk while Amelie climbed over the lowest part. They eventually arrived at their destination—a clear space beside the lake which had a panoramic view of open water, glistening in the sunshine. Tracts of unspoilt forest stretched along the opposite shore, lit up and freshly green.

'Where are we now? I need to get my bearings. Where is Helen's little beach and jetty? I don't see it,' Antonia fretted.

'Further down there, where the shore curves back in, there is the big bay which we can't see from here. Her house sits at the back, up beyond a large field. You remember?'

'Yes, I recall it now. I'm just trying to place things again. My sense of direction is not what it was. What is that, in the distance?' She squinted.

'Somebody is out fishing in a little boat,' Amelie said, raising her hand to shade her eyes.

'They will be after the first pike, no doubt,' Cleome observed. 'Oh look, it's Tarek, out with Josef.' Cleome waved enthusiastically. Amelie waved too. They were a long way out on the water, and appeared like tiny stickmen in the vast forest basin. 'They won't come over, it would disturb the fish if they started the engine,' Cleome said.

Tarek and Josef waved back before attending to their rods. Amelie's shoulders sagged. Cleome squeezed her arm and their eyes met briefly. Her grandmother recognised her budding friendship with Tarek. She looked down at her feet and pressed her lips together. A crisp wind stirred, rustling through dead leaves on the forest floor, and encouraging the bare branches above their heads to dance. It made the women's eyes moisten. The water's surface transformed, turning choppy within moments.

'It will be cold out there on the boat. They won't stay out for long,' Amelie said.

'You are probably right. I adore the fresh scent of the water at this time of year, when it has only recently melted. It promises that summer is not far away.' Cleome inhaled deeply, and turned to walk back between the trees. 'I love this lake. She has her own special spirit. I talk to her, you know, when I am fed up. She listens—and never fails to make me feel better.'

Antonia cut in, 'You always were such a hippy. You should have seen her in the sixties, Amelie. She had hair down to her waist, and wore a bandanna and strings of beads around her neck. She traipsed around the streets of London like a gypsy.' Antonia chuckled, rubbing her hands together in response to the chilly breeze.

Amelie said, 'But surely a lake is just a lake. It's geography. There's a dip in the rocks and the water collects. There's nothing more to it.'

'At one time I would have agreed with you, Am. But you live out here for a few years and you begin to connect so strongly with the landscape that you start to wonder about everything, and then with time, you see...'

'You need to get out more, sister.'

'All civilisations throughout history have respected the earth spirits. What is so arrogant about our culture that we think we don't need to, hey? Tell me that.' Cleome faced Antonia, her colourful coat and hand-knitted hat and gloves looking strangely at home in the wild environment.

'They worshipped because they were superstitious and didn't know any better. Science gives us proof of what is and what isn't true, while centuries of theologians have taught us religion.'

'Well, those are narrow points of view, if you ask me. You know, science has its place; but it is just *science*, when all is said and done. A limited discipline. It cannot possibly convey the sheer joy of sunlight dancing on water, like there, over on those tiny waves, where there's a sudden break in the cloud… or the exhilaration in the sweet scent of the pine needles that we all register, now that the frost has melted. Rational thinking is not the answer to everything! We would be very stupid indeed, to put all our eggs in one scientific basket. We sense the wonder, don't you see? We all sense the new season coming. We three have been cheerful today, and full of anticipation. The birds are singing again. Trassel is bounding through the forest. We all share it; we all feel it—whether we are a bird or a tree or a human being who is glad that the long darkness of winter is finally over; we all share the same relief and surge in energy because we are all part of this one magnificent whole life! You can't put that in a test tube and analyse it in a laboratory, can you?' Cleome's voice rang with conviction. 'And as for your theologians, don't get me started. They have ruined many more lives than they ever helped.'

'You always were a heretic, and "anti" any kind of authority!' Antonia sighed.

'And can you blame me?' Cleome boomed back.

The sisters stopped and glowered at each other. Amelie noticed the growing animosity between the elderly siblings. 'Come on, now. Let's keep walking,' she said, in an attempt to appease. 'I expect we are all getting hungry.'

Cleome continued to glare at her sister, who turned away and walked stiffly ahead of them.

'So, what did Patrick have to say earlier, during your phone call, Am? I forgot to ask you,' Cleome attempted to return the conversation to safer ground.

'He sounded down. I felt sorry for him, especially when I told him about our lunch and what a good time we had yesterday. They aren't doing anything today. It seems that Hilary has become depressed, and doesn't want to see anyone, not even at church.'

'Oh, nobody will be suffering more than Hilary,' Antonia chimed, glancing back over her shoulder.

'She will be making herself into a martyr, for sure,' Cleome nodded.

'Well, she has lost her son,' Amelie reasoned.

'It's true, of course she has. But we all know what she's like. She doesn't help herself, and will give little consideration to her husband's grief. It will all be about her.'

'That woman has always been a drama queen,' Antonia agreed.

'Listen to you two! I'm no fan of Hilary, but maybe we need to show her *some* sympathy.'

'You are right, we should bite our tongues. But poor Patrick—I can only imagine. He is the sweetest soul,' Cleome sighed.

'He has bought some new walking boots, and last Saturday he walked part of the Ridgeway with a Ramblers group. Hilary was not pleased because they went for a drink at a pub at the end, and she thought he should have come straight home to her. He had invited her to join in, of course, but she doesn't like walking. He said he is concerned because she is so bitter, and is looking for someone to blame. I know what she means; I have those moments when I could murder someone. But with her it's becoming an obsession, he told me. She wants justice. *Justice!* What does that even mean?'

'Well, there's probably a case for compensation,' Antonia interjected calmly.

'Hilary doesn't need any more money,' Cleome countered. 'She only wants others to suffer because she is suffering.'

'A payoff might help her to feel that justice has been served.'

'But it would be blood money!' Amelie exclaimed. 'And it won't bring Nick or Bertie back! It dirties everything! Surely you don't believe…'

'I don't,' Antonia raised a hand to forestall her, 'but it is the way the system works.'

'I can't see Patrick wanting that.'

'He won't want that at all. He has been a star, you know. I am dreading the inquest and I could not have prepared for it so well without his help,' Amelie said.

'We will all feel better when it is over,' Cleome agreed.

Once they had safely navigated the fallen tree again, Amelie strode ahead saying that she would stoke up the fire and make tea for them all. As the two sisters made their way back through the darkening forest, Antonia turned to Cleome.

'So, we agree you won't see her then? I don't trust her one bit, and you know you'll only get hurt again.'

'I know. You are right, and thank you for helping me to see more clearly,' Cleome said, her eyes glittering with sadness as she marched on

14

Waning Moon of Winds

They stepped out of the taxi in Percy Street into a fine rain. Helen squinted and looked around with interest. She had never been to Amelie's place before. She noticed that the biscuit-coloured house was part of a row, and the street was cluttered with cars. Several gardens were littered with blue, brown and green wheelie bins; others had been converted into parking spaces. Amelie's little patch had a low brick wall separating it from the street and the gate was missing from its hinges. Several shrubs hid her dustbins and while the grass was unkempt, the front door was a cheerful shade of duck egg blue.

Helen offered her hand to Cleome who climbed out of the taxi. They exchanged a grim glance at the prospect of what lay ahead. The inquest was a necessary procedure but neither woman relished the thought of it. Daniel helped the driver to unload their cases, and paid him, cautiously handing over two unfamiliar notes. Amelie, who had exited on the street side of the car, now scurried towards the blue front door, gripping the key so tightly that the whites of her knuckles showed.

Inside, she examined the bare pewter walls, familiar furniture, and varnished pine floor, and registered stale air in the unlived-in space. The living area was smaller than she remembered. The leather sofa appeared worn, and the bookshelves beside the chimney piece were stuffed with Nick's books—she had never noticed how chaotic they looked before. Bertie's toy box sat on the lowest shelf. She turned away. On the dining table lay a pile of unopened mail, a vase of multi-coloured tulips, and a note from Esme, saying that she had made up the beds, and left milk, bread, teabags and biscuits in the kitchen. Turning to look out through the French windows, she noted the neglected garden. Flowerpots housed bleached dead plants. Weeds grew between paving cracks.

'I will help to tidy up the garden while I'm here,' Helen offered. 'Come, show me where everything is. We'll begin with tea.'

'I am looking forward to establishing the facts at this inquest tomorrow,' Amelie told the others, determinedly. 'An accident like that does not simply *happen*. Something went terribly wrong, and we need to know what.'

That night, Cleome took the single bed in what had been Bertie's room. His cot was still there against the wall; his teddies lined up on a duvet cover which had been freshly laundered by the ever-thoughtful Esme. She picked up a small bear and pressed its fur against her face. Through the window, she caught sight of the waning moon, the traditional time of letting go. It felt like a cruel mockery, shining down on her now. How could she ever let go of this? If there was a natural order to things, why had death not taken her, who grew on like an old shrub, past its best? Why take a fresh, healthy child? She carefully replaced the teddy bear, and lowered herself onto the narrow bed, knowing that she would not get a wink of sleep. In the same way she understood that the universe would not always protect her from harm, she also had no faith in society or the establishment, and while she could see that it was necessary for a civilised culture to investigate an accident in the way they did, she did not expect any magical solutions from the inquest.

Amelie closed the door quietly behind her, and faced her old bedroom. It looked different now the invisible sparkle that had filled every corner had vanished, along with Nick's clutter and his distinctive vetiver scent—it was a sad room now, barren and waiting. She perched on the bed, and stood again abruptly, to open the sash window, and allow the chilly night air and noises of Oxford into the space. She slipped into her pyjamas, lifted the duvet and slid beneath it. The sheets had been washed by Esme and all trace of Nick was gone; it made her feel safer. She hugged the pillow, inhaling its laundry liquid fragrance. She would not allow herself to become emotional and focused instead on the prospect of the inquest and her certainty that it would bring her some answers.

As she waited outside Oxford Coroners Court, admiring old stone walls and graceful arched windows, Cleome noticed a mature tree that grew beside it, whose roots were encased in concrete. A canopy of bare branches reached for the sky but were restricted by the towering presence of County Hall on one side and the crenelated stone turrets of the courthouse on the other. She wondered how the plant survived in such an unlikely position when so much of its sunlight and soil was stolen. It must be resilient, she decided, and admired it.

The members of their group assembled on the wide paving beside New Road, and after quietly greeting each other, walked in a cluster towards the courtroom entrance. Dread balled in her stomach. She told herself firmly that it was her duty to be there. She had given birth to Kerstin; she would understand the reasons for her end. She pulled her purple shawl a little tighter.

They filed into the high-ceilinged courtroom which was sectioned into distinct areas—for the coroner, a jury when one was needed (there would none today), family and representatives. Rising at the back were a series of raked stalls—empty polished wooden benches for onlookers. A lone journalist, presumably from the Oxford Mail, sat high up at the rear of this edifice. Cleome took her place beside Amelie, Patrick and Hilary, while Helen and Daniel, Antonia, Marsha, Esme and Paul sat in the row behind them.

Nerves made Amelie light-headed as the courtroom staff filed in, and they stood for the coroner. Her almond-shaped eyes were bare of make-up above her fine cheekbones, and she had rubbed a balm over dry lips. As the wife, mother and daughter of the three subjects, she had an important part to play in the procedure that was about to begin, and she was determined to do her best. When the coroner allowed it, she resumed her seat and took a deep breath. Today, emotion would be parcelled up tight, and everyone would stick to the facts. She would get the chance to ask her questions, and to discover what had actually happened on that fateful October morning.

In the weeks leading up to the inquest, Patrick had gathered background information about Nick, Bertie and Kerstin, consulting her when necessary. He was the only family member brave enough to study the pre-inquest disclosure that outlined the multiple injuries suffered by each member of his family. Amelie had paled at the suggestion of it, and had been too much of a coward to read the reports; she did not wish to know medical details—she would too easily understand the levels of pain. She wondered that anyone could read such a thing, admired Patrick for being so courageous in his belief that somebody from the family had to do it, and was immensely grateful to him for sparing her. He had been a guiding light throughout the entire process, and she had trusted him to gain a good understanding of all the details. She sat next to him now and, noticing his veined hand resting at his side, she briefly covered it with her own, and met his gritty expression with an encouraging smile. Sitting beyond him, Hilary's flick-blade attention was caught by the gesture and her red lips tightened with disapproval.

As the coroner opened the inquest and the formalities got underway, Amelie's breath grew jagged. She listened to the bare facts of her mother's and Nick's lives read aloud to the court—their occupations, ages, state of health and so on. None of the details captured the special qualities of each person, and the account of Bertie's life was pitifully short. Behind the coroner's decisive voice lay a silence so deep that every sniff and shuffle could be heard throughout the courtroom. She forced herself to breathe properly so that she did not faint. She regretted that she had not prepared her own speech about the members of her family which would have said so much more. Cleome reached across and took her hand.

The inquest moved on, and they heard that although there had been heavy traffic on the A40 at the time of the crash, there were only three surviving witnesses. William Christopher Pegg, who wished to be known to the court as Billy, had been a passenger in the Mercedes Unimog lorry when it crashed. Joanna Pauline Ormorod was the driver of a Volvo travelling behind Kerstin's Audi, and had managed to steer her car out of danger and onto a verge. Alan Philip Morgan was the driver of a white van that had been travelling in the opposite direction to Kerstin, behind the Unimog. His vehicle had left the road and overturned but he had not suffered any serious injury. Others present at the scene had been unable to offer any clear or useful account of what had happened.

When it came to each witness giving their statement, Alan Philip Morgan's account was of little assistance; he simply reported seeing the lorry swerve for no apparent reason. Joanna Pauline Ormorod, the driver of the Volvo, described how she had witnessed the lorry cross the central white line and career into the Audi that travelled immediately in front of her. In a sharp reaction, she had steered her Volvo steeply to the left to avoid hitting the back of the Audi. She could not see any obvious reason why the Unimog had swerved across the central white lines and into oncoming traffic, and confirmed that the Audi was being driven in an appropriate manner and at a proper speed, and that in her opinion, collision with the lorry was unavoidable as it came out of nowhere and so quickly. After her Volvo had hit a dry-stone wall, and she realised that she was all right, she had clambered over the wall to get away from any further threat of danger, and it was then she realised that two vehicles travelling behind her had not managed to react so quickly, and had piled into the back of Kerstin's car.

When it came to Billy Pegg's turn to take the witness box, Amelie blanched when she realised that he was the man who had come to her front door in Percy Street, sometime after the accident. He had offered yellow flowers wrapped in cellophane, and she had thrust them back at him, and slammed the door in his face. She noticed that his hair was cut differently, and was now shaved around the back and sides. His fringe no longer hung over his eyes but was trimmed over arched eyebrows. He looked healthier than he had before but was still pale. He rested his hand on the wooden ledge before him, and confirmed that he was the passenger in the lorry driven by the deceased, Darren John Ackerman. When asked, he went on to describe how he and Darren Ackerman had finished work in Burford, and were returning to the tree surgery company premises in Witney, when the accident occurred. It was a clear day and driving conditions were good. Both men were pleased with the morning's work and were chatting in a friendly manner. He cleared his throat. 'Without any warning or apparent reason,' he explained, enunciating his words carefully and clearly, 'the Unimog jerked into the opposite lane and into the path of a white Audi travelling in the opposite direction. I had time to think to myself "what the heck?" but then everything happened so quickly, that is all I remember. Darren was not wearing his seatbelt—he hated them; it was stupid. In that split second, I hoped he would be okay because I knew that we were going to crash—and that was the last thought I had before we collided with the car. I think Darren tried to brake but I can't be sure; it all happened too fast.'

The coroner asked Billy Pegg to clarify whether there had appeared to be a mechanical problem with the Unimog or whether there had been some other distraction—sunlight, perhaps, or something at the side of the road. Billy replied that there had not been anything to distract Darren who was a good and careful driver and that there was nothing obviously wrong with the lorry but he could only assume there had been a fault with the steering.

When it was her turn, Amelie stood to address Billy Pegg. She fingered Nick's wedding ring on the gold chain about her neck, and took a moment to compose her thoughts.

'You came to my house approximately six weeks after the accident, and you told me that Darren Ackerman would "never hurt a fly" so why did he steer a fully-loaded lorry with a heavy trailer into a stream of oncoming traffic? Did he meant to cause harm?' She spoke slowly, each word clear as a bell.

'No, Darren never meant to cause no-one no harm,' Billy said firmly. 'He was not like that. He was a good man.'

'Then why did he plough a lorry into oncoming traffic?'

'I have often asked myself the same question. And the honest answer is, I don't know.'

Amelie shook her head. 'Are you absolutely certain about that?' she repeated.

'Absolutely. I have no idea why the accident happened but I am very sorry that it did.'

As there were no more questions, the coroner asked Billy Pegg to step down. He puffed out his cheeks and raked his fingertips back through his hair as he walked back to his seat.

A police spokesperson related how motorists arriving at the scene after the collision had alerted the emergency services. A report was read out that outlined how paramedics had declared Kerstin Elisabet Lindberg and Nicholas Patrick Tierney dead at the scene. The infant, Albert Patrick Tierney, had been airlifted to the John Radcliffe hospital but had not regained consciousness and had died shortly after admission. Post-mortem examinations found that all three victims had died as a result of multiple injuries. Toxicology tests on Mr Darren Ackerman found traces of alcohol in his blood at thirty-seven milligrams per one hundred millilitres of blood—well below the eighty-milligram drink-drive limit. Darren Ackerman's mobile phone had been recovered at the scene and was later shown as not being used at the time of the accident. Collision investigators had ruled out mechanical failure as being a cause of the accident. PC David Bush, who had prepared a report on the crash, said: 'It is not known why the driver of the Mercedes Unimog came to be on the wrong side of the road. There are a number of potential causes but there is insufficient evidence available to be able to categorically state which is contributory. Possible explanations include driver fatigue and driver distraction.'

No new facts emerged. The lorry had traversed the central line; and nobody knew why. Amelie's face hardened. The coroner recorded his conclusion that a road traffic collision had caused the deaths of Nick, Kerstin and Bertie, and announced, 'It simply isn't possible to say what happened but given the circumstances, it does seem likely that either driver fatigue or driver distraction are the potential causes. While we can find answers to lots of questions, sadly we can't always determine the details.'

Amelie seethed. She was depending on clarification, not guesswork.

After the inquest closed, the group assembled again on the pavement outside County Hall, squinting in the April sunshine. A bitter east wind whipped up litter from the gutter in New Street, and chilled legs and feet. Helen threaded her arm through Amelie's.

Amelie was white with fury. 'I am not happy,' she hissed. 'The coroner did not discover *why* the accident happened. That is what haunts me. *Why?*'

'It's important to establish facts and this inquest did not answer every question for me either,' Cleome agreed. 'Yes, two vehicles collided in such a way—but three stars went out, three souls were lost to the world that day!'

Hilary's coal-like gaze shone from behind her polished spectacles. 'I didn't believe a word that tree surgeon was saying. He was lying. Anybody could see that.'

'Come on now, darling,' Patrick soothed.

'Oh, stop trying to placate me!' Hilary snapped. 'He knew something he wasn't letting on. I could see it in his hooded expression. I am not going to let this go.'

Esme's face was pink from crying and Paul stood protectively close to her side. Marsha clasped her hands together, and stamped her feet against the cold. Antonia announced that she was driving back to the Cotswolds and said her farewells.

After a sleepless night during which Amelie tiptoed around the house and stared out at the narrow street, trying to work out what to do, she developed a strong conviction. She would not tell the others. While she waited for the right hour, she bagged up Nick's and Bertie's clothes, and books and toys for charity or, if they were not good enough, piled them into bin liners for the next rubbish collection.

Everyone helped and between them, they managed to sort through much of clutter in the house. At three in the afternoon, she ate a sandwich. Then she told the others that she was going out to meet a friend.

With assistance from Paul, her car had been fixed and valeted over the winter, and now smelled of air freshener. All the toddler detritus—the toys, squashed raisins and biscuit crumbs—had been safely dispatched. She drove out of the city, and parked on the designated road in Witney. She observed a lorry enter the tree yard laden with woodchip. Some twenty minutes later, Billy exited the premises, and got into his own vehicle. As he drove off up the road, she started her engine and followed him. His shabby red Nissan was easy to spot in the traffic, and she tailed it to Kidlington and through a maze of streets to a rundown housing estate.

He got out of his car while Amelie sat in hers. She watched him stride on skinny legs over balding grass to a ground floor maisonette. She drummed her fingers on the steering wheel, uncertain about the best way to approach him. As she gathered her thoughts, he reappeared, having changed into a pair of jeans that gripped his thin legs. He smoked a cigarette and clutched a couple of rolled-up plastic bags in his free hand as he set off up the street. Amelie slid out of her car and walked a short distance behind him, determined not to let him out of her sight. He made his way to a junction, crossed a busy road and approached a parade of shops.

Dense rain began to fall. Billy hunched his shoulders and Amelie cursed as droplets trickled down the back of her neck. He flung his cigarette butt into a gutter, and disappeared into a small supermarket. She followed, peering past other shoppers to watch him. He paused in front of a display of two-for-one bags of apples, and moved on. A little way down the first aisle, he grabbed a tin of ravioli off a shelf and a carton of milk from a cool cabinet, and then edged past a group of people towards another shelf where he selected several tins of own-brand cat food and a bag of cat litter. He doubled back, almost catching her unawares, and she swivelled and pretended to be looking for something on a shelf. He then stood in a queue, chewing the corner of his finger, with the metal basket at his feet. His watchful eyes scanned his surroundings. Amelie slid out of the supermarket, and pretended to be looking in an adjacent shop window while she waited for him to reappear. Rain soaked her thin jacket and splattered noisily on the paving stones.

Billy emerged, carrying a bag in each hand, and began to walk quickly towards home. Amelie strode up behind him, before her courage failed.

'Billy,' she shouted.

'Jesus, you made me jump! Oh, it's you.'

'I want to speak to you!'

'Leave me alone.'

'I want to know what really happened!'

'I've already said what happened.'

'No, you didn't. You lied. You're hiding something.'

'If you don't leave me alone, I'll call the police.' He paused and glared at her, rain flattening his hair, as they both stood beside the kerb. He turned and marched across the road and she jogged to keep up with him.

'Oh yeah, great move, Billy. You go right ahead and call the police. In fact, be my guest! I'd love it if you called them! I'd kick up the biggest stink anyone has ever seen until they completed a thorough investigation and an interrogation of the like you've never known! Let's face it, I have nothing else to do these days—since my whole family was killed. I have money to burn and nothing, *nothing* will stop me from making your life utter hell. So, you go right ahead and call the police! Make my day!' she threatened.

Billy stopped and considered her. A woman hurried past, hunched beneath a red umbrella. 'What do you want, exactly?'

'I want the truth.'

'I told you the truth already.'

'No, you didn't.'

'Well, you got all I'm ever going to say.'

'Listen, Billy!' She dodged in front of him, and stood facing him, blocking his path as rain streamed down both their faces. 'I know you're hiding something. I can see it in your eyes now. And I could tell at the inquest that there was something you were holding back. I'm a nurse and I know when someone is hiding information, or lying. I can spot it. You are covering something up.'

'Bully for you. Now let me past.'

'No, I won't. Not until I've said my piece. You came to see me that day. You were going to tell me something.'

'That moment passed when you slammed the door in my face.'

'So, there *is* something! I knew it! Look, I lost everything in that accident, Billy! For God's sake, listen to me! I have lost my reason to live. I don't know if you can comprehend that. I don't expect you to—but I have to understand what happened so I can find a way to move on. That's all I want, honestly.'

Billy regarded her silently, his leaden eyes narrowing.

Amelie went on. 'And let me make myself very, very clear: I will haunt you until I get the truth. I will haunt you for the rest of your life, Billy Pegg. I will stalk you, I will nag you, I will plague you. And I will not give up, ever, until you tell me whatever it is that you're hiding.'

'There's laws against that type of thing, harassing a witness.'

'There's laws about lying under oath.'

'I did not lie!'

'Yes, you did. We both know you did!'

'Well, so what if I did? What's a stupid oath anyway? What the hell does it mean? Everybody lies. You'd be bloody naïve if you thought an oath made any difference to anybody these days. People say whatever they need to say. Nobody gives a shit.'

'So, you admit it?'

'I'm not admitting nothing.' He dodged past her and continued up the road. She caught up with him again.

'Billy.' She touched him on the shoulder and he stopped, staring straight ahead with his chin raised in a defiant gesture that she was beginning to recognise. 'How would you feel if it was you? How would you feel if your mum and your whole family were killed in a crash? Can you even imagine it?' He shot her a glance sideways, and encouraged, she went on. 'I don't want any bother. I don't want to make a big scene or go to the police or try to sue you or anything like that—none of that will bring my family back—but I do need to know what actually happened, so I can try to make some sense of it, and get on with my life. Can you see that? I need to know what happened in the lorry that day.'

'Oh, shit. This will be the death of me.'

'No, it won't. Just tell me.'

'I have your word you won't go to the police?'

'You have my word.'

'You'd better come in,' he nodded over towards the maisonette. Amelie hesitated. 'I don't bite,' he muttered.

She followed him into a short corridor which smelt of cat urine. There was a strip of kitchen immediately to their left and a litter tray on the floor which needed emptying.

'Excuse me, I have to do this first. I can't have them being in a mess.' Billy put down the shopping bags and emptied the litter tray into a bin liner which he tied up tight and put outside before spraying the tray with disinfectant, fastidiously wiping every corner with a paper towel and tipping out the newly-bought litter into the tray. 'That's better,' he declared, washing his hands rigorously. 'Tea?'

Amelie nodded. A black cat with milky eyes sat on the worktop. Billy boiled a kettle and tipped hot water into two bone china mugs. He excavated a carton of milk from a bag on the floor and tipped some into each cup, squeezing the tea bag savagely against the side of each mug before handing one to her.

'He's blind,' he explained, following her gaze toward the cat on the worktop. 'And old. And black. Not much hope of finding a good home if you're a cat with a CV like that. And he scratches. Don't try to touch him.'

Billy gestured through a wide kitchen hatch towards a magnolia-walled room with a row of partially-closed curtains across the window at the far end.

'Go and find somewhere to sit.' He lit a cigarette, and followed her, putting his mug on the table before sweeping the curtains open. 'I keep them closed while I'm out to try to keep the heat in for them. They go behind there and bask in the sun, when we have sun. They like to watch the garden.'

A small table was pushed against one wall and another cat sat on it, flicking its tail. There was a sunken sofa and a large television. A door was open to a bedroom; Billy stuck his cigarette between his lips, and shut it. A third cat wound itself around Amelie's legs. A fourth cat rose from the sofa and mewed.

'You have a lot of cats,' she remarked.

'I rescue 'em,' Billy said, matter-of-factly. 'Black cats. Hard to find homes for them. People are too superstitious.'

Amelie was distracted. This was not what she had expected. Her desire to murder Billy was abating. She gathered in her anger. 'So?' she challenged, plonking herself on the plastic chair beside the table. Billy gently scooted the cat off the table and pulled up the remaining chair. They sat down facing each other.

'If you ever tell anyone I told you this, I will deny it. I will say you put the words into my mouth or I'll say I lied to get you off my back. Let me be perfectly clear: Darren was my mate and I will not have his name dragged through the mud for the only stupid mistake he ever made. He has already paid with his life for it. And if you think you're an obstinate bitch, you don't know me. I will never crack under pressure. I'm only doing this for your little boy, you get me? He didn't deserve none of it.' A tear appeared in the corner of Billy's eye, making him blink frantically.

Amelie sensed her advantage. 'Go on.'

Billy began. When he had finished, she was incredulous. 'Was that it?' she whispered, shaking her head. 'Is that all it was? He bent down to pick up a tobacco pouch?'

'Yep. It's the truth.'

'But you're kidding me. It has to be more than that. A thing like that doesn't just wipe out three lives.'

'Well, I know what you mean. But it does, obviously...'

'You must have missed something else like a faulty brake or maybe he fainted or something?'

'Nope. I told you. He was passing me the packet. It slipped out of his hands and he bent down to pick it up. That's it.'

'I don't believe it.'

'Me neither. But I've gone over and over it in my head, and you know, I didn't lose consciousness or anything. Nothing really happened to me except the seat belt did for my shoulder. That was it. *That was it.*'

'What sort of an idiot bends down to get something from the footwell while they're driving?'

'A tired one? Someone who wasn't thinking, just for a moment? I don't know. You tell me. Darren was fine that day, like he always is—was. Honestly, it was just all so quick, it happened in a flash.'

'I hate him,' she cursed. 'The stupid idiot. I absolutely hate him.'

'Yeah, I get that.'

Amelie had been a nurse long enough to know that accidents happen, and miniscule errors could result in catastrophe. She knew from experience that death lurked around everywhere, all the time. She understood that the things that happened were often unfair and unpredictable, but she had not been prepared for such a small thing, such an ordinary, careless trigger for the deaths of three of her own loved ones. The truth left her speechless. She had expected... she did not know what she had expected, but something bigger, more meaningful, than a dropped tobacco packet. She could not understand it.

'I need to feed this lot,' Billy announced and stood up.

She watched him through the hatch, as he set out a neat row of four freshly-washed bowls and dished out the cat food he had just bought. 'Wet food is their favourite,' he explained. The cats mewed. The flat was sparsely furnished but the cats, Amelie realised, looking about her in a daze, were thriving and had glossy coats. She felt disorientated, suddenly.

'I'm going now,' she announced, pulling her car keys from her pocket. She realised that she had left her bag and phone on full display on the passenger seat of her car, and wondered for a moment if they would still be there—and in the same moment, did not care.

'I did it for my brother. I told you because of my little brother,' Billy said to her as she paused at the kitchen entrance. 'He was two. A drunk driver.' He looked down at the lino floor. 'It wrecked my Mum's life. She was never the same again.'

Amelie glanced at Billy's distraught face and looked around his small kitchen. 'I'm glad you told me,' she said. 'I still can't believe any of it and I don't know what to think but I'm grateful to you. Oh, and be careful of my mother-in-law,' she added. 'She's a witch.'

He looked up at her then, with a question on his face. She nodded at him and let herself out. Outside in her car she slapped the steering wheel repeatedly and howled.

15

Waning Crescent Moon of Winds

Amelie drove out to the picturesque graveyard where Nick was buried. It stood at the end of a tree-lined, arrow-straight lane. Beside the ancient church were the graveyard and two large country houses; this small cluster of civilisation made a tiny island in a sea of well-tended fields. In the distance, the wooded Chiltern Hills shimmered like an unreachable shore-line. Overhead was a canopy of empty sky. A chilly wind circled her as she stepped out of her car. She strode to the spot where Nick was buried with her arms folded across her front. She was the only person there. A pair of red kites circled above her in the blue. She sat cross-legged on the cold grass beside Nick's headstone, with her shoulders hunched. She longed to make contact with him, wherever he was now—she had never been a spiritual person but was willing to open her mind to any possibility if it meant she could talk to her husband again. She plucked at the grass.

'Nick?' she whispered. 'Nick, are you there?'

Nothing.

'I don't know what to do, Nick. I miss you… I need your help.'

Nothing.

That evening, she changed into running gear and set off down Iffley Road. She was unfit and had to walk for intervals between spates of jogging, but eventually she reached Kerstin's house in Jericho. A sold sign was erected outside. She had never loved the house in the way that her mother had, felt nothing at the thought of never being there again, but a lump formed in her throat at the sight of it now. All her mother's ambitions: where had they got her? What did they mean now?

From Merrivale Square, she jogged down to the canal side, to the place where she and Nick had once lived in the narrowboat. The canal had transformed since the local authorities had changed the rules and prevented people from living on boats permanently. She looked around cautiously; it was not the safe area it had once been—it was a quiet spot now, hidden away in the middle of the city; pretty on a sunny day but eerie on a chilly evening in April. There was not a soul in sight. She heard cars driving over the bridge nearby.

Trusting to their shared history at the place, and memories of the first heady months of their love, Amelie closed her eyes for a moment and asked again for Nick to come to her. Miraculously, or perhaps not, a warm sensation circled her. She opened her eyes and narrowed them in an attempt to focus. Something shimmered, the trees rustled and the water appeared misty—and she knew that Nick was close. She perched on a nearby bench, fingered the ring on the gold chain at her neck, and spoke in a quiet voice.

'If there was anything I could give—our home and all our possessions, a limb or even two, my sight or hearing—anything I possess, to bring you back, I would give it with all my heart,' she said. 'You must know that. I expect you see it clearly; you always could read me like a book. If it were in my power, I would change the world to give you life again. I still love you, Nick, and I miss you.' She stood, drawn to watch light dancing on the water, in the place where it had all begun. She knew that her love for Nick would never end but that she had, somehow, to carry on without his presence. A gentle wind swept over the canal and caressed her, like warm silk against her face, and the city noises became a crooning din, and lights from canal-side cottages and buildings further along the waterway made a flurry of bright sparkles. She heard Nick's voice then, a whisper of the kind rarely heard; so clear, silent yet mysteriously audible, and coming from another place, she did not know where. 'Be brave, my love. Be happy,' it murmured, distinct in its hint of Irish brogue, unmistakably Nick and yet disembodied, ethereal and strange. And then his presence was gone, just as quickly as it had come, and she stood, alone again. In that same instant, Amelie learnt that Kerstin was long gone, dancing in some other world beyond the skies. And she knew that Luiz the hospital porter had been right that day, when he told her that Bertie had joined the angels.

For a moment, she felt a profound sense of peace and was warmed to her bones but as she began the walk back to Percy Street, her comfort and sense of belonging in the city dissolved. She no longer warmed to the places she used to love, seeing them in a different light. As she trod the familiar route through the streets, the sights offered her no solace. The city simply wasn't the same without her family in it. Relationships at work which had once seemed so strong had lost their bonds too, with only her rapport with Esme and Marsha remaining. Their friendship would survive, but many of the people she had once known were so busy earning a living and wrapped up in their families, carrying on in the same old ways, swept along by a tide that no longer included her.

Amelie did not confide in anyone about her experience beside the canal. She wanted to keep it secret, a private encounter between her and the spirit of Nick. Nor did she admit to the meeting with Billy as she still struggled to accept the unlikely truth behind the accident. The following morning, she and Helen took down more pictures and tidied away the last of the toys to give to Joel. Esme called in for coffee after a long night shift, and implored Amelie to consider resuming her career at the hospital. Frustration played around Esme's tight lips, and Amelie had to look away. She hated being a source of annoyance to the friend who had done so much for her. In a moment's weakness, and in an attempt to repay Esme all her kindness, she finally agreed to pay a visit to the ward. Esme was delighted and hugged her.

The taxi arrived to take Helen and Daniel to the airport, and after they had waved them goodbye, and Esme had left to get some much-needed sleep, she and Cleome set about tidying up, and washing the bed linen. Percy Street felt very quiet with just the two of them there.

16

Dark Moon

Her bones felt leaden. Traffic noise had woken her several times during the night. At seven o'clock, she struggled out of bed, made a coffee, and flung open the back door to let some fresh air into the house. She opened her journal where it lay on the table, and plonked herself down in a chair. *Sweden or England?* she scrawled, flung down the pen, and cradled her head in her hands. She did not know which direction to take. She was so uncertain, her life so groundless now, it was horrible.

Upstairs, her grandmother slept on, exhausted, she said, by the change of air and the aftermath of the inquest. Amelie moved quietly so as not to disturb her but every noise echoed in the new emptiness of the house: scraping butter on toast, the blade clashing against the plate when she cut it, the knife rattling down on the counter. Tears welled as she stuffed her breakfast into her mouth and chewed. With Nick's books gone and Bertie's toys given away, it was like living in a ghost house.

Her grandmother came downstairs wrapped in her dressing gown, her face creased after sleep. They sat and drank coffee together and then drifted through the morning by clearing out her wardrobe, and washing clothes and pegging them on the line in the spring breeze. Cleome left to visit the botanic gardens, and Amelie pulled on a blue dress, warm jacket and cross-body bag. She brushed her hair and rubbed a beeswax salve over her lips. She strode to the local shop and purchased a packet of lemon shortbreads then took the bus across the city, on the journey that she knew so well. When she disembarked at the John Radcliffe, it was shortly after three o'clock in the afternoon—

the quietest time on the ward, and therefore, they had all agreed, the best time for her visit. Sunlight shimmered off the glass as she approached the hospital building. Its steep edifice towered over her. Goosebumps broke out on her arms, her fear as real as it had been nine months previously, when she had sprinted to the entrance around the corner with two policewomen in her wake. She squeezed her eyes tight shut and took a deep breath. She must face up to her fear, she told herself firmly—she must not let irrationality take a grip on her life. This was the place where she had worked for many years before last October. Here, she had nursed hordes of children back to health. *Cling to the good memories, let go of the bad.* She clutched the bag at her hip with one hand, and marched inside.

The ward was bright and clean, and remarkably similar to how she had left it. Esme welcomed her with a hug. Marsha introduced her to a new member of the nursing team. Amelie looked around at the familiar space with interest, noting the young patients chatting with their visitors. A fondness for the place stole over her alongside a stirring curiosity to discover who the patients were, and what they were being treated for.

'Look at you—you look fabulous!' Marsha enthused.

As it was a quiet time on the ward, they were given permission to take their drinks and the packet of biscuits to a quiet side room which had comfy chairs and a low table bearing a box of tissues. As she sipped her tea and listened to her friends' chatter, Amelie relaxed a little. A paediatric surgeon, having heard of her visit, knocked on the door, and poked her head around it.

'Hello, how are you?' the doctor asked brightly.

It was the worst question, the one that tumbled from so many well-meaning lips, and made Amelie want to scream a roll-call of unpalatable truths: *I am broken! I am sad! I am terrified!*

'I'm as well as can be expected,' she replied, a smile flickering over her face as her fingertips sought the gold chain and Nick's wedding ring.

'Good to see you back,' the doctor said, and retreated.

Marsha looked at Amelie. 'Are you okay?'

'Yep.' Amelie inhaled, and then blew the air from her lungs. 'I'm not sure I'm ready for this,' she admitted.

Marsha smoothly asked what she had been doing since the inquest, and waited for her answer. Twin expressions of hope shone from her friends' concerned faces, and Amelie felt the pressure of not disappointing them. She talked vaguely, in a carefully-cultivated upbeat voice, about clearing out the house and "working out what her choices were".

After leaving the ward, she took the bus into the centre of town, imagining that she would wander around the shops and buy some much-needed new clothing. She had underestimated her energy level though, and how much the trip to the ward would tire her; she had cried on the bus as it travelled down the hill, partly with relief that she had managed to confront the John Radcliffe again. In the High Street, the spring air raced between ancient stone buildings, making her ears throb with cold. She ducked into the Covered Market, and gazed at busy, bright displays in windows. The sights dizzied her, and she quickly sought the exit into Market Street. Having never felt lonely in Oxford before, she found herself thinking that she could curl up in a doorway like one of the rough sleepers, and simply vanish, and no-one would notice. With her shoulders hunched against the fierce wind, she rounded the corner into Turl Street. This was how it happened, she realised, seeing a woman huddled in a bricked-in doorway. One moment like this, jammed with too much loneliness and despair, and your world might turn. She paused on the pavement and closed her eyes, held on to thoughts of Nick. He would not want her to give up. He would urge her to stay strong. A surprisingly warm breeze, laden with dust and diesel fumes, nudged between the stone buildings and circled her in a clumsy caress. Doggedly, she moved forwards and found the bus stop for home.

In the distance, the Chiltern Hills glimmered emerald in the sunshine. A lone blackbird sang a few notes from a leafy beech tree. Amelie placed a jar of tulips, gathered from the back garden in Percy Street, beside Nick's poignantly fresh headstone, and sat a while on the damp grass watching a bee working a clump of dandelions beneath the nearby hedge. She had no sense of him being there with her, and as she lifted her face to the sun and closed her eyes, she fancied that he was somewhere far away now, somewhere wild, beautiful and untouched—by a sea, lake or river—but he somehow knew she was there, missing him, and saw that she had gathered the tulips, just for him.

After a while, she returned to her car and drove the short distance to Patrick and Hilary's low stone cottage. She stepped out of the vehicle, and smoothed her skirt nervously. The latch of the garden gate stuck, as it always did, and she shoved it hard. She had not told Hilary or Patrick that she was coming, as she suspected that Hilary might put her off in some way, and it was important that the two women talk, however briefly.

When Hilary answered the door, her eyebrows shot up in surprise and the corners of her painted mouth turned tellingly down as she said hello. There had never been any love lost between the two women, and Nick's passing had changed nothing, it seemed. Her mother-in-law's eyes glinted disapprovingly behind her wire-framed spectacles as she invited Amelie inside. Amelie followed her down the familiar corridor to the kitchen.

'Patrick is in Ireland,' Hilary declared, 'but I expect you know that.'

'No, I didn't, actually. Is he over visiting family?'

'He's staying at the cottage in Sligo. You know what he's like about that place. I don't know what he sees in it. All it ever does is rain there.'

'Nick loved it too.'

'Oh, not that much. He preferred the bright lights, a bit of culture and good society. Ireland was always too boring for him.'

'Oh, but he adored Sligo,' she said. 'He loved Lough Gill, the fishing, and being out in nature there. We honeymooned there, remember?'

'Oh, that was just a passing phase.'

'He chose to live on a canal boat in the middle of a city because he missed Lough Gill so much,' she persisted, starting to feel irritated.

'One of his rasher decisions,' Hilary scoffed.

A fly buzzed, trapped against the kitchen windowpane. Ranks of wall cupboards made the room feel claustrophobic. 'Tea?' Hilary suggested. 'I don't have long; I need to go into town.'

'Thank you, but only if you have time.'

'So, what brings you here?' She pushed her spectacles up her powdered nose before filling the kettle.

'Well, I am here to sort out my paperwork—all the things I have been unable to face until now—and I am considering finding a job, although I don't know where, or when to begin. I haven't worked for almost nine months. It's time I did something.'

'I should imagine you're comfortable now. Your mother will have left you quite well off.'

'That's hardly the point.'

'You don't deny it though, I notice,' Hilary chuckled to herself and brushed a speck off her beige slacks before reaching for two mugs.

'I want to be useful, and try to do some good in the world—that's why I want to get a job.'

'How charming.'

Neither woman spoke while Hilary made the tea, and the silence was awkward, crammed full of unspoken emotions. Amelie took a mug of tea from Hilary when it was offered, and they adjourned to the kitchen table.

'How are you coping?' she asked, kindly.

'How do you think?' Hilary bit back. Amelie knew that there was nothing she could say to help her mother-in-law, or indeed, anything that would make her like her. She leant back in her chair and looked out of the French windows where the clipped lawn stretched towards a beech tree, not yet in leaf. A crow made a racket somewhere close by.

'Will you and Patrick stay on here now?' she tried, a reference to the fact they had moved to the village to be closer to Nick.

'I will. I will stay here to be close to my son's grave but Patrick is unsure. He does not know what he wants.'

'Me neither,' Amelie admitted.

'Oh, you're young. You will find somebody new,' Hilary said bitterly.

Amelie flinched, thought of Tarek, and then just as quickly, dismissed the notion. 'No-one can ever replace Nick,' she said, truthfully. 'I just hope we can all make some kind of peace with what happened, eventually.'

'How the hell would I ever make peace?' Hilary retorted, a red flush creeping down her neck. Amelie sipped the scalding tea, her hand trembled as she replaced the mug on the table and she used a second hand to steady it. She could not cope with Hilary's anger. 'I will not rest until I have got justice for Nick, and you and Patrick and everyone can go to hell with your bloody *peace*. You should listen to yourselves! I sometimes think I'm the only one who really cared!'

She stood. 'Thanks for the tea,' she said. 'I need to be going.'

'But you haven't finished!'

'Sorry, I forgot, I need to be somewhere. The dentist,' she lied. She pecked her mother-in-law's powdered cheek and fled down the corridor, along the gravel path and out of the broken gate. As she drove back into the city, she took a series of deep breaths. She did not think she would ever see Hilary again.

She visited the solicitor and dealt with Nick's life insurance company. Esme departed for a holiday in the Canaries. Cleome went to stay with

Antonia for a few days. Amelie dismantled the empty bookshelves in the living room and set about filling the holes in the plaster and redecorating. The effort of using a paint-roller left her arms aching. In the evenings, she tidied the garden, weeding the bed where tiny seedlings of love-in-a-mist, cornflowers and California poppies were sprouting from the year before when she and Nick had first sown them. The memory of working in the garden with him at her side, weeding and preparing the soil, and scattering the seed while Bertie played with his toys on a rug, made her feel faint. She knelt back on her heels on the cold coarse grass, and blinked up at the sky. How on earth was she going to move on?

On impulse, she drove out to see Billy. She felt irresistibly drawn towards him, and had no idea why this was, or how he would react to her visit. She took a bag of cat treats and a small toy for each animal, and knocked on his front door. He eventually answered, wearing only a pair of trousers. His torso was startlingly pale but below the t-shirt line, his arms were brown.

'I brought some little gifts for the cats,' she offered.

Billy looked down the length of his long nose at her, as if suspecting a trap. 'You'd better come in,' he decided.

As the sun was out, they sat outside on fold-out chairs that wobbled on a rectangle of uneven grass at the back of the maisonette. It was an unseasonably hot day. He offered her a beer, and thanked her for the cat presents. As they sat and sipped cold liquid straight from cans, their conversation centred on the weather—they had just had the hottest April day on record in London—and how the cats were coping. They discussed Theresa May and Brexit, the tax on sugary drinks; no words were exchanged about the accident or its consequences, and Amelie sensed that in some strange way, Billy understood what she needed. He did not ask the wrong questions or expect her to be getting on with her life as if nothing had happened. He gossiped on about the best way to treat cat fleas and the nightlife in Oxford, and Amelie soon felt more relaxed than she had with anyone since she had landed back in the city. She told him she might look for a new job.

'It's too early for you,' he replied, simply.

Instead of disagreeing, Amelie nodded. 'Your Mum—if you don't mind me asking—how is she, I mean… how did she go on?'

'It changed her,' Billy stated, gruffly. 'She's never been the same since.'

The chalky white emulsion made the living room look brighter. She gave away the old furniture to a charity shop, and bought a new sofa, one armchair, and a narrow dining table which she placed centrally at the back of the room. The lack of bookshelves made the sitting area more spacious—but nothing she did made Percy Street feel like home. With Cleome still away, she walked the streets of Oxford, stopping off at various cafés for a drink or a bite to eat, whenever she felt like it. She took her journal with her and scribbled down her thoughts. She waited for the solicitor to get on with what he had to do, and for the insurers to respond to the forms she had finally submitted. She sat on benches in the parks, and tried to slow her breathing as Marsha's meditation teacher had taught her at a session they attended together. Following the teacher's guidance, she focussed on one thing—the gritty tarmac beneath her shoe or the magnificent sequoia piercing blue reaches of sky.

Oxford was a dazzling illusion, she realised. She observed tourists and office workers scuttling or meandering in long streams of humanity, through parks and streets, and felt completely detached from them all. Life was not predictable, as she had once thought it was. Or controllable, as she had assumed. *Life was not safe.* She had believed that if you played by the rules, you won the game. She had sought solace in the notion that "the universe had her back"—but it didn't, and the contest was a smokescreen, and all the rules were nonsense. If her whole family could be wiped out in a minute or two, so could anyone's; the Chinese tourist taking photographs of All Souls College or the Bulgarian woman serving coffee were here by grace alone. Amelie herself only survived by chance. It was astonishing to see how vulnerable everybody was. Beneath the surface beauty and illustrious history of Oxford's ancient buildings and ordered lifestyle, violence and chaos were never far away.

Amelie wrote in her journal. *How come nobody is objecting? How come there is no revolution? How come nobody even talks about all this? I am woken up, and it is frightening, and also quite marvellous.* She lay in her bed at night, wide awake, alert to the truth she now saw everywhere. How could she ever slot back into her old life? She was not sure she could.

17

New Seed Moon

Cleome returned from her sister's, aggravated and secretive. Amelie was still unsure about what to do next. After talking it through with her grandmother, she finally abandoned the idea of applying for a job at the hospital; her heart was not in it and she knew that to resume her old role would not be fair on her young patients. She was not up to the job.

She now had Billy's phone number, and arranged to meet him for a walk in Port Meadows, one unseasonably hot afternoon, shortly before she was due to return to Sweden. He loped towards her in the car park; a tall gangly figure, his hair flopping in his eyes. He pushed it back, self-consciously.

'You need a hair-cut. I could do it for you, if you like.'

'You do realise I'm gay, don't you?' he challenged, ignoring her offer.

'I had wondered; but this is not a chat-up, Billy. I only asked you here because...' she faltered. 'Can't we just walk?'

He inclined his head in consent—it was one of the many gentlemanly gestures that seemed to come naturally to him—and they strode out, side by side.

'Because?' Billy prompted.

'Because maybe if you told me more about Darren Ackerman, I might be able to find a way to forgive him. I mean, I don't think I can—but I owe it to myself to try.'

'Oh Christ.'

'You're the only person I know who knew him,' she explained.

'You never give up, do you?'

'My father-in-law, whom I trust and who is a lovely man, rang me from Ireland. He says forgiveness is the only way forward.'

'Does he, now.' Billy blew his hair out of his eyes.

'Try me,' Amelie asserted. 'Just tell me something about Darren Ackerman.'

At her side, the lazy river glistened and sparkled in the heat.

'We've been through this before.'

'No, we haven't. Not really. I want to try to understand the man, to know what he was like. To see if there was a human side to him.'

'You are mad, you know that?' Billy put one hand on his hip.

'I'm just trying to understand everything.'

'But it will hurt you!'

'Nothing can hurt me more than I am already hurting!'

'Oh, all right,' he sighed. 'Well, if you insist. He was a very nice bloke. Divorced. Had a little boy he never got to see because his ex-missus was a selfish bitch. He loved trees. He loved going to the Isle of Wight on holiday—it was the only place he ever went. Same hotel, same pubs to eat in, every year. He was a good worker. A fair man. A good climber, too. Satisfied?'

'Climber?'

'Tree climber. He was good at what he did. Steady. Sensible. Had guts, you know? Had skills. Was thoughtful to the trees.'

Amelie moistened the inside of her mouth with her tongue and swallowed hard. 'Go on,' she said.

'What more do you want to know?'

'I don't know. Little things. Anything.'

'He liked pies. Those cheap ones you buy in a packet at the petrol station. He never ate properly, in my view—always some shite out of a packet.'

'Where did he live?'

'I never went there. Some little flat, over in Witney. Oh, and he liked art. He always went to some exhibition in London each summer. He went to art college once, years ago, but of course art doesn't pay the rent, especially when you have a little kid to support.'

'What sort of art?'

'No idea. He always paid his child maintenance on time. He would sometimes go without things himself to make sure he paid in full. That ex of his was taking the piss, if you ask me, but he couldn't see it.'

'Hmmm.' Amelie stopped walking, and tipped her head on one side. 'His poor son.'

'Yeah. He hardly ever got to see him too, like I say. Only when she wanted to go on holiday and her Mum wasn't around to help her out. It was appalling really.'

'Sad.' Amelie nodded. 'So, he doesn't sound especially... careless?' She held her breath.

'He wasn't. I keep telling you. He was a good bloke who made one stupid mistake. Well, two if you count that ex-wife of his.'

Tears gathered in Amelie's eyes. 'I don't understand how lives can end so quickly, for no reason. There was no malice or war or other violence. You know, I could understand it more if he was a psycho or if the lorry engine had exploded, or something like that, but this... dropping a tobacco packet... it beggars belief.'

'Yes, well, this is the real world we live in. Stuff like that happens. It's not like in the movies.'

The river's surface ruffled in a warm breeze. Water lapped the muddy riverbank. Green plants swayed in the shallows. A coot bobbed about nearby. Billy dug his hands into his trouser pockets and stood beside her, a little close, as if to protect.

'If he was still alive, I'd murder him. You know that? It's easier that he's dead,' she said.

'Yep.'

'You think I'm weird, don't you?'

'I'm not really one to judge,' he paused. 'But if you asked me, I'd say you're not weird at all. I think you're brave, actually, and one thing I can tell you is that if Darren was still here with us, he would do absolutely bloody everything he could to help you. He would never have got over what he done. I don't know if he could have even lived with it, to be honest. He wasn't one of those to blame the lorry or the weather or the other driver or whatever. He was a real man like that; he would have taken his responsibility on the chin, owned up, done his time.'

'You're not just saying that because he was your friend?'

'Nope.'

'Hmmm.' Amelie shook her head.

'I saw him die, you know.' Billy pushed his fringe back, and held it off his face with his long fingers as he stared out over the water. 'It happened in a flash. Bang! He was gone. Just like that. Big purple fruit grew on the side of his head and the light went out in his eyes. Honest to God, it was instant. It plays over and over in my head like a horror film, like maybe I could have guessed he'd try to reach for that tobacco packet, and I could have bent and got it for him, and prevented everything… You're getting me upset now.'

'Did you think that?' Amelie squawked. 'Did you see the packet and let him get it?'

'No, God, no! I didn't even notice the bloody thing. I never noticed anything until it was too late; that's the problem! I wish I had. Some nights I pray to turn back time and see the damned packet, and stoop and pick it up, and then Darren would have kept on driving and the crash would never have happened, and life would have carried on, you know. Everything normal and as it should be.' Billy frowned at the glimmering river.

They walked on. Amelie's attention was caught by sunlight flashing off the water's surface like an electric spark. It was as if the river was alive, in the same way that her grandmother described Lake Båven.

'My friend Marsha told me that you forgive people to make yourself feel better, not to help the person who did you wrong. You forgive them because forgiveness helps you to heal. It's not like you think it is, forgiving someone. It's self-preservation. You forgive someone, and all the knots in your heart unravel—eventually.'

'Well, I hope for both our sakes, she's right. Although I'm not sure I'll ever forgive myself.'

Amelie turned then, and gave Billy a brief hug. 'I forgive you, Billy. I don't blame you for not noticing the packet.'

Billy puffed out his cheeks.

'I wish you had though,' she added.

They walked a little further along the path in reflective silence, two new friends, comfortable in each other's company. 'I'm going back to Sweden,' she said eventually.

'I think that's a very good idea. And you know where I am, next time you're back.'

'I do, and thank you.'

Patrick returned from Ireland, and met Amelie and Cleome for lunch at The Trout Inn at Wolvercote, on the day before they were due to leave. They sat around a small wooden table in the busy pub garden, and ate fillet steak sandwiches in the sunshine.

'Hilary sends her apologies. I understand that you paid her a visit,' Patrick said to Amelie, a twinkle in his eye, as he dabbed the corner of his mouth with a napkin. 'She said you left without finishing your tea.'

'I'm sorry. I'm not sure we'll ever see eye to eye.'

'You have to understand that she's not herself.'

'I do, of course I do. But I think we both know she's never liked me.' Patrick looked down at his plate, his pouched cheeks flushing with embarrassment.

Amelie took a deep breath. 'Listen, there's something I need to tell you both, some information that I have been keeping to myself.' She circled the rim of her glass with her finger. 'There's never going to be a good time to say it, and I don't know how you will feel about it, and you would have to promise me not to tell Hilary, Patrick, and I appreciate you might find that hard.'

Patrick glanced up at her. 'Go on,' he said quietly. 'I've been half-expecting something like this.'

She told them everything about Billy, explaining how he had first come to her door with flowers, and she had shut him out, the way she had trailed him home from work and interrogated him, and how surprisingly, they had now become friends. She related what had happened in the lead up to the crash. As she spoke, Patrick looked away, and up at the blue sky overhead. He pressed his lips together tightly, as if to moderate an excess of emotion. Cleome's green eyes glittered furiously.

'Just a tobacco packet?' she whispered, urgently.

Amelie nodded, tears spilling from her eyes.

'Holy Christ,' Patrick said.

'I know.' She swept her cheeks with her fingertips.

'It must have been his time, well and truly.' Patrick bowed his head.

'But Bertie? My Mum? All three of them at once?'

'Heaven help us all.'

'You know, this world can be incredibly cruel,' Cleome said, drawing herself up to her full height. She summoned a waiter to bring a large vodka and tonic. Around them, other diners tucked in to plates of food, cutlery clattered against plates, a fly landed on the basket of bread.

'Thank you,' Patrick said, after a time. 'You are a good soul, Am. I appreciate you telling me. We'll get there,' he said, covering her hand with his for a moment before withdrawing it, slowly. 'It is not our place to question why such things happen—and *they do happen*, you know—everywhere, across this entire mad world of ours—unspeakable tragedies, all of the time, all over the place.' He raised his weathered hand, a worn leather watch strap fitted neatly around his bony wrist, and gestured vaguely towards the sky. 'It is not just us, you see. We must not take it personally. We have to somehow—God help us—*somehow*,' he searched for the elusive words, 'to *accept*, to *forgive*, to *trust*. And yet, in the face of it all, I have to admit, I sometimes quake with fury.' His eyes gleamed, two lamps beneath grey eyebrows.

'You are very wise,' Cleome said.

'The thing I go over and over again is, why did I not keep them safe?' Amelie whispered. 'I should have known when our car wouldn't start that it was a sign. It was the universe warning me that something would happen, and I took no notice. I should never have let Mum step in like that. I should have kept everyone home, and done my work that evening after Bertie had gone to bed. It was my selfishness, only thinking of my own needs, wanting to get my work finished so I could have an evening off; that's what caused it all. I was so desperate to get everyone out of the house, and look what happened!'

'Amelie, Amelie,' Patrick soothed. 'Come now, you know that's not true. Your mind is playing tricks on you.'

She broke down and sobbed, noisily. The couple at the next table looked over, and then quickly away, making faces at each other. 'If just one little detail had been different, it would never have happened. I could have changed something!'

'My dear, you are not thinking straight,' Cleome rested a hand on her granddaughter's forearm. 'Listen to me. All of us, we do our best. We cannot control everything, much as we long to sometimes. We do not get to choose what happens. The only power we have lies in our reactions to this heart-breaking and yet utterly marvellous life. Let's not forget that part. There is so much joy in the world too.'

Amelie blinked, and nodded. She took the clean cotton handkerchief that Patrick offered. 'I'm sorry,' she mumbled.

'You never, ever need to apologise to me,' Patrick said. 'The first person we have to forgive in these situations is always ourselves. Forget Darren Ackerman and everybody else that has anything to do with the accident. Forget them all, and forgive yourself, first and foremost. I too, wish that Nick had called me that morning, and I had driven them to the wildlife park. I blame myself that he never felt comfortable approaching me these past few years, and that he died uncertain about where my loyalties lay, God help me... I blame myself that I allowed his mother's attitude to your marriage to interfere so much with my own relationship with my son and your family. I stood back to keep the peace when I should not have done. I let her set the tone of things when I should have stood up for the way I wanted things to be. I lost so much time that I could have spent with Nick and you and Bertie in recent years, just keeping the peace with my wife. That's my regret. That's what I have been brooding on, over in Ireland. But I see that we don't always get things right, and I have to take responsibility for the choices I made and try not to beat myself up over them. Most days, it is still impossible and I am truly humbled by what it takes to live an honest life.'

'Nick knew you loved him. He saw the position you were in… And there's no way that what happened was your fault, or anything to do with what you did or didn't do.'

'Well, we will never truly know that now, will we?'

The trio sat silently for a while, lost in thought.

'Tell me, dears, what will you do when you get back to Sweden? Do you have any plans?' Patrick asked, eventually.

'I don't know. I will be glad to get away from the noise here, and people constantly *doing* things and rushing around like headless chickens. But I also need to work again, one day. I want to be useful.'

'I know just what you mean about the noise. It is shocking to come back here after the peace and tranquillity of Sligo. I am much better away from the hurry and chatter too. We are so fragile, after what has happened. And by the way, if it's money you're bothered by, I can always help you—you know that.'

'You've always been so kind to me, Patrick, and I thank you, but it's not that. What I need is a reason to get up in the morning, a purpose. I can't go back to the JR. I've visited and considered it, and I know there's no going back there now.'

That night, with their bags packed ready for the flight the next morning, Amelie struggled to get to sleep. Her mind was full of worries about whether she was making the right decision to return permanently to Sweden, and what she was going to do next. As she was drifting off to sleep, Nick's face appeared before her like a vivid image on a screen; it was very close to her, and his chestnut eyes met hers in a direct gaze. *Live on, Am*, she heard him say, in his inimitable Irish brogue. *Treasure your precious life while you have it. Savour every moment. Be grateful. Love again. Enjoy every single thing you can. Do it for Bertie, Kerstin and me. Do us proud!* And then, he was gone, just as quickly as he had come.

18

Waxing Seed Moon

Tarek whistled softly to himself. He had jogged across the damp field beneath *Båvenshult* and through the still forest to reach the rock-strewn glade at *Det Lilla Huset* and had now slowed to a walk to take in the beautiful location. Kaia and Trassel (who was staying at *Båvenshult* while Cleome was away) bounded ahead of him. He walked towards the homestead, rubbing his hands together. While by Swedish standards, it was a warm spring, he feared that he would never acclimatise to the weather in Sweden, and for a moment his thoughts turned to the springtime at home. He always pictured Raqqa as he had left it—a thriving city spread beside the glistening Euphrates, untouched by the ravages of war. While he had been growing up, at this time of year in Raqqa, sunshine baked the architecture each day, the skies overhead were a dazzling cerulean blue, and the streets were alive with chattering vendors and the constant passing of scooters and cars. He experienced a sharp pang of longing for the place he would never see again. Even if he were able to return one day, Raqqa was now so devastated by bombardment that it was being likened to Dresden after World War II. He had seen photographs on the internet. Many of the places where he had grown up no longer existed; razed to the ground by war, they were reduced to piles of pitiful rubble. His cheerful whistling petered into silence, and he halted and shook his head. Anger simmered inside him as it so often did, and the pain which rested like a hot stone in his chest made his heart pound. Some days, it was impossible to believe that the people whom he had once known and loved, the social structures of his youth—his school, the local football pitch, the cafés where he had drunk cola and coffee with his friends, the shops, and the myriad scents and sounds of home—had literally turned to dust. He despaired that the world turned its back on the ongoing tragedy in Syria. And while it did him no good to remember, a part of Tarek felt that he owed it to his country to never forget its beauty, and the precious life and peaceful values he had once cherished there. He rarely let his thoughts stray as far as his lost family—that was too dark a place to enter, and too threatening to his sanity, when he still needed to stay focused on survival. He reached for a cigarette from his overshirt pocket, lit one, and strode on.

As he approached the barn that housed Cleome's chickens, he sensed that something was wrong at *Det Lilla Huset*. The dogs had both disappeared. He glanced over at the red-painted house, and frowned. The front door was ajar. He threw down his cigarette and stubbed it out with his trainer. Cautiously, he advanced towards the house, thinking that perhaps Cleome and Amelie had come home a day earlier than planned, but in that case—he checked the car port—where was their car? After his long and troubled journey from Syria, his intuition was finely honed. He scanned the edge of the woodland before approaching the door, pushing it open a little further, and calling out, '*Hej*? Anyone home?' and then, 'Come, dogs!'

The dogs came back outside. Not wishing to intrude, Tarek did not enter the house but crept around the corner of the building whilst looking about for any signs of human presence. He slid past overgrown shrubs, and then saw what he feared: a window hung open at the side of the house and the pane was smashed. He froze, scanned his surroundings, and listened. He could hear no-one. He could not see anything else that was unusual. The dogs scarpered through the fringes of the forest, their noses to the ground in the usual way, unconcerned. He pulled out his mobile phone and dialled 112.

Since leaving Syria, he had dreaded any involvement with the authorities because he knew that with certain individuals, his immigrant status made him a prime suspect for any type of crime or misdemeanour, even in the fair, safe culture of Sweden. Nevertheless, he knew it was his duty to make the call, and while he waited for the police to attend the site, he steadied his nerves by calmly feeding the chickens and giving them their fresh water, and then lighting another cigarette.

There had been a long delay before their flight was able to take-off from Stansted, and so when Amelie and Cleome's plane finally landed at Skavsta airport, they were both relieved. After they had disembarked and made it through Customs, they were glad that the long day was nearly over and they were back on firm land again. Amelie drove them back to *Det Lilla Huset* while Cleome napped in the passenger seat. As she steered the car down the track and reversed under the barn, she noticed lights on inside the cottage. She turned off the ignition, and saw Tarek walking from the house towards them.

'I am sorry. I could not get hold of you to warn you,' he said. 'I am very sorry but there has been a burglary.'

Cleome woke up and climbed out of the car, and when she heard what Tarek had to say, she wailed and scurried into the house. Trassel had run out barking to greet her, and now raced back indoors beside her.

'The police say you have to make a list of what is missing,' he explained to Amelie, his dark eyes fixed on hers. He was calm but concerned, and watched her closely to see how she would react.

'Who would do this to my grandmother?' she asked.

'They don't know yet. They think perhaps it was someone looking for prescription drugs as they have left many of your valuables alone and there has been a spate of similar crimes in the area.'

'Prescription drugs, out here?'

'I know, it's crazy. But there's a lot of this type of crime about, apparently,' he said, striding beside her as she hurried towards the house.

Inside, Cleome paced from room to room, wringing her hands. 'The bastards!' she cried. 'Never, in all my time here, has this happened before. It has always been a safe place to live.'

'Let's sit down a moment, and have a cup of tea before we do anything,' Amelie suggested. 'It is done now. There's no point in rushing about.'

'After the police checked for finger prints, I was able to clean up,' Tarek said. 'I have tried to put some things back in their places for you, but other things, I did not know what to do with. There was so much stuff, spread over the floor.'

Cleome's eyes flashed, lividly. Her jars of dried herbs had been emptied over the floor, drawers and cupboards had been ransacked, their contents now haphazardly replaced on the table by Tarek. 'Tell me exactly what happened,' she said to him.

While Amelie set about making some tea, Tarek explained how he had discovered the open door and the broken window, and had called the police. 'They questioned me about every detail,' he went on, 'and took finger prints around the window frames and so on. They asked me who I had told about you being in England. I only mentioned it to one of the guys in the football team—a white guy—but honestly, it was just in passing because he wanted us to go running, and I explained how I was coming here. He is a nice guy. I can't think it has anything to do with him.'

'Of course, not.' Cleome touched Tarek's arm. 'I trust you implicitly. Oh dear, what a mess.'

'I will stay and help you clear up some more,' he offered.

Amelie, who had been listening to Tarek's account of the burglary, stopped making tea, and suddenly turned and fled up the stairs. She entered her bedroom and saw that her suitcase of precious things had indeed been opened. The lid was leant up against the bedroom wall but the cherrywood box containing Bertie's ashes had been placed carefully on the chest of drawers, photograph albums piled neatly on the floor, and Nick's jumper and some of Bertie's clothes were folded and placed back in the case. For a moment, she was confused.

Tarek knocked on the bedroom door and waited for permission to enter the room. He clasped his hands behind his back, and stepped over the threshold. 'I tidied it for you.' He cleared his throat and kept his eyes on the floor. 'The idiot had scattered everything everywhere and I could see… I knew how it would make you very upset so I made it tidy. I apologise if…'

'You don't need to apologise.' Amelie turned to him, and on seeing his stricken face, added, 'I'm very grateful for your thoughtfulness.'

'Right, well, I will go.' He gestured at the door, and disappeared.

She clutched at Nick's wedding ring on the chain around her neck, and bent to pick up a teddy which Tarek had propped at the back of the open case. She pressed it to her chest, and dropped to her knees. She ran her fingers over a photograph of herself and Nick on their wedding day, and closed her eyes.

She returned downstairs to join Cleome and Tarek, and after they had drunk tea and eaten a few biscuits apiece, they began the process of tidying up. They returned papers and string, cutlery and tea towels, and numerous other items to their various places. Helen and Daniel, on hearing what had happened, came to give a helping hand. Daniel checked window latches and made sure that the damaged frames were boarded up for the night. There seemed to be no logic to the break-in. The television remained in place, as did Amelie's laptop. It was as if the intruder had been searching for something specific in all the many drawers and cupboards or had simply been malicious.

By the time some semblance of order had been restored and the neighbours had left, it was past midnight. Unable to sleep, Amelie went into a cleaning frenzy, wiping down surfaces and mopping floors. Cleome prowled around her home with her eyes half-closed and her nose lifted. She took out a handmade bundle of dried juniper from a wooden box, and lit it, walking from room to room and allowing the smoke to drift into every corner.

'What is that smell? What are you doing?' Amelie grumbled.

'I am cleansing my home. There is darkness here, lurking. I can sense it.'

Amelie shook her head, and carried on wiping a doorknob with antiseptic. She did not want any germs from the burglar's filthy hands to be left where she or her grandmother might touch them.

Cleome, having cleared each corner of her home with the juniper smudge stick, then took an old aluminium pan from one of her kitchen cupboards. She poured Epsom salts into it and sloshed methylated spirit over them. Using a long wax taper, she lit the mixture so that flames danced in the saucepan. At a stately pace, she bore the flaming vessel ahead of her, offering it first to an area beneath the stairs, and then into each corner of the downstairs bathroom, before walking up the stairs, and into each bedroom.

'Shush,' she admonished Amelie, who stood with her hands on her hips, aghast, as her grandmother carried the pan of flames from one room to another. 'Be quiet now. I will explain later.'

Finally, the flames died down, and Cleome returned to the kitchen.

'That is it,' she declared, satisfied. 'They are gone.'

'What is gone?' Amelie questioned. 'That was not a safe thing to do!'

'It was better than the alternative.' Cleome's eyes glittered. 'The dark spirits. They have fled.'

19

Waning Seed Moon

Spring finally came to Sweden, touching every tree with her vernal wand so that branches burst into bud, birdsong rang out through the forest, and plants poked their tousled heads through the earth, lush and fresh-faced after their long winter sleep. Temperatures rose, unseasonably high as they had been in England.

Amelie cleaned the cottage from top to bottom. She moved the precious contents of her suitcase into a pine trunk on the upstairs landing, and stashed the case beneath the house eaves. She kept the cherrywood box containing Bertie's ashes where Tarek had placed it, on the chest of drawers.

Cleome escaped into her garden, tidying up after the long winter, cleaning out the summer run for her chickens, digging over her vegetable patch and planting neat rows of seed potatoes. While she could not labour for long hours like she used to, the activity lifted her spirits and she would occasionally perch on a boulder to recuperate, and turn her face to the sun.

They did not hear anything more from the police about the burglary, other than they were continuing their investigations. Apart from some painkillers and a small amount of cash, they had not noticed anything missing from the cottage so far; it was all rather strange. The broken window was replaced, and the door locks changed as a precaution. Cleome suspected vandalism for the sake of it; she fancied she could sense traces of it in the air, but she could not figure out the source. She kept up her rituals of cleansing the little homestead, smudging the place with smoking sage sticks, section by section, to rid it of opportunistic bad spirits. She left out more offerings of buttered porridge for the *nisse* (a practice which she normally did only at Christmas time) to appeal to the little sprite to keep her, Amelie and the animals safe. She was not sleeping at all well since the break-in, waking at the slightest sound.

On the 28th of April, when it would have been Kerstin's fifty-third birthday, Cleome and Amelie escaped to Stockholm for a day, and wandered through *Gamla stan*. There they ate a lavish lunch, before taking the water bus for a trip around the many islands that formed the archipelago outside the city. Cleome contemplated the tracts of dazzling sea that wove through the myriad beautiful islands, and gave thanks for her daughter's life. At her side, Amelie scribbled in the journal which she now toted everywhere in her practical cross-body bag, noting down a series of random words, memories and gratitude to her mother.

At Helen's suggestion, Amelie began to accompany her in her volunteer role with Doctors of the World. Here, Amelie saw another side to Swedish culture, and was moved by the plight of illegal immigrants who struggled to communicate their medical symptoms, and whose trauma was evident in their restless hands and nervous, strobe light smiles. Sörmland, for all its wild beauty and isolation, housed large communities of displaced people, some of whom like Tarek were entitled to be there and others who lived in the shadows. A quarter of the population of the local town Flen now comprised Somalis, Syrians and other asylum seekers. Tiny Flen had a history of welcoming immigrants from as far back as the Vietnam War, but decades of goodwill were turning to hostility in some parts of the town due to the sheer numbers of incomers and the strain on local resources. One national newspaper article even cited Flen as an example of the country-wide rise in right-wing extremism and racist sentiment.

One particular morning, Helen took Amelie on a home visit to a Russian immigrant family.

'You need to prepare yourself,' Helen advised as she switched off her car engine. 'I'm certain you won't have seen anything like it before as it seems to be a sickness confined to Sweden. My patient is a twelve-year-old girl who is suffering from a little-known condition called *uppgivenhetssyndrom*. Literally translated, it means Resignation Syndrome, but privately, I think of this girl as one of Sweden's Snow White Children.' Amelie raised a questioning eyebrow. 'My patient is called Revekka, and her family fled to Sweden when she was six. She was an intelligent child who soon learned Swedish, was popular at school, made many local friends, and so on—a normal, healthy girl, by all accounts. Her father sought asylum for himself and his family because the Russian security forces had threatened to kill him over some unorthodox religion he practices, but Sweden refused him residency as they said he could not prove that his life was in danger. That was six years ago. Believing they had no choice, the parents hid from the authorities but continued to send their daughter to school (which they can do here although many such illegal migrants don't risk it) and then the father tried to reapply for asylum a year ago, this time additionally claiming that Revekka and her younger sister Sophie would be psychologically damaged if the family had to return to Russia, as they had settled in to life in Sweden, and life here was all that they knew. When their application was rejected again, Revekka's parents became distraught. They feared for their lives if they were forced to return to Russia. As the date for their deportation drew close, Revekka simply took to her bed. There, she fell into a deep sleep and has not woken up since. That was eight months ago.'

'*Eight months?*'

'Yes, eight months. The first time I saw Revekka was the day after she had "fallen asleep" and her father had contacted Doctors of the World. It was the only way that he could get medical help for her as they are not registered through the proper channels for Swedish medical care, and he was very frightened about what might be wrong. I recognised immediately what I thought was happening—that Revekka was another Snow White Child.'

'You're kidding me?'

'I'm not. Since the 1990's, Sweden has seen many children like this.'

'I've never heard of anything like it before.'

'That's why I brought you. I knew you'd be interested. But I warn you, it's a strange situation.'

'That's okay. There's not much I haven't seen with sick children.'

'Let's go in then. I expect Revekka's little sister Sophie will translate for us. Her parents still struggle with speaking either Swedish or English.'

Inside the small bungalow, young Sophie and her dark-eyed mother Ellina greeted them with smiles, although Ellina also chewed her lip. She led the way to a bedroom off the main room, where she pulled a light quilt off Revekka, who lay on her back on a narrow bed with her eyes closed. Ellina undressed her daughter so that Helen could examine her.

Amelie, who thought she had seen everything during her years at The Children's Hospital, was startled by what she saw. The girl lay in a single bed which was pushed against one wall, with a feeding tube attached to her nostril. Her dark shiny hair splayed out across the pillow. Her skin was pale but had a healthy glow, and her relaxed face suggested that she was in no pain and at peace. Cards and photographs were sellotaped to the wall above her bed. At the foot of it was a ripped-open pack of extra-large nappies.

Helen opened the girl's eyelids with deft fingers. Revekka stared straight ahead. When a torch was shone into each eye, her pupils contracted. Her pulse and blood pressure were normal.

It was a warm day. The bedroom window was ajar, a tired-looking floral curtain billowed gently in a breeze, and from outside came the sounds of children calling to each other and a scooter racing past.

Helen asked for ice, and Ellina returned with a packet of frozen meatballs. Helen placed the pack on Revekka's bare stomach and tested her pulse and blood pressure again. In a normal patient, the ice would create fluctuations in these measurements but Revekka's vital signs remained constant. A tear spilled down Ellina's cheek as Helen gave Revekka a breast examination—explaining quietly to Amelie that one of her young patients had developed cancer while she had been "sleeping", and so she now routinely checked all of her "apathetic" female patients in this way. Amelie touched Ellina's arm to comfort her. Helen brushed the bottom of Revekka's foot and Revekka's big toe curled, indicating that there was no damage to her brain.

When the examination was over, Amelie helped Ellina to dress her daughter again while Helen wrote up notes. Revekka's arms flopped as Amelie fed each into a sleeve, and then carefully and gently buttoned her blouse. The women moved to the next room, leaving the door open so that Revekka was in full view, and might be able to hear the life going on around her.

The main room was spartan, with a short row of kitchen units, a table with four chairs, and a sofa that faced a television. Helen checked on Revekka's tube feeding routine and asked Ellina in basic Swedish, how she was coping. Sophie, who had been playing outside the bungalow door, came back inside. She chatted animatedly with Amelie, boasting that two teachers from her school visited every week to take it in turns to read stories to Revekka, and that Revekka's friends came and sat on the floor beside her bed after school while they looked at their mobile phones. She gabbled, as if attempting to reassure Amelie that everything was normal and fine. Amelie asked her a few gentle questions about school to help take her mind off her big sister.

'Will she recover?' Amelie asked, as they drove away.

Helen shrugged. 'It is possible that the family will get to stay in Sweden now that Revekka is ill. A few years back, a petition was signed by over one hundred thousand Swedes demanding that we stop deporting "apathetic children", as they are known. To expel sick children goes against every principle this nation holds dear, and many native Swedes were horrified when they realised what was going on. Of course, the flip side is that just as many are highly sceptical about the illness, and there is a raging battle going on about these cases in some sectors of society. Some people think that the children are being drugged or are pretending to be ill just so that their families can stay in Sweden. Of course, some immigrants are so desperate that they are doing just that and faking the condition, which doesn't help. But with others—like Revekka—to say her family are faking it seems to me to be unlikely. There are many medical tests, in and out of hospital, that these children are subjected to, and there is a body of growing evidence to confirm the diagnosis. Personally, I think,' she paused, 'I think these children have simply given up on life. It has become too much to bear, and my theory is that there's a part of the human brain which we don't understand yet, that shuts down when we are so overwhelmed that we can see no way out. There have been similar examples in other traumatised cultures that are just beginning to be written about, but nothing quite like these Snow White Children. They are uniquely Swedish. Revekka's family will find out soon whether their latest appeal for asylum is granted. It is still by no means certain. If they are successful, they must talk about it regularly in her presence, and in all probability, she will come around, although her brain might never be the same again—we never know about that.'

'It's incredible that recovery can come about, simply by hearing good news.'

'The logical explanation is that patients can still hear, even though they don't respond. And slowly, slowly, if they hear the good news enough times, the brain begins to heal. But this is just speculation. We don't have evidence that this is what happens other than there is this pattern to recovery.'

'And this *always* happens?'

'It does. Although some make a better recovery than others.'

'I find this very hard to believe.'

'You are not alone in that. But Revekka is my seventeenth patient—my seventeenth Snow White Child. I continue to do every test I can so that we can gain knowledge about the condition, and I'm not the only doctor working with these types of patients. There are a few of us; we all share information. The stories are always the same; the symptoms are always the same. There are sceptics, like I say, but I have yet to be convinced that these kids are pretending, and there's no way they are drugged. This is something completely different, almost beyond the physical.'

'Her soul is in despair. I could sense it in the room,' Amelie mused.

'You are sounding like your grandmother! But, yes, I know what you mean.' Helen fell silent. Sunlight shone on rusty pine tree trunks that edged the forest road, and shadows from dancing branches made patterns across the brightness. A cleansing pine needle scent wafted through the open car window, a natural source of comfort.

'This forest is the best medicine,' Amelie reflected. 'All the rules are different out here. I hope Revekka wakes ups and can appreciate that one day.'

'I think she will,' Helen said. 'Changing the subject completely, have the police caught your burglars yet?'

'No. It seems they were careful and left no prints, and as nothing much was taken either, we're not top of their list of investigations.'

'It's appalling, really. How is Cleome coping?'

'You know what she's like; she plays her cards close to her chest. I know she's bothered but she won't admit it.'

'Tarek is worried about the incident; he feels responsible.'

'He's not responsible!'

'I know—but you know what he's like and you can see why he would feel guilty.'

'He really does *not* need to feel guilty, at all.' Amelie was surprised by how much it concerned her that he might be upset, and vowed to reassure him. 'I must ask you. How did you actually meet him? You've never told me.'

'I met him when I used to take Josef swimming at the sports centre, several years ago. He had not long arrived in Flen, and was always kind and helpful but he struck me as lonely too, despite having found a good part-time job. I talked to him a few times, and I had a hunch that like many refugees, what he really needed was a new *home*. That simple. Somewhere he could start to feel like he belonged. So, long story short, I employed him to take care of Josef one summer, during the school holidays, on the days when he didn't have to be at the sports centre, and he was so good and Josef like him so much that at the end of that summer I invited him to live in the bungalow at *Båvenshult*, and to work part-time for me on a regular basis. I told him I would supply the paint etc and pay him to make the place properly habitable. He's been there ever since—over two years now—and he can stay for as long as he wants, as far as I'm concerned. He can drive, and is still a companion to Josef while I work. I hope that one day he will make his own proper home here in Sweden but part of his soul remains in Syria, and when the war is over, he wants to go back there. He is an inspiration,' she paused. 'He knows how to make the best of things, no matter what happens to him, probably because he came from a close and caring family. He is in deep mourning for them, of course, but he always tries to accept what happened and not fight it. Have you ever spoken to him about this?'

'No, not really.'

'He insists that the secret to happiness is to see beauty in the "holy mess of life" as he calls it, and to focus on what is true. He is much-loved in the community of Flen, you know. His character is so warm that he engages everyone, from all walks of life. Our society needs more men like him who can build bridges between the different cultures who live here now.'

They drove on past houses where blue and yellow Swedish flags flew from tall white poles. The fluttering emblems gave the impression of a proud nation, even though many of the old Swedish ways were changing. In the unexpectedly warm weather, people were out on bicycles. Beside the lake shore, a lone fisherman sat with a rod and a brave elderly woman took a dip. At Amelie's insistence, Helen dropped her off at the top of the track, and Amelie walked back down to *Det Lilla Huset*. The air was thick with insects, great clouds of them drifting at the edge of the forest. The landscape was preparing for summer.

When she arrived at the cottage, she was surprised to find Tarek there. Kaia was playing in the glade with Trassel.

'Hi, Tarek,' she said. 'What are you doing here?' He was dressed in jogging bottoms and a creased white t-shirt that revealed slender muscular arms. He also wore a baseball cap over his dark curls, and trainers.

'I thought you might like to come for a run with me, and we could take the dogs.'

'Is my grandmother here?'

'She has gone into town. She said to tell you she'll cook supper tonight.'

'That's nice. Okay, I would love to run but I am very unfit, you know. I haven't jogged since… since…'

'That's alright,' he stepped towards her, and went to touch her arm but then withdrew his hand. Reassurance shone from his eyes. 'I'm pretty unfit too.'

'Okay,' she agreed. 'Just give me a moment to get changed.' She went into the cottage and left Tarek sitting on the garden bench watching the dogs while she hurried upstairs. It was the time of year when the tick population was exploding, and everyone was advised to wear long trousers. She dashed about, searching for her leggings and a clean t-shirt, and feeling flustered that Tarek had called on her so unexpectedly. When she was ready, she locked the cottage door, and joined him outside. At this time of year, daylight spread her long fingers into evening-time, and postponed nightfall for a little longer each day. It was a beautiful afternoon for a run.

'I want to show you something special,' he said. 'And just tell me if you want to stop. I am training for the new football season so I usually do a mix of jogging and walking.'

'Okay, I will certainly need to stop for breath sometimes.' She laughed. 'Where are we heading?'

'To a special place, hidden deep in the forest and high on a hill over the other side of the road. I came across it by accident one day.'

'Sounds good. I've not been over that way before, that I can remember.'

Amelie had tied her hair up in a ponytail to keep it from falling into her face. She was glad she had chosen a long cotton top for protection against the mosquitoes which hovered, suspended in the forest air. She was happy to follow Tarek's schedule of short bursts of sprinting followed by walking. He normally ran early in the morning before the world was fully awake and he needed to get ready for work, he told her. Today was different because it was his day off. If she ever wanted to join him, all she had to do was message, and he would run over the field and through the forest to *Det Lilla Huset*, to meet her.

As they reached the top of the track, the whining noise of a strimmer disturbed the peace. Robban Bengtsson, with lank hair stuck to the sides of his face, swung a machine through a patch of long grass. The metal blades screeched as they hit hidden rocks and rusting car parts beneath the weeds. As they approached, he idled the engine and stared at them.

'Hello Robban! You are doing a good job there!' Amelie called to him.

'My father expects me to keep the long grass cut. It's full of ticks, and mother is afraid of them.'

'I agree with your parents; it's best to keep it cut around the house.' Amelie slowed to a halt, and Tarek stopped too, his dark eyes watchful.

'I don't like doing this work.' Robban remarked, his tone flat.

'I like to work in the garden,' she said. 'I keep the grass cut for *Mormor*. Just make sure you take regular breaks. You look a bit hot.'

'I did a job for Helen over at *Båvenshult*. Did she tell you?' He stood taller as he recollected. 'I took some aerial views of her farm. I'm working on editing them now. She hasn't seen them yet.'

'That sounds good. Listen we'd better keep going. We're going for a run.'

'Okay. See you.'

'That man never looks happy,' Tarek said, once they had crossed over the road and taken the track into the forest. 'I think his father is quite strict with him.'

Amelie glanced at the stubborn set of Tarek's jaw-line. She had never seen him riled before. 'You are concerned?'

'Yes, I am. When you have seen what I have seen, you know an anxious man when you meet one. Something is going on in that family; I can tell by the shadow in his face.'

'You don't know that. He has a learning disability that makes him a little awkward sometimes, that's all.'

'I do know it. I know it here.' He thumped his chest. 'And I listen to my heart.'

The forest was still and quiet. Clouds of insects floated in the rays of bright light that cleaved patches of dense shade. Splotches of vivid green moss, pale lengths of fallen wood and lichened boulders made a sensual tapestry over the earth. The dogs raced through the forest, never straying far. They ran on in silence, with Tarek leading the way. When they were part way up the hill, Amelie slowed to a walk and he slowed too. The dogs gathered beside them, their tongues hanging out.

'I have something to tell you,' he said. 'It is better that you hear it from me.' He stopped and bit his bottom lip, as if searching for the right words. 'The police. They question me. They think I burgled your grandmother's house.'

'No! What utter rubbish!'

'Yes, but you try telling them that. They claim they have a witness. You know, there are some people in Flen who will say anything about a person just because they are an immigrant. They are ignorant, and yet they are listened to.'

'My grandmother and I will never accept that. We will stand up for you.'

'Thank you, but it is not the point really.'

'No, I can see that. I'm so sorry.'

'It's not your place to apologise, but I appreciate what you say. I am concerned for my future here if I am formally charged.' They continued to climb towards the brow of the hill, talking as they picked their way past boulders and fallen wood, with the dogs panting in convoy behind them. Tarek explained that he longed to be accepted by Swedish society and to find a place in it, even if it was only for a short time until he could return home again. He was a peaceful, law abiding man who simply wanted to live a good quiet life, and was angered by the latest turn of events. Amelie listened, respectfully, feeling furious on his behalf. She told him she would do whatever she could to help, and so would Cleome. She felt guilty that they had not foreseen something like this happening when they had asked him to care for the place while they were away.

'What do your friends have to say about this?' she asked. 'Can anyone provide an alibi?'

'Unfortunately not. I was alone on the day of the burglary. Most of my friends are like you, and are really sympathetic but a couple—Ayah and Zain, the brother and sister that you met at Helen's are keeping their distance from me now. It is very sad. They are also getting in with a very bad crowd. I thought they were good people as Ayah is the younger sister of my girlfriend from home who died in the war, and Zain is her twin. I have known them for many years and try to help them because of our past, and because they are young, but sometimes they stir trouble, you know? And they are incredibly naïve.'

'I guess everyone is afraid, being in a new country.'

'Perhaps.'

'Surely you don't need to remain friends with them, if they are treating you in this way?'

'But we all come from the same place. You know, it counts for something, it matters.'

'There is something I will tell you in confidence which I think might help your case. I don't want you to mention it to my grandmother though, in case it frightens her.'

'Okay.'

'Earlier in the year when we had all that heavy snowfall, there was one night when we had a power cut at the cottage. It unsettled me and so I decided to sleep downstairs. After I had fallen asleep, I was woken by Trassel barking at the window. The following morning, the power was back on but when I went outside, a car had driven part way down the track, and there were footprints coming right up to the window. Maybe this incident will shed more light on the case. I didn't mention it to the police while my grandmother was there, but I will contact them when I get back. Perhaps it will take the focus off you.'

Tarek thanked her. They reached the clearing at the top of the hill, and stopped to take in the expansive view of undulating green forest, and in the distance, the sparkling lake. On the opposite side of the hill to that which they had just climbed, was a well-worn path down to a road. Obviously, it was a place that was often visited, but not normally by the route they had just taken. In the clearing, standing in a patch of mown grass, was a tall slab of stone engraved with ancient runic characters outlined in red. It was majestic, and somehow magical. The dogs collapsed onto the grass and lay panting beside it.

'I found out about it. It's called a runestone, and was put up in honour of a person from this area who took part in Viking expeditions, a long, long time ago.'

The afternoon sun bathed the tree tops in golden light. She could see for miles around. Amelie ran her fingers over the stone's surface, and imagined the history associated with the hill where they now stood. She wondered who had engraved the stone, what the mysterious hieroglyphics meant, and tried to imagine all the people who had come to see the stone, through centuries past.

'It is probably a memorial to a dead friend or relative. Probably one thousand years old.'

'One thousand?' She felt a growing sense of awe. It was very special to stand there, and to honour this lost stranger, whoever they were. She was struck by the realisation that all through time, there had been people like her and Tarek who had lost loved ones, for whatever reason. The reasons hardly mattered. It was the expression of love that was so important, and so humbling. She patted the stone.

Tarek touched the stone respectfully too, and then turned and leant his back against it, and studied the view. 'This is such a beautiful country. Very different from what I know but equally beautiful.'

The sun was sinking lower, and after they had caught their breath, they made their way back down the steep side of the hill again. Tarek led, and as they clambered down one particularly steep rock face, he took her hand, to help her balance. Even though it was a practical gesture, there was a flash of intimacy about it too, and Amelie felt the warmth of his fingers, long after he had let go. As the slope became less steep they began to jog again. When the land was flat again, the dogs tore off between the trees, chasing each other and delighting in the sheer joy of being out in the fragrant landscape. Amelie felt her spirits lift at the sight of the dogs running, and at seeing Tarek jog ahead, a short distance in front of her. She barely recognised herself, out here in the wild. It was as if the grief she always carried had slipped away for a while. She was discovering that she was not only a grieving mother, widow and daughter but that she was a living woman too. And she was beginning to realise that the living woman was stronger than she thought.

20

Ramadan

In her journal, Amelie wrote, *Running several times a week with Tarek. I don't have to think. He decides where we go, and what kind of a run we will do—straightforward jogging or interval training. I pour with sweat and it feels cleansing. I push myself to my limits. It passes the time and helps me forget. I don't know why, but I trust Tarek. And I really like being with him. I want to be with him all the time, in fact.* She paused, her pen suspended over the journal. She could hardly believe what she had just written, and was not sure where the words had come from. As a grieving widow, it was surely not right to harbour thoughts of another man, and yet she realised that she did, and that while her feelings were inappropriate in some ways, they were uplifting in others. Her emotion seemed healthy and natural, in many respects. She leant back in her chair at the desk in her bedroom, and remembered how, when she was back in Oxford, the spirit of Nick had come to visit her and whispered that she must embrace life, and live it to the full. She considered her mother and knew exactly what she would say. Kerstin would encourage her feelings for Tarek, wholeheartedly. She would tell her to "go for it" and follow her heart.

Restless, she abandoned her journal and went downstairs to where her grandmother sat, quietly knitting in her favourite armchair. What would her grandmother say if she saw what she had just written? Would she be shocked or disappointed? She remembered the day when her grandmother had touched her arm when they had seen Tarek out fishing on the lake but there was a big gap between that, and the conscious statement she had just written. At the prospect of ever telling her beloved *mormor* that she had feelings for Tarek, Amelie was dismayed, and even slightly ashamed.

'I'm going for a swim!' she called out.

Cleome called back, 'Enjoy!'

She stood on the floating platform tethered to the lake's shore at the bottom of the glade. A warm breeze drifted across the water's surface, and she lifted her nose to its fresh fragrance, like an animal reading a scent. She clasped the grab rails on either side of a metal ladder which led down into the water, and dipped her toe. In the subterranean world beneath the surface, young reeds swayed and tiny fish darted. The sun dazzled, sending reflected sparkles to play on the skin of her face. The world she was about to plunge into was inviting, pure and radiant.

Amelie leapt, and her long slender body plunged into the cool, bubbling arms of the lake. When her head broke back through the surface, she gasped and let out several small squeals of shock and joy. Sensing that she must keep warm, she did a steady breast stroke away from the raft, scanning the landscape that was so devoid of humanity. It was a wonder, a marvel, to push her bare arms through the clean water and feel it cool under her belly. The lake imparted energy and made her feel properly alive, for the first time in a very long time. She swam for about fifteen minutes, keeping close to the pontoon, before her arms started to ache with the cold. Returning swiftly to the ladder, she grabbed it and climbed out. After wrapping a large beach towel around her body, she sat cross-legged on the warm wooden decking, breathing raggedly.

'*Hej!*' a voice called behind her. Tarek loitered some distance away with one hand raised, and in the other, he held a full mug. 'Your grandmother sent me down with a hot drink for you. She told me you would need one.'

'Come on down,' Amelie called back.

He picked his way through the grass to the ramp that led down onto the pontoon. 'I don't wish to disturb your privacy,' he apologised.

'Don't worry. I just had the first swim of the year. Come and join me. I'll put these sunchairs up for us.' She stood and tucked the towel securely beneath her armpits. Tarek averted his gaze and looked out at the lake. She set up the chairs and took the mug from him before sitting down. 'Join me.' She gestured at the empty seat. 'Are you not going to have a coffee too?'

'It's Ramadan.' He perched on the opposite chair and narrowed his gaze to the horizon. His dark wavy hair lifted in the breeze; his beard was neatly clipped. 'I came to see if you wanted to go for a run but I guess not, if you have just been swimming.'

'No, I'm not ready for a run after that; but tell me about Ramadan,' she asked. 'I had a couple of friends at school who did it but I never really understood it.'

'Ramadan begins each year with the new moon in the ninth month of the Islamic calendar.'

'I didn't even know there was an Islamic calendar.'

'Yes, there is... Anyway, for the whole of Ramadan—about one month—we don't eat, drink or smoke during the hours from sunrise to sunset which is pretty challenging if you are living in Sweden and it's summertime!' His face broke into a grin, and he glanced at her.

'Well, to give up smoking is a very good thing, I'd say.'

'I know, I know. You always say that, being a nurse.'

'I say that as your friend, and I feel bad drinking this in front of you now.' Amelie tucked a strand of wet hair behind her ear. Her cheeks felt pink in the sun. Her freckles would be appearing.

'Oh please, don't feel bad at all. This is my choice. You having a coffee now is not a problem for me.'

'So, what is the thinking behind Ramadan? I don't think many of us non-Muslims understand why you would put yourself through such a thing.'

'Well, it is different for everybody. Even though I am Muslim, I am not a religious man so I am not too bothered about praying and so on—although sometimes I go to the mosque when I'm in the mood. I do Ramadan for self-discipline, to keep my body healthy, and to respect the traditions from my homeland. I think it's good to know a little hunger from time to time, not just take everything for granted. My mother was very religious. She taught me that the Qur'an was revealed during this month. Like many people, she believed that Ramadan is the time when the gates of heaven are open and the gates to hell are shut so her prayers were more effective, and if she prayed a lot, she would win more favour with Allah. I always think about my family at Ramadan, and I try to remember my place in the world and be humble. It is my view that religions make wars but that Allah is everywhere and is for everyone, if they want Him. The Allah who is here in my heart is peaceful, never a reason to fight. And I don't like being labelled by any of this, by the way. I am never going to be a label,' he grinned, and there was a spark of intimacy in their shared gaze, before she turned away.

'I agree with you there about the labels, and it's supposed to be healthy to fast regularly,' she said, watching the shimmering water, and hardly daring to turn back to him. His presence was making her heart race a little. It was not just the way his gaze seemed to search her soul but her body's response to him that was disconcerting. Longing swelled in her belly and she pulled the towel down over her knees. There was a mischievous energy at play around the two of them that seemed to have a life of its own.

'Yes, and Ramadan is good for the mind and soul too, don't forget. That is also why I do it.'

'Well, I admire you… and your English is very good.'

'Oh, I don't know about that.'

Friendship was deepening between the two of them, and as the conversation went on, a new warm emotion wove its way through every sentence they spoke in spite of Amelie's reservations. She knew it, and sensed that he knew it too. When he looked at her again, she became absorbed by the tender expression in his dark chocolatey eyes. His voice was soft, his Syrian accent endearing. 'And I must add that I am a practical man,' he was saying. 'At the moment we have daylight for seventeen or eighteen hours here. That length of time without any liquid is not sensible when I am teaching sport so I sip water at midday. It is not good, settling my fellow Muslims in the north of this country where they have twenty-four hours of sunlight now. I feel for them if they are religious and in a strange land where the sun never sets at Ramadan. It will be very hard for them.'

'It must make it impossible. How do they cope?'

'Some people stick to the daylight hours from their old homes. Others are incredibly disciplined.'

'Do you know many people doing Ramadan now?'

'Sure, I have Muslim friends in town and there's a small mosque in Flen where I sometimes go to pray but it's not easy, if I am completely honest—I am always remembering the joy in my family and our community back home in Syria. We would eat dates and drink water the way the Prophet Muhammed did; my mother would make special meals, and there was comfort in the prayers. These days Ramadan can make me sad if I think of everything that's gone. The whole way of life, smashed to pieces by the war.'

They were quiet then, for a minute or two, listening to the lake lap against the jetty. 'You are getting cold?' he asked suddenly.

'Oh no, I'm fine. This drink is warming me up.'

Tarek watched her carefully now, and she felt herself blush again.

'We must swim together in future!' he said. 'It's too hot to keep running. Would you like to swim with me one day soon when the weather is good?'

'That would be great.' She smiled, and as if it had a life of its own, her spirit soared. She knew that by encouraging Tarek she was approaching a crossroads in her recovery, and she was mindful that like her, he was quite vulnerable in some ways, but it was hard to ignore the warm encouragement in his eyes and his quick smiles that mirrored her own. She had a choice about the path she took, and a blossoming conviction about the one she would choose.

Something seemed caught at the back of the drawer in the side table as Amelie rattled it to push it shut. She felt around with her fingers, and then hooked out a strip of four yellowing black-and-white photographs.

'This is you! You are so beautiful! And who is this with you? Written on the back in pencil is *"London, 1978"* in your handwriting.'

Cleome, who sat knitting in her chair, looked up. 'Oh, I can't remember now,' she lied.

'Never mind. I'll leave them in here. Your young friend was very attractive too,' Amelie remarked.

Cleome's heart beat wildly. After Amelie had gone upstairs, she tiptoed to the drawer and retrieved the photographs. She spread a hand across her chest in an attempt to slow her heartbeat, and peered at the strip through bright pink reading glasses. She had forgotten about them, lost in the back of the drawer, but remembered the day as if it were yesterday. She recalled the shock of seeing Catherine's pitch-black eyes and the curly hair which grew down to her waist, that first time— it had been so hard to take in. Squashing close together in the photo booth. Her pungent Biba perfume. Giggling like schoolgirls. Being dazzled by the flashes. The entire clandestine visit, when she had snuck away to England, leaving Wilhelm at home to look after Kerstin. Wilhelm would never have understood, and she had been too afraid to test him. She and Catherine had sat in a café in Chelsea, later stumbled across the booth, and taken two sets of pictures; one each to keep.

Amelie must have slipped back downstairs and now called from the kitchen, asking something about potatoes, and Cleome hastily replaced the photographs and closed the drawer before replying. She could not settle back to her knitting after that, reliving all the pain that had come, soon after. She had turned to Antonia that time too—her sister, who for all her fierceness, could console.

Dusk fell so slowly that evening that it seemed the sun might never set. Amelie had gone out, and Cleome, left alone in the cottage, wandered from one room to the next, restlessly. She mulled over the photographs, and the card which she had hidden in a drawer upstairs along with the letter. It felt as if the past was closing in on her again, and she was afraid, suddenly. A heavy sense of discomfort lodged in her chest and pain shot down one arm. She felt nauseous and broke into a sweat. She cried out and reached for a chair and dropped down onto it, gasping. Fumbling in her pinafore pocket, she found her medicine and hastily swallowed it.

Amelie bore a hot dish before her, covered with tin foil. She wore the oven gloves from *Det Lilla Huset*. She could not knock on the wooden door as her hands were full, and so called out, '*Hej!*'

Tarek opened the door, and his dark eyebrows rose in surprise.

'I cooked a Syrian dish for you to eat after sunset,' she said. 'It's a bit hot.'

'That is very kind! Here, bring it around the side of the house. There's a table outside where I like to eat.' He slipped his bare feet into a pair of battered Swedish clogs, and led her around the side of the tiny cottage and through a gate to a wooden table set on timber decking. Close by was a shadowy paddock where horses rested, flicking their tails beneath the trees.

'What is it? It smells very good.' He leant forward to inhale the fragrance.

'Halal lamb and cinnamon stew. I have no idea what it will be like. I don't want to intrude but if you want, I can keep you company for some meals during Ramadan—when you are not with other people, and so on.'

'But you're not Muslim.'

'It doesn't matter. I won't do it to be Muslim, I'll do it because you have taken me out running and I owe you. It will be good for me too. You can teach me some halal recipes. I would like it. *Mormor* can join us sometimes.'

Tarek swatted a mosquito away, and looked out at the darkening field, as if struggling to suppress his emotions. 'Okay,' he agreed. 'Will you stay now and share this?'

'Yes please, if you don't mind. I'm starving!' She wore a long-sleeved top and trousers despite the warmth so that she did not get bitten by insects. Tarek lit incense coils to help keep them at bay, and they sat either side of the wooden table surrounded by the pixilated dusk, and ate the stew.

'This is very good,' he acknowledged. 'You know, before the conflict, my mother, grandmother and aunties would spend hours at the market, buying special food for Ramadan. We would look forward to it every year. I often wonder how those who are left behind in the bombed cities manage now? Ramadan is a period of generosity when strangers give food and take great care of each other, even offering gifts, like you have just done for me. Now there are severe shortages, even of basics like clean drinking water and electricity, prices have rocketed and everyone is hungry. Syrians at home will find it hard to offer anything to others, and besides, most people are too afraid to celebrate anything. I pray for them. I pray that they will survive, and peace will come to my country.'

'I hope people there will find a way to mark Ramadan like us, even if it is just with small things,' she agreed.

'You know, all these people in power? They think one more bomb will bring peace. All we ever hear is that they are killing people to get peace, using chemical weapons to secure peace. One more war will bring peace. Are they crazy? Do they not listen to themselves? How did a bomb ever bring peace, I ask you?'

She stared through a small copse of trees. Beyond it, stripes of lemon light from the sunken sun coloured the horizon. 'You are right,' she agreed. 'This world of ours needs to change. Are the police still bothering you, by the way? I told them about the footprints.'

'They have backed off as their so-called witness proved to be unreliable—but there have been more burglaries around here apparently, and I can feel them watching me, if you know what I mean. Plus people are gossiping. Even in my own community, they talk behind my back. They say there is no smoke without fire.'

'I'm so sorry. You know that *Mormor* and I don't believe the rumours for one moment. We know it wasn't you.'

'Thanks. I just wish I could prove it.' He finished his meal, and lit a cigarette.

The following afternoon, the sun beat down on the forest. It was unseasonably hot for the time of year. Cleome had left earlier that morning to meet a friend for lunch in Stockholm, and Amelie had the place to herself. Tarek messaged to ask if she would like to swim. As she waited for him to jog from *Båvenshult*, she felt as if she was being drawn by an invisible force towards her new destiny, and had little power over her own actions, if any. She suspected that she might feel guilty later on, but for the time being she was simply happy and excited. She did not feel especially nervous and got ready to meet him with the minimum of fuss. There was no point in dressing up. Her face was clean of the mascara she sometimes wore and her hair was simply tied back as it was about to get soaked and tangled by lake water. She removed the gold chain around her neck that threaded through Nick's wedding ring. She always took it off when she was swimming in case she lost it but this time, placing it down on the chest of drawers and leaving it behind felt significant. She stalled for a moment, touched his ring delicately with her fingertips, picked it up and kissed it, and then replaced it on the wooden surface. She took a deep breath, and pulled on a t-shirt and cotton skirt over her swimming costume, grabbed a towel, and when Tarek arrived at the cottage door, they headed down to the jetty together with Trassel scarpering ahead of them.

'I don't know about Muslim culture or Syria,' she puffed as she swam alongside him. She was hungry to learn more about him and the country he came from. 'So if you teach me about your world, I'll teach you about mine. Does that sound good to you?'

'Yes, very good.' He grinned, ducked beneath the water and swam several metres below the surface. Amelie smiled, and the sensation was so unfamiliar that she stalled and treaded water. When his head and shoulders broke through the water's surface, his dark hair was flattened. 'Now let me tell you something that has nothing to do with my culture but that I learned since I've been in exile, okay?'

'Okay,' she said.

'Grief is like a rucksack. You might have to carry it for a long time. Sometimes, when you have had enough though, you can take it off and put it down. And sometimes, you can take things out of the rucksack and leave them by the roadside. You won't have to carry everything forever but you will probably always be carrying something. That is what I have learned..'

Amelie turned on her back, and floated, squinting up at the sun. 'Good lesson,' she murmured.

'The world according to Tarek Mourad.' Tarek, also now floating on his back, laughed at himself.

'So what other wisdom do you have to offer me?'

'Pretend, if that's all you can do. It kind of works.'

While his conversation had serious undercurrents, he made it sound light and acceptable, as if devastating loss was an everyday fact of life. To her surprise, far from being tactless, his openness came as a huge relief.

Swathes of forest had turned fresh green in the finer weather. Nothing stays the same, she thought, nothing lasts, things always change. A warm breeze caressed her floating body. There were glimpses of happiness in her days now—during exchanges with her grandmother, or at moments out walking with Trassel, or like now, spending time with Tarek. She rolled over in the water, as did he. He smiled in the mischievous way he had, and she smiled back. Something about him gave her hope. As they swam out into the bay, he pointed over at the little house on the rock.

'Empty, as always,' he said. 'Such a waste.'

The water was not warm enough for them to stay out for long, and they turned back towards the jetty. He swam on his side, watching her with admiration glimmering in his eyes and a smile playing about the corners of his mouth. The tension between them grew stronger with every stroke they took, and they swam closer, side by side.

'Wait,' he urged, insistent but soft. She stopped, and they trod water, facing each other. He wasn't smiling anymore and wore a serious expression, anxiety lingering in his slight frown.

'I like you, Amelie.' His voice was low.

She looked into his eyes, the eyes that seemed to pull her towards him with their own magnetic energy, and found her own quiet voice. 'I like you too, Tarek.' His face broke into a radiant smile then. Sunshine sparkled on the water's surface around them as he raised one curved hand and gently cupped the side of her face. His fingers were warm. He leant forward and kissed her, his lips were also warm and wet with lake water, and his beard prickly. She had not been kissed for so long that it was as if her body realised what it had been missing, and awoke with a life of its own. It edged through the water towards him and they pressed together, the whole length of them, their legs entwining, exchanging instant body heat in the cool water. They kissed for a little longer before pulling apart so that they did not both sink below the water's surface. She did not know what to do next. They needed to swim back to the shore but she wanted the kiss to go on forever, it was so sweet and so tender.

'Let's race back and get warm,' he said, and she nodded and struck out through the water beside him.

Back on the jetty, they both shivered with cold as Trassel bounded around at their feet, delighted to have them both safe on dry land again. They laughed at her and wrapped themselves in thick towels before putting their arms around each other again, and holding each other close. She lifted her hands to his bearded cheeks and kissed him again. This time she could linger, and take her time, with her feet pressed down on the warm wood and the pontoon rocking gently as the lake water rippled beneath them. She found that kissing him was as natural and right as it had once been to kiss Nick. When they pulled apart a little, he pushed a damp tendril of hair from her face and gazed at her in wonder. 'You are a beautiful woman, Amelie,' he said and his dark eyes shone with tenderness and desire. 'I have been wanting to kiss you for a long time but I wasn't sure that it was right for you. Are you okay?'

'Yes,' Amelie nodded. She had rarely been so certain about anything before. She did not want to think about Nick now or to stop what she had started. There would be time later to work all that out.

'I can see in your eyes something has changed.' He studied her. 'It looks like you are here with me now, and not still lost in some other place.'

'Really?'

'Yes, but I wanted to be sure. I didn't want to learn later that I had been dreaming you were ready to be with me when you weren't.'

'There is one thing I must ask you.'

'Anything.'

'The woman at the Easter lunch. Ayah. In the blue hijab. She likes you.'

'Yes, she does. But she is not the woman for me. She is the sister of my old girlfriend, and has promised herself to my friend.'

A wave of relief rolled over Amelie. She had not realised how important it was to her to learn that Tarek was free and not involved elsewhere. The small worm of doubt that had plagued her, disappeared. They wandered back up through the glade, hand in hand with Trassel running in wide circles around them. The afternoon sun still lingered above the tree tops and warmed their backs. Overhead, the sky was clear blue. Around them, the forest was thronging with life—birds sang and everywhere there was fresh growth.

When they reached the cottage, Amelie saw straight away that her grandmother's car was parked in the barn. Tarek saw it too and let go of her hand. They exchanged glances.

'We haven't done anything wrong,' she said.

'I know but this type of thing can be hard for people to understand,' he replied.

'I know, you are right. I wonder where she is. *Mormor!*' she called, and had to admit to feeling relief when she spotted her grandmother over in the orchard, tending to her hens. She frequently went straight to them on arriving back at the cottage, and there was a good chance that she had not seen them kissing.

'I will go now,' Tarek said to her, as he waved to Cleome in the distance. 'Your grandmother will not think anything of us swimming together.'

'I don't have to answer to her, or anyone else.'

'I know, but people can be strange, and we need to be discreet.'

'My grandmother is a worldly woman. She would never gossip about us, you know.'

'I know, and for that I am grateful, but the immigrant community in Flen are another matter. They will have plenty to say, and they will blame you, not me.'

She nodded.

'We will see each other again soon,' he said. Amelie met his gaze, saw the intensity there, and then lifted her hand to wave farewell to him, as if nothing had just happened. She watched him turn and run back up the side of the glade, dodging between the boulders, and then waited for her grandmother to come over.

'Did you have a nice swim?' she asked.

'Yes, we thought it was too hot to go running,' she replied, truthfully.

'Very sensible,' Cleome nodded.

'How was the lunch with your friend?'

'Oh, you know, it was fine,' her grandmother replied with her eyes focused on the distant lake. Amelie sensed that she was holding something back but then dismissed the notion. It was probably her own subterfuge making her suspicious of everything.

As she stood beneath the warm shower, she touched her lips where Tarek had kissed her, and smiled. Back in the bedroom, she dressed quickly, roughly dried her hair with a towel, and reached for the gold chain to fix it back around her neck. Her good mood waivered. Could she be happy? Was it callous to be carrying on, and to find pleasure in another man? A sense of shame curled its octopus tentacles around her.

21

Wednesday 23rd May

The 23rd of May was Bertie's birthday. He would have been two.
Amelie awoke with a lurch. She squinted at the clock. It was ten to four. Bertie was born at two minutes past midnight. At this moment, two years ago, he had been nearly four hours old. She recalled the darkness outside the hospital window, the tender way she had cradled him in her arms, got used to holding him, had given him his first feed at her breast, the magical sensation of the milk coming, the way she and Nick were cocooned in a pool of light from the lamp over her bed, how they had marvelled at the sheer wonder of their little boy. She remembered those first quiet hours of his life, before the dawn had risen on another new day in Oxford.

Outside, the borrowed cockerel crowed, and the birds in the forest struck up a hectic, tuneful chorus. A compelling urge to be alone drove her out of bed.

Down at the pontoon, Cleome's small boat bumped lazily against a buoy. A light breeze rippled the water's surface, and sparked a thousand silvery reflections from the rising sun. Amelie, wearing a jumper and shorts, climbed down into the small vessel. She untied it from the mooring, set the oars into the rowlocks and, dabbing one into the water and then another, manoeuvred the little boat out into the open lake.

There was not a soul around and all she could hear was the plaintive call of a goshawk, the rustle of reeds at the water's edge, and the rhythmic splash and bubbling rush as she pulled the oars steadily through the water. There was no current pulling her one way or another—only the empty stretch of lake, fringed by dense forest and canopied over with brightening sky.

When she had rowed around the corner of the bay and out of sight of *Det Lilla Huset*, she pulled in the oars and sat in the gently rocking boat. Kneeling to look over the side, she watched fish swim amongst weeds in the clear water—the usual schools of tiny perch darted one way and then the other, and the occasional bigger slab of piscine flesh flexed its way past with nonchalant ease. After a time, she lay down in the hull, the wood hard and warm beneath her shoulders and hips. A tiny pool of water dampened one elbow. The boat felt like a cradle, and reduced her line of vision to the white blue sky above.

There was no way to make sense of losing a child. There was no escaping the ache of loss that had taken residence in her body. There was no justice, there was no reason or meaning or explanation that could soothe her. It all just *was*. And the only truth she knew was that she would never stop loving Bertie, even though he no longer shared this world with her. In the same way, she would never stop loving Nick or her mother. Love did not cease simply because a person had passed on. Nor should it, surely.

And yet, with him gone, she was so alone in the world. The boat rocked a little, water lapped against wood, the air wafted fresh and clean; the simplicity of the natural world curled around her. Lake Båven showed her, starkly, how alone she was but that there was still sweetness in life. Everything was as it was.

After a while, her back ached and she sat up and hugged her knees, looking about. Lake Båven showed her also that, if she chose to look at life with slightly different eyes, everyone was alone—and yet was not. Everyone was part of a swirling mass of crazy energy where things broke and died or got lost or injured or sick, and yet still the rest of life carried on. Tragedy was tidied up, swept away and dealt with, with almost indecent haste. New things grew, the sky changed from bright to dark and back again, the rain still pelted down on a winter's afternoon, the fish swam by, the birds cried overhead, the sun rose and set, the stars came out at night, sparkling like diamonds as they had done for centuries and would do for centuries to come. Lake Båven showed her the teeming, unending abundance of life and made her see how she was a minute speck in the hugeness of it all. The lake showed her this; that she was not important and yet that she was, that she was tiny but that she was somehow sacred too. She was a part of the churning, swirling mass of living creatures. Lake Båven showed her place in the scheme of things; she did not pretend or disguise anything or make up complicated stories about what must be done and when and how, in the way that her life in Oxford did. She did not trick her into thinking that because she worked hard in a noble profession, she would get a good life or could control what happened, or that because she paid her mortgage on time and was kind to her neighbours, she would be safe and secure and somehow avoid death. How come so few people saw life for what it was? Even as a nurse, she had not really accepted the truth of it. Her Oxford life had been a trick of mirrors, a game played blindfold where the importance of what you wore, where you shopped and worked, who you knew, what you knew, and how constantly busy you were, steered everyone, not just her.

Out in the little rowing boat, with no sense of what time it was or having to be anywhere or do anything: this was some kind of real truth. Her bones knew it. Her soul knew it. And perhaps, this simple sense of *being* could be an anchor of sorts?

She had lost her beautiful, soft-skinned boy whose blond curls had clouded his head like a halo, whose eyes shone quartz blue, who knew no malice, and was only just beginning his life. His perfect body had grown inside hers, and exactly two years ago, she had pushed him out into the world and fallen in love with him, so absolutely and utterly— a new kind of love, a first love, a pure love. All the other loves had paled that day—even, if she was honest, the love she held for Nick. It was only when she became a mother to Bertie and held him in her arms that her truth had shifted, and her heart had known for the first time the infinite, boundless, "I would give my life for yours" kind of love. In an instant, she had known that she would do anything for this little soul; she truly would have given her life if it meant that he kept his. She still would.

She sensed the familiar swell of emotion rise in her chest and sobbed noisily, swiping tears away with the back of her hand. How could she be given all that, and then have it plucked away? Surely it was cruelty of the worst kind? What had she done to deserve it? What had Bertie done? Nothing. She knew for certain that he had done nothing. Bertie had been blameless, innocent, thriving. He had been the perfect little boy.

And as Lake Båven cradled her and rocked her and absorbed her tears, and as the breeze caressed her and wrapped its gentle arms around her curved shoulders, and as the hawk cried and the fishes swam beneath her, a kind of peace slowly settled on Amelie. And in the same way that she knew the infinite love for Bertie which had filled every cell of her body, she also realised that this world, this natural world, offered her love too—a raw kind of love with no false promises or man-made rules. Looking around her at the sky, the lake, the forest: they were what they were; they did not promise food or shelter or any kind of sustenance and yet they offered her a true place in the scheme of things. There was abundance, beauty, nourishment if she chose it. Or there were biting insects, fear, and isolation if she chose that. She had a choice, still, about how she responded to it all. She could not control what had happened to Bertie, her mother or Nick. She would never be able to control what happened around her, but she could choose how to react, and in her choice lay her power, and in her power lay her hope. Lake Båven showed her this. She peered over the side of the boat, and down into the clear depths, and sunbeams sparkled on the surface, dazzling her. The risen sun warmed her damp jumper. The air was fragrant with nectar from the shore, and laced with the promise of freshness, a new beginning.

She gathered the oars and rowed back around the headland.

Tarek stood on the wooden raft, and bent to grab the end of the boat to help to moor it.

'I came to see if you want to run or swim. Your grandmother told me what day it is. She is out looking for you; she is worried. I am so sorry. Are you okay?' he asked, troubled brown eyes meeting hers.

'I think so, yes.'

'I went through the forest and I saw the boat floating empty on the lake. I thought there was some kind of trouble,' he went on, running his long fingers back through his hair.

'It's okay. I didn't mean to worry you or *Mormor*. I could not think of anything else but Bertie. I just lay down for a while.'

'You know me, I see awful things everywhere,' he said, with a nervous laugh.

'I know, I get that.' She rubbed his arm reassuringly. 'Sorry.'

'No problem. I try to be like a Swedish man, but in my heart I am still Syrian, with a head full of war.'

'My son would have been two years old today,' she whispered, blinking down at the bleached wood and fighting back more tears. Tarek moved as if to embrace her, and then conscious that her grandmother might see them, drew back. He brushed her hand with his fingertips, in a secret exchange. 'I know. I understand. I will call your grandmother. I told her you would surely be home soon.' He made the call, and Amelie exchanged a few words with Cleome too, and apologised for worrying her. Tarek and Amelie sat down on the jetty and dangled their feet in the water.

He smiled sadly. 'Tell me all about your son, and I will listen. I want to hear every detail.'

She glanced at him. Nobody had asked her to talk about Bertie, not once, since the accident. He nodded encouragement. 'He used to say the funniest things,' she began. When she faltered, he did not attempt to fill the silence, and she resumed, describing in detail her tousled-haired boy with his love of music and cuddles and animals, and life. When she was finished, it was like a weight had been lifted from her. 'I'm going for a swim,' she announced. She peeled off her clothes down to her underwear, and climbed down the ladder into the cool clear lake. 'Oh my God, it's gorgeous.'

'I'm coming in too!' Tarek said suddenly, and tore his clothes off too, before diving in. 'I love this country!' he cried, emerging from the water. 'I love this country where we are so free and can swim in a beautiful lake!'

While they were swimming, Cleome arrived with a tray bearing a flask of hot coffee, some cups, a bag of pastries, and a couple of towels over one arm.

'Here, take the towels, Am,' she instructed, adding, 'I'm sorry, Tarek, but it's breakfast time. You can take or leave the food as you want but I thought I should offer some sustenance.'

Tarek decided that on this one special occasion he would accept the offer of food after sunrise, and the three of them sat, enjoying warm drinks and sugary cinnamon buns. When they had finished, Cleome headed back up to the house, muttering that she had things to get on with.

'Something is bothering her,' Amelie said, her brow creasing. 'But she won't say what.'

'Maybe she is just worrying about her granddaughter. It's only natural, after all.'

'Maybe, but I think it's more than that.'

Tarek and Amelie lay on in the mounting sunshine drying their young bodies. Mindful that Cleome might reappear, they did not touch but exchanged warm glances instead. It did not feel right anyway, to kiss on this day of all days. As they lay and chatted, a strange humming sound arose from the tree tops at the side of the lake and disturbed their peace. Tarek sat up. A drone circled above them like a flying giant cockroach. He punched his fist in the air at it, and let out a stream of angry Arabic.

'Stop it, you son of a bitch!' he shouted.

Amelie stood up, shaded her eyes with her hand, and fixed a stern gaze on the flying machine. It swung around and disappeared back behind the trees.

'If anyone sees that and knows we are out here alone, it to make more trouble for me in Flen.' Tarek compressed his lips.

'No, it won't. Besides, who would Robban show it to? Nobody is going to be interested.'

'You are naïve. When it comes to an immigrant hanging out with a local white girl, a certain type of person is very interested and can turn nasty. His father certainly knows that.'

'I'm not sure Robban does, though. With his Asperger's, he won't realise the sensitivity, and would probably never show his father anyway. He probably thinks that filming us is a good joke and he's being funny. I'll have a word with him, tell him to erase the film.'

'I don't understand him at all. Maybe you're right. But if a video of us two lying here in the sun together ever did get around, it would make life worse for you as well as me in Flen, and I would not want that. Plus the fewer ripples in the pond at the moment with the police still watching me, the better.'

'It will be okay, I promise,' she insisted. 'I will speak with Robban.'

When they were both dressed and about to leave, Tarek turned to her. 'May I say something?'

'Of course.'

'You know the terrible pain you felt this morning? It doesn't stay forever. Some days already, I can forget it—not them, not my family and my friends; I will never forget them all my days—but *it*. I still remember, but it doesn't hurt so much. You cannot rush it, you don't get to decide, you have to wait—but this change happens.'

'In its own time,' Amelie nodded. She looked around her at the forest and lake coming to life beneath the summer sun, and understood that what Tarek told her was true. There was a rhythm to these things—to darkness and to light, to ice and to sun, to grief and to peace.

'No matter how bad the fears are, time is stronger,' he went on. 'Time is more powerful. Time heals us. You will see. You won't forget but your power will grow if you let it—like mine has. You will see.'

22

New Moon of Horses

Cleome did not need to read the news headlines to know that there was a heatwave in Sweden. It lingered over *Det Lilla Huset* like a heavy blanket woven from still sunlight, thousands of lazy insects, and the fragrance of roses climbing the cottage walls. Amelie mowed the grass wearing long trousers tucked into boots, her legs liberally sprayed with Cleome's herbal insect repellent to lessen the likelihood of tick bites. She created a wide pathway to the lakeside, and two others leading into the forest on either side of the glade. Ticks infested the long grass, and some carried Lyme disease or even worse, so it was imperative to keep walkways clear. Each evening before bed, both women checked their bodies from head to toe for signs of the tiny burrowing creatures, as well as thoroughly inspecting Trassel's coat.

Even though she was not sleeping well and was tired, Cleome insisted that after the grass cutting was finished, she would teach Amelie how to fish. While Amelie rowed them out over the water, Trassel stood in the bow with her paws braced against the hull and her nose to the breeze. They dropped a buoyed net across one corner of the bay and sat for a little while, enjoying the sunshine. Amelie told her grandmother that she had spoken with Robban Bengtsson after he had filmed her and Tarek sunbathing. In his naivety, Robban had not understood that his actions were inappropriate. He had asked Amelie all sorts of questions about what privacy meant.

It had not escaped Cleome's notice that when Tarek was around, Amelie's energy fizzed with the electricity of a woman in love. She detected shifts in the couple's body language that many would not notice—the glances, fleeting smiles and softened voices. While to her, signs of romance shone crystal clear, she respected the fact that the couple were not yet ready to talk about it, and guarded their secret fiercely. She knew how cruel gossip could be, and how whiplash from the human tongue often left the deepest scars.

Amelie picked up the oars again, and rowed them back to the shore.

Cleome had fished the lake every summer for years. She had a routine, and after leaving the net all night, she and Amelie rose early the next morning and rowed out to retrieve the buoys and gather it in. They inspected each plump *gös* that had been trapped before whispering "thank you" to them for sacrificing their lives so they could eat, and placing them carefully in a bucket. Back at the jetty, Cleome taught Amelie to scale and gut each fish with deft precision, using the sharp knife that she kept especially for the purpose in the small shed there.

As they made their way back slowly through the glade with Amelie carrying the bucket of fish, she issued a heavy sigh.

'What is wrong, *Mormor*? Please tell me. I hate to see you so distressed at the moment.'

'It's nothing,' Cleome shook her head. 'Just grief. You know how it is.'

'Are you sure? I've noticed you are making far more trips into Stockholm than normal. Is there something you're not telling me?'

Cleome spread her hand over her chest. Where to begin? She thought, desperately. 'There's nothing wrong, don't worry. I often have phases of going into the city. It livens me up a bit, especially as I spend so much time stuck out in this forest.'

'I sense it's more than that.'

Cleome focused her gaze on a patch of long grass, and frowned. It was typical of Amelie to recognise that something was different, in the same way that she had noticed sparks in the air whenever Tarek was around. The two of them were so alike—both intuitive souls who could read a person's mood at a glance. Amelie would not easily be fobbed off, and so she decided that she must divert her attention, lead her off the trail. 'I've noticed that you and Tarek seem to be getting along well,' she said.

'Ah.' Amelie nodded. Cleome felt immediately guilty for having exposed her granddaughter's secret. She could see how she struggled to reply.

'Of course, it's none of my business,' she said hastily. 'I'm sorry. I shouldn't be so damned nosy. You don't have to explain yourself to me.'

'But I want to,' Amelie blurted. 'Sit down at the garden table. Let me put the fish in the fridge and make us some coffee.'

When, after ten minutes, she returned with coffee and biscuits, she set them down on the wooden table and poured out the black steaming liquid from a jug into a pair of mugs. 'What do you know about Tarek?'

'I know that his girlfriend was killed by a sniper, right in front of him.'

Amelie winced. 'I didn't know that! How awful. He hasn't said anything.'

'It was the last straw, the reason he finally fled his homeland. Too painful, perhaps, to tell you about it—or knowing Tarek, more like he doesn't want to pile anymore sadness onto your plate. He is a kind and selfless man.'

'Yes, he is…'

'And devilishly handsome.' Cleome chuckled as her granddaughter blushed. 'He was quite the hero in the refugee camp in Greece, you know. He fought for better living conditions and for the children to get some kind of schooling. He raised money by putting photographs on social media and recruiting help from a charity. Don't ask me how it worked but he was clever, and he did it for everyone there, not for himself. It was a refreshing and impressive reaction to dire circumstances, I'd say.'

'He's modest about all that.'

'I'm sure he is.'

'He understands me, I think.'

'I can believe that too. But I think it's more than understanding; he has real feelings for you. I can see it in his eyes.'

Amelie blushed again. 'Do you think I'm awful, so soon after…?'

'Not at all.'

'Sometimes, I feel so guilty about taking any pleasure at all.'

'That's the way it goes. But guilt is not a feeling that we should pay much attention to. It can destroy us if we're not careful.'

'So you don't judge me?'

'Oh Am, not at all. And your secret is safe with me. I won't tell a soul.'

'Thank you. To be honest, right now I'd rather no-one knew. It's very early days and who knows what will happen.'

'Just be careful of those friends of his—the flirtatious one who wears a blue hijab. Helen has confided to me that she cannot warm to her or her brother, and it's rare for Helen to react to anyone in such a way. She must have good reason.'

'Tarek says they are trouble-makers too.'

'All the more reason to stay on your guard. And on the other side of the same coin, there is a resurgence of extreme right-wing attitudes in the area too. They are a tiny minority but still, there are some who will make a noise about a white woman dating an immigrant. The women at the knitting group, for example, can be racist, with Lotta Bengtsson being one of the worst offenders. It's nobody's business of course, and you must live your life your way; but don't be naïve. For all the progress we have made with our multicultural policies, it is a sensitive time in Sweden after the high influx of people seeking asylum, and feelings are running wild. Some are going back to the old divisive views we never thought we would see again.'

'There is always small-mindedness with some.'

'I know, and it will settle, but it's not a good time right now.'

The chickens made dust baths in the dry earth opposite the barn. While Amelie walked Trassel in the forest, Cleome picked young leaves, flowers and roots from her garden to dry in the paper bags that were pegged to a line of string, pinned across the kitchen ceiling. As she laboured, she brooded that she was foolish to keep her secret from Amelie. It was true that she had been going to Stockholm a lot since the middle of May, on the pretext of visiting the art galleries or meeting old friends—and she had only told her granddaughter white lies; she had indeed been to the galleries and had seen an "old acquaintance". Against all her sister's advice, and in some respects, against her own better judgment too, she had been meeting Catherine who had come to spend a month in Stockholm. Catherine had sent her contact details to Cleome, and suggested they meet up. For the first part of her holiday, she was staying in a smart hotel close to Old Town with views over the water and Skeppsholmen, and she had rented a room on Sandhamn, a small island in the archipelago, for the second half of her visit.

During their first reunion, they had updated each other with news from the decades that had passed since their last encounter, and asked carefully-worded questions. Subsequently, they had met for various lunches and wandered through shops and galleries in the city. On her last visit, Cleome had taken the ferry out to Sandhamn and they had basked in the sunshine, walked and chatted, and gradually got to know each other a little better. Cleome harboured a stupid fantasy of the great love that would be rekindled by these encounters, but in truth the meetings had remained guarded and polite, and she was left wondering whether they would ever bridge the hurt of the lost years. Were they foolish to even try?

She stood in her vegetable patch and lifted her chin to the sun, closing her eyes for a moment as her thoughts ran on. She longed for closure. She longed for peace. And there was only one way to get it, and that was not by avoiding the truth or staying hidden away at *Det Lilla Huset* forever. She needed to continue to get to know Catherine again, for better or worse.

Helen's car hurtled down the track towards her, leaving a cloud of dust in its wake, and interrupting her ruminations.

'What are you in such a hurry about?' Cleome called out, wiping her hands on her gardening apron, as Helen strode towards her.

'I have something to show you!' Helen's face was tight with exhaustion but triumph glittered in her dark eyes. 'Come here, close your eyes, and take my hand.'

'What sort of nonsense is this?' Cleome grumbled, interested despite her contrariness. She closed the gate to the orchard behind her, and offered her hand to her friend.

'No peeping now. No cheating,' Helen insisted, leading her across crisp brown grass to the driveway. 'Now wait here a moment, and keep your eyes closed.'

Cleome heard the car boot open, followed by a scuffle. She opened one eye craftily and then both, wide with astonishment.

'Oh my, isn't he beautiful!' she exclaimed.

'I knew you would cheat!' Helen clasped the red leather lead of a fine Afghan hound. Cleome extended her hand for the dog to sniff before stroking its fine-boned head. 'What is all this about, then?'

'A patient of mine died in the night. Nobody can take care of the dog. His name is Aslan. I know you've always loved the breed, so I said I would bring him away with me, as a temporary measure. To see what you think.'

'He has to be the most impractical dog in the whole of Sweden! Look at that hair! The ticks!'

'I know, and there's Trassel to consider too, but you don't have to keep him. You don't even have to take him on trial, if you don't want to. He will soon be adopted, I'm sure.'

'Then again, as a breed, they are excellent guard dogs,' Cleome vacillated, 'and I would welcome his help here. Of course, I will take him on trial!' she decided. 'Let me take the lead. Come here, Aslan. So you've had a bit of a tough time, eh? Well, you've come to the right place, you know. We understand about such matters here. Are you hungry? A little thirsty? Let's take you indoors and sort you out, shall we?'

'I have to dash.' Helen reached for her car door handle. 'Any problems, just call me, yes?'

'Oh yes, yes. Go carefully now! And stop rushing so much! The world will still turn without you pushing it around, you know…'

'See you soon!' Helen called through her car window, and started the ignition.

Aslan walked closely beside Cleome with his long elegant nose lifted to the breeze, and what looked like a triumphant smile across his muzzle.

The wooden walls of the cottage baked and creaked in the heat. A pulsing vitality came over the homestead; butterflies, crickets and bees grew busy in the meadow grass, and fish darted in the silky lake. Amelie watered her grandmother's vegetable garden, and inhaled the earthy sweetness as the fine spray met dusty soil. She recalled the first summer she had brought Bertie to Sweden, when he was a new-born baby. He had slept in a carriage pram in the shade beside the garden table, a white net protecting his skin from insects. He had lain flat on his back, pink-cheeked, his lips pouted, and his knees splayed wide in the way that babies lie. She had checked on him constantly, and often stood transfixed, simply watching him nap. She had stayed for a month, enjoying her maternity leave, and Nick had joined her for some of the time, only returning to Oxford when he had to, for work. Last summer, when they had come for another holiday, Bertie had just learnt to walk and had toddled through the forest, holding her hand. It had rained a lot. She and Cleome had moved all sorts of household items out of his reach. Their whole lives had revolved around him and his needs. Nick had bought a backpack and carried him on long hikes. They had given Bertie that, at least—they had given him the magic of two Swedish summers.

As she moved into her new life, she would carry all these memories with her and keep them alive. That evening, Tarek had offered to cook *iftar* for her. It was another step in their deepening relationship. She did not feel bad about meeting him for supper, now that she did not have to keep it secret from her grandmother.

They sat outside again in the warm night air with scented incense coils lit to deter the insects and citronella candles in glass holders set around the decking. She sipped a glass of red wine and nibbled on fat medjool dates before Tarek served bowls of thick harira soup with lamb and chickpeas. He had got the recipe from a Moroccan friend, and had wanted to try it for a while, he told her, as it was reputed to be excellent nourishment after fasting. He joined her with a small glass of wine for once, joking that it was a very special occasion and he was not a perfect Muslim. After they had eaten the delicious meal, all the while chatting quietly, Amelie fell silent and smiled into his dark eyes. She admired his confidence and strength of character, his kindness and stamina in the face of all that life had thrown his way, and her belly ached with longing. He leant across the table and kissed her, slowly and softly, his hands cupping the sides of her face. He ran his fingers up and down her arm.

'Let's go inside,' she whispered.

'You're sure?'

'Yes, I'm sure.'

He took her hand, and led her in through the back door to his tiny bungalow, closing it behind them.

In the morning, she awoke to the sound of him moving about in the small kitchen area. Fresh coffee scent laced the air. On seeing that she was awake, he placed a steaming mug on the table beside her, and then climbed back into bed and took her in his arms again. He drew her close, and she laid her head on his bare chest. She kissed his olive skin and looked up at his handsome face, and smiled. He bent and kissed her on the mouth. Outside, the first hint of sunlight brushed the landscape, and gently lit the room with its pale yellow hue. Swedish summer nights were indecently short. The air was warm and pine needle scents wafted through the open window. Birch leaves in the copse beside the cottage rustled in a breeze. Tarek ran his fingers up and down her spine.

'Your grandmother might be worried.'

'It's okay, she knows where I am.'

'Then she will know about us.'

'She does. I told her. I hope you don't mind. She is an intuitive woman; she had guessed.'

'I am glad that you do not have to deceive her to be with me.'

'I'm glad too. She will keep our secret too. You need not worry.'

'I know. I'm very fond of your grandmother and I trust her. She is nobody's fool. She knows what is important and what is not.' He pushed a strand of hair from her face and looked deeply into her eyes, as if searching there for a sign. 'You want me to make love to you again?' he murmured.

A smile crept over Amelie's face and she nodded, and wrapped her arms around his neck and kissed him.

'And you are okay with us? Being like this?'

She knew that he was referring to Nick, to the fact that she might be finding their togetherness strange or confusing or perhaps felt guilty or nervous or even slightly afraid, but she felt none of those things. Being with Tarek was the most natural thing in the world for her, and it felt right, as if it was meant to be. 'I've never been more certain of anything in my life,' she told him, truthfully.

He grinned at her.

'Our coffee will go cold,' she teased.

'I can make us more coffee.' He looked at her seriously for a moment. 'I can't spend the morning with you, as I would like to, though. It's Eid and there's a community breakfast with some of my friends in town. So we have a little time, but you don't mind if I leave you? With your grandmother's birthday party later too, it's a busy day.'

She smiled. She liked the fact that he was honest and stayed true to his roots. 'I don't mind at all.'

'You know how much this means to me?'

She smiled again. It's what she had wanted him to say but not been willing to mention herself. 'Me too.'

'Really?'

'Really.'

He laughed and rolled on top of her, and held her close.

Cleome was wide awake for most of the short night. The dogs dozed peaceably on large cushions on her bedroom floor. She knew where Amelie was, and prayed that everything went well for her, fretting a little that it might not, the stupid worries conjuring in her mind like even more biting insects. For most of the night, her tired body rested heavily on the bed, spread-eagled in a white cotton nightdress, her duvet cast aside. The heat made it hard to breathe and random fears circled in her mind. After Amelie had left for the late supper with Tarek, she had rung her sister in England where it was an hour earlier, and still an acceptable time to call. She had wanted to talk to Antonia in private before she left for the early flight to Skavsta, the next morning. During the conversation, she had confessed to meeting Catherine in Stockholm, and Antonia had been livid and cursed her, and said she was cancelling her flight and would not be attending her birthday party. She had hung up, and refused to pick up the telephone when she had tried to call her back. Cleome had lain awake half the night, upset and exasperated, and now faced explaining Antonia's absence to everyone at her party without, of course, telling them the true reason.

She levered herself up and sat on the edge of her bed, and ran her fingers through her tousled hair. Antonia's anger was unsettling. For all their differences, she trusted her younger sister, and wondered again if she had not been a fool to meet Catherine. It was true what Antonia said—that Cleome had been hurt by Catherine in the past and would in all likelihood, only get hurt again.

She made her way gingerly down the wooden staircase, gripping the rail, both dogs tiptoeing behind her. The cottage was quiet without Amelie and the lemon dawn cast shafts of light through the small windows, exaggerating the stillness. Cleome made herself a strong coffee and considered her situation. She understood her sister's fury but surely everyone—especially this person—deserved a second chance?

By sheer coincidence, the new crescent moon that marked the end of Ramadan arrived at the same time as Cleome's birthday, when a party was planned. Patrick stepped out of the taxi at *Det Lilla Huset*. Amelie hugged him fiercely. His hair was unkempt and curled over his collar, and the skin creases from his nose to the corners of his mouth had deepened. At her invitation, he had arrived to join the celebrations for her grandmother's seventy-sixth birthday.

'Come in,' Amelie greeted him. 'Let me wheel your suitcase inside and we'll have a cup of tea before I show you to your room.'

Patrick looked around him in wonder, at the abundant vegetable garden and the flock of squawking chickens that clustered nosily around the gate to the orchard. Trassel and Aslan had come out to meet him too, followed by Cleome who embraced him warmly.

'Happy birthday,' he said to her. 'I have a little something for you in my case.'

'Oh, you shouldn't have.' Cleome's face crinkled into a welcoming smile.

After a lazy afternoon spent drinking cool drinks and chatting in the shade beside the house, a barbeque was started down by the lakeside, and an abundance of citronella candles and spirals were lit as usual, to keep the hovering insects at bay. A table was carried onto the wide jetty and seats placed to overlook the indigo-coloured lake. The guests brought small gifts for Cleome which she opened sitting in her sun chair like a queen surrounded by cast-off wrapping paper. Tarek was given presents too, to celebrate Eid. He wore a new t-shirt from Josef. Amelie felt bad as she had not realised the tradition of present-giving, and had omitted to get him anything but he whispered to her that she had already given him the best gift of all. They avoided too much eye contact lest they give their secret away.

Daniel and Tarek tended to the fire in a pit on the bank so that it grew hot enough to cook on. As Amelie occasionally glanced over at him, she noticed that in unguarded moments he looked preoccupied, and she wondered if it had something to do with the night before. A small part of her feared that he might have regrets over what had happened between them.

Helen appeared at her side with a sheaf of aerial photographs taken by Robban Bengtsson's drone that she had finally printed out, showing *Båvenshult* and her beautiful land.

'He is actually a very good photographer. Look at the clear focus and detail here, and the way he has framed the buildings in the landscape. And see, he even got Tarek and the dogs in a few,' she pointed.

'Spying, I call it,' Tarek grumbled, overhearing the comment and catching her eye. Instantly, his lips curved in a warm smile before he gave his attention back to stoking the fire. Amelie smiled back, relieved that whatever was bothering him did not seem to have anything to do with her.

The evening air grew soupy with the earth's heat and humidity, and the colours of the landscape fused into shades of sepia and mauve in the encroaching twilight. Beneath them the pontoon shifted subtly on the surface of the water. Despite the sultry weather, most people wore long sleeves and trousers as added protection. Tarek was the exception; no insect went near him, let alone attempted to bite. He stood in shorts and a t-shirt, up on the bank beside the fire. She made furtive glances at his long, caramel-skinned limbs which the night before had been wound around her paler body. Josef and his friend pulled chairs out from one end of the table, took out their guitars, and strummed and sang. Daniel's sticky chocolate cake sat, centre-place on the table, beneath a net. As it was a special occasion, Cleome allowed herself one glass of iced vodka and tonic. Everybody joined her in raising a toast apart from Tarek who raised a glass of water and Helen who claimed a headache and drank apple juice.

Cleome teased her. 'A little vodka would smooth those knots on your brow. Just one, come on.'

'Not tonight. I'll stick with this, thanks. And changing the subject, where are all your knitting friends? They usually celebrate your birthday with you.'

'I did not feel like inviting them. They make everything so complicated.' Her gaze wandered to where Tarek stood, calling for another song from Josef and his friend.

'And did you not invite Antonia to come over?' Helen persisted. 'She usually comes for your birthday and *Midsommar*.'

'Ach, she is getting very crochety in her old age. We've had a little falling out.'

Helen rolled her eyes and shook her head.

'You didn't tell me that!' Amelie exclaimed. 'You said she was looking after a sick friend.'

'I might have told a little white lie earlier but don't fret, it's nothing to worry about,' Cleome shrugged, and took a swig from her glass. 'She'll get over it.'

The enticing aroma of fire-cooked salmon and beef burgers spiralled into the evening air. Several of the party swam to cool down before dinner, including Patrick whose eyes, while still full of sadness, glimmered with interest at the simple beauty of the unfolding scene. Over by the barbeque, Daniel wiped sweat from his brow with a handkerchief, and regaled Cleome with quotes from Christina Rossetti's birthday poem.

'Like Rossetti, you have a poet's soul,' he told her. 'I know one when I see one.'

'You flatter me!' Cleome scolded, fondly.

'I hope so.' He chuckled.

Tarek was taking a break from tending the fire, and Amelie wandered over and stood beside him on the ramp that led down to the jetty. She was careful not to give away any signals of their new intimacy but still sensing that something was wrong, needed to speak with him. In front of them, out in the lake, Josef and his friend swam, splashing each other and laughing raucously but Tarek's expression remained stern.

'What's up?' she asked.

'Oh, I am fine, no worries.'

'You don't seem fine.' She moved to touch his arm, but withdrew her hand awkwardly. 'Is something wrong? I expected you to be happy with it being Eid, and seeing all your friends, and eating proper meals again.'

'When they went to prayers this morning, somebody had painted graffiti on the door of the mosque. A swastika.' He shrugged and kept his focus on the far shore of the lake.

'The bastards.'

'You could say that, yes.'

She longed to put her arms around him and offer him comfort but with everyone there, it was impossible. Instead they exchanged a lingering gaze, and she saw the hurt and anger blaze in his eyes.

Later, when the meal was over, and the party finally ended, he returned to *Båvenshult* in the car with the others. She gazed down the track, watching the car's rear lights turn out of view, and then there was only darkness and silence again.

23

Summer Solstice

Cleome rose in the small hours of the longest day, before the rest of the household was awake. Just after dawn was her favourite hour, when the world was fresh and birds and other forest creatures gathered in her garden. After a cup of coffee, she dressed in turquoise trousers with a matching scarf tying back her hair and a green pinafore apron over the top, and ventured outdoors with the dogs. Silver bangles gleamed at her wrists. Her bright eyes flicked appreciatively around her property, as it basked in fragile sunlight. Trassel raced through the orchard grass, enjoying her freedom. Aslan followed, his regal head held high, and long coat streaming like the hair of a fashion model. He had acclimatised to life at the smallholding, and Trassel accepted him now, having snapped at his heels once or twice. Amelie had taken responsibility for grooming his coat, and while Aslan could appear aloof, Cleome was not fooled, noting his interest in his new home and the way his eyelids lowered with pleasure while he was being brushed.

She cut dill and parsley for drying, fed and watered the chickens, and collected warm eggs from a row of nesting boxes, running her fingertips over the smooth shells as she cupped each one in her hand. She took great pleasure in accepting these gifts from her hens in all their various shades from honey brown to white. With the day's offerings placed carefully on a bed of herbs in her trug, she paused and lifted her chin to the fragrant air, inhaling dried grass and damask rose scents. A hawk cried somewhere over the lake and bees buzzed lazily in the flowerbeds. She was feeling good. Catherine had written a card to thank her for all the time they had spent together over the past month. It seemed that the meetings had not been the flop that she had feared, or that Antonia had predicted. Catherine was back home in England now, and grateful for her stay in Sweden. A tentative seedling of truce had germinated during the past month, and tiny roots were spreading. A weight was lifted off Cleome's old shoulders and she chuckled aloud at the prospect of rubbing her sister's nose in this small triumph. After a moment's pause, she narrowed her gaze to check the windows of the house and slipped a small hip flask from her apron pocket. She took a hasty swig and screwed the top back on, licking her creased lips. Vodka warmed her veins and reinvigorated her spirit.

In spite of her happiness about Catherine's note, *Midsommar* was always a turning point in the year for Cleome. Swedes wildly celebrated the light, and she too gave thanks for the glorious sun that never quite set at this time of year; but at the same time, each year her prayers were tinged with melancholy. This was the peak, the summit, and for the remainder of the year, the only way was down, gradually, into darkness. As it was with all things in life, there was a balance of light and shadow, and after *Midsommar,* the scales tipped. She stopped and took out the card again, to re-read the precious missive, holding it in the direction of the sun that had just risen above the tree tops, in order to decipher each beautifully crafted word. As she re-read carefully, her initial joy over the success with Catherine was tempered by sudden insecurity. She realised that Catherine did not made any suggestion of meeting again. She knew it was her place to wait and see what happened next, and her hand trembled as it dawned on her that history might yet still repeat itself, and another meeting might not come for a very long time.

She tucked the card back into her apron pocket, picked up her basket, and walked back to the cottage with her lips pressed together. She would not brood but would press on with the day. That evening, Helen was hosting her usual celebration for her many friends and family at *Båvenshult.* It was an annual event when guests stayed over in tents, in secluded spots around her rolling gardens and orchard. This year, with the promise of a hot, dry evening, everyone would be jubilant. The party-goers would drink liberally, and skinny-dip in the lake at midnight. Their whoops and cries would rebound off the still water for hours. Cleome was no longer in the mood for it, and to make matters worse, Amelie had persuaded Antonia to come and stay for the midsummer party, and she was due to arrive at any moment. They had not spoken since the argument on the telephone, two weeks previously.

Back in her kitchen, after she had pencilled the date on each egg and stored them in the larder, she made another coffee, fed the dogs, and headed out for a long, quiet stroll through the forest. On her return, she found the house full of people. Amelie had collected Antonia from the airport. They pecked each other's cheeks dutifully, and then Antonia resumed her lunch preparation—she was always so organised, it was irksome, and took over the kitchen as if it was her own. Amelie cleaned as usual, moving swiftly, her long slender hands efficiently tidying and wiping down surfaces. Patrick, who had extended his stay with them, busied himself with a screw-driver at the kitchen table, attempting to fix her broken lamp. His head remained bent, and his gaze concentrated on his task as he bid her good morning.

'Are you all right, *Mormor*? You seem a little unsteady,' Amelie quizzed, sharp-eyed.

Antonia clattered soup bowls onto the table, proprietorially.

'I am absolutely fine,' she replied, stiffly.

Amelie trimmed her grandmother's hair so that it sat neatly on her shoulders, and framed her cat-like face. When she had finished, Patrick took his place on the chair in the shady part of the garden, and while she combed his damp hair, took a section between her fingers, and snipped at the ends, he explained how he was struggling to cope with Hilary's vengeful mood. Several of her friends were encouraging her to sue—to "get justice"—for Nick's death, and the situation was distressing him.

'Do you think I'm doing a disservice to Nick and Bertie by not supporting her legal campaign?' he asked, as she combed through his hair some more. Cleome and Antonia were busy elsewhere, and the fact that it was just the two of them, seemed to encourage his confession. Before she had answered, he added, 'The thing is that I have examined my conscience and concluded that the only way forward is—God only knows how—to find a way to forgive Darren Ackerman for his error.'

Amelie paused, comb and scissors suspended, and gently straightened Patrick's head with her fingertips. He continued, explaining that he had grown up with the troubles in Ireland, and knew that bitterness and revenge did not assuage anger but merely kept the flames alight. 'On my mind every day is the example of Gordon

Wilson, the man who lost his daughter in the Enniskillen bombing in 1987. I don't expect you've heard of him, but he was so dignified and brave in a speech he gave on the television news that it moved me (and half the nation) to tears. I will never forget it for as long as I live. It is his fine example that I cling to. He was so noble. After losing Nick, I googled Gordon Wilson, and memorised a few of his words from that interview, in an attempt to find solace. "I bear no ill will. I bear no grudge. Dirty sort of talk is not going to bring her back… I will pray for these men"—the terrorists, he meant—"tonight and every night." That's what he said. Can you imagine? The man prayed for the terrorists who had murdered his daughter!' Patrick paused and shook his head. Amelie stilled it again. 'Isn't that something? And d'you know, he was so *peaceful* and sure of himself… but the difficulty for me is that I love my wife, and she will not hear of forgiveness—indeed, she became so outraged when I suggested it that I worried for her health, and so I shut up. And now I am left keeping all my thoughts to myself, and feeling disloyal to her, and quite alone with it all.'

She had no answers for Patrick. When she had finished cutting his hair, she went for a long swim in the lake alone, and then took a shower to dampen her unease. There was so much unfinished business surrounding the accident. She was nowhere near being able to forgive Darren Ackerman. She felt terrible being in Patrick's presence after the night she had spent with Tarek. Her guilt and anger lay buried inside her like a curled snake.

She went out into the garden to find Antonia striding about with an apron tied firmly around her navy shirtdress, and a pair of secateurs held aloft. She cut roses, hydrangeas, honeysuckle, dahlias and wild chervil, together with various stems of greenery, and had so much energy compared to her sister, that it worried Amelie.

Her grandmother looked beaten down and frail. At the outdoor table, she twisted the blooms into wire frames to make a wreath for each woman to wear that evening, in accordance with Swedish tradition. Her hands trembled as she threaded the foliage. She stopped to rest as Amelie approached, her face pale. Amelie offered to give her a hand but Cleome refused, tutting as Antonia dropped more flowers on the table. The two sisters, while they worked to complete the wreaths together, had not spoken throughout the entire process.

As shadows lengthened, the group of four set out to walk over the shallow hill, through the swathe of forest and across the field to

Båvenshult. The dogs trailed in their wake. Patrick clutched a bottle of wine, and Antonia carried a cake tin with both hands, containing an elaborate meringue she had made from *Det Lilla Huset* eggs. Her wreath was pushing her fringe into her eyes and she blew her hair upwards at regular intervals. Amelie wore a blue floral dress that reached down to her shins, and had her wreath firmly fixed in place. Her arms smelt of Cleome's home-made citrus insect repellent, and she wore a shawl looped over both elbows. Around her slender neck was the gold chain bearing Nick's wedding ring. She contemplated the evening ahead, knowing that her love for Nick would never leave her but that she had to stop dwelling in the past, and open her heart to the life that lay ahead of her. Her eyes, that Tarek had yesterday told her were the colour of the Mediterranean in winter, took in the beautiful sights of the forest on the warm summer's evening. She could not wait to see him again, but they would both need to guard against showing any affection to each other. As they drew closer to *Båvenshult*, she heard music drifting across the field, and the noises of another party in full swing on the opposite side of the lake. Sound travelled over the water in uncanny ways: a whisper was caught on a breeze; a voice startled, even though it came from someone in a boat, far out on the watery expanse. Cleome called the dogs, and put Aslan on a strong leather lead. She had tied red bandannas around both animals' necks, in an attempt to make them look festive.

At the party, guests milled about and chatted. Amelie separated from her group, seeking respite from the sibling tension, and wandered through the crowd, clutching a glass of beer. Venturing into the house, she overheard Helen and Daniel having a furious argument in the kitchen, and hastily tiptoed outside again. She filled a plate with salmon and a scoop of potato salad from a table laden with food, and chatted with a couple from Stockholm while she ate. Leaving them, she helped herself to a glass of schnapps and stood in the garden, looking down the field towards the bay and the dazzling lake beyond. Helen appeared at her side, looking flushed and annoyed.

'What's up?' Amelie asked.
'Daniel is driving me nuts.'
'What has he done?'
'He is fussing. He fusses over me like I am some kind of invalid.'
'He cares, that's all.'
'Pah, he's stifling!'
'Have a drink, relax.'

'I'm not drinking tonight.'

'Oh?'

'Got a party to organise. Can't have the hostess plastered,' Helen said, and lifting a hand in greeting to someone, strode off again, leaving Amelie as abruptly as she had arrived. The *Det Lilla Huset* group appeared at her side, along with Daniel, who ran his fingers back through his thick white hair and nursed a beer.

'I will never understand women,' he lamented.

'Oh, come now, we're not that bad,' Antonia replied briskly.

'Is that Robban Bengtsson with his parents over there?' Cleome asked, peering across the garden.

Dusk had settled in shady corners of the garden like fine powder. Lotta Bengtsson stood on the perimeter of the gathering, wearing a floral dress and tight sandals. At her side Magnus Bengtsson cradled a beer and wore an irritated expression. His shirt was buttoned to the top, and his face glistened puce in the heat. Robban stood a little separately from his parents, looking agitated. Nobody talked to them, and Cleome, feeling sympathy for her neighbours, waved a hand in greeting.

'So, you will keep this beautiful dog then?' Daniel asked, his fingers seeking Aslan's coat.

'Oh yes, and I have told Helen. The family are relieved, apparently,' she said, turning back to him. Antonia rolled her eyes as if her sister were stupid. Amelie tiptoed away again, to exchange a few words with the Bengtssons. Magnus Bengtsson did not acknowledge her presence and averted his rubbery chin to avoid any eye contact with her. Lotta spoke about the lovely weather while looking Amelie up and down with a needle-sharp gaze. Robban simply waved and said, '*Hej*, Amelie,' before staring at his feet. Amelie moved on. She took a short cut across the orchard in search of Tarek. As she walked behind Daniel's *lillstuga*, and turned the corner of the small building, she almost bumped into him.

'You made me jump,' she exclaimed, drawing her shawl around her shoulders and smiling.

'Are you okay?' He touched her arm.

'Yes! I've missed you.' She smiled again.

'Me too.' They exchanged a fond and knowing look. 'You want to walk a bit, over here?'

'Sure.' They moved away from the main party, past some apple trees and across an open stretch of grass. 'So what have you been up to?'

'We cleaned the graffiti off the mosque door and painted over it although you can still see it so we will need to paint some more.'

'Such a pointless thing to do. Did they find the culprit?'

'No, and I doubt they ever will.'

'You look upset.'

'Well,' he paused. 'I have discovered that someone I know might have information about your burglary.'

'Who?'

'Someone I thought was a friend.'

'But who is it? Who would have information and not tell the police?'

'I can't tell you until I know for sure. Listen, perhaps I am speaking too soon. Let's forget it for tonight. Have you ever seen inside the old barn over there? Upstairs is a beautiful hall that was a meeting place for the local community, many years ago. People used to gather there for celebrations, Helen told me. Come, I'll show you.' He led her towards the huge barn where Helen and Daniel parked their cars, and logs were neatly stacked. They entered through a wooden door to a closed section where garden equipment was stored alongside bicycles, and there was an empty space where a boat was kept over winter. Amelie had never been inside the building before, nor had she registered that there was an upper storey. The air smelt of warm wood and a faint hint of engine oil. Dust motes danced in yellow evening sunlight that beamed through cobwebbed window panes in the back wall.

'Over there,' Tarek said, pointing. 'There are some stairs.'

She climbed the steps in front of him, clutching a hand rail, curious to know what was at the top. As she entered, she saw a cavernous hall with a beamed, vaulted ceiling. The floorboards beneath her sandals were worn smooth by footfall from the past. The space was still and warm, and the thick wooden walls muffled the noise of the party. Apart from two chairs and a table against one wall, the space was unfurnished. The atmosphere reminded her of a cathedral; there were long windows at either end, and a dormer in the sloping roof that afforded views over the vegetable patch, the large field, and beyond it, the lake. She strolled to the far end of the hall where sunlight made a slanted oblong of brightness on the bare boards. Peering out, she saw clusters of people in the garden below.

She turned back. 'I remember when *Midsommar* was so magical, when I was a child.'

'It still is,' he murmured. He moved closer to her and picked up both her hands and held them in his.

'If you say so.'

'You like this room?' he asked.

'It's lovely.'

'Come here.' He kissed her softly, cradling the sides of her head in his gentle hands. Her body reverberated with longing. He drew back and gazed deeply into her eyes. 'Something is bothering you?'

She removed the wreath of flowers from her head, and circled it in her hands. 'You know how it is?'

'I do.'

'I get so sad and angry sometimes, and I have so little control over my emotions. I try to hide it, but it's horrible.'

'I understand. But it's not good to remain like that.'

'So what do I do about it?'

Tarek shrugged. 'You are grieving and a part of you thinks it is okay to be angry and sad all the time. You feel alone and isolated, like you are the only one. At times you feel scared. You are hurting really bad.'

She stared at the floor. A tear trickled down her cheek and she smudged it away. 'I don't want to be like this today, but it's like I have no control sometimes.'

'It takes effort but it's important to always seek out the good stuff in life. I want you to know, you can be however you need to be with me though,' he added. 'I'm here. I am your friend. This year it's your turn to be sad. Next year, it might be mine. We will get through this time, together.'

She looked over at crepuscular rays glowing through the barn window, lost for words.

'You know what I do when I am so full of rage, I think I will burst?' He opened his hands to the air.

'Well, you certainly don't drink,' she joked, recovering.

'Ha, no, I don't. You are right there. I dance, by myself, a special dance from home that my Grandfather taught me. He was a Mevlevi, from Turkey. You've heard of them?'

'No.'

'In the West, you call it Whirling Dervish. My grandfather was a dervish, a spiritual man. You have heard of the Whirling Dervishes?'

'I've heard the name but I've no idea who they are.'

'Whirling is a special, sacred dance to connect with the divine energy. When you whirl, you put your right hand up—to touch heaven—and your left hand down to distribute divine healing on earth, like this. The whirling movement…' Tarek turned swiftly, his trainers making a shuffling sound on the wooden floor '…mirrors the turning motion which exists in the universe generally, like when planets move around the sun and even the invisible atoms go in circles. But enough talking! I don't have the costume; you will have to imagine—a flowing white skirt and a tall hat on my head.' He paused, took his phone from his jeans pocket and placed it on the table. He found the music he wanted, kicked off his trainers, and untucked the short-sleeved shirt he wore so that it hung loose about his hips. Music from lutes, mandolins, zither, and drums, issued from his phone. He stood still, his gaze altered so that he did not look at her or anything in the hall. He folded his arms across his chest and bowed before he began, slowly and smoothly turning around and around, his feet brushing over the wooden floor in their own regular, soft rhythm. After a moment, his arms unfurled gracefully so that he became the shape of a spiralling tree, and then slowly he dropped one arm and whirled, around and around and around, fast and steady. His movements were fluid and effortless, and yet deceptively precise. The sight of him spinning, combined with the hypnotic music, mesmerised Amelie. She wondered at the culture he came from, where grown men spun and danced to honour the divine. Life must be so strange for him, living in a secular country like Sweden. There was so much to learn about Tarek, his life and his values. As the music eventually slowed, so did Tarek, and his arms lowered and wrapped around his body, and he bowed again, perfectly in time with the composition.

Silence fell in the barn. Dust motes danced on in the evening sunlight.

'I want you to teach me this dance!' she applauded.

'I will teach you to whirl. But not now, after you have been drinking. You will get dizzy and sick.' More music began, and Tarek did a few more turns, as if trying out a different step.

And then, from outside in the garden, there came the sounds of some kind of commotion. Cleome was shouting. Amelie and Tarek stared at each other. He pulled on his trainers, scooped up his phone, and they ran towards the stairs.

24

Waxing Moon of Horses

Outside in the potato patch, the elderly siblings stood face to face on a grass pathway. A section of Cleome's hair had escaped from her floral wreath, and fell over one eye. Antonia's arms were folded beneath her bosom, and her lips were corrugated with fury.

'I did not want to give her up!' Cleome shrieked. 'She was stolen!'

'You were a child!' Antonia wailed back.

'*You* are parroting our parents. I was seventeen! I was not a child—young, yes, but not a child! I could have kept her. With help, I could have raised her!'

'You are being stupid.'

'You were only thirteen when it happened—how could you know what I was capable of? You were a prissy little virgin, and they wrapped you in cotton wool and told you all sorts of stories in case the truth about me tainted you in some way. You have never even had a child of your own! What do you know about any of these things?'

'I have always been more mature than you; that I do know.'

'Rubbish! You are living out the spell that our mother cast on you! She labelled you as "the sensible one" so that you would never make the same mistakes as me!'

'I make my own decisions, thank you very much!'

'Can you not see that they never gave me a choice? That the system for nice middle-class girls like us completely disregarded my mental wellbeing, or God forbid, my happiness? They told me I was psychologically unstable when I said I wanted to keep Catherine. They brainwashed me, insisting that I would "get over her" like I had some kind of illness. And eventually I believed them! Our parents and the doctor—they presented such a united front, such an authority, that I caved in. I should have persisted but there was nobody to turn to for help. Later I realised—when it was far too late—that I was right all along, and there were ways I could have kept her. I saw how they had lied to me to get what *they* wanted, to cover up *their* pathetic shame at church and in the village.'

'They did what they thought was best for you.'

'Why do you defend them? They were cruel. If they had been brave enough, they could have helped me; they were comfortably off. But instead, they bullied me and hid me away in that dreadful home like a dirty secret. Plenty of other girls with kinder parents got to keep their babies, but not me.'

'You're a dreamer! You always were! You have a romantic notion of how things would have turned out but you would never have coped! You would have been a single parent in the nineteen-sixties. You still don't understand the stigma that you and Catherine would have faced.'

'I would have given it a go, worked hard, done my best!'

'Oh, you do talk utter rubbish sometimes.' Antonia shook her head; her floral crown remained immaculately in place. Trassel and Aslan lay close by in the shade, panting. 'And let's not forget, she almost broke your heart before…'

'She was angry with me, and she had every right to be. I let the authorities take her. I didn't fight for her. I will never forgive myself for that. I'm not surprised she was livid, the way her life turned out.'

'She should have been grateful for the fact that she was adopted by a decent family!'

'Oh, do shut up! You know perfectly well that her adoptive mother is a narcissist who only wanted a child because it fitted in with her perfect marriage story, and after she got Catherine, she conceived two children of her own, whom she idolised. The children at Catherine's school knew she was adopted and taunted her that I had never loved her and had given her away, so she fought them and got a bad name with her teachers. Do you not remember? Catherine was a tall Latin beauty where her siblings were short and plain. When she came searching for me that first time, her so-called mother found out and played the blackmail card, saying how hurt she was. She still met up with me, of course, but she was torn. Technically she was a young adult when we met that first time but she was still immature.'

'And so, what now? She is suddenly going to be your new best friend?'

'That first meeting was a long time ago, and she was bitter on discovering that I had gone on to have Kerstin, and kept her. If she hurt me, it was nothing more than I deserved. Last year, she saw what had happened to Kerstin in the paper. She had traced Kerstin and considered approaching her at one time but had held back. She contacted me to send her condolences.'

'And now everything is roses?'

'Oh, for heaven's sake—she is fifty-eight years old now! She has raised three daughters and is recently divorced. She is menopausal and trying to understand who she is. She's angry, hurt and in pain. Her husband has left her for a younger woman. She says that being abandoned has always been her biggest fear, and it has happened again. Of course, it's not bloody "roses". I will never be a proper mother to her—it is too late for that—but I have spent a lifetime missing her, and now I am finally able to get to know her, just a little bit, and maybe even help her in a moment of crisis. For that I am eternally grateful—and nothing will stop me seeing her!'

Amelie and Tarek appeared at the entrance to the vegetable garden. The enclosure was hidden from view of the rest of the party by overgrown clumps of lilac and wild roses, and a picket fence that kept out the wildlife. The two sisters faced each other, poised as if ready to pounce. Heat radiated from the red-painted barn wall behind Cleome, emitting a dry woody fragrance, and making her hair stringy with sweat so that it stuck to the sides of her face. Antonia fanned herself with a manicured hand, and her cheeks glowed pink. Trassel scratched her belly with her back paw.

'What is going on here?' Amelie asked, incredulously. 'We could hear you two fighting like cats from inside the barn!'

'Never you mind,' Antonia warned.

'No, Antonia!' Cleome's lip quivered. 'I have had enough of all the lies and secrets. Enough! I shall tell her... Amelie, Amelie, my dear,' she paused as if searching for the right words. She hobbled over to Amelie and took her hand. 'I have something to tell you which might come as a shock. Let's find a quiet corner of the garden, perhaps over there, further away from the crowd.'

'I will leave you,' Tarek murmured, and disappeared. Amelie watched him go, and then returned her questioning gaze to her grandmother. The three women tramped in silence through the vegetable patch, trailed by the weary dogs, to the far side of the garden where clouds of humming insects gathered beneath a stand of pine trees, and Helen's land gave way to forest. There, Cleome told Amelie her story. In the distance, down beside the lake, several party-goers stripped naked, and splashed in and out of the water, calling to each other and crying out toasts to the summer.

25

Waning Gibbous Moon of Horses

She stood barefoot on the wooden jetty, looking out over the gleaming water. Her slim feet were the colour of sun-kissed sand, her toenails trimmed neat. The afternoon sun beat down on her slender shoulders, turning the skin pink. Antonia and Patrick had returned to England. Antonia had left under a cloud, again refusing to speak to her sister since the argument. Cleome had, moments before, rushed off to Stockholm to meet Catherine who was suddenly back in the country. She had hissed like an angry cat when Amelie had said she looked tired, and accused her of spoiling her fun, jabbing a gnarled finger in the air. Her reaction had been startling, and Amelie had faltered and reassured her that she cared and was concerned. Her grandmother had been restless for days, ever since the midsummer party—and ill-tempered too. She had told Amelie about Catherine, and the home for unmarried mothers where the matron had hacked-off hair and hands like a farm labourer's. How her mother had dropped her off at the kerb outside, and not said goodbye. That she was not like the other mothers-to-be, who smoked, chatted, and knitted baby clothes. During her stay, she had to rise early, wash, say prayers, and do chores all morning—cleaning or laundry, mostly. In the evenings, she sat in a recreation room and knitted. They had to get clothes ready for the birth, and put them in a special box to go with the baby to its new home. All the pregnant women worked until they went into labour, scrubbing floors or fetching buckets of coal from the cellar. There was no slowing down, even in the last days. When her time came, she was told that she needed to be induced at the local hospital. She was sent there alone in a taxi, terrified about what would happen. She had never been to the hospital before, and did not know what "being induced" meant. Nobody asked about such things in those days, she said. On the maternity ward, the nurses all called her "Miss" in a mocking tone, and after her waters had broken, she had cried, fearing that she had wet herself. She had been put in a room on her own for the labour, and told not to make a fuss. Each contraction had terrified her, as in her naivety she thought it might kill her baby. She said she had never been so scared. When the baby came, she yelled for help, and after Catherine was delivered, she was given stitches with no anaesthetic, and told not to make a fuss.

Amelie's heart ached for her grandmother. She felt terrible that she had felt compelled to keep such a heart-breaking secret for more than half a century, and furious on her behalf at the way she had been treated. If she was completely honest, the revelation that her mother had a half-sister was disturbing too, and she wondered what her mother would have done if she had known, and who Catherine was, and what she was like. It was strange to think she had an aunt whom she had never met.

She pushed her fingers back through her sweaty hair and looked about. The newspapers were reporting record high temperatures all over Scandinavia, and predicted that they would continue into the following month. The surface of the lake had a sheen like a mirror, and reflected the trees overhanging the shoreline in meticulous detail. She filled her lungs with the sultry air. After the earlier cross words from her grandmother, the glistening water at her feet offered solace and sparkle. She lifted her arms and dived in.

She spent the day alone, going about the chores around the homestead slowly in the intense heat. She swam again to cool off, and then showered and sat and waited for her grandmother to return. When she arrived, late in the afternoon, Cleome's face was pinched with exhaustion but there was a gleam in her eyes. It was a sign that Amelie recognised only too well—the glimmer of happiness. Her grandmother apologised for her bad mood earlier, and hugged Amelie, holding her for a few heartbeats longer than she normally would. Amelie made her sit down with a cool drink while she cooked them a simple supper to share.

They sat in the familiar kitchen with the windows flung open behind the insect nets to encourage whatever draught might sweep through the sweltering cottage. After they had eaten, Cleome confessed that she was indeed weary, and while she'd had a wonderful day, a small part of her had reservations because Catherine's mood vacillated. One minute she thanked Cleome for coming to meet her in the heat, and the next she was sulking about some unknown thing that she did not wish to talk about.

'Perhaps she is simply menopausal?' Amelie suggested.

'Perhaps.' Cleome sighed. She stood and fetched a new bottle of Russian bootleg vodka from the back of a cupboard, and poured a liberal shot into her lemonade. 'I find it very difficult when she is moody and silent. I feel guilty enough about her, without any extra pressure. And to be frank, she is ungrateful sometimes. Sure, she had it tough, but don't we all? I long to see her but I'm not sure it helps me. Perhaps Antonia is right?'

'I'm surprised Catherine came back to Stockholm so quickly.'

'Me too. Unfinished business, she says, but she strikes me as quite an impulsive character. She doesn't seem to work and has a lot of time on her hands now her daughters are grown.'

'How long is she here for this time?'

'She doesn't say. I'm not sure she knows.' Cleome spread her hand over her heart and took a calming breath.

'Are you alright?'

'Yes, yes. Just weary. I will sleep well tonight.'

She heard footsteps behind her, and turned. Tarek approached, clutching a rolled towel in one hand, and grinning. He kissed her quickly on the cheek. There was nobody around to see them, as Cleome had driven into Flen to do some food shopping.

'*Hur mår du?*'

'*Bra, tack.*'

He wore a creased white t-shirt with the sleeves rolled up and long denim shorts. His arms and legs were the colour of toffee. He flung his towel onto a sun chair.

'Your grandmother is out, so I can kiss you again,' he said, taking her in his arms. Amelie rested her gaze on his strong handsome face and the lips she had come to love. It still astonished her, the swell of feelings in his presence, and the way her whole being forgot its pain and sorrow when he was around. Tarek was like her own magic potion. He brushed his lips against hers before kissing her properly and pushing a strand of hair from her face. 'I'm looking forward to this,' he nodded at the water. 'To us having some time together again, at last.'

'Me too. I'll beat you in!' she cried, and turned and dived into the silky lake. A moment later, he followed, laughing as he surfaced, shaking his hair free of excess water. Keeping a couple of metres apart, they swam out across the bay, towards the first forested promontory where the house on the rock sat hidden by summer foliage. Occasionally, one of its windows glinted between the trees but the house remained empty, as it so often did. Amelie used a long breaststroke while Tarek employed a strong, slow crawl. Apart from the rippling sounds of disturbed water, the silence around them was palpable. Sunlight flashed off the lake's surface. At the shore, a dense swathe of reeds formed an impenetrable margin. Fish flickered through the deep crystalline reaches. They saw the small beach belonging to *Båvenshult* which lay deserted in the sunshine, and swam on, past the house on the rock to the next cove, pacing themselves with steady, rhythmical strokes.

Around the headland was another bay with a private jetty, the exclusive domain of a palatial summerhouse whose owners also rarely visited. It was very obvious when they were there as they left their belongings scattered everywhere. Seeing that nobody was home, they climbed out of the water using the ladder to the wide pontoon, and lay down on the baking wood, staring at the cerulean sky, and panting from their exertion.

When they had rested and warmed up again, they would swim back, but for now they lay on in the sun, relishing the heat and peace, and each other's company. A motorboat sped past along the far side of the lake, and Amelie waited for it to pass, and then began to tell Tarek about her grandmother's lost daughter and the terrible circumstances of Catherine's forced adoption.

She told him that when Cleome was seventeen, in the summer of 1959, her family were visiting Florence. While they were there, she met a young Italian man called Angelo who worked as a waiter in the café where the sisters sat each afternoon for an hour or two, drinking fizzy drinks and devouring *gelati* while their parents took a siesta, back at the hotel. The café was in one of the city's ancient squares, and they usually sat outside at a table beneath a parasol, and watched the world go by.

'*Mormor* says she can still recall the scent of the baked stone walls, and fresh ground coffee blended with cigarette smoke,' Amelie said. 'She was charmed by Angelo's smouldering glances, and the free dishes of *amarena* and *fregola* which he offered them. Antonia was twelve at the time, and apparently too focussed on the ice-cream to notice her sister's blossoming flirtation. Angelo spoke only a few words of English. One evening, my grandmother snuck out of her hotel bedroom to meet him. You can guess the rest.'

He stared up at the sky. The jetty rocked gently in the wake from the speed boat.

Amelie went on. 'After she had been back home in England for two months, her mother realised that she was pregnant, and kept her off school. In the late fifties, society was harsh, and middle-class English girls did as they were told. It never entered her head to protest, she says, or to insist that she went on with her education. She had wanted to go to university to study literature and poetry, but her mother made it clear that would never happen after the pregnancy because she did not deserve it. None of her family spoke to her. Antonia was told that her sister was poorly, and she must keep away from her. Her mother policed the separation.

'Her mother told her that she could not stay at home and they sent her to an Establishment for Unmarried Mothers run by the Church of England. It was situated in Essex, far away from the gossips who lived in their small village. Everyone was told she was in hospital. How her parents pulled that story off, my grandmother never knew. After the baby was born and taken away, *Mormor* went back home for a short time but she found it unbearable, and so she ran away to London.' Amelie paused. 'She says she never told my mother that she had a half-sister because she was ashamed of what she had done.'

'That is a very sad story,' Tarek remarked.

'Cleome met Catherine once when Catherine was eighteen but since then, she has not seen her for almost forty years—and now suddenly… after my mother passed away, she reappears, out of the blue. I can see why Antonia is so protective but it's horrible the way she has fallen out with my grandmother over this issue. They're still not talking to each other. I question Catherine's intentions too. *Mormor* gets exhausted after a day in the city in all this heat.'

'I will offer to help your grandmother with things around the house, like getting the logs stacked for winter. I know at this time of year, her thoughts already turn to the changing season. I did it for her last year, in good time so the logs get nice and dry. She will accept the offer, I think.'

'You're very kind.'

'She has always been good to me. These things go in circles.'

'We'd like to help you too, to clear your name regarding the burglary, once and for all. Did you find out any more from that person you mentioned?'

'No, but I am on the trail. I thank you but there's nothing you can do that will change anything, and in fact, you getting involved might make things worse. There's nothing the community likes to talk about more than when one of the men falls in love with a white woman.'

Amelie stalled. 'You said "falls in love"?' she said, and rolled on her side to face him.

He rolled to face her too. 'Yes, I did. Does that scare you? It is the truth. I know I am falling in love with you, Amelie.'

'It does not scare me at all,' she murmured. 'It is wonderful. It's what I want too. I'm falling in love with you, Tarek, despite everything. It's like my love has a mind of its own.'

He smiled at her and traced the side of her face with his fingertips. 'My beautiful Amelie.'

'You're very special to me,' she said.

'You're very special to me, too.'

She nodded. 'You know,' she said, 'you still need to teach me to whirl like a dervish.'

'It will be my pleasure.'

They kissed, a long and gentle kiss, and fell apart and lay on their backs again, holding hands. It felt so natural to be intimate with him, like honouring a truth that had recently dawned on her.

After they had swum back to *Det Lilla Huset*, Tarek left for work at the sports centre, promising to see her again the next day.

26

Waning Crescent Moon of Horses

Amelie and Helen set off on their usual rounds for Doctors of The World. They were due to visit Revekka. There was great excitement because her parents had finally gained permission to stay in Sweden, and not long afterwards, Revekka had awoken from her long, deep sleep. There had been much celebration in the community although Revekka was by no means fully recovered. Helen informed Amelie about what to expect.

She paused in the explanation and opened the car window to inhale some fresh air.

'Are you alright?' Amelie asked.

'Yes, yes,' Helen said.

When they got to the bungalow where Revekka lived, Amelie was apprehensive. The young woman's case had touched her more than she cared to admit. The small brick building sat forlornly on a plot of overgrown grass where dandelions bloomed in yellow abundance, and curtains were drawn across the windows. They were greeted by Ellina who told them that Sophie was out, playing at a friend's house. Since the last visit, Ellina had documented Revekka's progress in an exercise book, carefully dating each entry which she pointed to with a pink-tipped finger, while nodding anxiously. Three days after first opening her eyes, Revekka had sipped water from a spoon. The next day, she had taken a small amount of ice cream. The day after that, she had moved her hand. Four days later, she had attempted to turn over in bed. The curtains were kept closed as the light hurt her eyes. She remained propped up in bed, her mouth slack and her gaze unfocussed.

When prompted by Helen, she whispered that her body ached all over. Helen asked if she could examine her.

Revekka paused, as if struggling to find the word, and then in a soft voice and with a fractional shake of her head, murmured, '*Nej*.'

Helen grinned, and made eye contact with Ellina, who smiled bravely.

Back outside, with the visit finished, Helen explained that Revekka's refusal to be examined was a positive sign; she was re-drawing the boundaries around her body, beginning to think for herself again, and to govern her own life.

'I still cannot believe it,' Amelie shook her head. 'Her case questions everything I know about medicine.'

'There is more to this life than we see. It is not only our minds and bodies that become sick; I think our souls can too, and the medicine for a sick soul is compassion, nothing else.'

'That's an interesting theory.'

'As a doctor, I never thought I would draw this conclusion, and yet I do. It is such an education.' Helen started the engine, and they drove with the windows down to dispatch the intense heat from the car. 'As I have told you before, there are still many doubters about this condition, and there are some who are trying to fake it in order to get residency in Sweden which doesn't help, but there are still cases like Revekka's that astonish me.'

After they had finished their days' work, Helen agreed to a glass of iced tea at *Det Lilla Huset*. Unusually, she appeared to be in no rush to go anywhere, and sat gazing down the glade, past the long yellow grass that shifted in a gentle breeze, to the lake, shimmering in the distance. Her hair had grown a little longer, and dark waves framed her face.

'What is the matter?' Cleome asked, as her friend's fingers drummed the table top.

'Well, I have something to tell you both.' Helen paused.

'Spit it out,' Cleome encouraged.

'Daniel and I are... expecting a baby.'

Cleome replaced her glass on the table and gawped.

'When?' Amelie asked, excitedly.

'December.'

'Well now, there *is* a surprise. Congratulations!' Cleome beamed and staggered to her feet to wrap her brown bangled arms around her friend.

'I'm so happy for you,' Amelie enthused.

Helen remained silent, a distant look in her eyes.

'What is it? What's wrong?' Cleome quizzed.

'Nothing, nothing's wrong. The baby is fine, but you know I'm forty-four. I thought those days were gone for me, and there are risks, you know?'

'Oh Helen, Helen… It will be fine. We don't get to decide everything, you know. Something wiser is at play.'

'I am a scientist. I don't see these things the way you do.'

'What does Daniel say about it?'

'Oh, he is over the moon. He plans to reduce his working hours and be the main carer of the child so that I can keep my job. It will be his first child.'

'You don't sound very pleased?'

'I don't know what to think or what to do, if I'm honest. I was dreading telling Josef but he thinks it's "cool" so it's just me who has doubts. Ach, I will get used to it, with time.'

That evening, Amelie knelt on the landing floor and opened the pine chest. Sunlight slanted through the window at her side casting her shadow long over the polished floorboards. She extracted a photograph album bound with thick brown card imprinted with dozens of small golden hearts, and placed it on the floor beside her, unopened. That would be for another day—a stronger day. Next, she removed her favourite jumper of Nick's, smoothed the wool with her fingertips, lifted the soft fabric to her face, and inhaled deeply. She stilled for a moment, and then folded the garment and placed it to one side. Next, she picked out Bertie's teddy bear; the small honey-furred one that her mother had given him when he was born. She stroked its sturdy body and sat it on the floor. On she went, carefully examining each precious object, allowing memories to swirl and dance about her, joining the motes in the sunlit air. She processed each swell of emotion before replacing every item and closing the pine lid. She did not want to forget as she moved into this new phase of her life. She did not want to ever let go. She wanted to somehow live her new life while carrying her old life along with her. She ran her fingers back through her hair and took a deep breath.

There was one more thing she needed to do in order to be completely free to move forward.

27

New Moon of Calming

Very early in the morning, before the heat became intolerable, Amelie and Cleome walked solemnly down to the jetty. They had both showered and wore fresh, colourful dresses. Cleome's many silver bangles gleamed on her arm. Amelie had tied back her hair with a long scrap of cream lace. Trassel's and Aslan's coats were groomed free of tangles, and shone. The dogs trotted beside the women, noses to the air but keeping close, knowing, in the way that dogs do, that something special was needed of them. Amelie carried a large basket, and Cleome an armful of freshly-picked flowers.

At the jetty, they met Helen, Daniel, Joseph and Tarek. They had motored a boat around the bay, and were waiting for them. They too were colourfully dressed and had cleaned their boat especially. Kaia sat in the prow, and the dogs woofed and wagged tails on seeing each other. Amelie and Cleome nodded quiet good mornings to the others. Amelie set the basket and Cleome's flowers down in the hull of their own small vessel. She quietly instructed Trassel to sit where she always did, with Aslan behind her in the bow, and then took Cleome's hand to help her to a bench seat. Tarek climbed over into their boat too. Then, as they did not wish to disturb the peace with engine noise, each boat was rowed into the centre of the lake with Josef at one set of oars and Tarek at the other. They stopped at an agreed point, drew in the oars and roped the two boats together. At that early hour, there were no private leisure boats or enthusiastic water-skiers to disturb their peace.

Amelie took out a cloth, and on it, she placed the cherrywood box containing Bertie's ashes, the armful of flowers from the garden, two specially chosen books, and her phone.

'Shall we begin?' Daniel asked, with quiet reverence.

Amelie nodded.

'In the lake, we give Bertie a final place to rest. In our memories, we will not forget him. In the eternal love and mercy of God, he will be at peace,' Daniel read.

The boat rocked as Cleome reached for her book, and put on her reading glasses.

'Angels, in the early morning,' she began.

'Angels, in the early morning
May be seen the Dews among,
Stooping—plucking—smiling—flying—
Do the Buds to them belong?
Angels, when the sun is hottest
May be seen the sands among,
Stooping—plucking—sighing—flying—
Parched the flowers they bear along.'

She closed the book, and folded her glasses into her pocket. Tarek sat up tall, and after exchanging a glance with Amelie, began his reading.

'Peace, my heart.
Peace, my heart, let the time for the parting be sweet.
Let it not be a death but completeness.
Let love melt into memory and pain into songs.
Let the flight through the sky end in the folding of the wings over the nest.
Let the last touch of your hands be gentle like the flower of the night.
Stand still, O Beautiful End, for a moment, and say your last words in silence.
I bow to you and hold up my lamp to light you on your way.'

Tarek smudged a tear from his cheek with his thumb, and Cleome, noticing, contemplated all the loss that he had borne too. Daniel took his turn with another reading.

'You would know the secret of death. But how shall you find it unless you seek it in the heart of life? The owl whose night-bound eyes are blind unto the day cannot unveil the mystery of light. If you would indeed behold the spirit of death, open your heart wide unto the body of life. For life and death are one, even as the river and sea are one... For what is it to die but to stand naked in the wind and to melt into the sun? And what is it to cease breathing, but to free the breath from its restless tides, that it may rise and expand and seek God unencumbered? ...And when the

earth shall claim your limbs, then shall you truly dance.' Daniel nodded to Amelie who picked up her phone and selected her chosen song. The soulful voice of Eric Clapton singing Tears In Heaven filled the air with poignant melody. Tarek closed his eyes. Josef chewed his lip, and tried not to cry. Daniel reached for Helen's hand. Cleome put her arm softly around Amelie's shoulder. Aslan sat with his elegant nose to the breeze, and Trassel slept, curled up in a sunny patch in the bow of the boat. The song finished, and there was a moment's silence. Amelie then picked up a battered paperback, and found the page she was looking for. She gazed steadily at the cherrywood box which sat on the colourful cloth as she spoke, mostly from memory A.A. Milne's poem Us Two. She recited the words she knew so well, without faltering or needing the page open before her, as if to Bertie. It was a poem she had read him many times. When she had finished, she set down the crumpled paperback, picked up the cherrywood box, and carefully opened it.

Helen found Chopin's Nocturne No 21—the piece she had chosen to play—on her phone, and as Amelie and Cleome scattered Bertie's ashes over the lake's glimmering surface, Claudio Arrau's sensitive and poignant rendition rang out across the water. Light shimmered as the warm translucent lake welcomed Bertie's remains into her embrace. More piano music played, as Amelie whispered her good-byes. Cleome put her arm around her granddaughter's shoulder again, as Tarek and Josef, quietly and without any fuss, untied the ropes, picked up the oars, and rowed the boats back to shore.

It is done, Amelie told herself as she stepped onto the land again. It is finally done.

28

Waxing Moon of Calming

The grass around *Det Lilla Huset* looked dead. In the interminable heat, it had withered and browned, and now crunched beneath Cleome's sandals as she went about her chores, watering her plants and feeding the chickens, her dogs never far from her side. The cottage had been invaded by wasps. She had made several traps—jars of water mixed with a spoonful of jam, and fixed over with pierced paper tops. Each day, several wasps crawled in through the holes, easy prey to the sugary concoctions. They drowned in a sticky, satiated kind of heaven. It was probably not a bad way to go, she reflected.

Amelie had hummed as she went about her incessant cleaning that morning—abstract little tunes, merry and pretty. She always moved deftly, stirring and enlivening the air, her pointed chin held high. Kindness shone from her face like a sunbeam, even on her darker days. She was a special soul, Cleome reflected, gazing at the empty glade as it shimmered in the morning heat. She had now disappeared somewhere for the day, possibly with Tarek.

In the back of her mind was Catherine, who was staying on in Stockholm with no immediate plans to leave. Three additional granddaughters danced in her mind's eye: Catherine's daughters. What would they be like, assuming she ever met them? What would Amelie make of them? Life could be so complicated, and she did not always know the answers.

With her chores done, she carried a mug of coffee out to the wooden table in the shade. Insects hummed in the long grass which, dry and erect, awaited a forgiving breeze or rain shower that never came. The dogs slumped idly at her feet. The silence was deep, and she knew that it waited for her to fill its void with all her troubles. It nudged her to face the unpalatable truths that lurked deep in her being. After she had finished her coffee, she collected a towel and sauntered down to the lake. She swam religiously three times each day now, while Aslan and Trassel sat on the jetty, whimpering their concern. The doctor had told her to gently increase the amount of exercise she took, and to relax more and avoid stress. She had mentioned her pains but not told him about Catherine; she still did not trust male doctors, had never fully recovered after the rubber-lipped idiot in England had told her she was a "naughty girl" who could not keep her baby. So inhumane, and a liar too.

After the cooling dip, she drove into Flen for food, the car seat roasting the backs of her thighs and warming her old bones. Dazzling stripes of light illuminated sections of the forest road. During the journey, she missed discussing with Amelie what they would eat, and in ICA, the way that Amelie darted down the aisles, her attention focused on getting them everything they needed. She shopped well with Amelie, unlike the many times she had shopped with Kerstin. *Kerstin.* Never a day passed when her throat did not thicken at her loss. She still berated herself for having been so hard on her second-born child. She saw now how Catherine being seized from her had woven a wrong-coloured thread through her relationship with her younger daughter—and it had not been Kerstin's fault that her mother secretly mourned, not Kerstin's fault that she had been born blessed in a way that her half-sibling had not. As she drove, Cleome allowed the memories of arguments with Kerstin about school work, and household chores, and boys and clothes, to repeat over and over in her mind until she felt quite dizzy, and pulled the car over to the side of the forest road, and rested her head on the steering wheel in an attempt to stop the litany of all the mistakes she had ever made.

When she had put her shopping away and let the dogs out into the garden, she poured herself a strong drink, and took it out to sit beneath the trees. Daniel appeared over the hill, walking towards her with his determined stride. He had brought her another bottle of bootleg Russian vodka, and come to share his concerns about Tarek, whom he said was very agitated by all the gossip in town. The police still had not found the burglars and there had been a spate of further break-ins in the area. Daniel confided that he suspected Tarek had a soft spot for Amelie but Cleome kept a poker face and said nothing. She asked him about Helen's pregnancy and his face flushed with pleasure as he outlined their plans. They wandered down to the lake with their drinks. She told him about her meetings in Stockholm, and the fact that they did not always go as smoothly as she hoped. Catherine took her Italian heritage seriously and was irritated that Cleome did not know the surname of her father, or the exact square in Florence where he had worked.

'The way Catherine phrases it, my inattention does seem irresponsible. She is being denied her paternal heritage.'

'You must not be so hard on yourself.'

It was true, but nonetheless a sense of shame made her cheeks burn and her chest throb erratically. 'I suggested that perhaps with research, she might still be able to find out her father's name, but that was met with a haughty silence.'

'I have an idea.' Daniel pulled out the small notebook he always carried in his trouser pocket, and asked Cleome a string of questions. He jotted down her answers—general fears and feelings of inadequacy—using one or two words per page. He then carefully tore out the sheets and made a series of tiny paper boats from them. Putting a match to each small vessel, he launched them on the water where they burnt and disintegrated.

'There. You have let your troubles go.'

'That is pollution,' Cleome remarked.

'Of a necessary nature,' Daniel replied, with a warm smile.

He left to return to *Båvenshult*, and Cleome wandered back up to the garden, and continued to drink vodka and reminisce. The quietness of the homestead was all-embracing, the heatwave loitered like the unwanted guest at a party. At fifty-eight, Catherine's skin was like honey, her hair thick and dark with sophisticated streaks of grey; she was undoubtedly beautiful. She assumed that her father was a man of class. Cleome had struggled, and tried to explain that he was not the type to admire fine art or Italian cuisine, that ogling a Ducati had been more his style. They had wandered along *Drottninggaten* and visited one boutique after another, as was Catherine's preference. She stepped through the streets like an inquisitive deer, primed to flee. Cleome had taken some kronor, and bought her a scarf. She had accepted the gift with a charming smile.

She recalled Angelo, who did not know—and would perhaps never know—that he had an English daughter. She speculated on whether he was still alive, what his full name might actually have been, and whether he had gone on to marry and have a legitimate family of his own. For the first time, it bothered her that she had not discovered more about him. She recalled how they had smoked shared cigarettes and drunk red wine. From the second clandestine encounter onwards, they had repaired to his cousin's empty apartment overlooking one of the city's small and charming piazzas to have hot, sticky sex in a wide bed while a dusty net curtain ballooned in the breeze, and the chatter and life of the square went on beneath the open window. Angelo had skin the colour of milky coffee. His name had conjured impressions of romance and angels in her naive teenage mind. He had known a thing or two about the joy of touch and the slow art of seduction; rare qualities in her experience, and in a different league from the clumsy advances of English grammar school boys with names like Geoffrey or Derek.

She had not loved him. Deep down she had known that, even at the time—but she had definitely liked him, laughed with him, and been intrigued by him. Was her lack of love another mark of her disgrace? Even now over half a century later, on a bad day, shame at the memory of her lust weighed down her old shoulders, like a yoke. She had definitely not loved him; she had barely known him. They had exchanged few words; only touches, lingering gazes, warm wet endless kisses, and a series of exciting climaxes when, in thrall, they had gripped each other and held tight, as the vital bodily fluids were released. Angelo had known the deal too. He had not asked to keep in touch, had blown her a kiss as she strode away, back to her oblivious parents, that final time.

Despite everything that had followed, and the fact she had not loved Angelo, she had fallen helter-skelter in love with their baby, from the very moment she was born, all slippery and screaming, a shock of dark hair plastered to her scalp, and her tiny face puce. Her birthday was the 28th of April 1960, and in another twist of fate, Kerstin was born on the very same date, five years later. *Poor Kerstin.*

Cleome took a long sip from her drink. Aslan scratched himself. A hawk cried.

Eight days after Catherine was born, she returned to the home. Catherine was put into the nursery there, and Cleome's breasts were bound to stop her milk. She was not allowed contact with her but crept into the nursery each night, just to look at her. Ten days after being back, she was cleaning the stairs and happened to notice Catherine being carried out of the front door by a woman in a dark wool coat who had a tall man at her side. Catherine was crying; Cleome would have known her cry anywhere. She had not dared to run after her to say goodbye in case she spoilt something for her, but Catherine's parting cry had torn something from Cleome that she had never got back.

At the bottom of the glade, the light softened over the water turning it purple, and the reeds rustled in a gentle breeze. Maybe this was what the profound silence at *Det Lilla Huset* was asking her to face? The darkness, shame, and terror that was still stashed away, somewhere deep inside her ancient body.

Since the reunion with Catherine, she was more convinced than ever that what she and Angelo had done was not "dirty" or "wrong". What a nonsense her parents' reaction had been! God had not punished her, He had blessed her with a beautiful child who had grown into an educated, decent woman. It was the society at the time that had caused all her pain, not God, not her or Angelo, but other human beings— the authorities and her own family.

The silent landscape listened, encouraged. As the sky turned dark, she spoke into the silence, not in words but in the other, secret language. She prayed to be unburdened and finally forgiven, and in what might have been a trick of the light, she thought she saw her guilt spill out of its flimsy hiding-hole and pool at her feet— a black sticky puddle. Slowly, the tarry mess was absorbed into the earth.

Tarek and Amelie returned from Stockholm where they had spent a perfect day, touring the archipelago on the water bus, holding hands, kissing and cuddling, and not having to worry about being seen. It had been good, not having to keep their love secret. They had discussed when to tell everyone, and Tarek had told her there was something he needed to do first, but he would not say what. He said it was better that she did not know for now, and he would tell her at the right time. Amelie trusted him but was nettled. She wondered if he was apprehensive about their different races. He understood the current rise in inter-racial tension in Sweden far better than she did. Living out in the forest, it was easy to forget that beneath its perfect surface, Sweden struggled. Even the United Nations had released a report expressing concern about the level of racism and extreme right politics in the country—it had made international news.

He drove them back from the bus stop at Skavsta airport, and she asked if he would mind driving past the supermarket in Flen and waiting while she dashed in to get something. In the shop, she grabbed a box of tampons from the shelf and turned to find herself face-to-face with Ayah who was with two other veiled women whom she didn't know.

'Hi,' she said, and smiled.

Ayah did not return the smile. 'Why don't you just go back to England?' she said.

'I beg your pardon?'

'Go back to England, where you belong.'

'My mother was Swedish.'

'Ha, it makes no difference to me. You go home. You are not wanted here.'

'What is your problem? Tarek would be horrified to hear you talk like this.'

'You don't know anything about Tarek.'

Amelie raised an eyebrow and stared down at Ayah. She saw how young she was, the bitterness glittering in her kohl-lined eyes, and her barely controlled anger. One of the other women murmured something in Arabic to Ayah, and she softened but pressed her lips together, stubbornly. Amelie thought of what Tarek had told her about Ayah and Zain, how they were young and trouble-makers, and she turned and walked away. She would choose her battles but she would not forget Ayah's billowing hatred.

29

Waning Moon of Calming

On the much-awaited morning, after a night when a crescent moon had graced the sky with her perfect curve, the dogs heard the lone car crunching down the track long before Cleome did. They rushed off towards the sound, barking and stirring up a dust cloud with their paws. Cleome scurried in their wake, waving her arms so that her collection of silver bangles jingled. She wore a freshly-ironed cerise cotton top and patterned azure skirt. A yellow-printed scarf was tied about her head to keep her hair out of her eyes, and the multi-coloured woven pouch containing her hip flask bounced against her thigh.

'*Kom hit!*' she called to the dogs, and whistled like a sheep farmer. Trassel turned and raced to her mistress. Aslan took a moment longer before loping back, his blond coat lifting like the cloak of a prince.

It was not quite the welcome that Cleome had rehearsed. Catherine, however, did not seem to register the commotion. Her shiny estate car hurtled down the track to the barn and reversed swiftly and efficiently into a shady spot. Cleome hastened forwards, her polished red sandals already dusted with dry earth. Pausing a short distance from the car, she fingered the nugget of turquoise on her vintage silver necklace. The car door opened and a gazelle-like ankle emerged. Catherine pushed her sunglasses into her hair, and looked around. Her gold pumps gleamed in the dirt; she sauntered towards Cleome, and planted a kiss in the air above her ear.

Her daughter smelt of expensive perfume and sun cream. It never failed to astonish Cleome that she had given birth to a woman so unlike herself, and each time they met she felt a needle of shock. Angelo had been tall—surprisingly tall for an Italian—and had moved with the grace of a cat. He had been sallow-skinned with a mass of dark curls, all traits that lived on in his daughter.

'So, welcome! Here is my cottage and barn. Over here is the orchard, and down there is a pontoon beside the lake where we can sit later. Do let's get out of this burning sun. I expect you'd like a coffee after your journey. I'm not sure where Amelie has disappeared to. She's longing to meet you.'

Catherine gazed about, taking in the fenced vegetable patch, the chicken run dotted with apple trees, and the long yellow grass with the shady forest beyond. She nodded silently, as if the sight of the little homestead confirmed something deep inside her.

'After a drink, perhaps you'd like to swim,' Cleome gabbled. 'And then later when we get hungry, we are invited to a crayfish party at my neighbour's house. It's a great Swedish tradition, and there will be plenty to eat and drink.'

'I'll fetch my bag,' Catherine said, and Cleome watched as she extracted a beach bag from the car boot.

Amelie appeared, having been in the shower when Catherine arrived. Her fair hair hung about her face, wet and freshly-combed. The two women shook hands while Cleome watched, clasping her own hands. They went inside and made polite conversation about the weather and life in the forest while Cleome clattered about making a jug of coffee. The dogs stalked her, making the kitchen feel claustrophobic. Amelie put some biscuits on a plate, and carried everything outdoors on a tray. They took seats at the table in the shade, and Cleome offered Catherine her home-made insect repellent made from an old Sami recipe, and lit an incense coil. There were fewer insects at this time of year but she was anxious that her daughter did not get bitten. The dogs flopped down on the grass, and Trassel scratched herself inelegantly and at length.

Catherine brought out tissue-wrapped gifts from her bag—colourful scarves from an expensive shop in the city. Cleome and Amelie admired them and thanked her. She surveyed her surroundings. 'Do you not get bored, living in the middle of a forest all alone?' she quizzed.

Cleome smiled. 'Not for one moment,' she replied truthfully.

As she poured out the coffee while Amelie and Catherine made polite conversation, Cleome found herself distracted by yet more memories of Angelo and Italy, the scent of cigarette smoke, the taste of pizza dripping with tomatoes and herbs and long strings of melted mozzarella, the smell of stone buildings baking in the relentless sunshine, and the surprise of him kissing her toes, one by one. Would her parents not be proud now, if they had lived to witness Catherine's spectacular presence?

After coffee, Cleome showed her daughter around the house and the cavernous barn that was full of cobwebbed furniture, garden tools and pots, lengths of disused timber, and logs that Tarek had begun to stack for the coming winter. She pointed out each chicken in the orchard, chuckling as she explained that they were named after female poets. There was Emily Dickinson, the Rhode Island Red with a stutter, the observant and diminutive Pekin called Mary Oliver, and the splendid and glossy black Maya Angelou who reigned at the top of the pecking order.

Amelie studied her new aunt, surreptitiously. Catherine was as dark as Kerstin was fair, but there was a striking similarity about their jawlines, and the shapes of their mouths and eyes. They were both tall, and Catherine obviously loved fashion in the way that Kerstin had too. It was like seeing the hazy shadow of a ghost of her mother, being in Catherine's presence. While Catherine was looking away, Cleome secretly squeezed her hand. Amelie squeezed it back.

After collecting eggs and carrying them back to the kitchen, Cleome suggested that they walk down to the lake for a swim. Catherine asked to go upstairs so that she could change her clothes, and Cleome lingered in the hallway while Amelie tidied away the coffee cups, filled a flask with cool water and found some paper cups to take down to the lakeside. When Catherine reappeared, she wore a cream sarong knotted around her waist over a black swimming costume. The delicate fabric clung to the small pouch of her belly, and allowed glimpses of her tanned knees. She walked at Amelie's side as they wandered down the glade.

'I wish I had met your mum,' she confessed. 'I went to her funeral, to pay my respects to the little sister I never knew. I was so full of regret that I had never found the courage to meet her, and overwhelmed with sadness at her passing. I'm so sorry for your loss.'

Cleome, who had been walking ahead of them, stopped and turned as Amelie blinked back a sudden tear. 'I did not know you were there,' she exclaimed. 'You should have come up to me, said something.'

'It wasn't the right time.'

'No,' Amelie agreed. 'But thank you for your kind words about Mum. She would have liked to have met you, I'm sure.'

They had reached the jetty, and Catherine took a chair with plump cushions, and after settling, stretched out her forearms and leaned her head back, raising her face to the light, and closing her eyes. Amelie and Cleome glanced at one another.

'Are you not going to take a dip?' Cleome asked.

'Heavens, no,' she replied with her eyes still closed.

Amelie stripped off to her bikini and dived into the lake with an impressively small splash. Cleome followed, descending the ladder and easing her body into the cooling water. As she swam, her hands created a gentle rippling sound, and sunlight danced and dazzled. For a moment, she marvelled at the way everything unfolded—this beautiful life that she would one day leave behind, her legacy of another daughter and three yet-to-be-met granddaughters, all living on this heaving, abundant planet—a place where a woman could be seduced, and a man could spawn a daughter and three grandchildren without ever knowing he had done so. What a wild life it was, really.

And then there was Kerstin, and the fact that she was gone. Cleome turned onto her back, and floated. *Kerstin*. The familiar pain lanced her chest. How could she celebrate Catherine, how could she be joyful at her presence when Kerstin had died so unfairly? Distress pooled around her like multi-coloured oil on the water's surface before she reminded herself that Kerstin would not want her to be a victim to her grief. Kerstin was the type who would have told her to "get positive" and look on the bright side.

'Do you swim here every day?' Catherine called out.

'At this time of year, three times a day.'

'You must be fit.'

'At my age, you have to use it or lose it,' she puffed, rolling onto her front and resuming a steady, slow breast stroke.

Further out in the lake, Amelie swam like a fish beneath the water, occasionally surfacing, a speck in the wild expanse of water and forest.

When she climbed out of the water, Cleome glanced at Catherine, and noticed that a frown puckered her forehead above her large film star sunglasses as she perched on the edge of the sun chair. 'Is something wrong?'

Catherine sighed heavily, and tore her attention away from watching Amelie. 'My half-niece is a real water-baby.'

'She is. Just like her mother.'

'You know, what you have here is so complete.' Catherine waved her hand in the air. 'There are so many gaps in my life, so many holes, so many unanswered questions!' She gesticulated again, in a gesture strongly reminiscent of Angelo's demonstrative and voluble mother.

'I can see that you struggle.'

'Oh, you have no idea!'

Cleome did not know what to do or say to make things better, and so she kept quiet. Pain darted through her chest, and she realised that her medicine was up at the house. She did not like to make a fuss; she had brought this distress upon herself after all, and must bear it.

As they prepared to get ready for the crayfish party, Amelie was quietly excited at the prospect of seeing Tarek again. He had been working overtime while a colleague was away on holiday, and they had not had a chance to meet up since their day out on the archipelago. He had messaged her, telling her he loved her, and she had replied. She had never mentioned the altercation with Ayah in the supermarket, not wanting to distress him. She checked herself in the mirror and smoothed her summer dress, smiled at the secret knowledge they shared, and allowed her excitement to bubble at the prospect of seeing him again.

Her grandmother looked tired but she had put her best bright clothes back on after taking a shower, and had brushed her hair so that it shone silvery white. She wore the new scarf from Catherine and had even applied a little lipstick. She now strode to the car, keen to introduce Catherine to her friends. They were running a little late, as usual. Catherine was to drive them, along with the dogs, in her rental car. She sped down the track and onto the forest road, as Cleome gripped the edges of her seat. When they arrived at *Båvenshult*, the party was already in full swing.

'Welcome, welcome,' Helen called out, waving. 'I thought you were never coming!'

Cleome waved back. 'Sorry! Time has run away with us today!'

'Wonderful to meet you!' Helen said, taking Catherine's hand and sandwiching it between hers. Helen's skin glowed, and she wore a loose blouse over her growing belly, but she looked distracted, as if something was bothering her. As she hurried them towards the house, Amelie gave her a questioning look but she shook her head fractionally, bitterness passing over her face like a ghost.

Amelie was concerned and looked around for a glimpse of Tarek. In true Swedish tradition, some of the party guests wore paper hats and had begun to sing drinking songs already. Paper lanterns depicting the man in the moon hung in the orchard trees. She could not see him anywhere.

'The wasps were so bad earlier that we moved the food indoors, so please, follow me.' Helen led the way through the kitchen, across the hall, and into her dining room, whose three tall windows looked out over the field to the glimmering lake beyond.

Catherine raised a hand to her chest and gasped at the view. Helen handed out plates and paper bibs, in a rush. 'There's plenty left. We made sure to save you some.' Spread on the large table were the remains of dishes of crayfish seasoned with dill, little mushroom pies, blocks of cheese, a bowl of fermented herrings, and various bowls of salad. Catherine selected a mushroom pie, some cheese and salad for her plate.

'I will teach you how to eat the crayfish, if this is your first time,' Cleome offered. 'It can get messy, hence the bibs,' she winked. 'They are delicious, and well worth the effort.'

Helen disappeared. Catherine declined the crayfish, and after piling their plates with food, they returned outdoors and picked their way across the garden to a table where Daniel and Helen sat huddled together, ignoring most of their guests.

'May we join you?' Cleome asked, eager that Helen and Daniel should spend time with her daughter.

'Of course, of course.' Helen patted an empty seat. 'You must forgive us, Catherine. We've had some worrying news, and we're just trying to work out what to do. It's Tarek.'

Amelie froze and exchanged a furtive glance with Cleome. She did not touch her food while Helen explained that the police had interviewed him again, and that he was so furious, he had driven off that morning and not returned. They had tried to contact him but he had turned his phone off.

'Have you heard from him?' Helen asked Amelie.

'Not today, but he did tell me that some of the immigrant community in Flen suspect him of carrying out the burglary at *Det Lilla Huset*. Some of them have ostracised him. They don't trust the fact that he lives out here with you, and not with them, and have decided that he must be up to no good.'

Daniel and Helen looked at each other. 'He's told us that too,' Daniel said. 'He railed at their ignorance and the unfairness of the accusation. He blames their inability to integrate into Swedish life as the force behind their prejudice. He says some of them only want to stick together, with what they know, and the Swedish authorities don't help, making them all live on the edge of town.'

'I hope he doesn't do anything stupid. He was pretty angry earlier, and said he knew who was behind all the trouble-making and was going to speak to them,' Helen added.

'It's not just his own people who are stirring up trouble,' Cleome said. 'The knitting group witches don't have a good word to say about him either. I'm sorry, Helen, but they bitch about you, and say you're a fool for letting him into your life. It is one of the reasons that I don't bother with them anymore. I stood up for him and for you, but they are a bunch of small-minded bigots who make it perfectly clear to me that after half a century of living here, I am still not one of them. They are all scared after the latest spate of burglaries, especially Monika whose husband is a retired police officer; she is the ringleader. She sees criminals out to get her around every corner, and they all have brown faces.'

Catherine listened intently, while politely tucking in to her lunch.

'I wish we could do something to help Tarek!' Amelie cried. 'Where is he now, do you know?'

'No. That's what we were just discussing—whether we should attempt to find him.'

'I wish there was some way of proving his innocence. *Mormor*, I'm sorry I haven't told you this before but earlier in the winter before the burglary, someone was snooping around our place. They left footsteps in the snow. I reported it to the police but of course, the snow had melted by then and there was no evidence.'

'Really? How odd. I wonder if Lotta saw anything?'

'I asked her. She said she didn't see a thing.'

'Ah, but we can't rely on her, hiding behind her curtains the way she does. And besides, she's one of the knitting group. She gossips like the rest of them, and is a closet racist. She probably believes that Tarek did it too.'

Catherine had stopped eating and laid her cutlery down on her plate. Her cheeks were pink. 'I have something to confess, Mamma' she said. It was so powerful to hear the word "Mamma" spoken aloud that everyone turned to look at her. 'I am re-evaluating my life and learning to speak my truth as part of my therapy, as you know. This includes making amends for any wrongs that I have done. I have a new counsellor in London who is encouraging all this,' she explained as an aside to Helen and Daniel, circling her elegant hand in the air, as she spoke. 'So,' she blushed again and lowered her eyes, 'I need to confess something. I don't know how to say this, so I will just be frank: I came out here one evening last January while it was snowing. I was going to knock on your door but the cottage was in darkness and I thought you were out or had gone to bed early. It was before I wrote to you and we had agreed to meet up again. I had hoped to surprise you with an unexpected visit from me. It was a silly, romantic idea; I was not thinking straight. The dog was barking and then Amelie came to the window and I didn't want to interrupt, after... after, you know, what had happened. I lost my courage and realised it was terrible timing on my part, and that I was being incredibly selfish and thinking about my own needs and not about yours...and so I tiptoed back to my car which I'd had to leave up the lane due to the heavy snowfall. I left without knocking on your door. I am so embarrassed.'

Amelie's eyebrows raised.

'Well, I think it's very brave of you to admit that, Catherine,' Helen said firmly.

'Yes, it is thoughtful of you to confess. Thank you dear,' Cleome added, her eyes glittering with tears as she gazed across the table at her daughter's bowed head. She reached an arthritic hand forward and covered her daughter's soft fist, giving it a little squeeze. 'It's alright. We're all friends here. There's nothing to be embarrassed about.'

Catherine looked up again, a self-conscious smile on her face. 'Not something I'm proud of, but in the circumstances, I feel it needed to be said. I had felt an uncanny sense of belonging for the first time in my life when I watched you both from the edge of the crowd at the funeral, you know. And then when I came here to Sweden, and I saw that my mother lived in this pretty little cottage by the lake, it was like something out of a fairy tale. You can't imagine what it means to me.'

'Oh, I think I can.' Amelie smiled. 'And thank you for being honest.' She touched her arm. 'There's one less thing to worry about but it doesn't really help us with what to do about Tarek.'

'Catherine, you must forgive us for talking about something you know nothing about,' Helen apologised. 'It's very rude of us.'

'But you must be so concerned about your friend. Don't mind me, and anything I can do to help...' Her voice trailed off. She fanned herself with a jewelled hand as the afternoon heat pressed in.

'I think it is best that we wait, and trust Tarek. He won't do anything foolish.'

'I agree. He's strong and sensible.' Cleome caught Amelie's eye.

She still fretted, privately. After all that had happened in the past ten months, her nerves were not as strong as they once were, and she knew that in life, anything could happen. She tackled her crayfish with silent determination while her mind raced with imagined horrors.

As the afternoon wore on, there was still no sign of him. At one point, she excused herself and rang him secretly but his phone remained switched off.

After the last of the guests had finally left, the small group wandered down to the lake beach to relieve their nagging unease, and so that Catherine could see more of *Båvenshult*. On their return to the farmhouse, Helen's phone rang. She answered it promptly, pacing off into the orchard to take the call, and returning with a pale face.

'That was Lotta Bengtsson,' she said. 'Her husband is dead.'

30

Perseid Meteor Shower

Catherine dropped Cleome at *Det Mörka Huset* as Cleome insisted on consoling Lotta and Robban and offering to help them, and that Amelie must return home with the dogs.

After Amelie had said farewell to Catherine, she fed the dogs and then paced the ancient floorboards of the little homestead, unable to rest knowing that Tarek was still not back, and feeling shocked and unsettled by the sudden death of the neighbour. After an hour, her grandmother returned looking weary, and saying that she needed an early night. Magnus Bengtsson had suffered a massive stroke, Lotta was distraught and Robban, confused and quiet. Amelie asked if there was anything she could do, and Cleome shook her head. She then asked if she could take the car to see whether Tarek had returned, and her grandmother patted her on the arm.

'Of course, you can. He will be alright, you know, but I expect he will be glad to see you, so go. I'm going to make myself a drink and have an early night. Take a key with you, and here, take this packet of calming herbal tea. Tarek likes it and I bet he could do with some this evening.'

Amelie drove back to *Båvenshult* and parked her car out of sight from the main house, not wishing to betray her closeness with Tarek to Helen or Daniel. She saw that Tarek was still not home, and crept round to the back of the bungalow to wait for him on the decking there. She took a seat and listened to the sounds of the landscape—the rustling trees and a horse blowing in the paddock nearby. She chewed the corner of her finger and checked her phone, wishing there was something more she could do. After twenty minutes or so, she thought she heard a car approaching on the forest road, leapt up, and raced to the front of the little house. From inside the car, Tarek raised a hand in greeting. He parked the vehicle and walked towards her with his arms open. Relief washed over her as she rushed into his embrace. He prepared to explain what had happened, just as a second car came hurtling down the track and drew up outside the bungalow.

Ayah stepped out and unleashed a torrent of Arabic at Tarek, shaking her arm in the air, her young face contorted with fury. Another woman accompanying her, joined in the shouting. Tarek motioned towards the main house, and signalled to the women to quieten down. Wary of Helen's standing in the community, they lowered their voices. Ayah turned to address Amelie, hissing in broken English that she was a selfish white woman who was disrupting their community in Flen. Tarek intervened, saying that what had happened was nothing to do with Amelie.

'Why do you defend her when Zain is being questioned by the police, along with that other Syrian and our Somali friend, regarding the burglaries in the area, including at *her* house?' Ayah jabbed a finger in Amelie's direction. 'Zain blames her and you for leading the police to him. Is it true, you betrayed my brother?'

'Your brother is addicted to prescription drugs. That whole crowd he hangs out with are addicts. That's why they have been robbing people, and raiding people's homes for drugs and cash to buy opiates illegally on the black market or from the internet. That's why they pray on elderly and sick people who are more likely to have strong painkillers at home, and it's why they do not take valuables because they don't have the network in place to dispose of them. They are pathetic.'

Ayah's eyes flashed defiantly. 'You think I don't know this? You think I don't try to help my brother when he suffers terrible dreams after all we have been through? He needs those drugs just to get through the night, sometimes. He cries and trembles, haunted by visions from the war. And the Swedish are rich and they all have insurance. If we take their things, it hardly touches their lives, let's face it. People like her don't know they are born!'

Tarek's expression grew stern. 'You knew what he was doing, and yet you defended Zain and you were trying to frame me for his crimes. Why?'

'Oh, you can take it, you always survive everything, and it served you right for being with her after my sister died! I am the one you should have loved. I am from home, not her. She is an outsider.'

'I think you'd better leave, Ayah.'

She stalled and frowned as if experiencing an internal struggle, and then swept away with her little chin in the air, back to her car with her silent friend trailing behind her. She spun the car around in the driveway and sped off.

'Ayah was always jealous and spiteful, and Zain was spoilt. They were not like Nuwar at all,' Tarek said. 'I'm mortified that I have brought such trouble into your home. I'm sure they would have come here too, to take Helen's medical supplies, if it wasn't for Kaia. They are terrified of dogs. They will only have burgled your place because they knew Trassel was with me. And they would have done it out of spite too. I bet that's why they made so much mess. Ayah will have inflamed them.'

'But how did you discover it was them?'

'I noticed something about one of the aerial photographs that Helen had framed, of Båvenshult. I realised it was taken about the time of your burglary. When I checked, I appeared in some of the pictures, and so that proved it could not have been me who committed the crime. When I approached him, Robban was actually a very sweet guy, and keen to show me all the footage of that day. He had all the evidence the police needed to show the van coming to your place and who the criminals were. Being Robban, he did not understand the implications but when I explained to him how he could help the police, he became very excited, and handed over digital copies of the photographs and videos to me as well, quite willingly. (I am afraid I do not trust your police entirely, and so I wanted to keep my own evidence.) His father and mother came home, and so I left quickly because my business with Robban was over and I sensed immediately that I was not welcome in their house. I must thank Robban properly. He saved my skin.'

'So, that's where you were?'

'In the morning I was with him, and then I went straight to the police station and then I needed some time alone so I walked in the forest, and went and sat by the runestone for a while.'

'You know, Robban's father had a stroke, earlier this afternoon. He didn't survive.'

'I didn't know that. I am sorry. Poor Robban will be very upset.'

'He will, but his father was quite cruel to him sometimes, we think, so I expect he will be confused too. You must go and reassure Helen and Daniel that you are okay.'

'It's alright, I called her on the way home. She wasn't pleased that I had turned off my phone but it was distracting Robban, and then I forgot it was off.'

'Shall we go inside? Or would you rather be alone?' Her throat tightened. She longed to be with him, and to know that despite the forces that worked against them, their special connection remained unbroken, but she did not want to stay if he needed to be on his own for a while.

'Of course, I want you to come inside with me.' His voice softened, and he reached for her hand. She stretched her fingers to touch his, and her heart contracted as she registered his warmth. She had not realised how distressed she had become, fearing that something dreadful might have happened during his absence. She blinked back a tear.

'It's okay,' he said, drawing her into his arms. His familiar cedarwood scent smelt like home. Indoors, they did not speak. She touched her forehead against his chest and then wound her arms around his neck and pressed her lips to his.

'I was worried about you.'

'You need not worry about me, but I'm glad you're here, tonight.'

He rustled up a plate of leftovers from his fridge, and Amelie, still full from the crayfish party, sat with him while he ate. After he had finished, he went outside to smoke a cigarette while she made steaming cups of her grandmother's soothing herbal tea. Indoors again, he strummed his guitar quietly, humming tunes that were unfamiliar to Amelie but conveyed hurt and loss in the international language of music.

As she sat in the darkening room, happy to be in his company again and listening to his soulful sounds, she was grateful that he had come into her life; but after the day's events, with him absent and out of touch, she also realised how vulnerable she was again and how, by allowing herself to love him, she had opened herself to more pain and heartbreak too. A miniscule part of her still mistrusted her newfound love. She could no longer imagine life without Tarek but still, there was a tiny element of caution. Wary that she might be in too deep, or too soon, or on the rebound, she vowed to proceed carefully. There was the question of how everyone else would react too—Patrick, Antonia,

Helen, Daniel—people who mattered. Would they really give their blessing to the relationship, or was it asking too much?

As the herbs in the tea took hold, and Tarek put his guitar to one side and smiled at her, her misgivings fell silent. They lit candles and ran a bath to share while outside the sun finally set on a long day, and above *Båvenshult*, a Perseid fireball lit up the starry sky.

31

Waxing Dispute Moon

As August unfolded, and the moon waxed a little larger each night, the stifling heat lifted and there was an occasional shower of rain over *Det Lilla Huset*. Out walking in the forest, Cleome inhaled the promise of autumn—in musky scents from the earth and fingers of damp breeze that sometimes blew in from the lake. Change was in the air in many ways; Amelie was busy, organising what she called "a surprise".

Catherine was due to return to England again soon. Cleome stood at the top of the glade, looking past the yellow grass at the choppy water. A couple more trips to Stockholm, with the accompanying noise, rush and pollution, had worn her out. She pondered the fact that both Kerstin and Catherine loved city life, fashionable clothes and new shiny jewels. Kerstin had worked hard for everything whereas Catherine had never earned money in any meaningful way, having relied on her ex-husband to provide for her, and latterly a generous divorce settlement. She wondered whether the half-sisters would have liked each other.

At Magnus Bengtsson's funeral it rained heavily for the first time in many weeks, and finding it hard to mourn for her neighbour in any meaningful way, Cleome's attention wandered during the ceremony. She considered whether the downpour, combined with light showers over the preceding days, might have prompted a flush of chanterelles to bloom in the forest. With the heatwave, it had been a bad season for mushroom picking so far, but there was always hope. Amelie fidgeted throughout the service, and was keen to leave the wake as soon as possible. On returning home, she changed quickly, asked if she could take the car again, and left on one of her mysterious missions.

Cleome changed her clothes, made a hasty mug of coffee, and prepared to go out into the forest, imagining platefuls of freshly picked mushrooms fried in butter for their supper, or if they were plentiful, filling preserving jars with delicious pickle for the winter. She set out with a small rucksack containing water for herself and the dogs, a tin bowl for them to drink from, one sheath holding her coveted mushroom knife and another containing a long-bladed knife for gathering pine bark. Over her arm, she carried her foraging trug. Her hip flask was restored to the pouch on her belt.

She set out in her usual direction, and then diverted, heading deep into the forest where she rarely ventured but knew that she might find a good crop of fungi. She wandered further than she normally would, her sharp gaze alert for any signs of the golden mushrooms, the dogs scampering around her. Although she scanned every inch of the forest floor, she found nothing. She harvested pine bark using her long knife and laid shards in her basket. She paused in a small clearing for a swig from her hip flask, and bent to pour out a little water into the dogs' bowl. They lapped noisily while insects buzzed about their heads. Refreshed, the trio continued on their way through an area carpeted with ferns, fallen wood, granite boulders, and parched low-growing bushes. Up above, blue sky was visible through the leafy canopy but there were still no mushrooms in sight.

She re-joined the track to *Det Lilla Huset* close to the Bengtsson's place, and noticed that Robban and Lotta were home again, still dressed in their funeral garb and sitting out on metal chairs at the back of their dilapidated cottage. She called out a greeting to them and offered more consolation on the difficult day. Lotta told her she was glad it was over. Robban remained silent.

'I've had no luck with finding chanterelles,' she added, by way of conversation.

'Me neither,' Lotta Bengtsson commiserated. 'I think it is all the foreigners. They come out and raid our forest.'

'I have never met anyone foraging out here, let alone a newcomer to our country!' Cleome disagreed. 'It is the heatwave—climate change—that has created the dearth.' Her patience worn thin by her stupid neighbour, she waved a vague farewell and headed down the track towards home, anticipating the peaceful evening ahead with pleasure. The sun would set at around eight o'clock. She would eat a light supper, run a warm bath and have an early night after what had been a disappointing day.

As she drew closer to home, the dogs raced ahead of her, barking excitedly. Alerted, Cleome noticed that Amelie had returned, and a second car was parked in the car port under the barn.

Amelie walked out to greet her. 'I have a surprise for you,' she said, slipping her arm through her grandmother's. 'When I organised it, I didn't know that Magnus Bengtsson's funeral would fall on the same day so everything is more rushed than I had planned, and I know you must be tired. But come inside, I've explained to the others that you've had a long day, and we will keep the evening simple and relaxed.'

'The others? What others?'

'Come, you'll see.'

In the hallway, Cleome took off her rucksack, and set her trug on the pine chest. Filled with curiosity, she followed Amelie into the kitchen where Antonia and Catherine both stood up from the table and smiled at her.

'I thought it would be good for us four to get together, and for everyone to get to know each other a little better,' Amelie said.

Catherine's dark eyes shone with excitement. Antonia pressed her palms together, nervously. Amelie put her arm around her grandmother, and Cleome spread a hand over her chest. 'Oh, my! This is a surprise.'

'Take a seat and I'll get you a drink. I've got lasagne in the oven already as I knew you'd be hungry after hunting for mushrooms. Did you find any?'

'Not one. I must get changed into something smarter.'

'Only if you want to.'

'Well, no, I don't, not really. I just want to rest my aching legs.' She sank into a chair with a sigh, and reached a hand across the table to squeeze Catherine's hand. 'So, you have been introduced to your aunt?'

'Yes, Amelie has taken care of all that.'

'And it's a real pleasure to finally meet you, Catherine,' Antonia said, authenticity evident in her firm voice.

'Am, you are a treasure to arrange all this.'

'We are family now. They are staying the night out here so we can all get to know each other better. We don't get a second chance at life, I've learnt that.'

'It means a lot to me. I can't tell you how much.' Catherine shook her head.

The four women sat around the kitchen table, chatting and eating for several hours. After it grew dark, Amelie lit candles. Any tension Cleome felt slipped away as the evening unfolded. Her heart beat strong and regularly, and the small knot of pain deep inside her finally shifted at seeing her sister and daughter taking the first, tentative steps towards friendship. It was not perfect but it was a start.

32

Dispute Moon to Harvest Moon

Amelie and Tarek walked the dogs and swam in the lake regularly, although the lake was growing cooler. They held hands when no-one was looking, and walked without speaking if they did not feel the need. Their relationship grew naturally, evolving with the certainty of a sapling in the forest that spread eager roots into the earth while reaching for the sky.

Amelie still wore Nick's wedding ring around the chain on her neck, and when she asked Tarek if he minded seeing it there, he pulled open the drawer beside his bed and took out a fine cotton shawl with a pattern in vibrant reds and blues.

'It was Nuwar's,' he explained. 'I carried it with me from Syria. We had not exchanged rings or any such thing but I will always take this shawl with me, wherever I go.'

'We carry our lost loves with us while we tend to our new, living love.'

'That is my intention, too.'

'Whatever comes, we can still remember them.'

'It's the way it will be. They are like stars in our souls.'

Amelie thought of her past and knew then that it was gone. Her eyes filled with tears. He hugged, her, and kissed her gently, and told her he believed that loving again was not a betrayal. It did not mean that their old loves, for Nick or for Nuwar, were ended. The lost loves remained but they stepped to one side to allow the new, living love to bloom. 'If they are looking down on us, they will see that we have something really special here. But I won't pressurise you. You must come to me freely, of choice. We will wait, not promise each other too much, until you know through every cell in your body what it is you want.'

Amelie did not say anything to Tarek, but on hearing his words, a tiny shift occurred deep inside her, and she knew that it was permissible to love him. She fingered Nick's ring as the final piece slid into place.

Late afternoon sunlight poured in through Cleome's open kitchen window. She arrived at the cottage to find the dogs desperate to get out, and after eating a quick sandwich, walked them down to the lakeside. Catherine had returned to England, as had Antonia. Antonia was talking to her again, and had made her peace with Catherine's presence in their lives. Old wounds were healing, albeit slowly. The sound of water lapping against the wooden jetty, the cry of the hawk overhead, and the clean scent of the breeze were soothing. She stood facing the lake with her eyes closed and mumbled a short prayer of gratitude for all the blessings in her life.

It was the time of the full moon again. The magnificent luminous orb would rise over the lake that night, and her haunting light would illuminate the entire homestead of *Det Lilla Huset*, casting shadows and keeping the owls awake. Autumn lingered in the spaces between the trees and in the long brown grass. Migrating geese called overhead. The birch leaves yellowed and fell, revealing stands of white tree trunks.

The news that Zain had gone on the run after the police had questioned him left her uneasy. She feared that he might exact revenge on Amelie as a way of getting back at Tarek, and although she did not say anything to Amelie, her ears were pricked for suspicious noises, even during daylight. The evening before, after her swim, she had fetched the fish knife from her little shed under the pine tree, not liking the thought of leaving it down there in case it fell into the wrong hands. She now kept it in her bedside drawer.

She reflected on the changes at the Bengtsson's place. The garden had been tidied; gone were the rusting car parts, empty plastic barrels and rotting bits of wood. The grass, while still brown and stunted after the dry summer, had been mown short. A row of washing hung on a new line strung between two apple trees. The windows shone as if newly polished. When she had come across Robban in the forest, he had waved cheerfully. He was attempting to use his drone with more consideration for her privacy, he told her.

She heard Amelie shout her name, turned to look, and saw her waving. Her granddaughter ran down to the lakeside to stand beside her. After asking about her day, she said that she had decided to stay in Sweden for another winter. Given her blossoming romance with Tarek, her decision hardly came as a surprise to Cleome. She warned her that life in Sweden was no paradise, the winter ahead would be long, and like everywhere else in Europe, life was no longer as it used to be. Amelie asked again whether she could stay on at *Det Lilla Huset*, and a part of Cleome melted at her granddaughter's sweetness.

'I'm under no illusions. I can help you over the winter, and I can find work and forge a new life for myself, eventually. And at least I can be surrounded by all this,' she said, and gestured at the lake and forest. 'It's what I need right now.'

'Yes, my dear child. Yes—to all of it,' Cleome replied, her emerald eyes twinkling with joy.

'More importantly of course, I can be close to you.'

'Well, there is that.'

'It's what matters—it's the only thing that does matter.'

She patted her granddaughter on the shoulder.

They walked back up to the cottage with their arms linked. 'I think I am, but I still don't completely *know* whether I'm ready to be with Tarek, you know?'

'Do we ever really know one hundred percent? It's your choice how you want to live the rest of your life but I will just say that there are no medals for being the best widow. There are no wrong or right times, and there is very little sense in any of it. Follow your heart's voice, and honour your life.'

In the weeks that followed, they took many walks in the forest with the dogs, and Cleome taught Amelie how to forage for autumn mushrooms. Fires were lit in the *kakelugn* in the evenings. They were both changed, and both resolved to carry on in the best way they could. Sometimes they talked late into the evenings, imagining women just like themselves, sitting down together in some distant place, attempting to survive grief. They discussed the way that newspapers and story writers told of life's disasters and tragedies, of wars or natural phenomena or freak accidents, and the astonishing roll-call of death— but rarely wrote about how those souls who were left behind picked up the pieces; the nuts and bolts of survival, of carrying on and creating some meaning to each day, and scratching out some joy. Yet this was the vital, if less headline-making, part of the arc of life.

Often, they walked with Helen and Kaia, their cheeks turning pink in the first of the winter winds. Helen was thriving and her bump was visible now. Amelie continued her volunteer work alongside her. She was delighted when Revekka made a promising recovery. Revekka had begun to walk again, shakily at first. She could feed herself, and had returned to school. She still tired easily and could not do her schoolwork as well or as quickly as she used to, but her friends had welcomed her back. Occasionally, she still spoke Russian with her parents but mostly she refused, and insisted that the family speak Swedish in the house. The family fractures would take time to heal as Revekka resented her mother for not integrating into the local community, and Ellina who was a naturally shy woman, was still slow to try. When Helen had asked Revekka what it had been like to be asleep for so many months, Revekka had told her that it was like being in a fragile glass box, deep below the ocean's surface.

As temperatures dropped, Amelie and Tarek took up running again. Rumour had it that Zain was living illegally in Stockholm. The spell of burglaries in the neighbourhood had abated. The Swedish elections highlighted immigration as a huge issue and the populist, anti-immigrant Sweden Democrats gained over seventeen percent of the vote, five percent more than in the previous election. Amelie sensed fear flutter around Tarek like a pecking bird some days, despite his relentless bravery. He confessed that he longed for home but the war still raged, and for now he remained severed from his traditions and heritage. He had tried to give up smoking but sometimes sat out on the step of his little bungalow with a lit cigarette, inhaling deeply to settle his unease. He told her that he must trust in himself, in Allah, and in his new friends in Sweden. They were his future now.

On the first anniversary of the accident, the two survivors walked in the forest, and when evening came, lit dozens of candles in the cottage. Cleome set up an altarpiece in the heart of the home, her kitchen. She placed photographs of Nick, Kerstin and Bertie on a low wooden table in a brightly lit corner, set small bunches of aromatic rosemary, thyme and yarrow in tiny jars. She scattered calendula petals and camomile flowers over the altar, and burned sage. Amelie watched, intrigued and sensing that she had much to learn. They looked through photographs, made a special meal and set places for their absent guests, including bringing out the wooden high chair from storage for Bertie.

That night, the first hesitant flakes of snow swirled from a bank of cloud in the inky sky.

'I want to have a party,' Amelie announced.

33

New Dark Moon

She remembered New Year's Eve, when her emotions were raw and despite the effect of the war-like fireworks, he had managed to console her; the walk when he had shown her his dream house on the rock; his brotherly affection for Josef; his initial willingness to include his friends from home in his new life at *Båvenshult* despite their ingratitude; the sensitive manner in which he had tidied her belongings after the burglary; and the long-standing and mutual fondness for her grandmother. She made a long and thorough inventory of the past year. Some days there was still so much pain in Tarek's eyes; perhaps there was in her own too, she did not know. But one certainty emerged from her reflections: he was the man she wanted in her future. He knew loss and was not oblivious to its effects. He was not naïve like so many, but awakened by his tragedy, in the same way that she hoped she was too. And despite all these things, or perhaps because of them, he saw the brilliance in life, he appreciated life and was grateful for whatever blessing came his way; it was perhaps this quality that she admired the most. She wanted a soulmate, and in Tarek she had found one.

She went to visit him one chilly evening when the west wind ruffled the lake's surface with her tireless energy. Although he was affectionate as always, he looked at her gravely in unguarded moments, as if he waited for her final decision, a little fearful in case she turned him away.

They stood in the one-roomed bungalow where a curtain was pulled tight across the front window for privacy while the curtains at the back remained open and framed the shadowy trees. What were they to each other, she and Tarek? Lovers, certainly. Friends, certainly. But damaged people too, who needed to tread carefully with each other's emotions and tiptoe around each other's hurts and dreams.

Memories of Nick and Bertie from over a year ago floated into her mind, and she stalled for a moment, before sensing the warmth that she had felt before, a circling, a knowing, like nothing on earth but there all the same. Nick held Bertie's hand, was with him, wherever they were, and they were giving her permission. She heard Nick whisper, "Trust your heart," before they shimmered and were gone again, as quickly as they had come. She knew then what she needed to do.

She took Tarek's hands in hers, and swept by a wave of utter conviction, said, 'I want to be with you.' He looked at her as if checking that she really meant what she said.

'Really?'

'Yes, really. With all my heart. And you? Do you want to be with me?'

'Well, of course. I have known that since the night of the fireworks when we stood in the snow and you were so fragile and yet strong, and kind. I knew then.'

'Really?'

'Yes, really.'

Her laughter filled the wooden bungalow. She said she was planning a party at *Det Lilla Huset,* and invited him to come, but would not say why.

At the party, held in the downstairs rooms of *Det Lilla Huset*, Robban and Lotta perched on the edge of a sofa. They were unused to social gatherings and unsure about how to join in. Tarek chatted with them before moving across the room to talk to Josef. Cleome had confronted Lotta about her racist attitude not long after she had arrived, and told her that if she spoke that way again, she would be asked to leave. Lotta had blushed and said she did not realise how her words sounded, had not considered herself racist before, and felt embarrassed. Helen and Daniel stood near the *kakelugn* where all three dogs lay sprawled on a large rug. Daniel had resigned his post in Stockholm, and had moved into the main farmhouse where the decoration of a nursery was underway, ready for the arrival of the baby, due the following month. Tarek and Josef shared a joke together nearby, and Amelie passed around a big plate of canapés and then handed out flutes of champagne or sparkling elderflower for Helen and Tarek.

'What are we celebrating?' Daniel asked.

'All will come clear in a moment,' she winked.

Cleome came to her side and whispered, 'That boy loves you, you know. I've not seen him like this before, ever. He can't take his eyes off you.'

Amelie picked up a teaspoon and clinked the side of her glass to get everyone's attention.

'Dinner is almost ready. But before we take our seats, I have an announcement to make.' She smiled. She walked across the room, met Tarek's steady gaze, and took his hand. 'We, Tarek and I, are a couple, and we'd like you all to raise a toast—to us!' She lifted her glass and touched his, before leaning forward and brushing a kiss across his stubbled jawline. The light of Tarek's smile lit the entire room, and said more than any words could ever say.

Glasses were raised and applause broke out all round with even Robban clapping enthusiastically and Lotta tapping her palm. Josef patted Tarek on the back and grinned at him. Daniel kissed Amelie on the cheek and shook Tarek's hand. Helen hugged them both, and said, 'I knew it,' repeatedly, while Cleome slipped over to Tarek and said, 'Welcome to the family.'

34

Fourteen months later

New Year's Day and a Waning Crescent Cold Moon

Amelie's spirits were lifted by the sight of fresh snowfall. Weak winter sunlight radiated off the earth's bleached surface and brightened the landscape for as far as the eye could see. The whiteness was immense. Dark silhouettes of trees, overlaid with frozen crystals, rose from drifts of amorphous mist that rolled in from the lake.

She had bought the little house on the rock, known locally as *Huset på Berget* with her inheritance, when it had come up for sale the previous spring. Her new home stood high on the promontory, secluded by copses of pine and birch with views of the lake on three sides. The bitter winter wind was filtered by these clusters of tall trees. From the windows, all her views were of the vast lake, resplendent in the forest basin. To reach her grandmother's place took roughly an hour's walk through woodland and across the field below *Båvenshult*—or ten minutes in the little motorboat which she now kept moored to her own jetty during the summer months. Soon after buying the house, she had set about renovating it to make it habitable all year round, in the same way that her grandmother had with *Det Lilla Huset*, half a century before. It felt like this was what her mother would have wanted for her—to be happy, to make her own choices and to stand by them, to be secure, and have a place to call home. She loved the winter times, just as much as she did the summer, and was working up the courage to skate across the thick ice from one side of the bay to the other, so that she could visit her grandmother easily whenever the lake was frozen.

She was studying for her Swedish nursing license. She had residency in the country now and had always spoken the language fluently. One day, she would work again, but for the present time, she enjoyed being a student and volunteering with Helen. Deep down, she knew that she had to heal herself a little more before she would be able to heal others—and that process would take time.

She became godmother to Esme's second child, a little girl named Poppy Louise who had been born in Oxford on an auspicious night the previous January when there was a total lunar eclipse. Esme had laughed when Amelie mentioned this, and said she was turning into her grandmother. In some ways it was true; Cleome taught her about forest plants and moon cycles, and her tiny place in the massive scheme of wild phenomena.

Marsha visited *Huset på Berget*, and created a special meditation area in the garden, using fallen wood and rocks. She built it at the very tip of the peninsular so that Amelie could sit there, and be bathed in light at either sunrise or sunset.

Amelie kept the house in Percy Street, and gave the use of it to an Oxford-based charity to provide temporary shelter for homeless refugees until permanent places could be found for them. There might come a time when this situation would need to change, but for now she wanted to help displaced people, having learned from Tarek and Helen what a difference such a gesture could make.

She still wrote in a journal, and now collected inspirational pictures, quotes, and stories of people like herself who had lost one life, only to survive and begin another—none of them choosing to do so, but all of them finding the will to survive, and to cherish each day. Grief remained, curled up in the cellar of her being. Sometimes when she meditated she was able to visualise fresh air and daylight easing her sorrow in the dark place where it lay. One day she would bless the grief (for it had taught her so much about life) and ask it to leave—but she was not ready for that yet.

Cleome's daily life continued in a round of growing vegetables, making herbal remedies, walking her dogs, taking care of her chickens, and in the evenings, knitting, and reading poetry. She was invigorated by having her granddaughter living on the opposite side of the bay, and relished the sight of the little house, twinkling with light in the long hours of darkness. Catherine kept in regular contact, and mother and daughter forged a new path through life together. Like any path through the forest, it was sometimes rocky or strewn with unexpected hazards but for the most part, it made for an exhilarating walk. She had cut back on the bootleg vodka again, and now saved it for special occasions, and her angina attacks were coming less frequently.

Antonia had returned to Sweden the previous summer to meet Catherine again while she was taking another one of her trips to Stockholm, a city which she now claimed as her second home. Catherine's beauty had made Antonia shy at first, but after a time, she found herself smiling at this ebullient new relative. As the months rolled by, and Catherine kept in touch with her mother, Antonia relinquished the need to protect Cleome, and learned to trust that all would be fine.

Catherine researched her Italian roots, hunting for her father with, so far, no luck. Amelie had welcomed her "new" half-aunt into the family, and invited her to visit whenever she wanted. One day, she hoped to meet her second cousins.

'My daughter has much to learn,' Cleome remarked. 'But she has spirit; I'll give her that.'

Patrick spent much of his time in Ireland, not exactly leaving Hilary but no longer living under her spell. He re-discovered family ties, fishing, and the pleasure of retiring to the pub of an evening to sing the traditional songs of his childhood. With his legal background, he became involved in an organisation that offered mediation after road traffic accidents—to create a space where people could talk under the supervision of a professional, and not fight. In the little bungalow in Ireland, he developed a routine and pondered the mechanics of his recovery, and how he would go on. At Amelie's insistence, he had learned to Facetime, and had visited Sweden for a week, the previous May. Hilary did not join him. She liked to stay at the house in Toot Baldon, to be close to Nick's grave.

Billy left his job at the tree surgery company, and began work as a gardener at Lady Margaret Hall, one of the Oxford University colleges, tending thirteen acres of beautiful grounds and gardens which bordered the River Cherwell. He became engaged to his boyfriend.

Lotta's home at the top of the track was unrecognisable from the dump it had once been. The doors and window frames gleamed with fresh paint, the red wooden walls had been re-stained, and her garden grew abundantly and prettily ever since Cleome had taught her how to grow herbs and vegetables, and had shared her geranium cuttings. Robban Bengtsson had joined a photography group in Flen.

Baby Maja Sophia Johansson-Ivanov was now over a year old. She had been born two weeks early the previous December, on Santa Lucia's Day, the day when Swedes traditionally celebrate the light. The labour was quick and Helen remained strong. Little Maja brought much joy to her parents and half-brother, Josef. True to his word, Daniel now wrote poetry from home, and assumed the care of his precious only daughter. Helen was back at work full-time after her maternity leave.

Zain remained on the run, and Ayah had moved to Stockholm.

Tarek persevered with the free Swedish lessons offered by the government, and was re-training to be a teacher in his adopted country. He remained unimpressed by all the labels that people attached to him—Muslim, refugee, Syrian, and the latest: immigrant. Each word only told a part of his story, and fell short of being a fair description of who he was. He knew that he had to continue to adapt to everything that life offered him, and the love and compassion learned during his early life was an enduring compass that helped him to find his way. A culture that did not acknowledge the soul, such as that which he found in Sweden, still felt like a strange place to live, but he was getting used to it, and he could see that in their own way, most Swedish people were kind and thoughtful, and still full of divine life force, even if they did not know it. He still mourned the loss of his family, his language and his country although he had made contact with a cousin who was now living in Germany, and this brought him great solace. As the war continued to rage in Syria, his beloved homeland became a distant mirage.

As promised, he was teaching Amelie to whirl like a dervish, and he was trying to give up smoking but still enjoyed the occasional cigarette, sitting on a rock overlooking the lake. He lived with Amelie now, in his dream house, out on the promontory. With Daniel at home, Josef no longer needed his company so much. Each morning when he woke early to find Amelie sleeping beside him, he felt a rush of joy and gave thanks to whatever force had driven them together. He was sharing his life with the woman he loved and living in a place that could only be described as paradise on earth. He was so lucky and grateful that sometimes he could not stop smiling. He had lost one home but he had found another, for this house with Amelie truly *was* his new home. He belonged. He was where he was meant to be.

Amelie longed to learn to trust the ice over Lake Båven, and to skate on it, as did Tarek. The two of them practiced on long blades at the local ice rink, and had become friends with an outdoor guide, Björn, who taught them about safety and the technique required for skating outdoors.

On New Year's Day, after a hearty lunch at *Det Lilla Huset*, they stepped out onto the ice, wearing rucksacks that doubled as flotation devices and contained ropes and ice nails so that they could haul themselves out of the freezing water, in the very unlikely event of the ice breaking. They held on to each other as they slipped around and fitted long blades to their boots. When they were ready, they exchanged excited glances, clasped hands and set off together, gliding out over the frozen expanse in the dusky afternoon light, to the cheers of Cleome, Helen and Daniel, Josef and baby Maja, who all watched from the shore.

'Sometimes, the greatest love story is born from terrible tragedy—the love of life itself,' Cleome murmured.

Amelie squeezed Tarek's hand before letting go, and skated alone, out over the icy expanse, having faith that the lake ice would hold her. As she glided, with the wind in her ears, she felt free for the first time in a very long time. She sensed her mother's encouragement, Bertie's delight, and Nick's heartfelt applause. Her laughter rang out over the frozen water.

ACKNOWLEDGEMENTS

Firstly, heartfelt thanks to my dear friend Lin Hallberg without whom this novel would never have been written. Lin introduced me to her beautiful country Sweden over thirty years ago, invited me to visit so many times that I have lost count, and then answered about a thousand questions during the writing of SNOW ANGELS with humour and careful consideration. She read an earlier draft of the story with an eagle eye, and gave fearless advice. Here's to over thirty years of brilliant friendship. I hope we have many more years of fun together.

I would also like to thank the following:

Oliver Loudon and Ellen Danesjö for helping me with many obscure (but vital!) details on Swedish life, always with patience, insight and lovingkindness. I am so grateful and love visiting you!

Huxley, Oakley, and Laura Loudon—for your constant encouragement, love and support. It means the world to me.

Sparrows for accompanying me on research trips, your proof reading skills, calming influence and loyalty. You are my rock.

My trusty, talented, and sharp-eyed editor, Lorraine Swoboda. I am so grateful that you enjoy wielding a red pen with such pinpoint accuracy!

Debs and Denise for help with nursing matters in this story.

The remainder of The Forum Girls for your enduring support and good humour when I am writing, day in and day out—and telling you about it! In alphabetical order: Dell, Donna, Helen, Janet, Maeve, Mary, Nette, Pammie, Ros, Sandra, Shirley, and Welsh Deb. You are special friends indeed, and I cherish our daily chats.

My cover designer, the truly brilliant Jane Dixon-Smith.

And finally, Alfie, canine assistant extraordinaire.

CREDITS

During *Snow Angels*, the author quoted from the following (all works are in the public domain): Chapter 4, Amelie reads WB Yeats, *The Lake Isle of Innisfree*. In Chapter 27, Cleome reads Emily Dickinson, *Angels in the Early Morning*, Tarek reads Rabindranath Tagore, *Peace, My Heart*, and Daniel reads an excerpt from Kahlil Gibran, *The Prophet*.

ABOUT THE AUTHOR

Jenny Loudon is a British novelist whose work includes the bestselling love story *Finding Verity*. She read English and American Literature at the University of Kent in Canterbury and holds a Masters in The Modern Movement. She lives with her family in the English countryside.

Find out more by visiting her website: www.jennyloudon.com, or follow her on Instagram @jennyloudonauthor
facebook.com/jennyloudonauthor

**If you have enjoyed reading this book,
please consider rating SNOW ANGELS!**

A star rating and/or review on any of the following is much appreciated—Amazon, Instagram, Facebook, Twitter and Goodreads

THANK YOU!

Also by Jenny Loudon & available on Amazon:

The best-selling love story

FINDING VERITY

An unhappy woman. An unfinished romance. A sense that time is running out…

Verity Westwood, successful, married, and mother of two grown daughters, dreams of a more exciting life. Her husband is handsome but selfish, her interior design work leaves her cold, and her London home is comfortable but has no heart, now that her daughters have left.

When Edward Farrell, a nomadic American journalist from her past, returns unexpectedly, she is swept by the irresistible desire to fulfil her dreams of working as an artist, like her famous father before her. And after being caught in a storm on the Cote d'Azur, she vows to change her life.

What she does not foresee is the struggle involved, the ultimate price she will pay, and the powerful force of enduring love that changes everything.

Reviews for FINDING VERITY:

'Stunning… one of my books of the year.' *Anne Williams, Romantic Novelists Association Media Star of the Year 2019*

'A psychologically astute exploration of what it means to be a woman in the first quarter of the 21st century.' *JM Wheatcroft*

'Finding Verity is an amazingly good debut novel. The story is so engrossing I couldn't put it down, but at the same time, didn't want it to end.' *Whirlybird, Amazon*

'Engagingly written.' *The Crafty Green Poet*

'A bittersweet read.' *Bookworm Lisa*

www.jennyloudon.com

Printed in Great Britain
by Amazon